BOYSICK

MEREDITH MINCEY

ISBN paperback: 979-8-9928599-0-4
ISBN ebook: 979-8-9928599-1-1

to my younger self

CHAPTER ONE

"**B**UT SHE WEARS SHORT SKIRTS, I WEAR T-SHIRTS!" I passionately scream-sing at my mirror.

Blending in my concealer, I am still not fully psyched for my first day of school. Pushing some of my makeup off my cold bathroom counter, I sing, "SHE'S CHEER CAPTAIN AND I'M ON THE BLEACHERS!"

I feel like I am the *epitome* of Taylor's character from the "You Belong With Me" music video. I have the kind of frizzy hair and awkwardness young Taylor had. Seriously, just swap out her blonde hair for my brunette and her black frames for my contacts and *Voila*! I have been and always will be the nerdy best friend.

Personally, I don't know how Taylor Swift ever felt like the outcast of her high school. How could Lucas Till not notice her after YEARS of living beside each other?! It's good to know she eventually got her happily ever after in *Fearless* (Taylor's Version, obviously).

Beep. Beep. Beep.

Walking along the plush beige carpet of my bedroom, I move to turn off my alarm sitting on my baby green nightstand. I sleep like a ton of bricks, so I always have to set roughly twenty-seven alarms to make sure I'm up. And of course on the first day of school, regardless of the multiple alarms, I overslept by thirty minutes.

I glance at my full length mirror and give myself a once over. I pull at the hem of my denim mom shorts and fidget with my butter yellow t-shirt.

Smoothing out my tangled brown waves, I run back to the bathroom to finish getting ready.

While swiping on some blush and thinking of my junior year of high school, nervous and excited butterflies fill my stomach. Yeah, yeah they say that junior is the most stressful and what-not, but I think it'll still be a pretty good one. My classes seem interesting, my teachers look fairly chill, and I have almost every class with my best friend Lenny.

I've known Lenny for basically half my life. We met at a summer camp when we were eight, and we've pretty much been inseparable ever since. One day at camp, I was sitting out on the picnic tables making beaded bracelets when a freckled, strawberry blonde haired girl came running up beside me.

Huffing and puffing, she said, "I just threw a bunch of water balloons at Zachary, Brian, and Beau, and now they're after me! Can I hide under the table?"

After she dove under the pollen-covered picnic table, I tried to look casual as the group of boys ran right past me. They had no idea Lenny was hiding there, and it felt like a small victory to help out in tricking them.

I wasn't like Lenny. It was hard for me to open up unless I felt 100% comfortable. Hanging out with Lenny definitely rubbed off on me because I rarely feel the social anxiety I once did.

Even back then, I admired her energy and looked up to her unapologetic attitude. For weeks, the boys had been placing snails on the toilet seats of the girls' bathroom. I mean, they definitely deserved the water balloons to the face. She was the only one who actually had the guts to get revenge.

Eight years of friendship later, she's the Rachel to my Monica. The Leslie to my Ann. The Blanche to my Rose. The Lily to my Miley... or my Hannah.

You get the picture.

Grabbing my slate blue backpack, I bound down the stairs. Sitting at a counter stool is my dad, eating an enormous bowl of oatmeal. My mom walks over to the coffee pot, pouring herself her signature cup of black coffee.

"Hey, kid," my dad says, looking over at me. "Are you ready for your first day of junior year?"

I shrug, "I guess. If I think about it too much, I get pretty nervous. I have to go in early to switch out of my Graphic Design class," I groan.

Setting her cup on the edge of the granite counter top, Mom asks, "Why are you switching classes?"

"Because of how my credits line up, I could have a free study block. And I would so much rather have that with Lenny than take a class I don't need."

My mom shakes her head. "It's changed so much compared to when we were there."

"Whew," Dad says. "Makes me feel old."

Twenty-six years ago, my parents met at Caelee High School, and it was straight out of a movie. My mom, Sam, was the artistic hippie that didn't care about rules or school. My dad was the valedictorian, math nerd, and book worm. Top of his class and punctual as hell, you wouldn't think he would fall for my mom.

When Mom first met Dad, she was immediately intrigued. According to romcoms, opposites attract, and my parents are the perfect example of that. They started dating during their freshman year of high school, and it's been history ever since.

So you can imagine how I feel when I've *never* had a successful relationship like my parents did at *fourteen*.

Mom clips her short black hair back and grabs her Harry Styles tote bag. She stuffs her laptop, iPad, and sketchbook to take to her art studio, where she cultivates art from other local artisans and sells her own work. That artistic hippie has never left my mom, but motherhood brought on a whole new set of traits.

It's almost like my parents switched places once they had me. Now, my dad is super relaxed and chill, and my mom is eager to help me in any way that she can. Mom bought all my school supplies in May and painted my notebooks with different cartoon cats holding up my name.

You could say that she's *passionate*.

Even as they've "switched" roles, my parents still seem to complete each other. They match one another's highs and lows, and it's wild to me that they began such a strong relationship as high school freshmen.

"Okay, I'm heading on," Mom says and grabs her bag. She walks over to kiss Dad on the cheek and waves me goodbye. "Good luck today! I packed you a really good lunch which is in the fridge. I put extra brownies in there for you!"

See? Passionate.

I quickly toast my blueberry bagel and spread a thin layer of cream cheese on top. I eat too fast and feel like the lump of bagel is stuck behind my sternum. Hastily, I fill up my water bottle to try to wash down the bagel boulder.

Running over to the front door, I grab my sneakers and ask, "Don't you have to get to school soon?"

My dad says, "No, the first two hours are my plan period, so I'll head in at 10:30."

"Lucky," I mutter. I finish double knotting my shoelaces and head outside.

My dad is the IT guy and Computer Science teacher at Caelee Middle, so it's nice to know that if I ever needed anything for school, Dad is a quick two minute drive away.

Climbing into my Toyota Camry, I throw some of my clothes and random cups onto the floorboard. Normally, Lenny and I ride everywhere together, but since I had to go to the guidance counselor's office early this morning, I had to actually drive myself for once.

I plug in my phone to play my "Good Mood Songs" playlist. Even though this morning has been a little chaotic, that can't stop me from having a great first day of school. I pull out of my driveway, tapping my fingers on the steering wheel to the beat of "get him back!" by Olivia Rodrigo.

I'm finally an upperclassman! Lenny and I have talked about this since we started high school. We would finally be able to drive and have more freedom, rather than feeling like a "kid" during freshman and sophomore year.

While singing along to Olivia Rodrigo's revenge anthem, I fail to recognize the red lights in front of me. The car ahead has pumped the brakes, and I didn't even realize it. It catches me so off guard that for a second, I don't know what to do. My car barrels towards the giant SUV. Screaming, I slam my foot on the brakes.

My torso hurls forward but gets stopped by my seat belt. The gray belt seems to cut into me as I throw my arms towards the steering wheel. Everything in my passenger seat is thrown forward and falls into the floor with a loud *thump.* I grip the steering wheel so tight that my knuckles are white, and my palms start to sweat profusely.

Panting, I look up and see that the car has started to drive forward again. Scanning the rear fender, I don't see a mark or dent. Somehow I managed to slow down in time before getting into a wreck. Thank God because it's a spotless Jeep Wrangler- which I assume is brand new. That would have been way too expensive to fix.

And an awful way to start a new school year.

I turn off my car's volume, so I don't hear any more music on the way to school. I am putting myself on music timeout because I can't have another almost fender bender on the drive to school. My heart still races from having to pound my foot on the brakes at 7:42 in the morning.

Pulling into the school parking lot, I decide to not take my chances and park in a space at the back of the lot. There aren't any cars on either side of me, which means no opportunity to hit another car. Excuse me, *almost* hit another car.

Class hasn't started yet, but the school is open, so I can run into the counselor's office to change my schedule. Since it's been a hectic morning, I walk inside my school's coffee shop to treat myself before my appointment with the guidance counselor. Our school's mission is to "foster an environment of creativity and community" according to our principal, Mr. Brooks. One of my classmates, Maya, is really rich. Her dads own a logistics company, and they are *loaded*. They have donated a ton of money to the school, so there are Creativity & Community stations all over the building like a craft center, coffee shop, rock climbing wall, etc. I'm not too particular about the community and creativity stuff, but I definitely like to take advantage of the ample opportunities to get a coffee before class.

I walk over to grab my iced caramel latte that has "Marrelo" written on it instead of Marlowe. Would it really be a coffee without your name misspelled on it?

Heading towards the guidance counselor's office on the west wing, I pass by some teachers and the occasional student. No one wants to be here before class on the first day.

Entering the freezing cold office, I have to wait just over thirty minutes to get my schedule changed. I should've known it wouldn't be an easy process, given the morning I've had.

"Okay! Everything is switched," Mrs. Morals says.

I glance at my phone. It's 8:25, so I've just got a few minutes before the school day starts. Luckily, I *now* have a free block for my first period, so I can go see Lenny.

> ME: Just got my schedule fixed!
> Omw to the coffee shop

> LENNY: already here!
> saved you a seat

I walk back towards the cafe and see people mingling among themselves amidst the smell of vanilla and coffee.

Although my school might be kind of artsy-fartsy, it still has every clique imaginable. Sitting at the high top tables, the lacrosse team and their girlfriends laugh at some video on a player's iPad. Lounging on the bean bag chairs are a bunch of band kids, discussing what they think of the new band director. Towards the windows are a couple cheerleaders making a TikTok on full volume. There are a few AP students taking up the large center table, passing around detailed note cards, and anxiously talking about an upcoming class.

Then, there's me. I am not really in a certain "clique" per se. Obviously my closest friend at Caelee High is Lenny, and I've got acquaintances here and there. But, I am not really *in* a group. I'm not smart enough to be with the honors kids, not cool enough to be with the athletes, and not coordinated enough to be in anything relating to music.

I feel like I missed the memo about how to thrive in high school. It sounds counter-intuitive because some people hate the stereotypical high school life. But for me, I long for that *High School Musical* type of experience. Going into high school, I thought it would be more like an early 2000's movie where the "nobody" turns into the popular girl. Or she gets the guy. Or becomes the valedictorian. *Something* at least.

I see Lenny waving at me from a small table near the giant window. She stands up to give me a hug, and she's got on her iconic light blue

Chuck Taylors, white Gracie Abrams baby tee, and pastel pink shortalls. In Lenny's words, her style is that of a hippie Easter egg. Her waist length strawberry blonde hair hangs over one shoulder, making her look even more like Rapunzel.

She giggles, "I stayed up too late on the phone, and now I feel like a zombie."

"Let me guess… you were on FaceTime with Jacob?"

She smiles at me sheepishly.

Don't get me wrong, I am so happy for Lenny. She and Jacob have been together since eighth grade. In middle school, they dressed up as Lucas and Max from *Stranger Things*, and it's been history ever since. They are perfect for each other, and many times I third wheel their dates. But Jacob makes Lenny forget about what it's like to be single in high school… because she hasn't been single in high school.

"Yes," she says quietly. Groaning, she tells me, "And then I decided to spontaneously try to learn hand embroidery. I didn't go to bed until two!"

I shake my head lightly, "I need my sleep, but I honestly wouldn't mind a boyfriend to talk to at night."

She nods, giving me a sympathetic look.

As embarrassing as it is to admit, I am a sixteen-year-old girl who has never been kissed and never had a real boyfriend. I want to fall in love *so badly*. It's like guys think I have the plague. All throughout the year, I see Instagram pictures of high school couples who caption every lovey-dovey post with "loml."

I've pretty much convinced myself that I'm perpetually unlovable. I don't like to admit it, but deep down, I am terrified I will be alone forever. Yes, I'm only sixteen, but it seems like everyone around me is in love. High school sweethearts seem to know a love that I never will. And that's what's hard to explain to Lenny. She just thinks that I haven't found the right guy yet, but it seems to me that no guys are interested.

And in the rare instance that a guy is interested in me, Lenny becomes really overprotective. I know she's that way because she cares, but it makes it even more challenging to get into a relationship.

It's like the guys at my school have a monopoly over who gets to be in a relationship. All of us girls are just out here trying our best. When I meet a guy I like, I try to be myself. I try to seem interesting and friendly, but it's like every joke doesn't land and every conversation falls flat.

Since it is unconventional for the girl to ask the guy out, it feels like it's up to the guys around me to decide who I fall in love with. If a guy doesn't ask me out, then I really don't have a chance at a relationship.

I envy the girls that seem to get "picked" by guys. Good for them, but also *why can't that be me?* You know those people that seem to bounce from relationship to relationship? Like you can't remember them single for long enough before they get into another relationship.

"I need to update you on Jacob," Lenny says and starts telling me about a work fiasco he had.

After *a lot* of thought on relationships, the only thing I can reason is that it is something psychological. Some people must be born as more "relationship" people. And some people are just deemed "single" people. My parents are relationship people. Lenny is definitely a relationship person.

Unfortunately, I am a single person.

I don't want to be. I want that drive in movie, late night Target runs, celebratory football games, wearing his oversized sweatshirts kind of relationship. Every year, I get my hopes up, and I think I've found The One.

It's happened since I was a kid. I fall head over heels for a boy I barely know, and I immediately begin hoping and praying he somehow notices me. I *pine* over these guys who really don't know I exist. I build up our prospective relationship so much in my mind. I get in this obsessive, butterflies-in-my-stomach frenzy that I can't shake.

Last year, I seriously thought I would date Zayn Fisher. He had deep tan skin, curly brown hair, and freckles that outnumbered the stars in the sky. In math class, I would constantly catch myself staring at him rather than my algebra notes. Before I went to bed, I would come up with all these scenarios of us in the future together. Does that sound like a stalker? Definitely. I wasn't in love necessarily, but it felt like more than a crush.

Lenny said I wasn't lovesick. I was Boysick.

"- and Jacob was like, 'Oh my God, I can't believe that happened.' It was so funny," she finishes.

"Crazy!" I say while nodding along. Once again, I have zoned out of another conversation while thinking about boys. Typical.

It's not that I want to be such a brat about guys' lack of awareness of me, but I can't help it. I'm a hater first, girl second. I am completely open to the universe changing my mind. If the universe wants to bring me a guy to prove that teenage love can happen to me, by all means, please do so!

After talking with Lenny for a bit longer, we decide to head to our class a few minutes early. Our sneakers squeak on the tile as we walk down the hall, with the sound bouncing off the teal lockers lining the hallway.

With my iced coffee in one hand and my phone in the other, I am fully prepared for my first class of the day. I'm so busy looking at the differing door numbers, that I don't even notice that my shoe has untied, with the laces sprawled out like octopus tentacles.

In the second slow motion event of the day, I start to fall forward. My stomach drops as if I'm on a roller coaster. My left foot steps on the untied laces from my right foot.

I'm falling, and I see the floor coming closer and closer to my view.

With a *thud*, I fall face first. Trust me, it's not that comfortable to have a full body slam into the speckled school tile.

One class a few doors ahead of me dismisses early, so twenty-five people walk towards me sprawled out on the floor.

In my fall, I threw my coffee across the floor, leaving a sticky brown puddle around it. My hip throbs after breaking my trip.

"Are you okay?!" Lenny asks, rushing down to assess the damage. I get some weird stares from the few students in the hallway, but no one else comes to my aid other than Lenny. My face heats up so much, I'm sure it's the color of a tomato.

"Yeah, I'm fine," I say. Scrambling to my feet, I try to brush the dirt from the floor off my shorts. The faster I move on from this disaster, the less embarrassing it is. "I promise, I'm good."

"I'll go get some paper towels!" Lenny says, running towards the bathroom.

How mortifying. So far today I've overslept, I've almost gotten in a car wreck, I've had to painstakingly rearrange my schedule, and I've fallen on the nasty hallway tile.

Lenny and I mop up my iced coffee mess and hurriedly throw the mound of soggy brown paper towels into the trash. Just as we finish cleaning up, the bell rings. I quickly retie my shoes and head into the classroom.

Lenny and I settle into seats right beside each other in U.S. History.

Out of breath, I'm still a little flustered after my plummet to the floor, but I need to get that out of my mind. Other people start to trickle into the classroom, and I see a few familiar faces. I recognize a couple of football players, a few kids from SGA, and several kids from my English class last year.

In walks Maya Nguyen, the queen of the popular girls. She's Caelee High's Regina George, and she is adored by everyone. She is involved in every single club, so the teachers love her. She's the head dance captain, so she has an endless supply of girls begging to be her friend.

I'm only a little bit jealous of her.

She sits next to two other dance team girls, and they instantly start talking about how their summers were. She's loud and bubbly, and she just has that effortless attitude that automatically deems her popular.

"How are you and Kevin?" one of the dance team girls says.

Lenny looks at me and just barely nods: our universal sign to eavesdrop on their conversation so we can talk about it later.

"He's been fine," Maya shrugs, tossing her hair over her shoulder. Maya and Kevin have been dating on and off for almost two years now. Their relationship has been filled with drama from day one, hence why Maya's minions are so invested.

"You all are so cute," her friend gushes. "Also, have you seen the new guy that moved here?"

Maya shakes her head.

New kid? Lenny mouths to me. I just shrug my shoulders and look around. I don't see anyone new.

Caelee High isn't necessarily a big school, so everyone pretty much knows who everyone else is. If there's a new kid, it becomes a pretty big deal.

Then, speaking of which, someone walks in. A spark of familiarity hits me, and I can't place why.

"There he is," Maya's friend whispers. "I think his name is Beau."

Beau.

Beau Braxton?

The Beau Braxton?

I look at Lenny with a shock of horror on my face. I can't believe it. That's him.

ME: THAT'S BEAU FROM CAMP

LENNY: WHAT!!?!?!?!?!?!

Lenny and I met Beau at camp when we were younger. He was a part of the boys' group that terrorized all of us girls, but he was the shyest out of all of them. I took his quiet nature and ran with it. He reminded me of Edward Cullen, and I was determined to become his Bella. I wrote Mrs. Beau Braxton across ALL of my journals. I wouldn't shut up about him to Lenny. He was the first ever person I was Boysick over.

And now he's back.

When we were twelve, his family moved away because of his dad's job. I thought I would never see him again, and I took that to heart. I mean, I sang "The One That Got Away" by Katy Perry alone in my room, every day for two months.

I snap back into reality when I see him walk over to find a seat. He still has his soft black hair, and his brown eyes twinkle under the classroom's fluorescent lights. His parallel dimples make time slow to a halt.

He's wearing light wash Levi's jeans with a black tee and black Adidas Sambas. He looks like the Pinterest guy of my dreams. He looks so *grown*, as if he's just matured into this European model overnight.

"Beau?! What's it been, like five years?" Lenny asks, waving him over towards us. I seriously have the greatest best friend. I mean, she is already playing wing-woman, and he *just* walked in.

"Lenny? It seems like the last time I saw you we were having a water balloon fight," he smiles, shaking his head.

Lenny gestures towards me, "And-"

Beau catches my eye and says, "Marlowe! Let me guess, you guys are still inseparable." His voice is so much deeper; it seeps with mystery.

Hearing him say my name makes the butterflies in my stomach go crazy. I tuck my hair behind my ears, just trying to play it cool. I feel so giddy just hearing his quiet voice. My palms start to sweat as I feel his eyes on me.

"Yeah, pretty much," I say, flashing him my best girl-next-door grin.

Our teacher, Mr. Evans, walks in and greets the class. While he dives into his lecture and introduction, I keep zoning in and out while thinking about Beau. I just can't help it! What if we rekindle our childhood friendship? What if I finally get the high school sweetheart I've always longed for? What if I'm finally deemed a relationship person?

What are the chances that he moves back to Caelee County, after all this time? He seems like his quiet self that broods with intrigue, as if we are all still ten at summer camp.

The first time I started to like Beau was during a hot day in July. We were playing freeze tag, and Brian, captain of the boys' club, was after me. We were running through the playground, and I wasn't a very fast runner (not much has changed).

Brian was on my tail, and I was running out of energy. With the most force he could muster, he tagged me right between my shoulder blades. Instead of freezing in place, my body reacted to the shove the only way it knew how: **I fell.**

But instead of just falling on to level ground, I fell onto the uneven part behind the swing set. I just kept rolling and rolling, unable to stop myself.

"OW!" I yelled.

Looking down, I saw that I scraped my knee pretty badly, and I was utterly embarrassed. I heard snickering, and I looked up to see Brian and his friends laughing at me. Lenny was nowhere to be found, and I didn't know what to do.

Beau walked up to me and said, "Are you okay? Don't listen to them. Do you want me to get a counselor?"

I nodded, and he grabbed my hands to help me up. I felt his calloused palms from where he loved climbing on the monkey bars. That was exactly the type of Disney Channel moment I had always dreamed of. It didn't matter that all of his friends were laughing at us, he still decided to help me. I was mortified, but his small act of kindness made me feel so much better.

He didn't say much, but he also didn't leave until I was at the clinic. From that moment on, I saw him as my shy Prince Charming. As the summer went on, he never mentioned that afternoon in July. I think he didn't want my embarrassment to resurface. Although we never spoke of the incident again, I *never* forgot it.

Now, he's sitting in my history class, nodding along to whatever Mr. Evans is talking about. I find myself sneaking glances at him.

We could totally grow on what we once had. Okay, maybe we didn't "have" anything with each other when we were eight, but you understand.

I smile to myself. This could happen. Who knows, I might even post a cringe "loml" picture on Instagram.

Midway through planning the rest of our lives, I get a text from Lenny.

LENNY: you've got that look on your face

ME: What????

LENNY: you know the look.
your crush for Beau Braxton is so strong,
it is taking over your face

ME: Shut up no it is not!!!!

LENNY: it's fine. i am definitely here
for Beau + Marlowe 2.0

Yep, Lenny is right. I'm officially Boysick again.

CHAPTER TWO

After school, Lenny and I coast down the Tennessee roads in her obnoxiously clean Honda Civic. We have the windows rolled partially down to let in the August air. I've basically spent the whole day planning what Beau and I's future will look like as high school sweethearts. We pull into Lenny's driveway and see her brother's car parked there.

"Carter's home?!" she says.

We walk into her house, and I'm instantly hit with the scent of lime and fresh laundry. Lenny's mom is kind of a health nut and ingredient mom, which is the complete opposite of my house. Her mom, Sheila, is always fixing different foods for her kids to try, and she's constantly trying to get her home on the cover of some healthy living magazine. Meanwhile, my room is a black hole for all dishes, random articles of clothing, and who knows what else.

"What are you doing home so early?" Lenny asks her brother. Carter sits at the kitchen table, eating a bowl of Froot Loops. He just looks so boyish. He has a sand colored crewneck on, and his ginger curls are peeking out of the sides of his baseball cap.

"Mr. Fitz ended rehearsal early. Hey Mar," he says. Carter is the type of guy that can get along with anyone. He makes you feel like you are instantly best friends. He's a golden retriever of sorts.

Lenny and Carter can be very similar at times; their mom jokes that they are more like twins than just siblings. Carter is a senior and super social to everyone he meets. Jackson Stewart from *Hannah Montana* walked, so Carter could run.

Lenny is pretty much the same way. Her energy is captivating, and she can light up any room she walks in. Carter and Lenny's social nature helps me feel more comfortable being my socially awkward self.

Since I've known him, Carter has been the class clown, always finding ways to give Lenny and me a hard time. At summer camp, he would have a group of little kids following his every move, mesmerized by his entertaining personality. It reminded me of Peter Pan and the Lost Boys. There was once a six-year-old who had a huge crush on him, and it was obvious to everyone. At the camp's end of summer talent show, she dedicated her rendition of "Love Story" to him. He was beyond flattered and such a good sport about it.

You never knew what to expect from Carter, and that's still true to this day. At school, he seems to go through a different situationship every other week. While Lenny has been in a steady relationship for three years, Carter hasn't been able to keep a girlfriend for more than a month.

It's kind of bizarre when you think about it; for him to be so social and charming, it's surprising that he doesn't have a long term girlfriend. Whenever Lenny or I ask about it, he gets all shy and quiet. It's the one topic he won't say much about.

"Len, aren't you so sad your brother is growing up? Just finished the first day of my senior year," he says with exaggerated puppy eyes. He finishes his cereal and walks towards the kitchen sink.

"Yeah, yeah sure," Lenny says. "Marlowe said you all had Leadership together."

He nods and sticks his bowl and spoon in the dishwasher. "Yeah, Mar and I are going to rule that class," he winks.

"Oh, of course," I say sarcastically. "When is your Beauty and the Beast audition, by the way?"

"September 25th," he says.

"Well, obviously you are going to get a leading role. So Lenny and I will have to come to watch."

"I would love that," he says, as his upper lip quirks ever so slightly, as if he doesn't want me to see him smile about that.

Carter flops on the couch, ready to watch an episode of *The Office*.

That's his favorite show; to be honest, he is the reason I love it so much. He forced everyone around him to watch it a few years ago, and I instantly fell in love.

Lenny has asked me before if I've ever been Boysick about her brother. And to be honest, I never have thought of him that way. It's like Carter and I know each other too well for me to think of him as my Prince Charming. He's gorgeous, but he's just not gorgeous *for me*.

When Lenny and I are upstairs, she says, "Why do teachers think it's okay to give homework on the first day of school? That's breaking some sacred, unspoken rule."

"I know! I already have like thirty problems to review for Statistics."

Even though I am pretty stoked for this year, I'm a little nervous for the "junior year anxiety" that comes when college prep is shoved in your face. I haven't even taken the ACT yet, and according to my overbearing nerves, I'm not sure if I'll do very well. Part of me just wants to enjoy this year with my best friend and not think about the future too much, but the worry is always there, looming in the background.

"I can't believe Mr. Robbins wants us to write an essay by next Tuesday! From what other upperclassmen were saying, I thought these classes were going to be chill."

"As long as we have ice cream to reward ourselves afterwards, I'm good," Lenny shrugs. I can hear the graphite of the pencil scratch her paper as she starts to outline her essay.

"Yeah," I say, starting to color-code my U.S. History notes. Honestly, I'm going to need to put extra effort into that class. If I just daydream about Beau the whole time, I am sure to fail. But I just can't help it if he looks like an angel!

Highlighting my history notes really didn't take as much time as I thought it would. Opening up my planner, I just stare at my to-do list. I have something due in every single class.

The words seem to float off the page, putting me in some kind of trance. I am so overwhelmed with things to do that I feel myself fall into some kind of paralysis. It's like I am stuck, unable to will myself to finish my schoolwork.

I glance over at Lenny and see that she is immersed in her homework, and I don't want to break her concentration.

Swallowing down the lump in my throat, I pull out my Statistics homework that my teacher assigned and try to get started on it. With my heart still beating rapidly, I can't stop staring at my notebook. Just staring at my paper won't complete the homework.

Lenny's timer goes off after an hour, and I've only finished five problems. It didn't even make a dent in my assignment. But I am much too eager for a study break rather than sitting back down for another hour to finish this worksheet.

"Lenny," I say, with an eyebrow raised. "Should we go for an ice cream run?"

"The answer is always yes," she replies.

Lenny quickly texts Jacob to see if he wants to join us. Packing up our school supplies, we get ready to head to Twisted, the best ice cream place in town.

Twenty minutes later, we pull into Twisted with Jacob in the backseat. I'm filling him in on the Beau situation. He already knows about my Boysick tendencies.

"So you knew this guy when you were kids, he moved away, and now he just happens to show up at school?" Jacob asks.

"Yes!" I exclaim.

"Netflix needs to make a romcom about this love story," he says.

Lenny chuckles and rolls her eyes.

Jacob looks at me and says, "Speaking of Netflix, I started Arrested Development."

"What did you think?"

"It's hilarious! I was laughing so hard the entire time," he says. "I finished episode five earlier. It's the one where Gob chips his front tooth, so every time he talks, he accidentally whistles."

Gasping, I clap my hands excitedly. "I love that episode so much!"

He turns to Lenny, saying, "I can't believe you didn't think it was funny."

She shrugs, "I don't know. It just wasn't my humor."

"At least Marlowe and I can talk about it together," he says, flicking a braid out of his face.

We pull up to the drive-through window and order our usual: one strawberry with sprinkles for Lenny, one chocolate with peanut butter cups for me, and one vanilla with cookie dough for Jacob. I'm pretty sure

Lenny just likes the strawberry ice cream for the pink aesthetic. I, on the other hand, will never pass up something with peanut butter.

We park nearby, silence filling the car while we gulf down our delicious ice cream.

"Okay, I have an idea," Lenny says and clears her throat. "Hear me out."

I look at her skeptically.

"Maya posted on her story that she's having a party tonight. Her dads are in New York for some business trips. You should message Beau to see if he's going."

"You want us to just go by and crash a party?" I ask.

"It's not crashing a party. She pretty much invited the whole school," Lenny says. Maya's house is big enough to fit the entire student body.

"But why would Beau even go in the first place?" I ask.

"He just moved back to town, so I'd say he'll be at the party to meet more people. If he wasn't planning on going, then you can just convince him to tag along with us."

Nodding, Jacob says, "Sounds like a pretty solid plan."

"He'll see how amazing you are at the party and instantly fall in love," Lenny winks, enabling my Boysickness to grow.

"I don't know," I murmur. Indecisiveness tugs at my chest. "What if it's awkward?"

"Well, if he's awkward or weird, then we'll drop him," Lenny says. In a true best friend fashion, she's overprotective so that I won't be let down.

"It would give you more time with Beau rather than just in class," Jacob pipes up. Even he knows how badly I want a relationship.

What would young Marlowe from Camp Caelee want me to do?

With an exhale, I say, "Honestly, it might work. Let's do it."

When we get back to Lenny's, I raid her closet to find a cute outfit. I had changed into an oversized tee and comfy shorts after school; that definitely will not cut it if I want to impress Beau.

"That's cute," Lenny says as I rifle through some crop tops. I hold up a light green tank top, and she nods.

"But I don't want to be cold later tonight," I say. "I've got to be prepared for anything. Beau could be so swept off his feet, that we might hangout *after* the party."

Am I a hopeless romantic? Yes.

Am I ashamed of it? Most of the time, no.

"What about this?" she asks, holding up a white linen button down.

"Like open?"

"Yes, more like a cardigan," she says.

I do some more digging through her closet until I've found the perfect summer-y party outfit. This reminds me of the *Princess Diaries* scene where Mia is picking out an outfit before her party with Josh. Maybe Beau and I will have better luck than Mia did with Josh.

Jacob heads downstairs while I change into the green crop top, white button down, denim shorts, and Lenny's white Doc Martens sandals.

"This is so cute!" she exclaims.

"Thanks Len," I say, giving her a hug. I glance one more time in the mirror and try to smooth down my wavy hair.

Swiping on another layer of lip gloss, I say, "I'm ready."

In the car, Jacob takes the backseat again, and Lenny connects her phone, so Conan Gray can blast throughout the car.

"Okay, Jacob. I need some advice on how to make Beau like me."

I turn around and see him pondering this. "Well, one of the first things I noticed about Lenny was how extroverted she was. She made me laugh, which I loved."

"Awww," Lenny blushes. She scrunches her nose and does a little head shake. It's adorable to see them so in love.

"I feel like guys either like a girl to *make them* laugh, or they want the girl to laugh *at them*. You've got to figure out what Beau wants."

"Like, I'll laugh a little harder at his jokes to flatter him. And maybe try to tell him some jokes of my own," I say, wiggling my eyebrows.

"Oh dear," Lenny says chuckling.

"Okay, what else?" I ask Jacob.

"What do you mean?" he asks.

"I need to step up my flirting game if this is going to work. Normally I just bat my long eyelashes and call it a day, but I need to add more to my flirting inventory."

Jacob laughs, and Lenny says, "Well, I've not hardcore flirted in a few years, but I was always more of a physical touch kind of gal."

"Mmmkay..." I say, motioning for her to go on.

"Like a playful touch of the arm, standing a little close, or going in for a hug."

"So, you're telling me everything was calculated with us?" Jacob asks with an eyebrow raised and his dimples on full display.

"Oh, of course," Lenny teases. "I'm a mastermind."

I roll my eyes at those two and tuck away their pieces of advice. I really feel like I have a chance with Beau. Maybe the party tonight can be the first few steps towards a relationship.

CHAPTER THREE

After confirming with Beau that he'll be at the party, I text Maya for her address. Caelee County is mainly filled with middle class families, but there are several wealthy neighborhoods on the west side. Of course, Maya lives in one of them.

I really shouldn't be so brutal to Maya. Obviously, the saying "empowered women empower women" is something that Lenny and I live by. There's just something about Maya that I can't stand.

I've known her longer than I've known Lenny. Maya and I met in kindergarten, where she was instantly the teacher's favorite. Throughout the years, I saw her win the spelling bee, wow the crowd at the talent show, and attract all the boys as if she's some kind of magnet.

When we were in elementary school, our family or friends could send us roses on Valentines Day. In fourth grade, I got three: one from Mom, one from Dad, and one from my teacher. Maya got sixteen: one from all eleven boys in our class, two from her dads, one from our teacher, and two from teachers she'd had in previous years. I'm telling you, this girl is adored by all.

Driving by her house, we see that it is littered with cars, so we just park at the adjacent street. The neighborhood is insane; every house looks like a mansion or something out of HGTV. Her neighbor even has golden lion statues in front of their gate.

We walk over to her back yard, and it's filled with people mingling. Surprisingly, this party scene kind of reminds me of the school cafeteria.

Everyone is already in their own groups, talking with their friends as if anyone else is irrelevant.

Sweaty bodies are everywhere, and I keep turning my head, trying to find Beau. The music is too loud, and I feel the bass rattle through my bones. Looking over some obnoxious people dancing, I keep glancing around for him.

Target: Located.

Beau is standing over by the pool, drink in hand, and he's talking to one of the football players. I can practically see his long eyelashes and rosy cheeks from here. I look over to Lenny because obviously I need her to be my hype woman before I go over there.

Lenny sees the desperation in my eyes and says, "You got this! You look so cute. That effortless girl-next-door vibe. Jacob and I are going to get drinks!" She squeezes my arm.

Waltzing over to where Beau stands near the pool, I say, "Hi Beau."

"Hey Marlowe," he says with a small smile traced on his lips, and I legitimately almost melt. The football player turns to go refill his cup.

"How was your first day at Caelee High?" I ask, trying to seem more social than I really am.

"It was pretty good. It's kind of weird to see people after I haven't seen them in a while, but then again, it's nice to see a bunch of semi-familiar faces. I mean, you know me," he says, his bronzed skin seeming to glow under the moonlight. "I'm not exactly the most talkative guy out there, so it'll take a while before it feels like home again."

You know me. He literally admitted how well we know each other! And he knows that I won't judge him for his shyness. I mean, without Lenny, I would be a hermit stuck in my shell.

I remember when I first heard the rumor at camp that Beau was moving away at the end of summer. I didn't want to believe it. Why did he have to leave? Why couldn't it have been one of his annoying friends that moved?

At camp, I went up to him after our afternoon snack break and asked, "Someone said you were moving away. Is that true?"

"Yeah," he said and looked at me with those sparkling brown eyes.

"I'm so sorry!" I said, giving him a hug. It was kind of out of character for me to just reach over and hug him, but I really didn't want him to forget about me.

"It's okay," he said. "My parents are getting me a phone before we leave. So, I'll still be able to text everyone."

"Oh good! Well, let me know when you get it. We can text when you are gone," I smiled.

He ended up leaving camp before I even got his number.

"Yeah," I say, snapping back to the party and trying to think of something else we can talk about. His phone buzzes, and he looks down at whoever is texting him.

I've got to get myself together. If I really want Beau and I's relationship to become something more than just my imagination, I need to step it up. I mean, I think it's a sign from the universe that the first ever guy I was Boysick over COMES BACK TO MY TOWN!

I'm already halfway through high school, and I've yet to have a single successful relationship. Obviously, what I've been doing isn't working.

Maybe I need to be more like Lenny and go after what I want. I can embody her extroverted nature. Summoning all of the girl power energy that's within me, I decide to shoot my shot. I can do this. I don't need to wait around for a guy to ask me out. Right?

"So um… if you ever want to study history together, let me know. I have the first block free, so we could get coffee or something."

A few seconds go by and he's still engrossed in his phone. "Mhm? Oh, I am so sorry. I didn't realize you had said something," he says, glancing up with an adorable smile of oblivion crossing his face.

Well, thanks Universe. Now I have to embarrassingly shoot my shot for the *second* time.

"I have the first block as a free period so if you want to go to the coffee shop or somewhere we could study together? For history? I've heard Mr. Evans is nice, but the class itself can be stressful at times and I've been struggling with my homework," I ramble on. *Get it together Marlowe.*

"Sure. Yeah, history isn't my favorite, so I need all the help I can get," he says. The evening sky accentuates his dark eyebrows and angled cheekbones.

"Cool," I say, secretly proud of myself. Beau is being so sweet right now. Lenny would be over the moon for me.

"Hi Marlowe," a syrupy sweet voice says behind me.

I turn around to see Maya with her blonde hair in a bun like some kind of makeshift halo. I mutter a hello back to her.

"I don't think we've met," Maya says with a cheesy smile and looks at Beau. "I'm Maya."

He introduces himself, pushing his dark hair out of his face. I want to scream at her for interrupting us.

After a few minutes of meaningless conversation with Maya, someone calls her, and she walks back into her house. I look at Beau, expecting him to roll his eyes at her fake personality. It was glaringly obvious that Maya was just exerting her queen bee status.

"She's hot," Beau says quietly.

HUH? Beau *cannot* like Maya. It can't happen.

"She has a boyfriend," I say quickly, waving a dismissive hand.

He nods, and his eyes are trained towards Maya's house. Looking down at his cup, he says, "I think I'm going to get another drink. Do you want anything?"

"I'm good! Designated driver tonight," I say. Sirens go off in my mind about Beau thinking Maya was hot. The more he talks to her, surely he'll see that she has a terrible personality. You can think someone is attractive without actually having a crush on them, right?

His eyes twinkle, and he starts walking into the house. I exhale and look around. Just as I am about to text Lenny the details of Beau and I's five minute conversation, I hear, "CAROLINE!"

I look over, and it seems that time has slowed down *once again*. A blonde headed boy comes running at me, grabs my waist, and catapults us both into the water. It takes me a moment to figure out what happened.

I am in the water.

I am soaking wet.

I am in Maya Nguyen's swimming pool, soaking wet with my clothes on.

"WHAT ON EARTH?!" I yell.

The blonde guy emerges from the water, with hazy eyes and soured breath. "Oh, my bad. I thought you were my sister's friend."

"What?!" I scoff and head towards the pool's stairs. I hear laughing from the sides of the pool. This is so embarrassing.

"Yo, my bad!" he says, which doesn't help the situation at all. Who thinks of pushing a girl into the pool? Never mind a girl they don't even know?

I see a dozen phone flashlights on as the blonde guy's friends record my utter embarrassment. Even after ringing out my shirt, I am absolutely drenched, and my phone is now useless. I try to click it on, but nothing works.

I look around for Lenny and Jacob, but they aren't in the backyard. Reluctantly, I head into Maya's house to try to find them.

Immediately when I walk in, I'm met with the intense smell of weed, and there is a couple aggressively making out on the couch. Nearby, there is a group of guys playing foosball towards the kitchen, and a couple of girls beside them are doing some kind of TikTok dance.

I walk around all over the kitchen and living room, and I don't see Lenny at all. It feels strange to just wander around Maya's house, but I don't know what else to do. Walking upstairs, I see someone throwing up in the hall bathroom. Yeah, no. I don't deal with vomit.

After several minutes of searching, my head is spinning. Glancing down at my arms, I see the army of goosebumps lining my skin. I head back downstairs and decide to just walk back to where we parked. I'll just chill in Lenny's car and watch *Parks and Recreation*. I'm on my seventh rewatch, and I'm about to hit the episode "Flu Season." That can be my plans for the rest of the night.

Now that I'm back outside, a gust of wind hits me with the smell of fresh air. The breeze is nice, but it sends a million more chill bumps down my arms. I feel like I'm wearing ice packs as clothes.

Walking over to Lenny's car, I pull at the handle.

It dawns on me a little too late that I don't have her keys. Now what am I supposed to do?

Squatting down in front of Lenny's Honda, I decide to just wait for them to come back. It shouldn't take much longer right? *This* is why I don't go to parties. At least I got a cute moment with Beau to justify this not so great night.

With my knees to my chest, I decide to pull out my phone to watch the blossoming relationship of Ben and Leslie.

But wait. My phone's off. *Oh no.*

"Mar?" I hear someone say.

Looking up, I see Carter standing in front of me, with the silhouette of his ginger curls and a Dr. Pepper in hand. He must've seen me eyeing the drink because he hands it to me.

"Is there anything in it?" I ask.

"Nah. Dr. Pepper is good enough it doesn't need to be spiked."

I smile and take a sip while he sits next to me.

"Why the sudden urge to leave such a great party?" he asks with a sarcastic tone and goofy grin.

"I was really hoping to talk with someone, and I accidentally took a swim in the process," I say, motioning to my wet outfit.

"You must be freezing," he says.

"Yeah, I'm pretty cold." I shake my head, "I couldn't find Maya inside to ask for a towel."

"I have a blanket in my car. It may not dry you off, but it'll keep you warm," he says, shrugging.

"Thank God," I say, walking over with him to his car. He parked over at Maya's guesthouse, and luckily, no one is around now. Carter opens his trunk, digging around for the promised blanket. He pulls out the soft quilt, lined with fuzzy green and navy plaid. Even though it came from his car trunk, I can still smell the fresh laundry scent on the blanket. Since they grew up in a clean freak household, Lenny and Carter are the opposite of slobs.

He holds up the slightly wrinkled blanket. In one swift motion, Carter lifts his arm above my head and drapes the blanket over my shoulders. I smile at him.

"Better?" he asks.

I nod. "Thanks."

"So this guy you wanted to talk to, were you able to show him your classic Marlowe charm?"

"He's quiet, so it'll take a while for it to become anything serious," I tell him. Bending down, I adjust my wet shoes, thankful for the warmth of Carter's blanket. "Nothing really happened with the guy."

"Let me guess," he says with a smirk. "Was it Beau Braxton?"

I snap up and look at him. "Did Lenny tell you?" I ask, startled.

"No," he says, chuckling. "I think you forget that I was at camp with you, Mar. Everyone pretty much knew you were in love with Beau. I heard he was coming back in town and knew you would flip."

My jaw is on the floor. I mean, yes eight-year-old me was pretty obsessed with Beau, but I didn't think it was so obvious that even *Carter* would notice.

I shove him. "And you didn't warn me? Carter, you're supposed to be on my side!" He just laughs and shakes his head. Carter's laugh always surprises me. It's loud and infectious, as if he just can't contain himself.

Anytime I'm not feeling well or I've had a bad day, I love going over to Lenny's house. She is there for me, acting as an ear while I rant about my day. Many times, Carter notices my unpleasantness, and he tries to cheer me up. He will say a stupid joke or do something silly, and most of the time, he ends up cracking himself up. When I hear his laugh, I can't help but to giggle to myself. It's one of those laughs that is funnier than the joke.

"I guess I shouldn't even be worried about who is on whose side. I have zero chance with Beau. He told me that he thought Maya was *hot*," I tell him, rolling my eyes.

"She already has a boyfriend. C'mon, you're *the* Marlowe Ford. You could totally slide in," he says with a wink.

"Carter, *how*?! There's no way I could compete with Maya. Look at this," I say, gesturing at the giant mansion we were at.

"Okay, that doesn't matter. And do you need some kind of flirting training?" He chuckles. "You know I'm kind of a ladies man."

"Lenny and Jacob have already tried to help in that department," I say, tucking my hair behind my ears. "But honestly, yeah. You *are* pretty charismatic."

He shakes his head. "No- I was joking. I'm not this ego-maniac douche."

"I know, I know," I say. "But, you could help me actually get Beau! You even said so yourself that I've had a crush on him forever." Everyone knows Carter, so he could easily be a double agent for me.

"Like, you want me to be your wing-man?!" he asks, surprised.

"Please, Carter? I'm your sister's best friend! Just see if you can bring me up in conversation or something."

He sighs and taps his chin dramatically. He finally says, "Okay."

I squeal and give him a hug. I don't even care that my hair is wet and I'm wrapped in Carter's trunk blanket… Beau could be my future boyfriend!

CHAPTER FOUR

It's officially the end of the first week of school, and I have *not* grown tired of seeing Beau everyday. Every time I see him, he's got a new outfit that makes me absolutely swoon.

This is a little embarrassing to admit, but I've memorized his class schedule based on where he walks to class. And… I've changed my path to each class so I could run into him everyday. I know it's a little pathetic, but I want to see him *as much* as I can.

In U.S. History, the course is very content heavy. So, there isn't much time to mingle among us classmates. I have to get creative on how I can talk to Beau.

Speaking of History, Mr. Evans walks in and addresses the class, "Hey guys. I know most of you are juniors, so it's ACT season for you. Mr. Brooks has started an ACT prep program for all juniors and seniors that is completely free. I would recommend forming groups to study together."

Lenny and I exchange glances because *obviously* we are going to study together. I really want to get a good score on the ACT, but knowing myself, I will probably freak out in the testing room. I just hate the pressure that comes with standardized testing.

Since third grade, I've had to complete an end of the year exam to assess my learning. I always hated taking those exams. I would feel more confident in my performance if the assessment was on projects instead of a test score. I've never had a standardized test with this much pressure or emphasis. If I could barely get through my end of the year exams in elementary school, how will I be able to stomach the ACT?

Mr. Evans rolls through the rest of the lecture, and the idea of the ACT is still tugging at the edge of my mind. I thought I would somehow be able to avoid the junior year stressors, but it has inevitably entered my life. How am I going to be able to study on top of everything else I have going on?

Wait.

I could feed two birds with one scone. Digging into my backpack, I pick up my newly fixed phone to text Lenny. Thanks to my encounter with Maya's pool, I've had to wait around until my dad could fix my water-logged one. I've felt so old school and disconnected, as if I need to communicate with Lenny through mailing pigeons. I haven't even had the chance to fully debrief with her about what happened at the party.

> ME: We need to form a study group...
> What if I invited beau???

> LENNY: ummmm yes!

> LENNY: do it!!!!!

"Alright, that's it for today. I'll see you all tomorrow," Mr. Evans concludes after the lecture. I pack up my bags and head over to where Beau is. Lenny follows behind me.

"Hey Beau," I say shyly.

"Hey," he says.

"So Marlowe and I were going to form a study group to prepare for the ACT. And we were wondering if you want to join?" Lenny pipes up.

"Sure. I honestly haven't even started looking at it, so a group would help."

"Perfect! We can text you the details when we figure out time and stuff," I say.

"Here," he says, handing me his phone. I type in my number and create a contact for Lenny. She nudges my arm, letting me know she's proud that *I just did that.*

Giving Beau back his phone, I flash a smile. Suddenly, I hear some footsteps come up behind me. "Can I join?" a high, feathery voice says.

Slowly turning around, I see that Miss Maya Nguyen has invited herself into our conversation. Lovely.

Beau looks over at Lenny and me, waiting for a response.

"Uh, yeah," I reluctantly say. Maybe if Beau sees Maya in our study group, he'll get a good glimpse of her annoying personality. At least I hope so.

"Yay!" she squeals.

It takes everything in me to not roll my eyes.

• • •

"But, you know that Maya has always been like this. We've known this forever," Lenny says after I just spent twenty minutes ranting about the study group situation.

"I know, it's just so frustrating!"

From Beau's eyes, Maya is a swan, and I'm the ugly duckling. I am Mia Thermopolis *pre-Paulo* transformation. Speaking of, we are actually watching *The Princess Diaries* at Lenny's house.

Stretching out on Lenny's living room couches, we have heaps of snacks all around us. It's a tradition that anytime we are going to watch a movie, we have to have an endless supply of all things carbs.

Right as Anne Hathaway finds out she's related to royalty, Carter walks in.

As I pause the movie, Carter walks over and asks, "Any Beau updates?"

"Ehhhh, some bad news. We are in a study group together, but Maya managed to weasel her way into it."

"Oh no," he says in solidarity.

"I know right?!" I tell him.

"Well if it makes you feel better, I did try to talk you up to him."

"Really?!" Lenny and I say at the same time.

"Yeah, I saw him at the coffee shop. We talked a little, and he asked about Len. Naturally, I brought you up, and he said he had seen you around. He goes, *'Talk about a glow up, damn.'*"

"WHAT?!"

"He thinks I'm cute?!"

"MARLOWE!!!!" Lenny says, shaking my arm. "AHHH!"

"Carter, this is amazing!"

"You're welcome," he says with a shove. "You can pay me back later."

"Anything you want, it's yours," I say. My heart is racing; for the first time it feels like my Boysick feelings are actually getting me somewhere.

After watching me for a beat, Carter stays downstairs with us as we resume the movie. *The Princess Diaries* is probably my top favorite movie. I love the way Michael is always there for Mia. Like, he would do anything to help her. It's nice to see a guy crushing on a girl; usually in movies, it's only the girl that's ever chasing the guy.

Maybe, I just don't know it yet. Beau could be crushing on me as much as I am on him. This pining could be mutual.

It may have just been a momentary lapse in judgment when he said Maya looks hot. If he thinks that *I* had a glow-up, then maybe I'm still in the running.

It worked out for Mia Thermopolis, didn't it?

CHAPTER FIVE

I t's Tuesday night, and I'm frantically running around my house to make sure it looks presentable for Beau. That's right, *BEAU BRAXTON IS COMING TO MY HOUSE*!

Maya's house was not an option because her dads were remodeling the kitchen. That's right, they were putting even more money into their million dollar mansion.

We were going to have the ACT study group at Lenny's house this time, but Carter had other plans. He was going to bring a girl over to meet his mom. *Carter, who never has a serious relationship, is inviting a girl for a "meet the parents" dinner.* Lenny and I were in shock. I guess I need to start asking more about his love life, instead of just having him help with mine.

Hence, the meeting is at my house. It's not that I'm embarrassed about my home or anything, but I rarely have anyone over other than Lenny. My dad is an IT guy for a middle school, and my mom is a freelance artist. So you can imagine what my house looks like.

On just about every counter or table top is some kind of tech device that is my dad's. And each room is painted a different jewel-toned color, thanks to my mom. Our living room is deep dusty blue, with pops of mustard yellow all around. There are unique pieces of decor sprinkled throughout our space, where my mom has supported local artisans.

Most people make fun of only-children and say they have a boring childhood because only-children don't have siblings to play with. My childhood was anything but boring. My adolescent years were filled with color and imagination. My dad and I would build forts in the living room, while my mom and I made planters for our wildflowers growing in the garden. From meeting Lenny, they instantly loved and welcomed her into our odd little family. Lenny and I's upbringing is completely different, but she never acts like it. Whereas her mom always had the bright white living room spotless, Lenny was judgment free about my cluttered, overstimulating house.

Ding- dong.

Okay, that's the doorbell. Okay, that could be Beau. You're fine. You're perfectly fine. It's just that your crush is coming over to your house. No biggie.

I open the door, and Maya and Beau are standing there, study materials in hand.

"Hey! Come on in," I say.

I guide them into our kitchen, where they sit their stuff down, waiting for me to say something. Luckily, my mom comes in to break the awkward silence.

"Hey! I'm Marlowe's mom, Sam."

"Hello!" Maya and Beau say politely. Surprisingly, Maya hasn't said anything passive… yet.

"There are some cookies I made earlier on the counter, and ice cream in the fridge. I also set out a bowl of chips and french onion dip. I wasn't sure what you would be in the mood for. Help yourselves to anything!" Mom says.

I hear the door open and Lenny joins us in the kitchen. Eyeing Beau in my kitchen, Lenny gives me an excited nose scrunch. I try not to blush, hoping that Beau doesn't see how starstruck I am by him.

"Well, we can go ahead and get started," I say while sliding into a chair. Beau sits down beside me, and our legs accidentally bump into each other, which sends the butterflies in my stomach into a frenzy.

"Oh sorry," he says.

"You're good," I say while nudging his leg back with a small smirk.

He smiles and bumps mine again. I give him a teasing grin.

If this isn't love, I don't know what is.

Interrupting the moment that Beau and I were having, Mom comes back in and asks, "Do any of you want a soda? There are cans in the fridge if you want some!"

Giving her big eyes, I try to signal that she doesn't need to empty our entire refrigerator in front of Beau.

"I'm good. Thank you though!" Lenny says sweetly, pulling out a bottle of green juice from her bag.

"I'll go grab us one," Beau says to me.

Beau comes back from the kitchen and hands me an ice-cold can of Sprite Zero. He says, "I had to, for camp's sake."

"Oh my gosh! I remember," I say, looking up at him. My chest fills with gratitude, and I'm sure he can see the red hearts in my eyes.

When we were at camp, the counselors would put on a small diving contest between us campers. You had one chance on the diving board to impress "the judges." Some kids would go up and do "The Pencil," where they just jump straight down. Some would jump with their arms and legs out to the side, calling it "The Starfish." Some of the guys would jump into a straddle, calling it "The Nutcracker." The name speaks for itself.

When I went up, I would jump with my signature front somersault in the air. It almost always wowed the counselors, and personally, I felt like an Olympian afterwards.

Beau was known among camp as having the best belly flop; it was true. He would jump, lay flat in the air, and fall against the water. A huge *smack!* would echo around the pool. His quiet nature was pushed to the side, as he was brooding, daring, and ready to win the prize.

To whoever won the contest, you could go pick out a soda from the vending machine in the counselor's lounge. Beau and I won in the top five a few times, and we always picked out a Sprite Zero. The other soda choices weren't that appealing; the counselor's didn't stock anything with caffeine for fear that the campers would start catapulting off the walls.

So, Beau and I would crack open our chilled Sprite Zeros and sip on them like the champions we were. I still love that soda to this day- Beau just unlocked its origin story from my memory.

Beau chuckles, snapping me back into the moment. "Yeah, those were the days."

If he's thinking back to our camp days, does that mean he thinks about me like I think about him? Do the memories and what-ifs revolve around his mind, like soap suds circling a drain?

"I suck at science, so can we start with that?" Maya says, breaking up our camp recollections.

"Sure," Lenny says and pulls a workbook out of her bag. "This is Carter's book from last year when he was taking the test. I brought it over for us to work through. I also stopped by Mr. Brooks' office and picked up the other workbook."

We all flip through the books and settle on some problems to work through. The thing about the ACT that is so hard for me to understand is that it is *designed* to trip me up.

What's the point in that?!

We practice a few of the science problems and work our way through some math questions. After a while, Maya breaks our concentration by taking a selfie with her study supplies with the hashtag "girlboss." Excuse me while I vomit.

"Holy crap, it's already been an hour! We should take a break," she says.

"I didn't realize we had been doing it for so long," Lenny says.

"Are you going to the pep rally on Thursday? It's the first football game of the season and everyone will be there," Maya asks us, changing the subject.

"Yeah, I'll be there," Beau says.

"Marlowe and I will be there too!" Lenny pipes up. I give her a small smile because she really is the best wing-woman ever.

"I'm trying to learn more about sports. Don't hate me, but I've only been to three football games before," I say.

"What?! No, you have to go! The team should be really good this year," Beau says excitedly. His eyes light up like a mirrorball in the center of the dance floor.

Beau isn't the stereotypical jock you'd think of when you think of a football fan. He reminds me of football players from the 1950's. He's got that James Dean aesthetic and tall, athletic body.

He starts telling me about the other team we are playing and the highs and lows of high school football. It's so cute when he talks about something that he's passionate about because it's clear he's on cloud nine.

He pulls out his phone to show me highlights from his favorite college team. I have no idea what's going on in the video or what play is being made, but I watch because it's Beau. I scoot in closer to see his phone, and once again, I accidentally bump his leg. Smiling softly, he looks over at me and nudges my leg back.

Is this our "thing?"

OH MY GOSH I COULD MELT.

"But yeah, Marlowe. You should totally come to the game," says Maya, breaking Beau and I's connection for a second time tonight.

"The dance team has been working so hard on our half-time performance, and we want there to be a really good turnout," she says.

"I'll be there," I say.

"Good!" Beau says. I smile, wondering what our football hangout will look like. Will this be our last hangout as *just friends?*

Am I being a bit delusional? Proudly.

After a couple of hours of studying, Maya starts to pack up her stuff. She claims she has to be somewhere. You know, the queen is needed everywhere!

Maya leaves and winks at Beau before heading out the door. That's so like her to flirt with another guy while she has a boyfriend. I watch Beau's face to see if he has any trace of emotion after Maya's flirtation. I need to do something to "one up" Maya's wink.

"Well, I should probably go as well," Beau says, as he starts to stand. He grabs his hoodie and raises his arms to slip it over his head. The hem of his shirt lifts above the waist of his jeans. A smooth patch of tan skin is exposed, and I feel my breath catch in my throat.

"I can walk you out!" I say enthusiastically. I hop up and lead him towards the door. Stepping out onto the porch, I look up into his chestnut colored eyes. The sun is starting to set, and it casts an orange glow onto my house's tan bricks.

"Thanks for coming by tonight," I say, tucking my hair behind my ears.

"Thanks for hosting. I'm glad we've made a little group."

"Yeah," I say. I need to make a move. STAT. "Well, I'll see you at the game!"

He smiles and nods. I stand on the tips of my toes and reach my arms upwards, going in for a hug. Beau steps forward, and he hugs me around the waist. He smells like cinnamon and leather. His fingers are gentle against my lower back, and I could pinch myself.

He looks down and gives me another small smile before heading down the stairs. He hops into his Jeep, and I wave to him as he drives away. My cheeks feel sore and pinched from so much smiling.

"LENNY WE HUGGED! WE HUGGED!" I squeal, running back into the house.

"YAY!" Lenny celebrates with me. She grabs my hands, and we jump around in a circle like little kids at a birthday party.

"He's just so dreamy," I say and look out the window. Although he has driven away, he's still here in my memories. The smooth black hair, the dark eyebrows, the brown eyes, and the patch of tan skin I stole a glance at.

THAT DAMN PATCH OF SKIN.

CHAPTER SIX

enny and I start walking towards the football field, and I'm immediately overwhelmed. I definitely missed the memo because everyone around me is decked out in neon. There are glow sticks, face paint, and signs all around. How am I going to find Beau in this crowd?

"Jacob just texted me where he is," Lenny says while grabbing my hand and pulling me through the crowd of people. It smells like sweat and old nachos.

I feel like everyone here knows that I don't belong. I know that people probably aren't staring, but I *feel* like they are. I mean, I am wearing athletic shorts and a white sweatshirt, so I kind of stick out in a sea of neon.

We make it over to Jacob and scoot over to the few seats he saved for us. While Lenny is catching up with her boyfriend, I scan the crowd to look for Beau. I see a group of guys towards the front of the bleachers with blue paint all over themselves. Among that group, I catch a glimpse of a tall guy laughing at something his friend is playing on his phone.

I tell Lenny what I'm about to go do and head down the stairs. If I can just sit by Beau the whole game, that will give us the perfect opportunity to talk more. Weaving in and out of cheering people, I keep my eye on Beau.

Tapping on his shoulder, I say, "Hey!"

"Marlowe! You came! What do you think?"

"It's a lot to take in. But I have no idea what's going on in the field," I chuckle, crossing my arms in front of my chest.

"Here," he says as he has some people move over so I can stand next to him. My stomach is currently doing one million cartwheels.

Beau starts to explain the rules to me. He doesn't explain in a condescending way at all. It's like he is just sharing his genuine love for football with me. I am probably coming off as an airhead because I pretty much know absolutely NOTHING about football. But hey, I was raised by an artist and an IT guy, so what do you expect?!

LENNY: YOU ALL ARE TOGETHER AND HE'S SO CUTE AND YOU ALL ARE SO CUTE AND I JUST CAN'T HANDLE IT

ME: I KNOWWWW

Halftime arrives, and Beau says, "Do you want to go get some food?"

"Yes! To have the full high school football game experience, I need to try the concession stand."

"Obviously," Beau says with a smirk.

We walk over to the food, and Beau lightly places his hand on the small of my back to guide me where to go. Weaving in and out of people, I can't stop smiling.

Beau tells me what's the best to order, walking up to the concession stand. It's pretty much a booth full-size Lunchables with all the salt and processed foods. He gets nachos, and I pick out a pretzel.

"Let me go run up to where Lenny is. I left my purse with her," I say, glancing back in her direction.

"No, don't worry about it. I got it," Beau says as he pays for our food.

BEAU JUST PAID FOR MY FOOD.

I REPEAT. BEAU JUST PAID FOR MY FOOD.

I know this isn't a date. But HE PAID FOR MY FOOD! That has to mean something.

While we are getting some napkins, I look over and see Carter walking around with Phoebe Burns. She must be the one that Carter brought home to meet his mom.

I wave to him, and he waves back with the hand that isn't intertwined with Phoebe's. It's kind of weird to see Carter outside of Lenny's house. On a *date*.

Speaking of dates, Beau and I definitely aren't on a date. Definitely not. Right?

"Thanks for the food!" I say as I take a buttery, salty bite of the pretzel. It's pretty stale, but with Beau next to me, it tastes like the best food I've ever had.

"What do you think?" he says eyeing me

"Dewicious," I say with a mouth full of pretzel. He chuckles, the dimples peeking out of his cheeks.

While we're eating, Beau recollects on his time playing football with his friends at camp. I could listen to his deep voice until the end of time. Right before we head up to the stands, Beau bends over and picks a flower.

Handing me the yellow dandelion, he says, "Here."

"Aw, Beau!" my heart pounds against my rib cage. "Thank you. Is this a reference to camp?"

"Yeah," he says sheepishly. This whole date is a call back to our childhood days... and I'm here for it.

When we were younger, I was absolutely obsessed with making flower crowns (a phase most ten-year-olds in 2016 went through). Lenny and I would spend what seemed like hours picking wildflowers on the edges of camp. Then, we would weave the stems together for a make-shift headband. We even sold some to the little kids for a nickel a piece.

One day, Lenny was gone from camp because she had a dentist appointment. Since I never really hung out with anyone else at camp, I sat at a wooden bench and made them by myself.

Little Beau had walked past me, noticing the fact that I was alone. About twenty minutes later, he came back and handed me a sand bucket. Inside, were dozens of yellow dandelions he had picked for me. I wanted to cry when I saw them.

Once again, I saw a flash of this affectionate kid who was so different from all his friends. Normal guys just weren't that nice. Well, except for Carter, but he was my best friend's brother. So he didn't count.

Beau's sweet demeanor and kind gesture meant so much to me. That day, I felt my heart grow three sizes for him.

So now, seeing him hand me a small dandelion tells me that he remembers our camp days. I put the small flower in the pocket of my athletic shorts and thank the stars that Beau is back in my life.

The cheer team just finished performing their halftime routine, and the dance team enters the field now. I immediately see Maya, front and center of course. Even all the way up in the stands, I can see her siren eyes and plump lips. I know I should be a girl's girl and not the jealous type, but it's so difficult to not compare myself to her.

A few minutes into the hip hop routine, Beau says, "She was right. They are really good this year."

"Mm hmm," I murmur. His comment reminds me of Demi Lovato in *Camp Rock*. Only red flag about Beau so far: his total obliviousness to how awful Maya is.

But then again, Beau did pay for my food. I can excuse his friendship with Maya for that. And I'm refusing to remember that he said Maya was hot. Ahem- that definitely did *not* happen.

The team finishes their performance, and I scoot a little closer to Beau. Our arms aren't necessarily touching, but we are close. Almost thigh to thigh.

"Hey! Get in for a picture!" Beau's friend Harry yells. We all slide in so we are in frame, and Beau slings an arm around my shoulders effortlessly- as if it's just second nature.

It's getting so easy to imagine a future with him. For Harry's picture, I don't even have to try to smile. I am already beaming from ear to ear. I will have to stalk Instagram to find that picture later to show Lenny. Obviously.

Now that halftime is over, the game has started again. Beau's face lights up as if he is a kid on Christmas morning. He's cheering and screaming for our team to score. He told me before that our team was good this year, and he was right. We end up winning by a landslide, and I would say that's pretty good for my first Caelee High football game attendance.

Smiling, he turns to me and says, "I'm going to go congratulate Maya. Thanks for coming."

Beau leans in for a hug, and I thank him for the invite. The sweat from tonight makes his hair smell salty. His long fingers hover over my sweatshirt, and he pulls away, biting his bottom lip.

Looking at me up and down, he says, "See you later, Marlowe."

"Bye," I tell him and replay that hug twenty times in my mind. Watching him walk towards the dance team, my palms sweat with nervous energy.

I head over to Lenny and Jacob, trying not to think about Beau giving Maya that exact same hug.

CHAPTER SEVEN

walk into Leadership class, yawning from my exhaustive schedule this semester.

I feel so much pressure from school right now. In each class, my teachers seem to be on edge, which makes me feel even more anxious. Sometimes in the middle of class I'll catch my heart racing from simply thinking of my to do list. It's all just too much.

Carter comes in and waves a hello. His freckled cheeks turn up into a smirk as he sees me.

"Alright class! We'll get started," Mrs. Lin says. "Now that we've introduced the basics to leadership, you all will get started on your year-long project."

Caelee High is on a traditional high school block schedule where we have different classes each semester. Oddly enough, Leadership is one of the few classes that lasts all year long. So this project better be good, especially if it lasts us until May.

"You will pair up with a partner and create something that will better our school, our staff, and our students. This can be a club that you create, a system that you propose, or a physical addition to our campus."

Looking around the class, I am not sure who I should pair up with. I am *not* going to get a partner that is going to just freeload off everything I do. I mean I could always partner with Carter, but I doubt he would want to do a year long project with me rather than his guy friends.

Mrs. Lin spends the rest of class showing us examples of what past students have done for the project. Apparently, the school's coffee shop was a proposal made by a group in Leadership class. Thank you to that group because what on earth would I do without my daily iced coffee?!

"So, on Monday, I need you all to come to class with some ideas for the project and who you are going to work on it with."

As we pack up to leave, people start walking over to their friends to pair up. Honestly, I might just see if Carter wants to do it together because I'm already at his house 24/7.

"Hey, Carter! Do you want to pair up?"

He looks up from putting his computer away. "Of course, Mar. I already assumed we would work together," he winks.

I giggle. "Sweet!"

"I don't really have any ideas on what to focus the project on. But I can start brainstorming," he says, running a hand through his red curls.

"That's fine! We can figure it out later," I tell him.

Leaving the classroom, I turn to the left and run into my new favorite person: Beau.

"Hey," I say with a smile.

"Hey Marlowe! How's it going?"

I start to tell him about my day, and I'm surprised by how engaged he is. He's nodding along and only checked his phone a couple of times while I was talking. It might not sound like much, but that's kind of rare to find with guys my age.

"Also, you've got a free block for first period, right?"

"Yeah I do!" I say, surprised he remembered my schedule.

"Do you want to work on some stuff for history? I know we've got that quiz coming up next week," he says.

"Yes! We have so much going on. I'm starting to feel that junior year grind," I say.

"Tell me about it. Okay, I'll text you!"

He is going to text *me*! I feel like I am always the first to text anyone! AND he must've liked hanging out at the game because he wants to meet up again.

• • •

BEAU BRAXTON: hey marlowe this is beau

ME: Omg hi!! When do you want to hangout??

BEAU BRAXTON: does monday sound good

ME: Of course!!!

BEAU BRAXTON: ok cool

"He's texting you, isn't he?" Lenny says.

I'm nestled on her couch, and with this accusation, I start to bury myself deeper within the cushions. Peeking out from a blanket, I say, "How can you tell?"

"You are doing the texting smile," she says as she mimics my closed lipped grin.

"Shut up!" I laugh, throwing a pillow at her.

"Ha, you know I'm joking. I'm really happy with how well this is going for you," she says, shimmying her shoulders and punctuating her words with a sing-song voice. "I haven't seen any red flags yet."

I nod. Could that be a sign that Beau and I are endgame?

"AYO!" Carter shouts from the hall, running and jumping onto the couch next to me. "I saw that picture of you and Beau at the game. Going well?"

"Hey Carter," I giggle. "And yes! But it wasn't a date exactly. More like date-adjacent."

Lenny says, "I wish we could just ask him what he's thinking."

Carter studies me. "Is this your hint for me to get more info?"

Lenny and I look at each other sheepishly, and she says, "Maybe…"

"Okay, I can try to talk to him. Anything else while we're at it?" he asks.

Giving him a guilty half-smile, I say, "Well, I could use a guy's input. What do you usually do to hint to a girl that you like her? Like what signs do you give?"

"Hmmm," he thinks. "Usually I'll want to hangout with them as much as possible. And I'll try to talk to them, or ask about their day. I just want them to feel heard and appreciated."

I'm not sure Beau has done *all* of that but we've at least hung out and talked some. While on the subject, I ask about Carter's new relationship with Phoebe.

"She's cool. We're in Theater together," he shrugs. "Phoebe is the head costume designer this year."

"You can tell she has good style," I chime in.

"Is this situationship going to become official anytime soon?" Lenny teases.

He bites the small white scar on his bottom lip that he got from falling off the tire swing when we were younger. Side-eyeing his sister, Carter says, "I don't know!"

If he brought Phoebe home to meet his mom, this must be getting pretty serious. Once I can lock down Beau, maybe we can all go on a group date.

Lenny grabs the remote and opens Netflix.

"Do you want to watch something with us?" Lenny asks her brother. "I was kind of thinking of rewatching To All the Boys I've Loved Before."

"Yeah, let's do it," he says, scooting closer and moving some pillows.

Maybe this could be a date Beau and I go on later: get together and watch classic movies on the couch.

With some cuddling of course.

CHAPTER EIGHT

"Latte for Marlowe!"

I grab my iced caramel latte from Caelee High's coffee shop, anxiously waiting for Beau. We agreed to meet at 10:00 AM to study together. He's just running a little late.

I pull at the yarn woven into my sweater and tap my foot endlessly. I was really worried about what to wear today since it's technically our second one-on-one hangout. This morning, I spent fifteen more minutes on my makeup trying to *perfect* the clean girl aesthetic. I even wore my favorite Rory Gilmore-esque sweater to look my best. All weekend I thought of this moment. Beau couldn't escape my thoughts. I found myself grinning while thinking of his smile, his laugh, and even his bushy eyebrows.

Trying to pass the time, I decide to scroll through Instagram, and wouldn't you know it, the first photo that pops up is Maya's. She's standing with a group of girls and guys, with Beau standing right beside her. I heard she had a party this past weekend, but I opted not to go this time. Beau looks really happy in the photo, but I'm sure he's just being more friendly with her because he's drunk.

I'm almost positive that's what is happening.

"Hey," I hear. Glancing up, I see Beau looking absolutely gorgeous in his matching beige sweatsuit. His hair is more floppy today, shading his eyes a little.

"Oh hey!"

"Sorry, I slept in," he says with a small smile. Aw, he feels bad for being late. I knew it had to be an accident.

Diving into our study session, I show him some of the notes I worked on over the weekend. It took me forever to define all the vocabulary terms for this module because I still feel the procrastination settle in when I study. But thinking about meeting up with Beau definitely helped with my motivation.

"Whoa, these look great," he says. Leaning over to take a picture of my notes, his hair falls forward onto his face, and the ends of his black hair softly brush his high cheekbones.

Changing the subject, Beau asks, "How have your classes been? I didn't see you at the other football game, so I assumed you had a lot of schoolwork."

"I've been pretty stressed. I'm constantly in a whirlwind of trying to catch up on homework. But I need to come to another game! I had a really great time last time," I say, meeting his gaze.

"Yeah, you should. We are playing our rivals in a few weeks. You've gotta come with us," he says. "The private school that I went to before Caelee didn't have a football team. Until I moved back, I didn't realize how much I missed watching it."

You've gotta come with us. I smile to myself. Is he asking me out? OMG.

"Yeah, I'll come!" I say.

"I'm thinking of going to travel to watch them play regionals in a couple months. I think they have a shot to win it all."

"Really? That's awesome," I say.

"Oh, I was going to ask you," he starts to say, looking at me through his dark eyelashes. "Do people normally go to the dance team competition that same weekend? I didn't want to show up if it would be kind of weird."

Mmmkay. I'm not sure where he is going with this.

"Um, well I've never been," I say. "So, I don't really know."

"Oh, okay. I wasn't sure," he chuckles. "It's like I have to relearn the Caelee County social norms."

"It must be strange coming back years later after everyone has seemingly grown up," I reply.

"Exactly. So I didn't want to be a complete weirdo and show up if no one does that," he says, fidgeting with his sweatshirt sleeves.

"But yeah, I don't think it would be weird to go. Like, I would love-"

"Can I ask you for advice?" he interrupts. Beau is being so intriguing right now. He's got a glint in his eye that I haven't seen before.

"Of course," I say with a smile. Tucking my hair behind my ears, I focus on his heavenly brown eyes. My heart beats like a jackhammer in my chest, erupting every single one of my senses. It feels like we are the only ones in the whole coffee shop. Or the only ones in the whole school.

"Well, since we are friends I thought I would ask," he begins.

OH MY GOSH.

OH MY GOSH.

IS IT HAPPENING?!

IT'S HAPPENING.

He's going to ask me out.

I nod, beckoning for him to continue. I am quite literally on the edge of my seat. Those mile long black eyelashes flutter as he looks at me and says, "I really like Maya, and I kind of want to shoot my shot."

Oh.

Ohh.

Okay.

He likes Maya.

"Oh! Yeah? No, Maya is great! I'm sure she would be flattered," I say, quickly. I physically feel myself sink lower into my seat. My stomach double knots in on itself.

"I'm not trying to be a homewrecker or anything, but I heard that she and her boyfriend are very on and off," he says, biting his lower lip.

Fidgeting with my thumbnail, I tell him, "Yes, they are very on and off, but I will say that she becomes even more popular when she's single. So, you'll probably need something more than just going to her dance competition to stand out."

He nods. "Yeah, I was thinking of talking with her more in our study group."

"That's good," I say, leaning forward in my chair. "It's just that every guy likes her, so you'll need to show her that you're different from all of them. And when I say every guy, I mean *every guy*."

I can't afford to lose Beau again. I was just so heartbroken when he left town five years ago. Now, it's like life is dangling a happily ever after in my face just for Maya to take it all away.

How can I get him to see me and not her?

Let's face it- Kevin and Maya are broken up every other month. According to how it's been in the past, Maya and Kevin will break up, and every guy at school will try to win over a newly-single Maya. The guys line up like they are courting her from *Bridgerton*.

If Beau likes Maya, then he'll go after her as soon as he can. I need to figure out a way to lock Beau down before Maya gives him an opportunity to go after her- all under the guise of being his wing-woman.

I can't be worried about what's logical or mature to do. I have to go to the extreme if I really want to make sure Beau won't leave me again.

Maybe it is because I had just watched the movie last night. Maybe it's because at this moment, Beau is looking a lot like Peter Kavinsky. But all I can think about is Beau and the fake dating scheme in *To All the Boys I've Loved Before*.

According to one of my favorite romcoms, I should come up with a fake dating scheme. If I could convince Beau to date me, with the guise of helping him get with Maya, we could fall in love ourselves. After doing a bunch of "couple-y" things together, we are bound to fall in love.

Right?

This plan is fool-proof.

I look around the coffee shop to make sure no one is in earshot of our conversation. I take a deep breath and wipe my clammy hands on my skirt. This is so not like me. But if Beau is interested in another girl, I really don't have a shot with him *at all*. So, this is my only option. I have to step it up.

"Um, I have an idea," I say hesitantly. I let out a shaky breath, hoping he can't hear. "What if we, like, fake date? Like in books? You can stand out and get her attention that way."

A slow beat passes. He looks at me as if I just sprouted two heads.

"Huh? The books I read don't really have that," Beau says with a halfhearted chuckle and confusion still painted over his face.

"Okay it's in movies too! The Proposal, Anyone But You, How to Lose a Guy in 10 Days, and To All the Boys I've Loved Before," I rattle off. "What if you and I fake date?"

"I'm confused. What does that even look like?" he asks, his forehead creasing. "How would that help the situation?"

"We just act like we are dating. Like we post together and people would see us together at school. But we both know it's fake," I say, pointing between the two of us.

He nods. Running a hand through his hair, he says, "But how would that help me get Maya? She's with Kevin, so what would make her want me if I was also in a relationship?"

I lean over the table to softly say, "It'll make Maya crazy jealous. She'll see you with me and realize you all have relationship potential." I smile, trying to disguise the lies seeping through my teeth. "Maya and Kevin break up all the time. Once you spark her interest, she'll break up with Kevin, and we'll call off the fake dating plan. Then, you and Maya will live happily ever after," I smile.

He nods again. Beau still looks skeptical. I don't blame him. "But what's in it for you? Why would you help me with this?" he asks.

Oh. Um. *Because I'm Boysick for you? Because I hope Maya and Kevin never break up, so I can keep you to myself?*

I quickly scan the coffee shop, trying to come up with a believable excuse. Why would I do this for Beau? What's in it for me?

My eyes land on the beige cork board above the cafe's high-top tables. A poster for my mom's art gala is pinned and hanging sideways. Every season, she does a really formal gallery to try to sell some of her most valuable pieces. It's a big deal for her and her studio.

"My mom has this gala in a month and a half. It's pretty formal, and I need a date for it," I ramble. I honestly don't care about going with anyone. It's my mom's time to shine.

"Oh. Your mom still owns that art studio?" Beau asks, remembering the small detail from when we were younger.

"Yeah! And the gallery is a good way for her to make money to put right back into the studio. So we could fake date, and I'll help you get Maya. Then you could come with me to the gala," I say, trying my best to embody a used car salesman.

Beau rubs the side of his chin. He's still not fully convinced.

"Also! You were saying it's been a little bit harder making friends since you've moved back. If people hear you are in a relationship, that automatically bumps you up a few rungs on the Caelee High social status ladder," I fib.

Beau purses his lips together, debating. Who doesn't want to hear that fake dating could make them become more popular?!

Beau slowly shakes his head, taking all of this in. "I'm not sure that is a good idea."

"You said so yourself that we are friends, right? So it won't be weird. We just act like we are dating, and it catches Maya's attention. She'll be enamored with us and won't even realize she's falling for you! And then I get a date to my mom's gala. Win-win situation."

Beau still looks skeptical. His bottom lip twitches, as if he's got something on the tip of his tongue.

"So let's say we fake date. For how long?"

"I don't know. A month and a half?" I ask. My voice comes off a little shaky, as I try to pull off this unrealistic scheme. "My mom's art gala can be the deadline."

Beau shakes his head, "This is weird though."

"No! Haven't you read Better Than the Movies? I promise this happens all the time," I say with a smile. "If you don't want to do it, then no problem! But I feel like it would be a good way to get Maya's attention. She has the guaranteed knowledge that you'd be a great boyfriend because she'll see you with me. Once she and Kevin break up, she'll be thinking of you instead of all the other guys."

It's interesting that Beau has noticed that it seems like the guys dictate who dates whom at Caelee High. He's intimidated by the other guys who are interested in Maya. But he has no idea how irresistible *he* is.

Beau nods. I add, "I'm just trying to help a friend out."

"I'll think about it. Can I get back to you?" Beau asks, as if it's some sort of official business transaction. I feel like I need to shake his hand or something.

"Of course. Hey, what are friends for?" I wink.

Beau chuckles, shakes his head, and walks over to order a coffee. I think he may actually agree to the fake dating scheme. I mean, it's kind of genius on my part. This worked out for Laura Jean and Peter. This worked out for Wes and Liz. So who's to say it won't work out for me?

I pull out my phone to text Lenny my master plan.

ME: I have so much to fill you in on!!!!

ME: For one, Beau has a crush on Maya...

LENNY: WHAT NOOOOOOO

LENNY: EW I HATE HIM NOW

LENNY: HE TOLD YOU
HE HAS A CRUSH ON HER?!?!?!

LENNY: RED FLAG RED FLAG RED FLAG

ME: Wait let me explain

LENNY: NOOO!! HE'S A JACKASS!!!

Well, crap.

I should have known not to start it off this way; it's just like her to say that. If I'm Boysick over a guy and he does something questionable, Lenny is the first to jump ship. She is there to give me a reality check if I'm being delusional over a guy who isn't good for me.

Lenny will be super harsh towards a guy, so I can realize that he's being a jerk. But she doesn't need to be harsh in this situation! Beau isn't being a jerk at all. He's especially not being a jerk if he agrees to my fake dating plan.

ME: Are you being serious lol

LENNY: YES MARLOWE WE HATE HIM NOW

LENNY: public enemy number one

LENNY: we ride at dawn!!!

Oh no.

Now, I guess I have to keep the fake dating idea to myself. I don't want her to give me a reality check over my romcom trope scheme. If she doesn't like Beau anymore, she will think fake dating is the worst idea ever. She wouldn't get it.

But *I* get it. This could really work. To hold hands with Beau all the time? To hug him? TO KISS HIM?

This could be the cure to my Boysickness.

CHAPTER NINE

Sitting in Lenny's kitchen, we devour the intricate charcuterie board that took us way too long to assemble. Munching on a pretzel with hummus, Lenny says, "I heard from my dad yesterday."

"Yeah? How was that?" I ask. Lenny's parents got divorced when she was nine, and as expected, she took it pretty hard. Paul, Lenny's dad, had cheated on her mom. I remember Lenny and Carter's face when they told me that their parents' happily ever after had come to a crashing halt.

Now, Paul lives thirty hours away and is married with three kids. Oh and the wife? She's the mistress from the affair eight years ago. Lenny and Carter only see their dad and his new family on major holidays.

What a douche.

"Evelyn is pregnant. Again."

"What?!"

"Yeah," Lenny says quietly.

"How are you feeling?" I ask.

"I honestly feel kind of numb about it. I saw him on Father's Day, and he was the same as he's always been. Surface level questions. More interested in the new kids. More interested in Evelyn," she shrugs.

"I'm really sorry, Len," I say, walking over to give her a hug. I really hate it for her. I know she tries to hide how much it hurts her.

"It's fine," she says dejectedly. "I wasn't trying to dampen the mood."

Lenny deserves a dad who doesn't treat her like this. I love her so much, and I just wish she could see that her dad's behavior isn't a reflection of who she is.

The front door opens, and a few seconds later I hear, "ANYBODY HOME?!"

"Hey Carter!" Lenny yells back.

Coming in from the hallway, Carter sees me and says, "Mar! I didn't know you were here!" His boyish smile lights up the room.

"How's it going?" I ask.

"Well," he hints. "Guess who's the new Beast in Caelee High's production of Beauty and the Beast?!"

"No way!"

"Carter! That is so great!" I say.

"Thanks," he blushes. His freckles fade as his cheeks redden. "I'm really excited! Rehearsal starts tomorrow."

"Yay!" I say, happy-clapping.

"We need to celebrate," Lenny says.

"Oh, for sure," Carter smiles.

My phone pings on the granite counter top, and I see Beau's name. Quickly picking it up, I read Beau's text.

BEAU BRAXTON: hey do you want to meet up for ice cream tonight

I can't even help myself. I practically shriek after reading his message.

"What's wrong?" Lenny asks, looking startled.

Sucking in a breath, I mentally run through my options. I can lie, saying that it's some other notification that made me squeal. I can tell her the truth about everything- me still liking Beau and my proposed fake dating plan. Or I can run out of the room and avoid her question all together.

No, I can't do any of those.

I can't just fully lie to her. But maybe I can get her to not hate Beau by telling her half-truths.

"Beau just asked me to go out with him for ice cream!" I tell her, wide-eyed.

Lenny gives me a puzzled look. "I thought he was a jerk, and you said he likes Maya?"

"Well, he's not, and he must have changed his mind or something," I say. "Sorry, Carter. I didn't mean to interrupt your thing."

"No, you're good," Carter says casually. His gaze lingers on my face. "Go get that ice cream."

I turn to Lenny, saying, "Forget what I said yesterday. Don't automatically dismiss him."

"That just makes no sense. Why would he tell you he likes someone else, then ask you to get ice cream the next day?" she says, skeptically. "What happened to public enemy number one?"

"I don't know. But he's Beau! The same Beau we've known forever. I have to go and see what he's thinking," I say.

"Yeah." After a few beats of silence, she says, "Sorry, I shouldn't be so mean towards him, but I don't want you to get hurt. If someone crosses you, they cross me, too."

Smiling, I text Beau I'll meet him at Twisted in thirty minutes. I rush home and throw a quilted jacket over my baby tee and favorite pair of jeans. I reapply deodorant, quickly touch up my makeup, and braid my hair. You know- the essentials.

On the drive over, I practice how I'm going to greet him. A casual, *Oh hey Beau!* Or more bruh girl by saying, *What's up Beau?* Or just sweet *Hi there!* Or just *Hello!*

Talk about a mind warp.

I pull into the Twisted parking lot and text Beau that I'm here.

BEAU BRAXTON: hey i just pulled in i'll head inside

ME: Ok! I'll go in!!!

I see Beau with his forest green and navy flannel. He pushes his dark hair back as he looks around the parking lot for me. Our eyes meet and he softly smiles and raises his hand for a small wave.

"Hey Beau!" I say, as he opens the door to Twisted for me.

"Hey," he says. He looks… apprehensive?

We look at the array of ice cream flavors, and I'm waiting for him to say something. I don't even know why I'm looking at the other flavors because I know I'll just end up going with my usual.

"What do you normally get?"

"My favorite is the chocolate with peanut butter cups."

"Ooh, that sounds good," he says, looking down at me with those deep brown eyes that remind me of decadent dark chocolate with caramel swirls.

Once the employee finishes scooping out our ice creams, I walk over to the cashier to pay. I walk a little slowly because I'm not exactly sure if this is a date. I don't believe that the guy has to automatically pay for a date. I'm a strong independent woman who can pay for myself! I just think whoever asks to hangout or go on the date should pay. So if I were to ask Beau out, I would pay.

But is this a date? I get out my wallet and try to pump the brakes on my mini thought spiral.

"Wait, what are you doing? I'm paying. Obviously," he says with a smile.

"Aw," I say, while looking up at him. His near-black eyebrows and eyelashes look so striking against his smooth bronzed skin. "Thanks, Beau."

"Of course," he shrugs and pays for our ice cream like it's no big deal. We grab our cups, spoons, and napkins, and I start heading over to find us a table.

"Hey, actually I was wondering if we could eat in the car? I wanted to talk about your little scheme," he says with a small quirk of his upper lip.

Biting my inside of my cheek, I nod. We walk over to Beau's Jeep and hop in. He turns on the car, and the seats start to warm up. The September evening air plus the ice cream makes me a little chilled. Now with the seat warmers, I feel like we are just nestled next to a fireplace on Christmas Eve.

Beau takes his first bite of ice cream, and I look at him expectantly.

"What do you think?" I ask him.

"Probably the best ice cream I've ever had."

When we were at summer camp, some of the biggest daredevils would climb up on the structure of the swings. It took full upper body strength and a ton of courage. When someone successfully climbed up the top of the swing set, it was a ritual to toss them up a popsicle or ice cream bar of their choice. Most of us nine-year-olds had terrible aim, so we ruined a million of those sweet treats.

I tried over and over again to climb up at the top, but I could never manage it. Lenny tried to help me up so many times, but I was just too clumsy to make it work.

Beau noticed that I always attempted to climb up, and he came over to Lenny and I one day. He was so attentive and thoughtful even when he was in elementary school.

"Hey," he said. "Do you want me to help?"

I looked at him with my mouth open, and I glanced over at Lenny. To my young mind, this was the biggest grand gesture I could have imagined.

"Sure!" I told him.

"How do we want to do this? Usually Mar just stands on my knee," Lenny piped up.

"Okay, um-" Beau started to say as he deliberated on what to do.

"What if we grab your feet like cheerleaders do? We can hold your feet and then extend our arms so you can reach the top."

"That should work!" Beau exclaimed.

Lenny and Beau crouched down and linked their hands together to form a place for my feet. I put each of my hands on their shoulders, and I stepped into their nestled arms. I tried to situate myself so I wasn't hurting their fingers. Honestly, our form was pretty great for amateurs.

"Okay, are you ready Marlowe?" Beau asked, looking up at me.

"Yeah," I squeaked.

After counting down, Lenny and Beau slowly stood up, and in turn, I rose closer to the beam of the swing set. They were fully standing up, and I was on top of their hands in a makeshift cheerleader move.

"You got it!" Lenny encouraged.

I reached up and grabbed onto the top beam of the structure. I used all my might to pull up, as Lenny and Beau pushed up on my feet. I was able to steady myself and lift my feet up to grab onto the bar- koala style. After doing a few more swinging and pulling moves, I somehow managed to sit atop the beam.

Finally! I couldn't believe I had actually done it. My stomach fluttered with pride and nerves from being up so high.

"Ah! Look! Thank you guys!" I shouted down to Beau and Lenny.

"Of course! What do you want? I'll go grab your ice cream!" Lenny said.

"A Dreamsicle please!"

"Make that two!" Beau exclaimed with a smile. He jumped and pulled himself up effortlessly. He made it look so easy. We were sitting side by side on the top of the swing structure, and it felt like a scene from a movie. Just two love birds sitting on their perch.

"So," Beau says, transporting me back into his car. "About Maya."

"Yes," I say, eager to hear what he has to say.

"I think it may work. I mean, if it doesn't it'll just last for a month between us. So, it's not really a huge risk."

"Exactly," I say.

"So, let's do it," he says, laughing a little. "Should we set- I don't know- ground rules?"

"Yeah!" I say, giving myself flashbacks to Lara Jean and Peter from *To All the Boys I Loved Before*. "It can be like ways to help us stay on track with the plan."

"Okay," he agrees.

"To get her attention, we have to hard launch it on Instagram. She always flaunts her relationship with Kevin there. So, we'll turn the tables."

He nods. We've got to announce the relationship pretty fast in order for me to pull this off. It's not a fake dating trope if we aren't public about it.

"And I guess we should probably really sell it in History and the study group. So she doesn't doubt it."

"Yes!" I say.

"So maybe we can see if Maya takes notice on Monday and just go from there."

"Should we take a picture now? To post on our stories?" I ask, trying not to seem too eager.

"Good idea," Beau says and pulls out his phone. We take a selfie holding our ice cream cups, and Beau goes to Instagram. He drafts the post for his story and shows me for approval.

"So tag me, and then I'll repost it. Like with red hearts."

"This is some kind of science," he smirks and lifts one brow.

I giggle as he posts our selfie onto his Instagram story. Like a can of Sprite Zero, bubbles fill and float around my stomach. It may be a little lame that I'm getting this excited over a fake dating plan, but I just can't help it.

It's *Beau Braxton!*

I repost his story to mine, and I make sure to add the intentional three red hearts.

"Okay. Step one is complete," I say.

"Yeah," he says. His hair looks perfectly swept away from his face.

"Well, thanks. I guess I'll see you Monday," I say, giving him an awkward side hug from the passenger seat.

Beau squeezes my shoulder from the side hug and tells me goodnight. Walking out of his Jeep, the evening breeze ripples through my hair like an afternoon hammock swinging back and forth. I can't believe this is my life. As I get back into my car, I hear my phone start to ring.

"MARLOWE!" Lenny screams a millisecond after I accept her FaceTime.

"Hi?" I say tentatively as I try to bite back a smile.

"Do you have something to share with us?" Lenny says as she points the camera towards Jacob. "What's with hearts and Beau on your story?"

"Um," I stammer.

"I thought Beau liked Maya? I thought we hated him now?" Lenny asks with big eyes.

Let's be honest, I could never hate Beau Braxton.

"So it turns out he doesn't actually like Maya. He wants to date me!"

"WHAT?!"

I fib, "I think he liked both of us when he told me about Maya the other day."

"That's kind of weird," Jacob says over the phone. "Why would he tell you about her if he likes you?"

"He was just trying to figure out how he feels. And it's not weird," I tell him.

If you think that's weird, wait until I tell you about the fake dating thing.

"Marlowe, what's with the hearts on your story? Are you all together?" Lenny asks.

I could come clean right here. That's it's my masterful plan to fake date Beau until that dating isn't so fake anymore. But Lenny and Jacob just wouldn't get it.

Those love birds have been each other's first everything, and I don't see them breaking up anytime soon. Lenny would suggest I meet a guy the "traditional" way, but not every girl is lucky enough for "traditional" to work out for them.

If Lenny and Jacob are already wary of Beau, they are *not* going to be on board with me scheming to fake date him. I need to get them to slowly warm up to Beau. So, I'll just sing his praises, and once he and I are officially dating and done with the scheme, I'll come clean to Lenny and Jacob.

"Well, I guess tonight was our first date," I say, tentatively. "So, yeah. Beau and I are dating!"

"Oh my gosh," Lenny says, her eyebrows shooting to her hairline.

"Promise me you guys won't just write him off because he was weird about Maya. This is my Boysick dreams coming true!"

"You're right. It could be worse. At least he isn't Michael Cera and in love with his cousin," Jacob says, referencing *Arrested Development*.

I chuckle, nervously waiting for Lenny's response.

"I don't want you to get hurt. I just need to get him liking Maya out of my head," Lenny says and shakes her head quickly. "Sorry, I'm being a bad best friend. I really am happy for you, Marlowe."

"You're not acting very happy," Jacob chuckles.

Lenny huffs at him. Looking at me, she squeals, "Weeeeee!! Is that better?"

"I heard some screaming. Is everything okay?" I hear a voice say.

"Carter, guess what?" Lenny says.

"What?"

Lenny points the camera at him and says, "Check Instagram. Marlowe and Beau are kind of dating now!"

"No way," he says, his brow creasing.

"Yeah," I say sheepishly. Yes, I am lying, but it's so nice to think of this alternate reality as my real life. And Lenny is already starting to like Beau a little more, so that has to be a sign that I'm doing something right.

"You little mastermind," Carter says with a smirk.

"HAHA!" Lenny cracks up.

"What if I told you none of it was accidental?" I sing over the phone.

"And the first night you saw me, nothing was going to stop me!" Lenny sings back. We finish the phone call singing Taylor Swift (no shock there) and plot what Monday is going to look like.

I drive home, and the plan seems to be the only thing occupying my mind. Beau Braxton is my fake boyfriend.

Beau Braxton is my ~~fake~~ boyfriend.

CHAPTER TEN

BEAU BRAXTON: hey do you want to meet up
before so we can walk into history together

ME: Yes!

I catch Beau walking up to the vending machine, and he just looks so dashing. He's got these gray pants paired with a white long sleeve. He is the literal representation of my boyfriend Pinterest board.

Yes, I have a boyfriend Pinterest board.

"You ready?" I say to him, raising my eyebrows.

"Of course," he says quietly. His dimples seem to taunt me as I look up at him with a flirtatious grin. Beau holds his hand out. His long, slender fingers are stretched out towards me, waiting expectantly.

I look at his hand for a second before it hits me. I slide my hand into his, and we lace our fingers together. His hands are soft and seem to double the size of mine.

Beau leads us into the classroom, and I accidentally lock eyes with Maya. She quickly casts a questioning glance at Beau. I saw that Maya viewed my story yesterday, so I know she's seen the staged ice cream photo. Beau gives my hand a squeeze, and we go to our normal seats.

Oh my God! Lenny mouths. I grin at her, my dimples practically jumping out of my cheeks.

Mr. Evans dives into today's lecture, and I can't help but notice the stolen glances Maya gives Beau. Even though we are in a fake relationship, I feel weirdly protective of him.

Mr. Evans passes through each slide of his presentation while we all try to keep up. I scribble down some notes into my spiral notebook, but it's hard to pay attention. I keep darting my gaze between Beau and Maya.

Class drones on, and I am eager to see what Beau does after class. Mr. Evans dismisses us, not before giving us two journal entry assignments.

"Hey, have you finished that Chemistry homework?" Maya asks Beau sweetly.

"No, I haven't," Beau says. "It's not due until Friday, right?"

"Yeah! So we have time," Maya says, glancing at me.

Beau smiles down at me and looks over to Maya. "Do we want to do another ACT study session?"

"I'm down!" Lenny pipes up. We all walk towards the door, trying to figure out what the next plans are.

"We can do it at my place," Maya says. "The kitchen remodeling is done."

"Cool," Beau says. He steps over to me and gives me a full body hug. He's so tall that I feel my chest press against his torso. His fingers lightly brush my back. "I'll see you later?"

"Yeah," I say with a grin.

The perks of fake dating!

After lunch, I walk down to the second floor to head to Leadership class. Biting my bottom lip, I attempt to suppress my smile. I cross my arms in front of my chest and try to look "normal." I have no idea how to act like myself after I spent the last class acting as Beau's girlfriend.

"Mar!" Carter says, walking into Leadership. "What's up?"

"Nothing much," I say, my giddiness brewing behind my eyes.

Carter smiles softly, studying my face. Even though I have no evidence to back it up, I feel like Carter can see right through me. I have no poker face when it comes to him.

In a change of subject, I ask Carter, "How are things with Phoebe?"

"Oh, I think we are just going to stay friends."

"What?!"

"I don't know," he shrugs. "I think it's pretty mutual. We are still hanging out, I just don't know if there's a real future between us."

"Oh. I'm sorry. I know you liked her a lot."

"Yeah," he shrugs again.

Mrs. Lin walks in, holding a stack of folders. "Okay, everyone. Let's get started with your project preparation," she says. "I have some survey results from last year. We had several groups interview students about their requests or concerns about the school. This way you can get information from a variety of students."

After dismissing us to brainstorm, Mrs. Lin passes out the folders with the survey answers. Carter and I rifle through them for a few minutes before drawing up similarities between some of the results. A lot of people were impressed with the social engagement opportunities Caelee offers, but they were still getting overwhelmed with school.

"Okay, I see a lot of people dealing with stress from school. Like, homework, testing, and college prep," I say to Carter.

"Me too. I think it's very common for our age to become anxious with all of the responsibilities of being a student," he says.

"I don't know what we could propose that would offer something different. Caelee just got a grant to provide free ACT help."

"And they have a lot of college prep stuff offered to seniors. But, it doesn't help my overwhelmed ass," Carter jokes.

"I get that," I say.

"Maybe we could do something that starts earlier. Like support for all students, not just targeted at upperclassmen."

"Oh, I like that!" I tell him.

Ping!

I look down at my phone and see a text from my fake boyfriend.

BEAU BRAXTON: hey just wanted to say thanks for today

ME: Awww ofc!

BEAU BRAXTON: you are the ultimate wingwoman

BEAU BRAXTON: really helping me get maya

ME: Hehe!!

If only he would stop focusing on "getting" Maya and just see me.

I turn my focus back to Carter. We really need to finalize an idea for our project. I pull out my computer and browse through some students' past projects.

"I think something about stress relief is a really good idea. And it's pretty relatable to everyone. So it could be of interest to the whole student body," I tell Carter.

"Yes! Every year I've had some kind of major stressor or point of anxiety. And it seems to be the only thing I can think about."

"I haven't really felt this much school stress before this year. It's definitely a lot," I say, nodding. I take a deep breath.

Carter opens his mouth, about to say something. He pauses. Carter looks at me gently and says, "You know I'm always here for you, Mar. Anything you need. Or if you ever want to talk. Just know I'm here. I wouldn't lie about that."

My chest heats up, warmth spreading up to my neck. I know Lenny is always there for me, but it's so reassuring to know Carter is also in my corner. He's so genuine, and looking into his eyes now, I *know* if I needed anything, he would be there.

"Thank you, Carter. That really means a lot."

"Of course," he replies. "Just telling the truth."

I reach over to squeeze his arm. He really is one of my closest friends. He was even supportive when I told him about my crush on Beau.

Crush. That's what this feels like. My feelings for Beau are crushing me to a pulp- so much so that Carter's even pitching in to make sure I'm okay.

CHAPTER ELEVEN

"Do you need a ride? Or is your boyfriend Beau driving you?" Lenny asks with a smirk. I can see through FaceTime that she's french braiding her hair. We've got another ACT study group session tonight. It's at Maya's house again. Sometimes I wonder if she hosts just to show off her family's mansion.

We've met with our study group for a few times now, and I've definitely noticed a difference in my confidence. Don't get me wrong, I am still really nervous about taking the exam. But after hours and hours of studying, the amount of stress has lifted ever so slightly.

Also studying with Beau makes me feel at ease. I mean, it's *Beau.*

I texted him to see if we wanted to ride together. It may look a little suspicious if we show up separately since everyone knows us as a newly established couple.

He texted me back saying it would be a good idea to ride together, but we didn't really make plans further than that. I love Beau's quiet nature and how he isn't super extroverted, but sometimes it makes creating plans kind of difficult.

"Let me text him to double check," I answer Lenny.

ME: Hey do you want to pick me up or should I ride with Lenny?

BEAU BRAXTON: you should probably ride with lenny because idk if I'll have time to swing by your place

ME: Oh ok no problem!!

Even if we don't ride together, it can still be fun at Maya's house. I'm only a little ashamed to admit that I've been practicing flirting and laughing in the mirror. I've got to make sure I'm on my game in front of Beau.

"Okay yeah. I'll need a ride," I say to Lenny through the phone.

"No problem! I'll be there in ten minutes."

I throw on a brown turtleneck and Lenny's light wash jeans. Slicking my hair into a ponytail, I give myself a once over. I tug on my jeans and readjust my top. I want to look my very best when I see Beau. I hope he knows I'm not that same dorky girl he knew when we were young.

Glancing out my living room window, I see Lenny pull into my driveway and head to meet her at her car. As I climb into the passenger seat, Lenny squeals, "Look at my shirt!"

She turns towards me and gestures to a small embroidered daisy.

"Did you do that?"

Lenny nods, smiling ear to ear. I say, "Lenny, it looks so good! I didn't realize you started learning embroidery."

Her smile falters ever so slightly. "Yeah, I'm pretty sure we talked about it."

I shrug.

When we finally get to Maya's house, I see that Beau's car is already there. Maybe next session we can plan earlier to ride together so I can get more time with him.

"Hey guys!" Maya says cheerfully, opening the door for us. She's got on a baby pink tennis dress paired with some expensive looking sneakers.

As we walk in, Beau peers out of the kitchen, and I feel like his eyes light up once he sees me. A smile tugs on his lips, and he walks over with smooth, long strides.

"Hey!" I say, going in for a hug.

"Hey Marlowe," he says slyly and wraps his arms around my back.

His touch sends shivers down my whole body. It's probably no big deal to him, but I feel electricity running through my veins. I try not to make it obvious that I'm taking in his scent- spicy cinnamon and cardamom. He smells like my favorite mug of a warm chai latte.

"You look cute," he says, pulling back and interlacing his fingers with mine. Oh. My. Gosh.

Beau Braxton has GAME.

I stifle a giggle and try to play it cool. I have to remind myself that Beau and I have different end goals. He wants Maya. I want him.

"So, what should we start with?" Maya asks, breaking my train of thought.

"I'm good with whatever," Beau says casually.

"I've been struggling with the English portions," I pipe up.

"Yeah, let's start with that one," Lenny says.

We sit around the table in Maya's breakfast nook. Maya and I settle in on either side of Beau, and I make sure to scoot my chair as close as possible without seeming like a weirdo.

We divide up some ACT worksheets, and Lenny puts on some instrumental music. I find myself glancing over at Beau in between problems, and sometimes he catches my gaze. We exchange a small smile, and it feels like we are the only ones in the room. It's us against the world.

I set my pencil down and rub my eyes, trying to give myself a brain break.

"Are you done as well?" Maya asks.

"Oh I-" I start to say.

"Could you help me in the kitchen? I picked up some specialty doughnuts from the new shop downtown. I thought that could be our sweet treat for the night," Maya smiles.

See, this is the thing about her. She'll do something nice- like buy us doughnuts- but I know she'll do something later to ruin it.

"Uh, yeah I can," I say. I glance over at Lenny to give her big eyes. Why did Maya single me out?

I head into her gold adorned kitchen, and Maya pulls out four ceramic bowls. She gets out vanilla ice cream from the freezer and starts to scoop some into each.

"If you'll get that platter over there," Maya says, pointing. She directs me to place the doughnuts out while she finishes getting the ice cream. "So, tell me about you and Beau."

I didn't realize she had taken that much notice of my (fake) relationship. It's always been the other way around, where I notice every ounce of attention she gets.

It started back in kindergarten. Maya and I were in the same class, and we were pretty good friends. We played well together and sat with one another at lunch. Our teacher even referred to us as "M&M."

But pretty soon after school started, I began to notice how much recognition she got from our classmates. Originally, I was simply annoyed by it. I couldn't understand why she was the more popular "M" in our duo.

Five-year-old Marlowe's final straw was towards the end of our kindergarten year. It was a breezy spring day, and our class was walking in a single file from music class. We passed the other kindergarten class who was on their way to take music right after us.

A few girls in the other class's line complimented Maya's ripped jeans. One said, "Maya, I love your ripped jeans! You look like a teenager."

Maya beamed from ear to ear. The biggest compliment you can give an elementary schooler is to say they look older.

Maya flipped her hair and said, "Thanks! They are from Justice."

The other girls started gushing about how much they loved Justice. I had never shopped there before, so I felt like Maya and the girls were speaking a language that only they knew.

"What about mine?" I asked, motioning to my khaki pants.

I should have just kept my mouth shut. *Why did it matter what they thought of my pants?*

"Ha!" one girl laughed.

Another girl piped up, "Those look like a boy's pants!"

The group of girls erupted into fits of laughter. I looked down at my pants. I didn't think they looked *that* bad, but clearly, I was wrong.

I looked at Maya, waiting for my friend to stick up for me. She smiled at the group of girls and chuckled along. She chuckled!

My very first friend in kindergarten aided in people making fun of me.

When I got back inside our elementary classroom, I thought, *I'll show those girls that these pants are just as cute as Maya's.*

I went over to the back wall to get some scissors out of my cubby. I took the lime green scissors and cut a few slits in the khaki fabric around my knees. I made DIY distressed khakis.

Feeling proud of myself, I went up to my teacher and asked if I could go back to music class to show those girls my new pants. Mrs. Brown looked down at my pants horrified.

"Marlowe! What did you do?" she gasped.

"I made my pants into girls' pants. Now, they look like Maya's and not like boys' pants," I shrugged.

"Oh my goodness," Mrs. Brown shook her head. "No more arts and crafts privileges for the rest of the week. You'll have to earn back the opportunity to use your scissors again."

"But-"

"Go get your scissors and put them on my desk," she replied.

"Ugh," I huffed. I turned around to Maya, waiting for her to stick up for me. At the time, I would have done the same for her.

She looked down at her feet. I couldn't believe it. For the *second time* that day, Maya didn't have my back.

I clenched my fists and stormed to the back of the class towards my cubby. That was the final straw. I wouldn't sit back and be friends with someone who didn't stand up for me. I wouldn't keep brushing off everyone's favoritism towards her.

Later that day, Maya tried to act like everything was normal. As if we were fine. I wasn't going to let her fake niceties work on me. From that moment on, I harbored enough resentment towards Maya to fill up an entire Justice store.

And don't even get me started on how much trouble I got in with my parents when they found out I went all Edward Scissorhands on my khaki pants.

I was laughed at, and I lost my arts and crafts privileges. She didn't have the decency to stick up for me even though I did all of that to be more like her.

Maya was dead to me.

A few years later, Lenny moved to my school, and I learned what a real friend was like. Even though I had Lenny, I never forgot what happened that day in kindergarten.

"Marlowe?" Maya says, breaking me from my elementary school memories. "I said to tell me about you and Beau."

"Oh, sorry," I say, tucking my hair behind my ears. "We really reconnected once we got back into town. You know, we were pretty close when we were younger."

It's not lying if you're just embellishing the truth, right?

"That's sweet," she says, but her words don't quite meet her eyes. "He seems really into you."

I blush. So it's not just me! I feel like Beau is doing a little more than just acting when it comes to our brand-new relationship. He's charming as it is, but when he's directing that charm at me? I could melt.

"Thanks. I haven't really dated much, so it's exciting," I say. I try not to let my face give away how happy I am. I've got to be a cool, chill fake-girlfriend.

We walk back towards the others carrying our sweet treats for the night.

"Whoa, you didn't have to bring all of this," Beau says.

After we finish eating, Lenny and I start packing up our things to head out. It's already getting late, and I don't have the brain capacity to start on another worksheet.

"Are you riding home with Lenny? I don't think I'll have time to drop you off," Beau says.

"Yeah! No problem," I tell him, trying not to look disappointed.

Maya tells us goodbye, and Beau walks Lenny and I over to the door. I look over at Lenny and say, "Meet you over at the car?"

She smiles and nods. As she walks away, Beau pulls me into a hug. His strong arms support me as I lean into him.

"I just wanted to say thanks," he says. His husky voice sends chill bumps down my arms. "I'm going to stay here for a bit. But I just wanted to thank you again. You are the best."

"Of course," I smile, my cheeks warming up with his compliments.

"Goodnight," he says, kissing me softly on top of my head.

BEAU JUST KISSED THE TOP OF MY HEAD.

BEAU JUST KISSED ME.

My plan is working. Beau would never do that if he just saw me as a friend, right?

I tell him goodbye, and he heads back into Maya's house. Running over to Lenny's car, I see her beaming from ear to ear.

"Okay, I was wrong about Beau. That was so cute!"

"Isn't he so sweet? I can't stop smiling," I say, feeling my sore cheeks.

This is going better than I could have ever imagined.

CHAPTER TWELVE

enny's lavender wood wick candle crackles as we power through a few hours of homework, sitting side by side at the kitchen bar stools. I feel the cold granite counter top under my elbows as I prop up my head. Lenny works on her French vocabulary, and I try to finish up my English essay. Lately, it feels like my life only consists of studying, and I'm over it.

Even my parents have noticed how different this year's workload has been. It takes me double the amount of time to finish my to-do list, and I get so annoyed with them for having the TV on while I'm trying to do my homework. Even all the way in my room, I can hear them watching *The Big Bang Theory*. Never mind that I'm trying to learn about the actual theory, they just *have* to laugh at Sheldon at full volume. It's safe to say they've noticed I've been more crabby from school stress.

Lenny huffs and reads my mind, saying, "I'm so tired of this!"

"I know," I say. "Do teachers think we have unlimited time?!"

Raking a hand through her hair, she says, "If I see another French word, I'm gonna puke."

I hear my phone ping and see Beau's name pop up.

BEAU BRAXTON: how's your day been i feel
like i haven't seen you in forever

ME: Good! IKR I kinda miss my fake boyfriend!!

Beau wasn't in History the other day, so it's been a few days since I've seen him. It makes me feel warm and fuzzy inside that he's been thinking about me as well.

BEAU BRAXTON: maya is having a party at her house next weekend do you want to come with me

ME: Of course!!! See you then <3

BEAU BRAXTON: sweet

"Beau just asked me to go to a party with him!"

"Well, I would hope so," Lenny says. "If you're dating, you should automatically be his plus one to everything."

"Lenny!" I say, slumping my shoulders. "You promised you'd be nicer to him."

She groans. "Sorry. I just can't stop thinking about how he told you he liked Maya."

Well, if you keep talking about it then I won't be able to stop thinking about it either. And Beau's crush on Maya is banished from my mind.

"I'm trying to be nicer. I swear," she says.

Deep down, I've always known that Lenny turns on my crushes because she's protective of me. She even does it to Carter's situationships.

Once, Carter had a thing with a girl Kayleigh, who was a year older than him. She had her driver's license already, so she was going to pick him up after school to hangout. Kayleigh's plans changed, and she forgot to tell Carter that she wouldn't be able to drive him anymore.

Carter waited for her to pick him up an hour after school before

Kayleigh realized her miscommunication. Lenny was so upset on Carter's behalf that she never spoke a word to Kayleigh again. Not even after Carter had broken things off- Lenny held her grudge.

Hence, all of my worries about Lenny liking Beau. I have to make sure she's 100% on board with him before I tell her about the fake dating.

Someone knocks at Lenny's front door. "Come in, it's unlocked!"

Jacob walks in, holding a container of cookies. Lenny jumps up in surprise. "Are those for us?" She says, wiggling her eyebrows.

"Yes," Jacob says, his lip twitching into a smile. "My sister wanted to try a new recipe, so I currently have one hundred and sixty cookies at my house. I had to bring over her best batch."

"We can go grab some almond milk to go with these," Lenny says. I pack up our work, thankful for the snack break. At this point, I'm pretty much solely running off of coffee and desserts. Jacob asks, "Do you want me to see if Carter wants any? Trust me, we have plenty to spare."

"Sure! But he isn't home. He's dog-sitting for the Johnsons down the street," Lenny says.

"I can drop some off for him! I love the Johnsons' dogs," I say. They have two adorable dachshunds named Henry and Summitt. Seriously, they are too precious for this world.

I walk outside and head down the sidewalk to see Carter. The sun is starting to set in an orange and peach hue that makes me feel like I live in a painting. The green manicured lawns paired with the warm toned sky sets a magical ambiance within the neighborhood.

I'm sure Carter is the best dog-sitter; growing up, he always was obsessed with animals. When we were at summer camp together, Lenny and I were obsessed with the idea of fairies and woodland creatures. We watched the *Tinkerbell* and *Pixie Hollow* movies on repeat almost weekly. Lenny would always dress up as Rosette, and I would be Fawn.

Since we were consumed with the idea of nature and fairies, we would build "fairy cottages" around the woods at camp. Carter started helping us because he loved woodland animals. We would walk around the woods collecting pine cones, wildflowers, acorns, leaves, twigs, and the occasional four leaf clovers. Carter, Lenny, and I would then find hollow areas or cutouts in trees to build the cottages. We would make little furniture pieces or decor out of our nature finds. Imagining what the fairies and small animals thought of our cottages, it made our pretend play all the more fun. We would leave a fairy cottage one week and come back the next to find that our little fairy furniture moved around. Looking back, I know it was just from weather or something, but at the time, we all thought it was reassurance of magic.

After hearing my knock, Carter opens the door. "Mar! What's up?! C'mon in."

I smile. He always seems to be in the best mood. "Jacob's sister baked a bunch of cookies, so I brought you some! I think they are sea salt caramel and chocolate chip."

"That sounds amazing," Carter says. I place the container on the kitchen counter top and hear the pitter patter of dog feet. Henry and Summitt come running up, absolutely overjoyed to see company. Henry is a classic black and brown dachshund, while Summitt is a speckled long haired one. They are so cute that I could cry.

"Summitt! Henry!" I say. I bend down so I can give them both a proper belly scratch.

"I was actually about to just take them out for a walk. Do you want to join?"

"Of course," I say. Carter is that type of friend that you can go do anything with, and you know it'll be fun. I don't ever have to worry about what to say or what I look like with him.

Heading to the door, Carter and I get the dogs' harnesses on and walk outside. Luckily, I'm walking Henry; Summitt is known to try to pull you off the sidewalk.

"Have you listened to the new Backseat Lovers' album?" Carter asks and accidentally brushes my arm with his.

"Not all of it, but yes! It's so good."

"I know right!" Carter exclaims. His face practically lights up while talking about his favorite band. "What on earth would we do without music?"

"I don't know," I say, shaking my head. Summitt starts to veer off of the sidewalk, and Carter has to redirect the panting pup.

"I saw on Instagram that they are going to Nashville next summer. We need to go. I've been wanting to see them in concert for forever."

"That would be awesome," I say. "Speaking of music, how is the show going?"

"It's alright. I am so excited to be the Beast. I'm just a little over-whelmed, but I know that's normal," he sighs.

"I'm sure it's a lot. I seriously couldn't imagine balancing all your responsibilities. Do you have a favorite song you're learning?" I ask, raising my eyebrows.

"'Evermore' for sure," he says. "But 'How Does A Moment Last Forever' is also good."

"Those are both really great. You know Belle was my favorite princess growing up?" I ask.

"Yeah, I do! You remember that one time you borrowed my yellow t-shirt to use as a make-shift Belle outfit?"

I can't believe he remembers so many little things from our elementary school days. "That was so long ago," I say.

"Yeah," he sighs. We reach the end of the cul-de-sac and decide to head back towards the house.

"Well, I will definitely be at your show. I know it'll be amazing," I tell him, with a little nudge of my elbow.

"Thanks," he chuckles. He scratches the back of his neck. "So, what's been going on with you?"

"I feel like I'm drowning in homework right now."

"I can understand that," he says sympathetically.

"I just- I don't know. I feel like it's a lot of pressure. Y'know? I feel like adults tell us to cherish our youth because it goes by too fast. But then we're under adult-level stress from school, work, and just the idea of growing up," I say.

"That's it! And I don't feel equipped to handle any of it."

"Me either."

Carter looks over at me. "Are you doing anything that may help your stress? Like journaling or something?" The setting sun casts an amber glow onto Carter's face. His freckles glow against his fair skin.

"No, I haven't. That's a good idea," I say.

"It's helped me," he shrugs and bumps my elbow with his again.

Carter is one of those people that seems to always be genuine. Always caring. Always understanding.

Talking with him has made me realize that I need to pay more attention to my stress. Before it gets the better of me.

CHAPTER THIRTEEN

Pulling my only crop top on, I glance back at the mirror. Beau is about to pick me up to take me to Maya's party. Lenny plans on meeting us there with Jacob.

I spray myself a few times with an all natural vanilla perfume my mom got me last year and check off my mental checklist. Makeup looks good. Perfume is on. Outfit looks great.

With some Wallows songs playing softly in the background, I can't help but overthink about the whole Beau situation. Yes, fake dating was bound to get messy since I had real feelings for Beau. But lately I've felt like something has changed. He's been touchier and more flirtatious than we ever were before. And I don't think that's just to make Maya jealous.

When he hugs me and when he kissed me on the head, I felt like he was doing that for *me*. I mean, Maya wasn't even there for the forehead kiss! He didn't have to do that.

Maybe this is what it feels like to finally blossom into a relationship person. Throughout my whole life, guys have passed over me and wanted girls like Maya. Even Lenny- I love her to death- but why couldn't I have met the love of my life in eighth grade like she did?

Because of the stupid societal norm that guys ask the girls out, I've always had to wait around for a guy that never shows or is not into me.

I remember last year in my world history class, my teacher gave us assigned seats. I was assigned next to this guy James. He had just moved to Caelee two years prior, and I didn't know him well. He was super cute with his layered brown hair and wire framed glasses.

The first few weeks of class, James never spoke. He was always on his phone, and he wouldn't make any effort to talk to me.

When we had to do partner work in the class, I would have to take initiative on everything. I was always the first one to talk or the one to do most of the work.

I assumed he was *super* introverted. I would sit there, trying to look perfectly poised and approachable. He was just so cute, and I really wanted him to notice me.

After fall break, our teacher changed the seating charting, so James and I weren't sitting together anymore. He was now sitting next to a girl, Betty. She was super sweet, but that's not what most people noticed. She had blonde hair and blue eyes with glass-like skin. Once James started sitting next to her, he *suddenly* became really talkative. I would always look over to see what they were doing. Typically, James was starting conversations, flirting with her, or trying to subtly touch her arm.

Turns out James wasn't just super shy, he just didn't want to talk to *me*.

I was Boysick over a guy that barely made any effort towards me. And why? Just to get my feelings hurt in the end? I racked my brain to think of why all my efforts eventually failed.

But I guess none of that matters anymore. I'm turning into a relationship girl.

BEAU BRAXTON: hey i'm here

ME: Coming!

I hear a faint honk and head downstairs. My mom sits on a stool at the kitchen counter, studying her laptop. She's been trying to find a local vendor that can make cute tote bags to sell at her studio. I see her flipping through the images of this one artist that makes Y2K themed tote bags. My mom pauses at a Powerpuff Girls tote and looks up at me.

"I love those!" I say, eyeing her computer.

Honk.

"Who's that?" Mom looks towards the door. "Lenny knows she can come on in."

"Oh, it's Beau! We are going to Maya's. She's having a little get together," I say quickly. "Lenny and Jacob are meeting up with us later."

Mom eyes me and closes her laptop. "Is this a study session?"

I fidget with the hem of my crop top, trying to pull it lower to meet the waistband of my jeans. "No, it's like a normal hangout."

Standing up, she walks over to the refrigerator and pulls out carrots and ranch. I glance over at the front door and wonder how I can escape this conversation as quickly as possible. I'm not sure why my mom picked *now* as the time to interrogate me.

Crunching on a carrot, she says, "But you can't stand Maya."

"Yeah, but she invited Beau and me."

"Oh. Things seem to be progressing with Beau. So when do we get to officially meet him? Not just from a study session?" my mom asks, raising her eyebrows.

"Later, I promise! I really have to go," I say, straightening my shirt again. "I'll be back before midnight."

"Okay, but be careful!" she calls, as I head for the door.

Beau is parked in front of my house, and I see him glancing down at his phone. I open the passenger door, and he looks up and smiles.

"Sorry, I'm late!"

"No problem," he says, as I sit down and buckle my seat belt.

Beau's straight hair is tousled towards his face. I love the combination of his black hair and tan skin. He's like if Jacob and Edward had a baby in *Twilight*... which is basically my dream man.

He's got on a heather gray jacket with black jeans. He reaches over to flick up the volume, and Drake's newest song fills the car.

"You look," he pauses. "Really good."

I blush so deep that my cheeks turn to embers. There's been a switch between Beau and I, and I'm absolutely loving it.

"You look really good, too," I say. I gently place my fingertips on his forearm, feeling the soft jacket and the lean muscles underneath.

He smiles, glancing over at me before moving his eyes back to the road.

He chuckles, "This whole thing has actually been kind of fun."

Fake dating me is fun?! Beau, just imagine if we were actually dating.

We make some small talk about how our days went and what we are doing the rest of the weekend. I steal glances at him every now and then, as I take in his angular jaw and peach lips. We pull into Maya's neighborhood and drive by mansion after mansion. It's almost fully dark now, with the streetlights and headlights casting a yellow glow around her house.

Getting out of the car, we head towards the house. Beau opens the front door and slips his hand in mine. He looks over at me, and I give him a small nod. An unspoken pact: fake boyfriend to fake girlfriend.

Maya's dads own a logistics company, so they are constantly traveling. Hence, Maya's well-known and parent-free ragers at her house. I can hear the bass rattling the furniture from the living room. Smelling the sickly sweet scent of strawberry, we pass a group of friends vaping. Beau leads me into the kitchen, where some guys are pouring drinks.

"Do you want anything?" Beau asks, his eyes glowing under the kitchen lights.

"Surprise me," I tell him.

He grabs two bottles of Corona from the kitchen, opens them up, and hands me one. I take a sip. The funky bitterness slides down my throat and settles into my stomach. I've never been a beer girl.

Beau and I walk into the living room to watch the intense game of table tennis. People are yelling and rooting for the guy to beat the girl he's facing off. Beau watches them and chuckles, running a hand through his hair.

"Hey guys!" Maya says. She reaches her arms toward me, expecting a hug. I lean in and give her a tentative hug back.

"Thanks for inviting us," Beau pipes up.

"Babe, I was looking for you!" says a guy with sandy hair that flips in all the right places.

"Oh," Maya says, as the guy slings an arm around her shoulders. "Beau, I don't know if you've met my boyfriend, Kevin."

Kevin gives Beau a halfhearted flick of the wrist that barely qualifies as a wave. Beau nods, sticking his hands in his pockets.

"They are in the ACT study group I told you about," Maya says.

"Oh yeah," Kevin slurs. I don't know how he got this drunk because the party *just* started.

Luckily, I've managed to avoid Kevin Owens throughout my time at school. I think the universe felt bad enough for me that I've had a class with Maya almost every year since kindergarten, so I've been spared from Kevin's obnoxious personality.

Obviously, I know who Kevin is. He's the exact male version of Maya, so practically *everyone* at school adores him. Imagine the worst characteristic from each of Rory Gilmore's boyfriends, and that pretty much sums up Kevin.

"Where's my kiss at?" he asks, leaning towards his girlfriend.

Maya kisses him as if they are in her bedroom and not the middle of a party. Beau and I awkwardly peek at each other, while Maya and Kevin are nearly making out in front of us.

"Let's go this way," Beau says and pulls me out of the living room. He looks genuinely disturbed by Maya and Kevin's PDA.

Looking around the room, I try to see if I recognize anyone else. Just as I do, I hear a squeal that resembles my name.

"Marlowe!" Lenny grins.

"You're here!" I say, and she shrugs it off. Jacob comes up behind her, red Solo cup in hand.

"You look cute," she says quietly. She eyes Beau a few feet behind me and whispers, "Is this outfit for a certain someone?"

"Of course."

Lenny goes into telling me about what she and Jacob have spent all day doing: going to the craft store to get embroidery thread and then helping Jacob's sister with her recorder for the elementary school recital.

Squeezing Beau's arm, I leave with Lenny to walk around the party and gossip. Jacob heads over to the table tennis to show off his skills.

"So, is everything still going well with Beau?" Lenny asks.

"Yeah, it is. I don't think I'll ever get used to being with him," I say, shaking my head.

"That's how I feel with Jacob. Like, I just have to pinch myself sometimes because he seems too good to be true."

After walking around the house and our nostrils officially filled with the smell of weed, we head back into the living room towards Beau.

"I think I'm going to play some ping pong," Beau says. I nod and stand off to the side. Watching your boyfriend play games at a party is definitely a rule in the Girlfriend 101 book.

Lenny and Jacob disappear somewhere, and I walk over closer to Beau's table. I take a couple of sips from my beer, trying not to wince as the bitter liquid goes down. I feel a little awkward, and I'm not really sure what to do with my arms. Using my drink as a crutch, I try to not look too out of place.

Beau makes playing table tennis look effortless. His long and lean arms reach out as he makes each hit. It's like he's in a slow-motion action movie montage.

Half an hour goes by, and Beau quickly smiles at me in between each round. I smile back at him, and my stomach feels light with nerves. I glance down at my phone a few times to pass the time.

Feeling a hand on my shoulder, I turn around to see Lenny and Jacob. Hand in hand, she says, "I'm going to drive us home. Do you need a ride?"

"No," I look back at Beau. "I think Beau will drop me off."

"Okay," she says, giving me a quick hug. "Keep me in the loop!" she winks.

I wave goodbye and turn back towards Beau. He eyes me and walks over. "Sorry, I didn't realize how long I'd been playing. Bored?"

"Not too bad," I wave off.

Smirking, he asks, "You wanna explore?"

I agree, and he leads the way through Maya's home. People are scattered everywhere. I can't believe a house can hold this many people.

"I talked to Maya earlier, and she was acting weird. I don't know what was up with her," Beau says.

"Really? That's odd," I say. They must've talked when I was walking around with Lenny. I wonder if she's backing off from Beau because she sees him and me together. I would hope so.

We peek into the bonus room, and I see a bunch of guys and girls watching a college basketball game. Walking around upstairs, we look into a couple more bedrooms. There are people everywhere. Beau heads into a guest bedroom and pulls me in to see that no one is there.

Finally, some alone time with the two of us.

I glance around the room, taking in the wall art and designer bedding. Beau sits down on the bed, and I follow suit. His brown eyes gleam with intrigue, and I'm already dreading this moment ending.

"I just wanted to thank you again. You've been great," he says. "With the whole Maya thing. The fact that you would do this for me," he gestures between us.

"Beau, of course. I mean, you're one of my oldest friends," I say, nudging closer.

"I know. But not just anyone would be so caring," he says slowly.

I smile and scoot even closer. Our knees are almost touching now. Time has slowed down just for the two of us.

"I've really enjoyed spending time with you lately," I say quietly.

"Me too."

"Yeah," I breathe, feeling a little buzzed from half of the beer I drank.

"It's really made me think about things," he tells me.

"Oh?"

"Between us," he says quietly. "You and me."

"Oh," I say again. Searching his eyes, I try to figure out where he's coming from. Thinking about things between us? Thinking in a good way or a bad way?

"You and me," he repeats, leaning in and smiling faintly. Taking the cue, I lean towards him. He cups my jaw, and I breathe in his warm, autumnal scent. His lips touch mine softly. Such a gentle touch- his lips on mine and his fingertips on my jaw.

We kiss. My first kiss ever.

With Beau Braxton.

We start out slow with small kisses, fluttering between our lips like hummingbirds in the spring. I place a hand on his shoulder, pulling him closer. As our lips part, I can taste the beer he drank earlier. The bitterness only seems to add to the electricity between us.

He starts kissing me with more intensity. More passion. Beau slides a hand to my waist. I can feel his cool fingertips on the bare skin between my crop top and jeans. I lean back towards the bed, bringing him towards me.

Sprinkling me with affection, he lightly kisses my nose, my lips, and my jaw. I can't believe this is happening. Putting my arms on his shoulders, I run my hands through the back of his hair. He squeezes my waist, and I feel my breath catch in my throat.

This is so hot.

He puts a hand behind my neck and steadies me with the other hand on my waist. His teeth lightly score my bottom lip, and I try to match his energy by kissing him back with more power. His fingers trace my back, and his lips lock with mine. I don't exactly know what I'm doing, but I just try to follow his lead.

He's in the middle of kissing my neck when I hear a familiar ringtone. "Wait," I say, pulling back from Beau. His eyes dart between mine as he questions me.

"What's wrong?" he asks, his voice husky.

He rolls off of me, and I lean over the bed to grab my purse I set down earlier. Digging through my bag, I take out my phone and see that Carter's calling me. I click my phone off. I'll call him back later.

"Sorry, I thought it was my mom calling," I tell him quickly. Although it kills me to admit, it's 11:00 PM now, which is getting close to my curfew.

"I need to head back home soon," I tell him, jutting out my bottom lip.

"Oh, okay. I can drive you back," he says quickly. He starts to grab his keys and smooths out his shirt. "I only had a few sips of my beer."

"Thanks, Beau," I say. I try to catch his eyes to gauge how he's feeling. He looks a little exasperated, as if I prematurely woke him up from a trance. If it were up to me, I would obviously stay here with him all night. But it took years of convincing my mom to extend my curfew to midnight.

"Sorry. I mean, I would love to stay. I just don't want my parents to kill me for coming in late."

"No, I get it," Beau nods with a small smile, extending his hand for me. I take it, lacing my fingers around his.

He walks me out of the party, I feel like I'm riding on a conveyor belt at the airport. I'm passing by everyone around me, but my mind is still stuck in the guest bedroom with Beau. We say goodbye to Maya and head back towards Beau's car. We settle in, and he places his hand on my knee, as if he's done it a million times before.

This feels like a scene from a movie. We just made out at Maya's house party, and now we are assuming the roles of (real) boyfriend and girlfriend. My knee twitches under his touch. I feel like an imposter.

Beau calms my worries without me even having to say anything. He blushes and says, "I had a great time tonight."

"Me too," I say as the streetlights illuminate the drive.

He pulls in front of my house and parks so I can walk up the stairs.

He leans over and kisses me on the cheek. "I'll see you later, Marlowe."

My face heats up instantly. Grabbing my things, I quietly head inside. I peek into my parent's room and let them know I'm home.

"How was it?" my mom asks.

"Good! I'll tell you about it tomorrow. I'm exhausted," I tell her.

She nods, and I tell her and my dad goodnight. Running upstairs, I can't shake the feeling that I just survived a tornado. Images of Beau and I swirl past me, so much so that I'm feeling a bit dizzy.

Beau picked me up. We flirted. We made out. Which was my first kiss ever. And now I'm supposed to go back to my everyday life as if nothing has changed?!

Everything has changed.

I change into my pajamas, which consists of my dad's old sweatshirt and a pair of thread bare knit pants. I open up my phone and scroll for a few minutes, before realizing I have a bunch of missed notifications. After I missed the call from Carter, he left me a voicemail.

"MAR! What's up?! Um, I just wanted to talk with you about Leadership. I had an idea for helping with student mental health. I feel like we really connected the other day. You know, when we were talking about our stress and anxiety. I thought we could do something with that for our project. You know that dingy lounge on the second floor? We could propose to make it more like a mindfulness space. I don't know! Just let me know what you think. I thought we could look into it during class. Anyway. See ya! Peace out."

I smile down at my phone and text him that I love the project idea. Everything in my life seems to be finally clicking into place, like a heart shaped locket closing shut.

Going to bed, I hope when I wake up that I'm still living this dream.

CHAPTER FOURTEEN

In between class changes, I DoorDash some chicken noodle soup and hot tea to Lenny's house. She texted me earlier that she wouldn't be at school because she woke up with a migraine. I figure some warm food and drinks should help her feel a little better.

I didn't get a chance to talk to her yesterday, and I haven't seen her all day today. I had to call her about Beau and I's steamy stolen kisses rather than having an in person rundown. I could tell she was genuinely happy for me. Although she might not be crazy about Beau right now, Lenny knows more than anyone just how long I had waited for that perfect kiss moment.

Each time I think about Beau and I in the spare bedroom, my face heats up and my palms start to sweat. I don't really know where we stand now. I mean, it's apparent to both of us that this is a fake relationship. But that make out session definitely blurred the lines. We're now in this weird, undefinable limbo.

Heading into Leadership class, I see that everyone is already pairing up with their partners and working on the proposals. I've heard from some classmates that they are thinking of adding to the cafeteria, investing in better art programs, or building more parking spaces for their year-long projects.

I eye Carter, and he waves me over to the table.

"Hey you," he says. His hair is looking extra curly today. He's got on a Patagonia fleece pullover with gray sweatpants, and he looks so comfy.

That's the thing about Carter: his granola-surfer boy aesthetic always makes him look comfortable and huggable.

"How was your weekend?" I ask him.

"Good! A lot of hours in rehearsals, but good overall." He rubs his eyes, and I notice the dark circles under them.

"I'm sorry," I say. I hate to see Carter this stressed out.

"No, it's fine! Don't worry about me," he says with a smile.

"Maybe if we can get this project knocked out of the way, it can be one less thing on our plate. You know, so we don't have as much to do."

Mrs. Lin opens up the lecture by reviewing the project's provisions. We have to detail the purpose of our project, as well as our targeted demographic. Will this help students more than teachers? Does our project help others outside of ourselves?

Carter and I start typing up our proposal and answering Mrs. Lin's questions.

"So obviously our project is mainly targeted towards students," I tell Carter.

"Yes! I mean, teachers can also use the calming room. But if we cater it towards students, I think it will have more of an impact."

"Agreed," I say.

"So, if we try to have the school remodel the old student lounge, then they wouldn't have to build onto the school. So that may be a positive factor because it's probably not as expensive," Carter says while typing. His face seems to light up as he types. I can tell he's so passionate about this. I mean, he's passionate about everything. But the mindfulness room will help the both of us, as well as a lot of our peers.

"Exactly. And no one even uses that old lounge, so we could argue that it's more sustainable as well. Because we probably don't have to use as much building material in a remodel rather than an addition to the school," I say. I quickly find some articles that discuss bringing life to old spaces rather than getting rid of the spaces entirely.

"In Theater, we always make our props and backgrounds in brighter colors because it stands out more. It's more pleasing to the eye, and it will most likely get the audience more interested in what we are performing. So, we can have an opposite approach with this. If we use more muted colors, we can create a more calming and less stimulating space."

"I love that idea! We could have the walls painted in neutrals and pops of muted colors in the furniture," I say.

"So for furniture, what are we thinking? Overstuffed chairs? Floor pillows?" he asks.

"Yes and yes," I tell him. "I think the more inviting and comforting the room is, the better."

Nodding, Carter types all of our ideas up on a document on his computer. While he's doing that, I search for some statistics about how stressed high school students are.

"I was also thinking, could we get some yoga mats and a TV in one corner of the lounge? So students can practice yoga or meditation. Or even the TV could play calming music. Or white noise," I say. "Or, if the school didn't want to buy a TV, we could get a projector and mount it to the wall," I say, thinking out loud.

"That's perfect! Mar, you're a genius," he winks.

"Well, you're the one who came up with this idea," I say to him. He pauses and smiles at me for a second. His bright eyes convey a new level of understanding between us, burning a hole right through my chest.

"I was also wondering. After we talked the other day," he says. "When I told you about some of my anxiety? I stress over the future, so I tend to thrive in a state of nostalgia. I love kid shows from my childhood. Shows like Little Bear or Winnie the Pooh are so calming. Watching them really helps my anxiety."

"Aw, Carter! That makes sense about the shows. It was a simpler time for us, and the shows themselves are calming and not as stimulating as our phones."

"Yeah," he says quietly.

"I'm sure those shows would be beneficial for others, too. We could propose that shows from our childhood are available to watch on the TV. Winnie the Pooh, Little Bear, Wonder Pets, etcetera!"

"Yes! I love that," Carter says excitedly.

He continues typing as I find some more articles to support our project. Mrs. Lin walks around to each table to discuss each group's idea. She starts to head our way.

"Hey guys! What are you thinking?" she asks us.

Carter and I take turns telling Mrs. Lin about our project proposal. She nods along with enthusiasm. We explain our personal connection to the project and talk about our own increased stress levels.

"Wow, this is awesome! Sounds like a great plan, and I can't wait to see how it turns out. If you've got any questions at any time during the project, let me know," she says.

Carter and I exchange a look of relief.

Before we know it, class is already over, and we've developed a solid plan for our project. I stuff my notebook and laptop into my backpack as Mrs. Lin dismisses us out of class.

"Hey, I had a lot of fun walking the Johnsons' dogs the other day," Carter says, looking up through his amber eyelashes.

"Me too! I love them," I say, pushing out my bottom lip.

"Well, I was thinking about going to the animal shelter after school to walk some of the dogs. Do you want to join?"

"I would love to!" I say.

"Do you want to meet up in the parking lot after dismissal?" Carter asks.

"Yeah! Okay, see you then," I say as Carter and I part ways to head to our different classes.

"Bye, Mar," he says with a glimmer in his eyes.

• • •

CARTER: Hey!! My class got out early so
I'm already over to my car. If you stay outside
of the front doors, I can swing by and pick you up

ME: Perfect!

I walk towards the double doors at the front of the school, heading closer to the chilly autumn air. Pulling my backpack strap tighter, I scan the parking lot for Carter's car.

His navy SUV pulls in front of me, and I jog over to him. Opening the car door, the smell of sandalwood hits me. Carter just always smells like a fresh, clean surfer guy.

"Hey you," he says happily. He's got one hand on top of the steering wheel and the other on the center console. He looks so effortlessly casual.

"How were your other two classes?" I ask. I put my backpack below me and nestle my way into the car's cushioned seats.

Carter starts to pull away, his Sex Wax car air freshener swinging as the car moves forward. He drives to the left so we don't get caught behind the line of buses beside the school.

"My other classes were pretty good. Theater has been crazy, but I'm still loving it. Acting as the Beast is so much fun."

"I can't imagine the work you've put into the musical," I tell him.

"I constantly have the songs on repeat in my head. It's like I go to bed, and I'm still dreaming about Gaston's mob song," he chuckles.

I look over at him and nudge his elbow with mine. I start humming the tune of the dreaded song.

"No," he groans dramatically. "It's going to be stuck in my head for the rest of the day."

I giggle at his exaggerated dislike of the Disney songs I know he secretly loves. When he's fake-pouting, he's gets this small wrinkle between his eyebrows that's pretty endearing.

Carter pulls up to the Caelee County Animal Shelter and parks at a spot near the door. He turns off the car and says, "One second."

He walks around to the trunk of his car and digs around for something. I grab my purse and zip up my slate blue jacket. Getting out of the car, I walk over to Carter. He grabs two reusable totes full of dog toys, bones, and bags of treats.

"Oh my gosh, Carter! What's this?" I ask, motioning to his animal shelter donations.

Carter blushes, and I can see the skin on his neck growing into a faint shade of maroon. He says, "Oh. I had some money saved up, and I wanted to bring them some toys." He shrugs, as if it's just no big deal.

Most of the guys I know are pretty stingy. Which is fine, I mean go save your money! But also don't be a dick about it.

Freshman year, I went to the movies with this one guy, Justin Ward. He mentioned so many times that it was a "friend hangout." As if he wanted to make it blatantly clear that he was not taking me on a date.

When we got to the movies, he offered to buy us some snacks. I declined, trying to be polite. He insisted, so I picked out Reese's Pieces and a medium Dr. Pepper. He ended up ordering more and got popcorn for the two of us to share.

I genuinely thanked him a few times because we were 15 and neither of us had jobs. So, I thought it was a big deal for him to pay for my food. After the movie, he asked me to Venmo back for *all of the snacks*. It was like he was trying to return the merchandise of our "friend hangout."

That was our last hangout. He stopped talking to me later, saying that he just wasn't "feeling it" anymore.

So, for Carter to spend his own money on shelter animals is truly out of the ordinary. To free up his hands, I grab one of the totes full of treats, and we both head towards the door.

When we enter the lobby, I smell the comforting aroma of dogs and the sour stench of citrus cleaner.

A lady with purple hair is sitting behind the desk. Raising up from her chair, she asks us, "Hello! Can I help you all with anything?"

"Hey! We had some donations to drop off. And we didn't know if you were open for dog walking?" Carter says. The apples of his cheeks push upwards as he smiles softly.

"Of course! Oh my God," the purple haired lady says, eyeing our tote bags. "I can take those."

We hand her the tote bags, and she sets them behind her desk. She gets up and motions for us to follow her.

"I'm Alice, by the way," she says, holding the door to the backroom open for us. "We really appreciate volunteers like you. And don't even get me started on the dogs. They love it!"

"I can't wait," I whisper to Carter.

It's nice to hangout with him outside of school. I never think twice about hanging out with Lenny one on one, but this reminds me that I need to make more of an effort with Carter.

Alice opens up a side door, sticking her head in. She peeks back out and says to us, "So some of the dogs are having quiet time right now. We'll have to see which ones you can walk."

"We'll walk any of them," Carter says, pushing his curls out of his face. He holds the door open as we venture onto another hallway.

Once again, Alice pokes her head through a door, checking to see which dogs are napping. Smiling, she turns to us and says, "There are a couple in here! Just wait right there, and I'll bring them out."

Carter and I stand side by side as we wait for Alice to come back with the dogs. Our arms are almost touching.

Alice opens the door and comes back with two of the cutest dogs I've ever seen. One is a small, scraggly looking Chihuahua mix, with ears that almost double his little head. The other is a black lab mix, who comes through wagging her tail so much, as if she just can't contain her excitement.

Pointing to the small Chihuahua, Alice says, "This one is Pickles. He's eleven, but he definitely doesn't act like it!"

"Aw," Carter says, crouching down to the floor. Pickles immediately runs over to Carter. Panting, he tries to jump up to Carter's knees. Alice hands the leash over to him, and Pickles starts adorably running around in a circle, taking the occasional break to lick Carter's ankles.

"He loves you!" I say. Alice nods, and Carter looks over the moon. He just won the lottery.

"This is adorable!" I say, pulling out my phone. I take a quick picture of him playing with Pickles. His bright smile shines against the beige walls and tile of the shelter.

While Pickles is orbiting around Carter, I walk over to pet the black lab. "And what's your name?" I ask. She's got the biggest brown eyes, and she is five times the size of Pickles.

Alice pipes up, "This is Lily! She's super sweet. She was brought in about a week ago. She's basically like a teddy bear."

Lily walks over and nudges my hand, directing me to pet her. I scratch the top of her head, and she leans into my palm. She starts wagging her tail again, and I swear one swipe would fully take Pickles out.

"Are you all good?" Alice asks us.

Carter looks at me, and I nod. "Yeah! We're ready!"

Alice leads us out the back door and shows us to the dog park behind the main building. Pickles' little feet patter against the floor as he tries to keep up with Lily's long stride.

Stepping outside, we head over to the sidewalk with the two dogs. Carter's arm occasionally brushes mine as Pickles walks in anything but a straight line.

"They are so cute," I whine.

"I'm actually obsessed with Pickles," Carter says, looking down at the scrawny caramel colored pup.

Changing the subject, I ask Carter, "Have you ever thought about doing something with animals as your career? You clearly like working with them, and you would be great at it. Like a veterinarian or something?"

He pauses, and I see a look of hesitation behind his emerald eyes. His brow furrows a bit, and he bites his lower lip. I didn't realize it, but that was a loaded question.

Pickles somehow gets his leash twisted around Lily's leg, so we have to take a second to untangle the two. Rubbing the back of his head, Carter finally says, "To tell you the truth, I don't know. I would love to, but I just don't know."

"Well, you have plenty of time to decide," I say, trying to offer some comfort to an obviously troubling subject.

"I think that's what I'm worried about. I have so much imposter syndrome, and I'm worried I wouldn't be good enough for it. And you know how I mentioned how overwhelmed I can get with stress?"

I nod. He continues, "I'm so afraid that will happen with my career. Like, I will graduate and get into the workforce and realize I'm not good enough."

"Carter," I say, putting a hand on his arm.

"I just- I don't know. I'm scared of wasting eight years of my life on a career aspiration that I'm not meant for. It's like my brain spirals if I think about not being good enough and time passing me by. As if I'll somehow be stuck and constantly trying to catch up."

"So, with your stress about imposter syndrome, do you think that puts extra pressure on yourself about college or career decisions?" I ask him.

"Definitely. It just freaks me out thinking of it all. I'm so worried about wasting *years* of my life on something I won't be good at. And I would feel like I'm lying to the world by acting like I was good enough for it. I know it doesn't make sense."

A silence fills our stroll for a moment while I ponder his words. "I know you struggle with the idea of being good enough, and it's a topic of anxiety for you. I'm not going to belittle that or act like it's not a big deal. Because I can imagine that it's incredibly anxiety inducing," I tell him. "And it may not help or mean anything, but *I* think you are good enough."

He nods and quietly says, "Thanks, Mar. And it does mean something."

I smile at him. "You are one of the most dedicated people I know. You are so passionate. I totally understand the imposter syndrome. Trust me, I get it. But I want to let you know that I believe in you," I say, intently.

"Marlowe," he says, actually using my full name. I look over at him, and I can see his eyes start to well up. He clears his throat and says, "That really means a lot."

"I believe in you, Carter," I tell him. To lighten the mood, I lightly shove his elbow with mine. He smiles, and he bumps his elbow back at me.

Pickles walks over to the grass beside the sidewalk and turns over to his back. He scoots around on his back, with his tiny legs flailing in the air. "Oh my gosh! Look at him," I say.

Carter pulls his phone out to take a video of Pickles rolling around on his back. "I want to adopt him. Like so badly," he says with puppy eyes.

"Sheila might let you," I say.

"Don't tempt me," he chuckles. Carter bends down to scratch Pickles' exposed belly. He jumps up and starts to dance around Carter's legs again.

"He loves you," I say to Carter.

"I love him," Carter says. "Come here little guy," he says, picking Pickles up.

Lily takes this moment to plop down on the sidewalk. Her double chin seems to bounce up and down as she pants from our stroll. Pickles licks Carter's nose and cheeks, while Carter scratches his frizzy fur.

I snap some more pictures of Carter. He looks ecstatic and like a little kid. He's got this look in his eyes, as if nothing could ruin his mood.

Carter puts Pickles back down, and we take a few more laps around the park. The leaves on the trees are starting to turn into that marmalade shade of orange. The dogs keep trotting ahead of us, with their tails wagging and falling into a rhythm.

We start to head back towards the building, and Carter grabs the door for us. The dogs run over to their water bowls, while Alice walks back over to us.

"I really want Pickles. I may have to stage some kind of presentation to convince my mom to let me adopt him," Carter says and looks down at the scruffy Chihuahua.

After getting a drink, Pickles runs back over to him and flops over so

Carter can give him more belly rubs.

"Look at him!" I whine, snapping more pictures of the little dog. His scraggly curls create a halo around his pointy ears.

Lily starts walking slowly back over to her bed. She reminds me of an oversized stuffed animal.

"Okay, if I don't go now, I will actually take him home with me," Carter says and hands the leash to Alice. "I promise I'll come back!"

Pickles looks up at him, wagging his tail. Alice thanks us for volunteering, and we head back to Carter's car.

"That was so much fun," I say getting into his car. "Thank you for letting me tag along!"

"I hope you don't feel like you were *just* tagging along. I wanted you to come," he says looking through his eyelashes.

The corners of my mouth turn up as I try to bite back a smile. Carter really is the sweetest.

As we pass the trees driving back to the school, Carter taps the steering wheel along to the rhythm of Noah Kahan's "Stick Season."

I glance down at my phone and see a couple of text messages I've missed.

BEAU BRAXTON: hey

BEAU BRAXTON: i just wanted to say again that
i really appreciate you doing this whole fake dating thing

Oh my gosh! Beau just double texted me. As Carter pulls into the school, I quickly text Beau back.

ME: Of course!! What are friends for?!

BEAU BRAXTON: haha do you want to hangout this weekend i feel like we need to get to know each other better if we are going to keep this up

I grin to myself and look over at Carter. He's parked next to my car. I put my phone away and say, "Sorry, Beau was texting me."

"How are things," he pauses, "with Beau?"

"Good! I'm really happy," I tell him.

He offers me a warm smile and says, "I'm glad you're happy."

"Thanks," I say. "I had fun today."

"Me too," he says.

Grabbing my bag, I tell Carter goodbye and head over to my car. I get settled, buckle my seat belt, and text Beau back.

ME: Yes!!!!! See you then! Can't wait

I look over and see Carter is still in his car, waiting for me to leave. He mouths, *I'll wait until you go*. I nod and wave to him as I drive off.

CHAPTER FIFTEEN

Pulling on my perfectly worn Levi's and a dark brown sweater, I finish getting ready to hangout with Beau. It's been a couple of days since we last texted. To say I'm excited to see him is the understatement of the year.

I run down the stairs and see my dad watching *The Big Bang Theory*. Of course, he has the volume turned down when I'm *not* doing homework.

He pauses the TV, and says "Are you hanging out with Beau tonight?"

"Yeah. He's picking me up soon," I say.

"Are we meeting him? Your mom won't be home until later."

"I think you'll meet him tonight. If he's coming here to pick me up, he'll probably stay and chat for a bit before we go."

"What are you guys doing?" he asks in a classic Dad Interrogation way.

"I don't really know. Beau said it was a surprise. And something to help us get to know each other better."

"Oh, that's nice," he says, nodding.

My phone buzzes, and I hate to admit how eager I am to see who's texting me.

BEAU BRAXTON: i'm here

ME: You're welcome to come inside!!

BEAU: no it's okay i'm parked
across the street

ME: Okay no worries! Be down in a sec

I read Beau's texts to my Dad, and I walk over grab my crossbody hanging beside the front door.

"He's not coming in?" Dad asks.

"Nope. I have to go!" I say, as I head out the door and jog over to Beau's car.

Opening the gray door of Beau's Jeep, I say, "Hey Beau!"

"Hey," he says. "You look pretty."

Oh my gosh.

Oh my gosh.

Am I dreaming?!

"You look nice as well," I say, eyeing his denim jacket and henley shirt. His dark hair falls away from his face, framing his features perfectly.

"So, what do we want to do?" I ask him.

"Well, I know we both like to read, so I didn't know if you wanted to go to the new bookstore that opened up? June Avenue Books?"

He really is my dream guy. He's so attentive, remembering our shared love of books and offering to take me to a new bookstore.

My eyes grow wide, and I can't help but squeal. "Beau! That would be awesome! That's the nicest thing ever."

His brow creases because he's taken aback by my excitement. "Ha, I'm glad. I also didn't know if you wanted to go to the drive in movie that's down the street? They're playing *The Karate Kid*. If you want to go."

"Of course!" I gush.

He starts to pull away and head downtown towards the bookstore. I feel almost lightheaded with giddiness. I'm anxiously picking at my fingernail polish as Beau turns up the radio. Some rap music I don't recognize fills the car.

"So, how's school been?" I ask over the music. "Like with your workload and everything?"

"It's been good," he says. "I'm really happy my family moved back to Caelee. I think it'll always feel like home." He glances over at me with those gorgeous brown eyes.

"I'm glad. Considering I've never lived anywhere but here, I can't imagine moving around so much."

"Yeah, it was hard when I was younger. But now my dad works remotely, so we were able to move back here. And it's a guarantee that I'll be here for my senior year. I really didn't want to move again in high school."

"That's good! You'll be able to stay here another year and graduate with everyone," I smile at him.

"Yeah," he says with a small smile back. His eyes crinkle at the edges, making his dark eyelashes look even longer.

Beau pulls into the parking lot of June Avenue Books and turns off the car. Glancing over at me, he asks, "Ready?"

"Yeah!" I say happily.

He opens the door for us, and I'm instantly hit with the smell of pumpkin and warm vanilla. Tall bookshelves line the walls with multi-colored spines just waiting to be picked up.

"I'm already obsessed," I tell him. I walk over to the romance section and he follows. Due to my Boysickness, I'm an absolute sucker for a romcom novel, and I always need to add more books to my shelf.

I pick up novel after novel and read the back or the inside cover. Time seems to slow down when I'm in a bookstore. I could stay here for hours.

Grabbing Rachel Lynn Solomon's new book, I cradle it in my arms, fully expecting to buy it no matter the price. Her books are my happy place. I glance at two other books that caught my eye- each with an adorable pastel cover.

I look over at Beau, and he's leaning against a shelf, looking at his phone. He's staring at something intently, and I swear he could be a model.

"We can go to another section. I already have enough picked out," I say, holding up the three books in my basket.

He nods, his coral lips pressed together. He leads the way to the science fiction section. Beau's height matches that of the bookshelf, and it makes him look even more like a 6'2 Prince Charming.

"No way!" he says, his face lighting up.

"What is it?"

"They have this special edition cover of *Dune*," he tells me, holding out the polished matte hardback. He runs his fingers over the embossed title, a grin peeking out of his cheeks. It's absolutely adorable to see him geek out over his favorite book.

"You should get it!" I tell him, brushing his arm with my fingertips.

"I think I will," he says. Tucking the book under his arm, he uses his other hand to slink into mine, fingers intertwined with each other. I grin at him, feeling my cheeks heat up as we walk to the front counter.

"Hey there!" the bookstore worker says.

"Hi!" I reply as he rings up my books. My TBR is already five miles long, but what's wrong with adding a few more books?!

After the worker bags my books in an adorable paper tote, Beau checks out with his copy of *Dune*. Walking out of the wooden doors, Beau's hand finds mine again. I want to squeal, feeling his fingers wrap around mine.

"What do we want to do now?" I ask him. We've got a little under an hour before the drive in movie begins.

"I'm down for whatever," he says, climbing into the driver's seat.

I quickly look over at his backseat, and his charcoal gray skateboard catches my eye. "You skate?"

"Yeah," he nods, with one corner of his mouth upturned.

"I've always wanted to learn," I say, giving him a flirtatious smile. "Do you want to teach me?"

He grins and says, "Of course I'll teach you, Marlowe."

Just hearing him say my name makes my heart skip a beat. He puts the car in gear and drives over to the skate park that's not too far away.

"So how long have you been skateboarding?" I ask him.

"Um," he says, "since I was thirteen, I think."

"How did I not know this?" I say.

Laughing, Beau parks the car, and we head towards the skate spot. He puts the board on the ground and turns towards me. He says, "First thing you are going to want to do is figure out which foot to put in front of the other. I like using my left foot in front."

I look down at my feet and practice planting them on the asphalt, as if the ground below me is the skateboard. Beau studies me as I try to mimic what he showed me. His eyes glow with intrigue.

"I think I like the right foot in front of me," I tell him.

"Sweet," he says. The corners of his mouth wrinkle as he's amused with how much of a beginner I am.

"So, what's next?" I ask him.

"Next you're going to focus on getting on the board. When I was first learning, I couldn't easily get started. I was too clumsy," he chuckles.

"Oh no. I never outgrew my uncoordinated phase," I laugh in return.

"No, you got this," he encourages.

Beau looks at me and starts with his next set of directions. He says, "Okay, so you are going to walk up to the board and put your front foot forward. So, for you, it would be your right foot."

I nod along, and I try to act out what he's saying before actually getting on the board.

"Then, you are going to step onto the board and give it a push with your back foot," he says.

"Okay," I say once again trying to act out his instructions.

"Here, I can show you," Beau says. This reminds me of when the boys would get competitive trying to show off for the girls at camp.

Beau puts his left foot on the board, steps up, and pushes off with his back foot with ease. He rides around the park effortlessly. He leans slightly to turn the board in the direction he wants to go. He looks like this tall, lean, graceful skater boy. His dark hair flutters in the wind as he rides through a curved path.

He comes back around towards me and his eyes light up when they catch mine. "You're so good," I say.

He shrugs off the compliment. "Not really, but thanks," he winks.

HE WINKS. I think my heart just palpitated.

"Are you ready for it?" Beau asks me.

"I think?" I giggle.

He holds out his hands under my forearms to steady me as I put my right foot on the board. "Ah!" I yell, as the board starts to move under me.

"I got you, don't worry," he says, as his hand quickly brushes my waist.

"Here, point your front foot forward," he says. I do so, and he says, "Good! Now, push off with your back foot."

Gripping onto his hands, I lightly push off the ground with my back foot. In turn, the skateboard moves forward a few feet. Beau walks beside me, in line with the board.

"Look at you!" he says.

"Am I doing it?" I squeal. "I'm totally doing it!"

Beau laughs and continues to hold my hands. Now, he's leading me around on the skateboard, as if we are some kind of tandem person-skateboard hybrid.

"Ah!" I shout, starting to lose my balance. The skateboard shoots out from under my feet, and as I start to fall, Beau catches me.

Beau catches me.

He *catches* me.

"I told you, I've got you," he says. His brown eyes turn caramel as the setting sun casts a golden glow across the skate park.

My breath hitches in my throat.

Beau helps me regain my footing, putting his hands around my waist to pull me up. A beat passes. We are just standing in the skate park, his hands on my waist and my mind absolutely spinning.

I search his eyes for a cue. His eyes are set on my lips. He pulls me closer, and I move my hands around his neck. He's a whole head taller than me, so I stand on my toes. He leans his head down. I smell the peppermint on his breath and his lips look so soft.

His lips touch mine so gently, and the small act reminds me this is not a dream. It's everything I've ever wanted. His hands come off my waist to cup the bottom of my cheekbone. His fingertips lightly graze over my skin. I shiver under his touch.

It didn't really hit me at the party that I'm kissing Beau Braxton. That Beau Braxton was my first kiss.

Turns out he's my second kiss as well.

We fall into a rhythm, with him going between kissing me gently then with more intensity. He pulls away for a second, and I lean in for more. He tastes so sweet, and I'm hooked. I never want to stop kissing him.

I feel like I'm light as a feather, and I could just float right out of this skate park. He runs his hands through my hair, and he angles my face towards his, looking down at me.

"Beau," I say breathlessly.

He smiles slyly, and says, "We're going to be late for the movie."

"I don't care," I whisper. He chuckles and grabs my hand, with the skateboard in his other.

He leads me back over to the car and opens the door for me. I am obsessed with this version of Beau. He's so affectionate and caring. I'm almost positive our fake dating has officially become real dating.

My Boysickness has actually gotten me somewhere.

It's kind of quiet once we get back into the car, and I don't really know what to say. Beau takes us over to the drive-in movie, and he steals the occasional glance over to me in the passenger seat.

We've arrived just on time, and Beau pays for both of our tickets. He pulls his Jeep into the closest empty spot. There are some workers walking around with carts of snacks. One guy walks up beside Beau's window.

While Beau rolls down his window, the worker asks, "Can I get you all any snacks?"

Beau looks over at me, offering me whatever the guy has in his cart. I suppress a smile because this feels like something an actual boyfriend would do.

"Do you have any Chex Mix?" I ask. The worker nods and holds up a bag.

"Okay, we'll take two of those," Beau says and pulls out his wallet to get cash. After handing the guy a five, Beau gives me one of the bags of Chex Mix.

I pull out my phone and tell him, "Let me Venmo you right now while I'm thinking about it. How much was my ticket?"

"Marlowe," Beau chuckles. "I'm not going to let you Venmo me for this."

Blushing, I don't know what to say. "Thanks."

Suddenly, I'm very aware that it's just the two of us in his Jeep.

"What kind of gentleman would I be if I let you pay?" he said with a smirk.

He's insinuating that this is a date. This is a date, right? I'm not crazy.

The movie starts, and Beau switches on his radio to the station that plays the audio for the movie. We sit there in silence for a few moments as the first few scenes of the movie play.

I've already eaten half my bag of Chex Mix, minus the pretzels, and I feel like I should make conversation with Beau. This isn't a movie theater, so we can talk freely. But I also don't want to seem annoying if Beau is trying to actually watch the movie.

"Beau, I've had a really good time tonight," I tell him.

He turns to me, and his chocolate eyes twinkle even in the dark of his car. He smiles, and I can smell the spicy leather and Early Grey scent that is Beau's signature aroma.

"You're pretty cool, Marlowe," he says. He gives me a small smile, and he inches closer. I can even see his adorable crowded bottom teeth.

I awkwardly laugh and avert my eyes. I'll never get used to receiving a compliment from Beau Braxton. I feel his long fingers touch my cheek and turn my face towards his.

"I really like you, Beau," I whisper.

"Yeah, I like you too," he says.

I'm still pinching myself to see if this is a dream. Beau sweetly runs a hand through my hair. My chest swells, and my feelings leap out of my throat.

His lips hover over mine, almost tauntingly. I'm too impatient. I lean in and press my lips to his. He runs his other hand through my hair, and I move my lips away from his. I kiss the tip of his nose, his cheek, and his razor-sharp jaw.

I've never felt this way before. This is *more* than just my Boysickness. This is something more. And why waste time by hiding my feelings?!

"Beau," I say, looking past his dark eyelashes. "I don't think I *just* like you. I think I'm falling in love."

He pulls back, eyes growing wide.

I know it's our first date. I know we aren't even official yet. But I've known him forever, and these emotions are more than my typical feelings for a crush.

"What?!" he asks, his voice more curt than usual.

"I think I may-"

"No, I heard you. I just- I don't know. Wow," he says. He blinks several times, shaking his head slightly.

"I'm sorry if I caught you off guard. It's okay if you don't feel the same way right now. I know it's kind of soon," I tell him.

He scratches his eyebrow and looks at me puzzled. Suddenly, the air in his car is too warm, and I fight the urge to scratch at my throat.

Moving in his seat, Beau says, "Yeah it's soon. Marlowe, we haven't even finished our first date."

"I know but-" I stammer.

"I'm really thrown off right now," he says, taking a deep breath. "I just need a break."

"Yeah, I totally get that," I say quickly. I should have known that he would get weird about this. Beau has never been the most outspoken with his feelings.

Typically, Lenny acts as my reality check, keeping logic in my world. Recently, I've chosen to hangout with Beau over her, and that lack of rationale is clear tonight.

I know I probably shouldn't have bombarded him with my feelings. But what was I supposed to do? Keep my feelings inside? Bottle them up?

I couldn't just act like I wasn't head-over-heels Boysick for him.

"I'm sorry," I whisper, tucking my hair behind my ears.

Beau nods, pursing his lips. "Is it okay if I take you home?" he asks. "I just need a break."

"Yeah, of course," I tell him. I stop myself from reaching out to touch his arm. I understand- I really do. Everyone needs a breather at times.

Maybe stepping back for a second will be good for me.

Maybe.

CHAPTER SIXTEEN

finish pouring my strawberry banana smoothie into a metal tumbler and grab a reusable straw. Fidgeting with my sage green corduroy button down, I try to get it to sit right on my shoulders. I tuck in one side of my button down into my jeans and slip on my Birkenstock Bostons.

I'm still on the highs and lows from yesterday. My stomach is turning with nerves like a washing machine with too many clothes inside. Last night when he dropped me off, I had to journal about everything that happened with Beau. I just needed to get everything that happened on paper so it didn't anxiously bounce around in my mind.

I'm so nervous to see Beau today. What will our interactions look like? Should I hug him when I see him? Should I say something specific to him?

He hasn't texted me since he dropped me off, so maybe not.

Lenny messaged me while I was out with Beau last night that she could pick me up for school today. Of course I agreed so I could spill all the details from Beau and I's date.

I keep going back and forth about telling Lenny about my fake dating plan. I mean, Beau and I are basically official now. He just needed a breather last night. He should be good after that.

Lenny is my best friend and my other half. I can't help but worry about what she thinks of my confusing romantic life.

I stuff my notebooks into my backpack and head downstairs. My mom is in the kitchen, pouring herself a cup of black coffee that resembles motor oil.

"How was the movie?" Mom asks.

"Beau and I had a good time together."

"Next time he needs to plan better so he can actually come into the house to meet us," she says, both eyebrows raised.

"That wasn't his fault," I roll my eyes. "Don't let that ruin your image of him. Remember how sweet he was when I was younger? At summer camp?"

"Okay," she says. "I just don't want you going out with any boy that's too scared to face your dad and me."

I look at her with my arms crossed and dramatically roll my eyes. She chuckles and grabs her bag before heading out the door.

"See you tonight! Love you," she says.

"Love you too!" I call back, shaking my head at her. That was just such a *Mom* thing to say. Of course she's more concerned with Beau acting like a traditional gentleman.

I finish filling up my water bottle and grab my lunch for the day. Lenny texts me that she's a few minutes away. While waiting for her, I decide to just go ahead and text Beau. After the date we had, there's no reason to be awkward.

ME: Good morning!!

BEAU BRAXTON: hey

I feel a rock in my throat. Seeing Lenny's car pull up into the driveway, I grab my stuff and head out the door.

Before I'm even settled into the passenger seat, Lenny starts squealing and shaking my arm.

"MARLOWE!"

I giggle at her excitement over my blossoming love life. Lenny is the definition of a girl's girl. She really is my biggest cheerleader.

"Yeah?" I say, blushing and putting my hands over my face.

"YOU HAVE TO TELL ME EVERYTHING!" she shouts in the car.

I let out another laugh. "Lenny, it was perfect. Literally perfect!"

"Ahhhhh!" she squeals as she starts to back out of my driveway. "So start from the beginning. I want all the details."

"Well, we went to the bookstore first, June Avenue Books. Side note- we need to go sometime. It was so cute there!"

"Oh, we definitely will. But back to Beau!" she says.

"Since we are both big readers, we looked around the bookstore and picked out a few things. He came with me to the romance section, and I walked with him to the sci-fi section."

"Aw, that's sweet!" Lenny says.

"Anyways, once we got back to the car, I saw his skateboard in the backseat, and I told him I'd always wanted to learn how to ride. He agreed to teach me, so we drove to the skate park a few minutes away."

"Wait, I can't even imagine Beau skating," she shakes her head.

"I know! Football loving, James Dean looking Beau is a skater! And he's really good," I say.

"Okay, so you got to the skate park?" Lenny prompts me.

"We got to the park, and he taught me how to skateboard! Kind of. He would hold my hand and help me along. It was so cute."

"Oh my gosh!" Lenny croons.

"And I lost my balance at one point and he caught me. He caught me, Lenny!" I squeal.

"What?!"

"Then," I pause for dramatic effect. "We kissed while the sun was setting!"

"WHAT?!" Lenny says with her fist pounding the steering wheel.

"I know! It was so romantic! Like we just shared an intimate kiss in the middle of the skate park."

"That's straight out of a movie," Lenny says.

I blush even more. I can't even believe all of this happened yesterday.

"So then we went to the drive-in movie. He paid for my ticket and bought a bag of Chex Mix for me."

She squeals again.

"I offered to pay him back, but he didn't want me to. He's just so nice. Anyways, we started kissing some more in his car."

Lenny laughs. "Nine-year-old Marlowe would be freaking out at this news."

I giggle and agree with her. "Yeah, honestly. But I'm so nervous about seeing him. Like, I don't even know how to act."

"Oh my gosh," Lenny says.

"The only thing was that when I shared my feelings for him, he got kind of weird. But Beau's always been the more quiet type, so I'm sure he just isn't used to people opening up to him."

"Well, what did you tell him?" she asks.

Looking at her sheepishly, I say, "I told him I thought I was starting to fall in love with him. And he was just taken aback."

Lenny stares at me.

"What?" I ask innocently.

"You're kidding," Lenny says slowly.

"No, I'm not. I wanted to tell him how I feel."

"Marlowe," Lenny shakes her head. "You did not tell him you were in love with him *on the first date.*"

"Well, I wanted him to know how I was feeling."

"No. No, no, no," Lenny says.

"What's wrong?" I ask. I don't understand why both her and Beau's reactions are in the same vein. People always confess their feelings in romcoms, and it's perfectly fine.

"That's delusional. He must be totally freaked out," she says.

I tell her, "I thought it was cute to stay delusional."

"Not in this situation!" she says, shaking her head quickly. "Just give him a break and time, and he will come around. But moving forward, *never* tell a guy that on the first date."

"Okay," I say quietly. I don't get what the big deal is. I was literally just sharing how I felt in the moment.

Lenny pulls into the school parking lot, and we get our bags to head inside. We grab a booth, set our stuff down, and order our usual.

While waiting for our coffee, Lenny says, "My mom is seeing someone new."

"Oh! Good for Sheila," I say.

"Yeah! Mom really likes her, but she doesn't want us to meet until they've been dating for a bit longer. You know how she is. Even though Carter and I are basically adults, she doesn't want us to get attached to someone if it won't last."

"That makes sense," I say, grateful for the subject change. I felt weird having Lenny disappointed in me. "What's her name?"

"Ashley. I already tried to stalk her on Instagram, but she has a private account," Lenny says, making a face.

"Well maybe it will keep going well, and you'll meet her soon."

"Yeah maybe," Lenny shrugs.

"Have you heard anything else from your dad?"

"Not really. Evelyn is already planning the gender reveal. They invited Carter and I to the party, and I don't know how to tell them that I'm not exactly thrilled about getting another half sibling. Like, it'll just pull Dad farther away from us."

"I'm sorry, Len," I say. "What can I do to help?"

"I don't really think there's anything that can be done," she says.

"I disagree. I mean, we could make a Burn Book. Or, I'll grab a pillow for you to scream into," I tell her, as she chuckles.

"No, it's fine," she says, shaking her shoulders. "Whatever. We should probably get started on the homework."

I pull out my statistics work and try to start on some problems. It's been a little easier for me to complete my work on time, but I still feel overwhelmed. I have to map out all my work and to-do lists in order to organize my responsibilities. It's like I need to brain dump onto a sheet of paper so that I can complete everything.

We only spend fifty minutes in the coffee shop, but it feels more like fifty hours. Once we hear the bell for class change, Lenny and I pack up our stuff and head to U.S. History.

Anxiously biting my lower lip, I'm sure Lenny can tell I am still a ball of nerves about seeing Beau. I'm nervous around him as it is, but throw kissing into the mix?! I don't even know how to act.

Lenny squeezes my arm reassuringly as we head into the classroom. Beau is already sitting in his seat, averting his gaze. His hair is extra ruffled this morning, making him look a little less polished than he normally does. He's also got a vein in the center of his forehead that looks like it's threatening to pop.

As Mr. Evans walks in, I settle into my normal seat, diagonally across from Beau. Maya walks in and sits right next to him, as if I'm just irrelevant.

"Hey guys," Mr. Evans says. "We've got the first ACT coming up in a week and a half. Make sure you are still meeting with your groups to study. This program is a really good resource for students to use. I wish I had something like that in high school."

Lenny leans over to whisper to Maya, Beau, and me. She says, "We should probably meet up before next Saturday. I'm free tonight if you guys want to come over to study for a bit."

"Yeah, I'm free," I whisper back.

"I can't go," Beau says quickly.

Maya pipes up, "Yeah, I can't go tonight either. Sorry."

"Oh," Lenny nods. Turning to me, "Well, you can still come over and we can work on it for a little while. I've got Jacob's sister's school recital this evening. But we should still have time to at least study for an hour or so."

"Okay!"

Maya and Beau don't look back over at Lenny and I for the rest of class. I'm sure it's because Beau still feels a bit awkward. That's totally understandable. I just wish I knew when he would be feeling back to normal.

• • •

Right when I walk into Leadership, Carter sees me and shouts from across the classroom, "MAR GUESS WHAT?!"

"What?!" I say, surprised.

"I went to go see Pickles at the shelter, and he's still there! Which I guess is bad because he needs a home. But that means I still have a chance to adopt him."

"Yay!" I exclaim. "Have you talked to your mom about adopting him?"

"I mentioned it, and she was on the fence about it. She knows I'm responsible, but since I don't know where I'm going to college, she's hesitant. Which I understand. But there's still hope," he says, his grin still tracing his lips.

"Yeah. That's tricky. Was Lily there?" I ask, referring to the giant teddy bear black lab.

"No, she got adopted!"

Mrs. Lin walks into class. "Hello everyone! I hope you are having a good day so far."

She walks over to her computer and pulls up a picture of a 3D model of the school's coffee shop. She says, "Today, you are going to start mapping out your 3D prototype for your proposal. Over here, you can see the original prototype some students made for the coffee shop downstairs."

Honestly, the 3D model is pretty impressive. It looks like the students made it out of a cardboard box. Using bottle caps, popsicle sticks, scraps of fabric, yarn, and toothpicks, they made all of the furniture on a miniature scale.

Once Mrs. Lin finishes telling us what our prototype should look like, Carter and I turn to each other to start brainstorming ideas for our mindfulness space.

"My mom definitely has some big cardboard boxes at the studio," I say. "And she probably has a lot of crafting supplies that we could use."

"Sweet!" Carter says.

I pull out my laptop to look at Pinterest for some miniature furniture ideas. Carter pulls out a piece of paper, and he maps out what the layout of the room could look like.

"Wait, that looks really good," I tell him.

He cheeks redden ever so slightly. "Thanks."

"Ooh, look at this!" I say, turning my computer screen over to him. It's a picture of a yoga studio that's decorated in muted colors and warm lighting.

"I really like that," he says. "We could cut up some foam sheets and roll them up for miniature yoga mats."

"Perfect!" I say.

Once class is dismissed, I tell Carter that I'll be over at his house tonight to study for the ACT.

"Nice! Is the whole group coming?" he asks, as we walk to our next classes together.

"No, it'll just be me tonight."

Carter smiles. "Okay, sweet! See you tonight."

After my last class ends, I text Lenny to see where we should meet up to leave for her house.

LENNY: I'm in the front lobby

ME: Walking there now!!

Heading down the stairwell, I see Lenny standing by the water fountain in the front office. She waves me over, and we start to head out to the parking lot.

After a few minutes on the road, Lenny pulls into her garage, and we go inside. I can smell the all natural lime and eucalyptus candle burning on the dining room table.

Sheila, Lenny's mom, is at the kitchen island, rolling out some beige colored dough. "Hey! How was your day?"

"Good!" Lenny and I both say.

"I'm making some vegan cookies. If they are done by the time you finish, you are welcome to them," Sheila tells us.

"I may get some tomorrow. After our study session, I'm going with Jacob to Jenna's recital."

"I didn't realize that was also tonight," Sheila says.

Lenny nods, and we head over to the dining room table. While setting out the test booklets, Carter comes down the stairs.

Eyeing me, he says, "Mar, I haven't seen you in *forever*."

I laugh, and that makes him grin. He walks over to the couch and scoots some of the pillows over, so he can lay down on the sofa.

"Do you care if I hangout here? I won't bother you, I swear. I was just going to reread over my lines," Carter says, looking at Lenny and me. He holds up his small script booklet for *Beauty and the Beast*.

Lenny's living room and dining room is an open floor plan, so although Carter would be sitting pretty far away from us, he would still technically be in the same room while we're studying.

"I don't care," I shrug, looking over to Lenny.

"Yeah, that's fine," she says. "Just don't randomly break into song and dance."

Carter chuckles and says, "You got it."

"Can we work on math first? I'm struggling," Lenny asks me.

"Yeah, I was about to suggest math, too," I say.

After an hour of studying where I could practically hear the clock ticking with each second, Lenny and I finish the math worksheet. "What did you get for number three?" Lenny asks. "I got 5a."

"Oh, I didn't get that," I say, slumping my shoulders. I haven't felt this defeated since the *Hannah Montana* episode where Miley chooses Jake over Jesse.

Why is this so difficult for me? I could rip up my paper and pull out my hair. Lenny's version of struggling with math is my version of understanding it. She doesn't get how difficult classes have been for me this year.

Moving on to another problem, I say, "I had trouble with number eight. What did you get?"

"I got 50."

"I got 33," I whine. "Let's get the answer key."

I'm actually going to cry if I get another question wrong. Can't I just get a sliver of Lenny's brain? Can't I do one problem right?

Lenny rifles through some papers. "For number three, answer is 5a. Number eight is 50."

"Ugh," I say with my head in my hands. Of course my answer is wrong. "Okay, let's go through the rest of them."

Forty questions later, my paper is riddled with red pen, trying to correct all my mistakes. In elementary school, I used to cry at the kitchen table while my dad went over my math homework. His way of doing math was completely different than the way my teacher had taught me. My fingers hurt from clenching them into fists, then having to repeatedly unclench them to erase my wrong answers.

I didn't realize that the canon event would repeat itself and follow me into high school with Lenny.

"It's okay. Don't worry about it," Lenny says. "This sheet was more difficult than the others we've worked on."

"Is this how the actual ACT is going to go?"

"I don't know. But we still have a week and a half to study. So, it'll be okay," Lenny reassures me. "We got this!"

Working on a few more problems from another math sheet, the same thing happens. I overthink every problem and end up getting several questions wrong. To my relief, Jacob rings the door, saving me from another round of unbearable worksheets.

"Oh, that's Jacob! So I guess we can call it a day," Lenny says.

"Yeah," I sigh. My brain is melting after completing all those problems.

Lenny hugs me goodbye, picks up her purse, and grabs Jacob's hand as they head out to the car. "Marlowe, obviously you can stay here as long as you want."

After they leave, I flop onto the couch beside Carter. "And then there were two. What do you want to do?" I ask him.

"Hmmm," he ponders. "Do you want to go get some food?"

"Yes!" I say, sitting up. "Where should we go?"

"I'm good with anywhere," he says. "You pick."

We climb into his car, heading to my favorite Mexican restaurant in town. I'm always in the mood for some chips and salsa.

Carter's beaded necklace and air fresheners swing from his rearview mirror. I look over at his side profile, his copper colored freckles standing out against his pale skin.

"Lenny said that she told you about Evelyn's pregnancy," Carter says with an exhale.

His comment catches me off guard. "How are you feeling about it?"

"Well, I was wondering if I could vent to you about it. I don't know, I just thought you would be able to help me figure everything out."

Feeling my eyes crinkle at the sides, I softly smile at him. I'm touched that he thought of talking to me about this.

"Yeah, of course," I say. "Carter, you can vent to me about anything."

"Well, since it'll be their fourth kid together, I feel like I shouldn't be so thrown off about it. But I just don't know if I'll ever get used to my dad having a whole other family besides Lenny and me."

I nod. I know Carter's relationship with his dad is already a little strained, and I'm sure Evelyn's pregnancy doesn't help.

"I know I'm probably just being difficult about it. And I shouldn't get jealous or whatever. But I can't help but feel like this will put even more distance between my dad and me."

"I'm sorry, Carter. And you aren't being difficult about it. Your feelings are valid," I tell him.

"Thanks," he blushes. "And Dad has been pressuring me a lot to go to his alma mater for college. But I don't even know if I want to go to CalTech."

"That's so stupid. He shouldn't push you to go to his college."

"Exactly! I don't even know where I want to go. And I definitely don't need my dad breathing down my neck to go to his old stomping grounds," Carter shakes his head.

"High school is stressful enough as it is. Add picking a college into the mix, and it's even worse! Then add your dad pressuring you?! That's awful. I'm really sorry, Carter."

"It's okay. I mean, I'll figure it out. It's just frustrating," he says.

I nod. He turns to look at me and asks, "How has everything been for you? I know you were telling me about your stress with school."

That's so sweet that he remembered. "It's just so much right now," I tell him.

"Yeah," he says. "I hate growing up."

"Me too. It's like we have to have everything figured out. I'm sixteen! Like, we are expected to act a certain way and look a certain way," I say.

"Exactly! It's ridiculous. They tell us we better have gotten good grades in high school because if we didn't, how the hell are we going to make it in college?" Carter says.

"Yeah! You've got to get a good grade on the ACT, so you can get into a good college. Then, you've got to get a good scholarship. And find your right major, so you can work in the right career. Then, you have to marry the right person and start a good family. And have a good life," I huff.

"I couldn't have said it better myself," Carter says. "It's like life passes by too quickly, and we don't have time to stop for a second and look at where we are right now."

"Yes!" I say. It's so reassuring to hear from someone who thinks the same way I do. "Growing up sucks."

Carter nods in agreement. "Growing up sucks."

I look over to him and see that he's already looking at me. "We'll figure it out."

"We will," he winks, pulling into the restaurant parking lot. He finds a spot near the front door, and he starts to parallel park in between two cars.

"You're going to parallel park?" I ask him incredulously.

"Obviously," he says.

"You can actually do it?"

"Of course I can."

"You, Carter Taylor, who has the worst aim in bowling, can fit your giant SUV into that tiny spot?" I say, raising my eyebrows.

"Mar, have some faith in me," he says. "I'm the best parallel parker in Caelee County. Actually in the whole world."

"Sure."

"I'm being serious. My mom taught me well."

I cross my arms and tell him, "Well, my parents never taught me."

He looks shocked. "Your parents never taught you?!"

"That's what I just said."

"You can't even parallel park?" he asks.

"That's what I just said!"

"Well, that settles it. I'll just teach you," Carter says confidently.

"Now?!" I can't keep in my laugh. "Carter, I would destroy your car."

"No, it's fine. I'll teach you. Be prepared for a driving lesson after dinner."

Rolling my eyes, I grin at him as he perfectly parks in the tight space. We get out of the car, and Carter zips up his crimson hoodie. He grabs the door for the both of us, and we file inside.

The waitress shows us to our seats and places a tray of chips and salsa between us. Right as we sit down, I immediately take a chip and dunk it into the red salsa.

"Oh my gosh, so good!" I say. Carter grabs a chip and scoops up some salsa for him.

"It really is," he says.

We laugh about stories from when we were younger. Conversations with Carter are always filled with smiles, laughter, and early 2000's pop culture references. Everything is just easy and effortless with him.

Before I knew it, we'd been at the restaurant for two hours. Climbing out of the booth, we head up towards the front to pay for our food.

Carter grabs my ticket, and he pulls out his wallet to pay. I lightly grab his arm, stopping him from paying for my food.

"Carter no! I got this."

"Um, no. I'm not letting you pay," he says.

"No!" I say, grabbing the tickets from his hand. He tries to take them back but fails. In turn, he squeezes the side of my waist, and I let out a loud snort.

"Carter," I say in between giggles. "No, I swear I'm paying."

I turn to the cashier, who has watched what is basically a tickle fight unfold. "Here's my card. I'm paying for both."

She nods, and turns to run my card. I look over at Carter and stick my tongue out, as if I'm in first grade. He grins and shakes his head.

"You know I'm going to get you back for that," he says, raising his eyebrows.

"No you are not," I say, grabbing my card and receipts back from the cashier. We thank her and head back outside towards his car.

"Here," he says and throws his keys towards me.

Reaching out to grab them, I say, "What?"

"You are driving home, so I can teach you how to parallel park," he says, like it's just a normal, everyday occurrence.

"Huh? No way," I say, tossing his keys back to him.

With a look of mischief in his eye, he emphatically lays his keys on the hood of his car and runs over to get into the passenger side.

I gawk at him. He hasn't lost his childlike goofiness.

Begrudgingly, I snatch his keys off his car and walk over to the driver's side. Opening the door, I tell Carter, "Sheila will kill me if I wreck your car."

"You aren't going to wreck my car," he replies.

"What if I do?"

"You won't."

"But I might."

He shrugs, "You won't."

"You are too confident in my driving abilities," I say.

He chuckles, and I start the car. I back up a little and pull away from Carter's initial parallel parking. I look over at him and ask, "Where should we go? I am *not* parking around other cars. We'll have to find a cone or something."

"Hmmm," he thinks. "What about back at my house? I'll pull the trash cans out of the garage, and we can use those."

"Okay," I say reluctantly.

I start driving us back to Carter's house, and I realize that I'm not feeling all the anxiety that I was earlier. With Beau, I was just a bundle of nerves and had knots in my stomach.

"So, how is everything going with Beauty and the Beast?" I ask him.

"Good! I really like our cast. And although I'm pretty nervous about being the lead, I'm also really excited."

"Yay! That's good."

"You're coming to my show, right?" Carter asks me. His green eyes double in size when he looks over at me.

"Yes! I can't wait," I say, looking back to the road.

I pull in front of Carter's house at the base of his driveway. He says, "Okay, wait right here. I'll be back."

I put the car in park, and Carter runs up to his house. A few minutes later, I see Carter walking down the driveway and pulling two big trash cans towards the car. He places them on the side of the street, making sure to leave enough space for me to be able to park.

Carter opens up the passenger door and hops back into the car. "You ready?" he asks.

I nod. "I can't believe we are doing this."

He chuckles and says, "Okay, so you'll drive up beside the trash cans until your back fender is in line with the front trash can."

"Okay," I say, slowly inching beside the trash cans.

"If these were actual cars, you'd make sure that your side mirrors were lined up with theirs. But with this, just edge up enough so that the back of the car and the trash can are parallel to each other."

I drive up a little more. In the dark of the car, he says, "Okay, now you are going to turn the steering wheel fully to the right and begin to slowly reverse."

I do as he says and fully turn the steering wheel to the right. Changing the gears, I start to reverse. I barely lift my foot off the brakes.

"Good! Keep going," Carter encourages.

Luckily the street light illuminates the neighborhood enough, so I can actually see what I'm doing. Plus, it really helps that Carter is breaking down all the steps.

"Look at you! Okay, you'll normally stop when you see the car behind you in the left side mirror. But obviously in this case, it'll be once you see the trash can."

"Oh gosh," I mutter, as this is always the part I dread. In one fell swoop, I could back up too much and run his car right into the trash can.

I see the trash can in my mirror, and I stop reversing. Carter says, "Good! Okay, now you are going to turn the wheel straight and reverse."

"This sure does have a lot of reversing," I say. Carter chuckles and puts a hand behind my headrest as he checks to see how much room I have to back up. "You got it. Keep going. Okay stop."

I let out an exhale. I turn to Carter to see what to do next. He says, "So, now you are going to turn the steering wheel to the left and keep reversing."

I follow his instructions and turn the wheel to the left, while slowly backing up. I'm actually parallel parking!

"Atta girl!" Carter exclaims with a wide grin on his face.

I giggle. "Okay now what?"

"So you'll edge up a little bit and straighten up the wheel."

I do so, and I'm shocked. I actually just parallel parked in between two trash cans. With Carter's help, of course.

"I did it!"

"You did it!" he says.

I high five him and say, "Thanks for teaching me."

"Of course. We'll have to practice some more to make sure you really master it," he says jokingly.

"Oh, definitely," I say sarcastically.

"It just means we have to hangout more," he says with a shrug. He looks at me with his auburn eyelashes, and at this moment, I really understand how good of a friend Carter is. I'm lucky to have him and Lenny in my life.

"Definitely."

CHAPTER SEVENTEEN

I've checked my phone three times every minute. I know Beau still wants some distance after freaking out over me sharing my feelings, but I still expected him to come with me to my mom's event tonight. That was the deal when we originally made the fake dating plan.

If I know Beau, he'll come. He wouldn't stand me up.

Zipping up my sapphire blue satin maxi dress, I mentally prepare for tonight. Not only am I a ball of nerves about seeing Beau, but I know tonight will be really stressful on my mom. She's been planning this gala for a few months now; it's a way for her to sell a larger variety of art, which helps fund the studio.

I brush through my hair once again, setting my comb back on the bathroom counter. Putting on my small silver hoops, I check myself out in the mirror to make sure I look perfect.

"Are you about ready, kid?" my dad calls from the living room.

"Coming!" I yell, grabbing my purse and phone. I glance again. No response.

My dad and I climb into the family car, and I rub my arms, trying to keep warm from the late October air. Mom's already at the studio, I'm sure running around to make sure all the refreshment stations are perfect and that the art looks pristine.

"I really hope there's a good turnout tonight," I say.

"There will be. Your mom always manages to go above and beyond," Dad says, smiling to himself.

"I invited some of my friends, and I'm pretty sure most of them will be able to make it," I say, looking out the window.

We pull into the parking lot and brace the autumn breeze as we walk towards the gala. There's cafe lights strung around the awning, making the New York-style studio look even more New York.

Opening the front door, I'm hit with the familiar scent of orange and cedar, my mom's signature aroma. Even though it's ten minutes until the gala's start time, there are already a few people browsing around.

My mom's art friends are walking around and seeing their colleague's work. I spot Lenny's mom, Sheila, walking around with a lady, and they are both admiring this giant painting my mom worked on for months.

I haven't even seen the finished product of this one. It's enormous, and it practically looks like a pair of french doors. In an abstract fashion, Mom painted teal, orange, cream, charcoal, and royal blue swirls across the canvas. The colors all look like a tornado of exotic bird feathers, as each spiral intertwines with another.

It's absolutely stunning.

"Hi Sheila!" I say.

"Hey there, Marlowe," she replies with a smile. Motioning to the lady beside her, Shelia says, "This is Ashley."

"Nice to meet you," I tell her.

Turning to Ashley, Sheila stage whispers, "She's my kids' favorite person."

I giggle, feeling my cheeks grow warm. Turning back towards Mom's painting, I say, "Wow. This is amazing."

"Right?!" Ashley says. "I love it."

Since the canvas is so large and the details are so intricate, this is one of the most expensive pieces my mom has ever tried to sell. It's almost $10,000 and that kind of price point is not common for Caelee County. But my mom loves this painting. Even if it doesn't sell, keeping it in the studio would at least allow people to see her talent.

Speaking of which, my mom comes out from the backroom to greet everyone. I see some people setting out champagne, finger sandwiches, and chocolate covered strawberries, which I'm sure my mom is delighted to see.

Eyeing us, she waves and heads up to the front. She grabs a microphone and as some people finish getting inside she says, "Hello everyone. Thank you so much for coming to this season's art gala."

My phone buzzes. My stomach drops.

BEAU BRAXTON: no i won't be there tonight

How can a sentence in all lowercase make my stomach coil in on itself?

I shouldn't be surprised. We are taking a break. He didn't have an obligation anymore to come. But still. I had hope.

Several people around the room start clapping as my mom introduces the other artists that are participating in the gallery. "This gala features myself- Samantha Ford- Rebekah Moore, Lois Jorgen, and Frankie Andrews."

As Mom calls out each name, the other female artists step forward and wave to the studio visitors. After my mom's preface, everyone sprinkles throughout the room to view the local art pieces.

Trying to distract myself from Beau's text, I walk toward the side wall to see Frankie's portraits of realism. Soft instrumental music wafts through the studio's speakers.

Feeling a tap on my shoulder, I turn around to see three of my favorite people in the world. "Lenny, you came!" I squeal, giving her a hug.

Her long hair is perfectly curled, framing her lilac chiffon dress like a strawberry blonde curtain. Jacob stands beside her in all black dress pants and dress shirt, mindlessly tugging on one of his braids.

Carter stands a few steps behind them with a black and white suit on. His copper curls are more tame today, and his rosy cheeks glow under the studio's ambient lighting.

"Thank you all so much for coming," I say to each of them.

"Of course! We wouldn't miss it," Lenny says. Her gaze dances over my face, and she says, "Is everything okay?"

I should've known that Lenny would be able to tell that something happened. If I give her a few minutes, she'll probably be able to guess that Beau's absence is the reason I want to curl up into a ball in the corner of the room.

"Oh, yeah. I'm fine. I was a little stressed since it's a big event for my mom. Everything is fine," I say, not able to meet her eyes.

I look over to Carter, and he nods softly. With a close lipped smile and soft eyes, he says, "You look beautiful, Mar."

My breath hitches. He looks so genuine.

"Aww," I say, jutting out my bottom lip.

"You really do," Lenny says, squeezing my arm.

"Thank you so much," I say, blinking to stop my eyes from welling up with tears. I cover my face as a tear escapes my lower lashes.

"No! Don't cry," Lenny says, pulling my arms away from my face.

"Marlowe," Jacob says. "This will cheer you up. I got to the blind attorney episodes in Arrested Development."

"Oh my gosh!" I smile. "Those are my favorite."

"Julia Louis-Dreyfus is hilarious," he says, chuckling. "When Tobias tried to break into her house, I lost it."

I giggle, thinking about David Cross in the floral bathrobe. "I still can't believe you didn't think it was funny," I say to Lenny.

She shrugs. Carter pipes up, "I'll add it to my watch list."

"You need to!" I say, as Jacob says, "Do it!"

People brush past us as the studio becomes more crowded. Lenny asks, "Do you want to walk around and see everyone's work?"

Nodding, I follow the three of them as they head to the left wall, which holds many black and white paintings.

"Also, I met Ashley! She's super nice," I tell Lenny and Carter.

Referring to their mom's girlfriend, Carter says, "We got to meet her yesterday. I really, really like her."

"Me too," Lenny smiles. Slowly, we walk to each painting, and all are drastically different from one another.

"I love how your mom showcases all female artists," Lenny says. "I need to ask her if she knows much about embroidery. She could help me master this new design I'm working on."

I nod, and my mind drifts back to Beau without permission. We turn into the next room and see a familiar blonde girl in a pink midi dress.

"Maya?" Lenny says, and the girl turns around. What is she doing here?

"Oh! Hey guys," Maya says warmly. "My dads are here to buy some new artwork for the new living room remodel. So I decided to tag along," she shrugs.

"I thought you just finished your living room remodel?" I ask.

"No," Maya shakes her head. "That was the kitchen remodel."

"Oh," Lenny and Jacob say at the same time.

A lump in my throat forms out of nowhere. Swallowing it down, I say, "Well, thanks for coming. I know Mom really appreciates all of the support."

A beat of silence passes between us.

Carter pipes up, "Well, she deserves the support! She's literally amazing. I remember when I was younger- fourth grade I think it was- I needed help painting a planter for art. I accidentally cracked mine in class, so the teacher sent me home a blank planter to paint at home and bring back. Obviously, Mom and Dad weren't the most artistic, so Sam helped me out. We painted caterpillars all over the planter, and it's still in my room somewhere."

I look over at him, silently thanking for ending the lull in conversation. He meets my eyes and gives a small quirk of his upper lip. Although his eyes are cool forest green in color, they blaze with warmth like embers in a fireplace.

I croon, "Carter, that's so sweet."

"Dude, how do you have the best memory?" Jacob asks.

Carter chuckles and looks away towards the door. My mom stands next to the ivory-colored table and gets a glass of champagne. Seeing me, she waves us over. Lenny and I follow, as Carter and Jacob stay to talk with Maya.

"Sam! I love *everything*," Lenny says, giving my mom a hug.

"Is it all going well?" I ask.

Lowering her voice, Mom tells us, "You are not going to believe this. The big painting just sold."

My mouth is agape. "The giant one?!" I say.

"Yep," my mom slowly nods.

"Who bought it?" I ask.

"Minh and Josh Nguyen," my mom says. She points her head to Maya's dads standing near one of Rebekah's paintings.

"Oh my gosh," I mutter. Of course they can afford to spend ten grand on a painting. Obviously, I'm thrilled for my mom. But I shouldn't be surprised that the richest family in Caelee County can throw their money everywhere.

"Sam, that is amazing!" Lenny says in a sing-song voice.

"Thanks girls," my mom says. "I'm going to go mingle for a bit. But I'm just over the moon!"

I squeeze her arm as she walks over to some other studio visitors. Lenny looks at me with surprise. She says, "Was that the one that was like $10,000?"

"Yeah," I say, shocked. Maya's life is something I will never understand. Obviously, I see her in name brand and designer clothes almost everyday. And I've been to her enormous house (and guest house). But seeing her dads buy Mom's most expensive painting just confirms how out of touch Maya is.

"I'm going to go save Jacob," Lenny tells me, chuckling. "He's shy enough as it is, but Maya scares him. He's probably gone mute." Nodding, I head over to my dad who is standing near the back wall.

"Hey kid," Dad says. He looks like a bodyguard, just watching everyone stroll through the gallery.

"Did you hear about Mom's painting?"

"The Nguyens are very generous," he nods.

I agree, suddenly hearing a familiar voice head towards my direction.

"Jameson!" Carter says, going in for a high five. My dad chuckles, and they "bro hug." As bizarre as it is, Carter and Dad are on a first name basis. I guess that's what happens when they've known each other for half of my life.

"Carter! How are you doing?" Dad asks.

"Good. This year has been a little stressful, but I know that's the case for a lot of seniors."

My dad nods. Sipping at his champagne, he asks, "How is the musical going?"

"Good and stressful as well," Carter laughs. "That's basically the mantra of my life."

My dad laughs. It's nice to see the two of them catch up. Lenny's family and my family just mesh so well together. Carter's familiarity with my dad makes me *almost* forget the fact that I was stood up tonight.

Almost.

CHAPTER EIGHTEEN

Grabbing my chocolate chip bagel from the toaster, I start to head up to my room for some mindless television. It's just me in the house today because my mom has to work late, and Dad has a faculty meeting at the middle school.

I place my bagel on my nightstand, and I flop onto the vintage floral quilt on my bed. The swirls of green, yellow, and blue make a symphony of colors for me to bury under.

Opening up my laptop, I pull up *The Office*. I was craving a good episode to watch after seeing Lenny and Carter so much this weekend. Jim and Dwight's antics will always remind me of Carter.

Browsing through the third season of the show, I click on the twenty-third episode, "Beach Games." Michael takes all of the Dunder Mifflin employees to the beach for the day. Everyone in the office was expecting to just relax, but in a classic Michael fashion, he makes them team up and compete against one another.

Each game the employees participate in is absurd and out of the ordinary. Pam, the receptionist, is instructed to take notes about what happens during the day. Towards the end of the episode, Pam gets annoyed with having to sit on the sidelines throughout all of the games. She decides to walk over a trail of hot rocks in order to prove something to herself.

The spontaneous walk stirs some courage within Pam, and she decides to confront Jim about their friendship. She tells everyone in the office that she feels invisible. Directly to Jim, she says she called off her wedding because of him.

In an emotional moment, Pam adds, "I miss having fun with you."

Wait.

That gives me an idea.

I really do miss Beau. I miss joking with him during our ACT study sessions. I miss taking pictures with him to post to our stories. I miss him teaching me to skateboard, with his hands steadily holding my arms. I miss seeing him in class, which was the highlight of my day. I miss feeling like he was just as excited to see me. I miss *him*.

Something shifted after our drive in movie date, and I'm determined to get back to normal. I know the idea of making us official is scary to him, but can't he see the amazing connection that we have? Can't he take that chance?

And even if he doesn't want to fake date anymore, my drive in movie confession shouldn't ruin the actual friendship that we had. I'm fine with ending our fake relationship, but I can't stand the way he's been avoiding me.

He was completely fine with fake dating me. Clearly, that was initially to get Maya's attention, but I really don't think he likes her anymore. He went on a date with *me*. He kissed *me*. He liked *me*.

So what changed?

Beau doesn't know what he wants. So, of course, me confessing my feelings scared him. I think Beau needs to know that someone is going to support him no matter what. He's moved around so much, so he's not used to the commitment of a girlfriend. I want Beau to know that I'll be in his corner. I'll be there for him when no one else will. Even if that idea scares him.

When we were younger, it seemed like he was everyone else's cheerleader. Yes, he's really shy, but he would have energetic moments at camp. He was- and still is- super competitive, so he loved cheering on his team in any sport.

There was one time at camp where we were all racing on the water slides. Someone would count down, and we would all slide down to see who could get to the bottom the fastest.

I wasn't normally good at the sports or games we played, but for some reason, I had a knack for racing on the water slides. I could finish before everyone else by a few seconds, and I felt like a real champion. I basically considered myself to be an Olympian at water slide racing.

On a warm June afternoon, I was up against Brian. He was Beau's friend and the leader of the boys' club. Even at age nine, he was so arrogant. Brian was the type of guy that was good at every sport, and he knew it.

"Come on Marlowe!" Lenny said, hyping me up before my race with Brian.

"You're going down!" Brian shouted at me. His blonde hair fell in wet ringlets against his forehead. His swimming trunks looked more like swimming capris with blades of grass stuck to his shins.

"No way!" I shouted back. I went over to Lenny to do our good luck handshake, ending with three snaps and a head roll.

Beau was standing at the bottom of the slide, so he was the designated referee. Obviously, he was really good friends with Brian, but I trusted that he wouldn't be biased. I mean, we were friends too!

"On your mark!" Beau yelled from the base of the slide.

I took a deep breath and looked over at Brian. He scowled and stuck his tongue out at me. Beau said, "Get set!"

"There's no way I'm going to lose to a girl!" Brian said to his friend. I just scoffed at him. His swimming trunks were so low now that I could practically see his butt crack.

"Go!" Beau screamed.

I immediately dove onto my stomach and started sliding down at record speed. My trick was that I would swing my legs around midway down the slide, so I could go on my back. It shaved off seconds from my time! Moving from sliding on my stomach to sliding on my back is what made me the water slide legend.

Now that I was sliding on my back, I straightened my legs and pointed my toes. Zipping past Brian, I reached the bottom in a fast *swoosh!* I splashed against the puddle of water at the bottom and looked up. Beau was beaming at me with his bright eyes, I could see the pride written across his face.

"Marlowe!" Beau said. "That was awesome!"

Giggling, I said, "Thanks! I can't believe I beat Brian."

"You beat him by a landslide," Beau praised. "You really are the champion at this."

"Ugh! You cheated! I know you did!" Brian yelled. "And why are you on her side? We need a new referee!"

Beau rolled his eyes and shook his head. As Brian marched back up to the top of the slide, Beau whispered to me, "I know you didn't cheat. You're just that good."

I was drenched in the soapy water that coated the slides, but I felt like a million bucks.

"Hey!" Brian shouted. "Are you coming?! I call for a rematch!"

"You better get up there," Beau said. "I'll get someone else to judge. But I know you'll win again."

I laughed and started running back up the hill towards Brian. We rematched all right. He insisted that we go against each other again to see if I was cheating or if the referee was judging unfairly.

I beat Brian another five times on the water slide.

Thinking about that fond camp memory brings a smile to my face, and giddiness fills in my chest. Beau was the best supporter at camp. Why can't he be my supporter now?

I've decided it. I'm going to pull a Pam. I'm going to really tell Beau how I feel. I'm going to say that I've missed having fun with him. Even just as friends. And it's ridiculous that he's icing me out after the amazing date we had.

I'm going to be courageous and take a risk.

Mark my words, my Boysickness is finally going to get me somewhere.

CHAPTER NINETEEN

While getting ready to meet him, I think back to everything that has led up to this. Every moment. Every interaction. Every flirtation.

I just like him so much. I'll tell him that. I'm NOT going to say that I'm falling in love because that scared him off the first time.

Putting the small silver studs in my ears, I try to rehearse what I'm going to say. I can't just try to wing it and expect it to go perfectly.

Hey Beau. Please don't freak out again. But I like you a lot. Wanna actually date?

Hey Beau. Don't you remember I was such a good kisser? Why don't we make this official?!

Hey Beau. Remember we've known each other forever? So why the hesitation? Why did you get scared when I confessed my feelings? Let's kiss and make up.

Hey Beau. If you're worried that I'll break your heart, don't be. I would never do such a thing.

Hey Beau. I'm Boysick about you. I've been Boysick about you for so long, and all I want to do is be with you.

Please.

I finish swiping some blush on my cheeks and take one last look in the mirror. In *To All the Boys I've Loved Before*, Laura Jean and Peter fake date each other and then end up actually falling for one another.

They survive the third act conflicts. They fall head over heels and end high school passionately in love. Maybe that could be Beau and me. We could finally be high school sweethearts.

I hop in my car and text my parents to let them know I'll be at Beau's house. I'll call Lenny after Beau and I's conversation to tell her the good news. I'll explain everything and finally be able to share my whole fake dating scheme. Beau and I will probably be official, so it'll be like water under the bridge. She won't be overprotective if we are officially boyfriend and girlfriend. This has to work.

It has to.

I start driving over to Beau's house, and I can't even listen to music because I'm so nervous. I feel jittery, and my chest hurts. My palms are clammy, and my clothes are too tight.

This is so out of character. This is so not me.

But I can do this. I can do this. I can do this.

I started to tell him my feelings that night in his car, but he cut me off. This time, I'll explain better. He won't get weirded out. I just know it.

Pulling into Beau's neighborhood, I try to shake the nervous feeling in the pit of my stomach. I pass by each dogwood tree and turn onto the street his house is on.

I parallel park on the adjacent street (thanks Carter) because there's a couple cars in his driveway. Glancing at the clock, I see that it's 5:03. So his parents probably aren't home or just now got home. If someone's at the house, I can just pull Beau aside, and we can talk on the porch or something.

I have to do this tonight. I have to confess my feelings. Again.

I walk over to his house, and I take the stone pathway up to his front door. I smooth out my shirt and take a deep breath. I can do this.

Ding dong.

A few moments pass. Trying to peek in the window, I can't really make out anything in the house. I don't want to be annoying, but I really need to talk to him. And I'm pretty sure he's home because his Jeep is in the driveway.

Ding dong.

"Coming!" I hear Beau call out from inside. Shuffling my feet, I wait for him to answer.

He opens the door, and his face looks flushed. He runs a hand through his tousled hair. For the first time since I've known him, Beau looks unkempt.

"Sorry, I just woke up from a nap," he says. "What are you doing here?"

"Do you care if I come in? I wanted to talk," I say with a small smile. "It's an emergency."

"Oh," he says. "Yeah. Is everything okay?"

"Yes," I say.

Beau leads me inside, still looking confused. "Can I get you anything? Water or something?"

"Water would be nice," I say as he heads back into the kitchen. Sitting down on the couch, I look around his house. Considering they just moved back a few months ago, their house looks very cozy.

Pictures of Beau and family vacations line the back wall, and a fluffy blanket is draped over the sofa. Pops of red sprinkle throughout the living room, with decorative vases and throw pillows. I look up at a portrait of Beau when he was probably ten or so. He looks exactly how I remember him from camp.

His dark hair is shorter in the picture, and he's grinning at the camera, showing off the small gap between his two front teeth. His bronzed skin pops against the light blue of the photo backdrop.

I hear some water running from the hallway, but that's probably from the washing machine. He must have come home and started laundry after school because there are small piles of clothes in the middle of the hallway.

Beau comes back into the living room, cup of water in hand. Handing it to me, he says, "Um. So, what's up?"

"Thanks," I say, referring to the water. "Well, I wanted to talk to you about *us*." I try not to put too much emphasis on the word, but I can't help it. Beau and I have felt like an *us* since the day we met.

"Okay," Beau says slowly. He runs another hand through his hair. "What about us? I thought this was over."

"I know I freaked you out at the drive-in movie. I know that. I shouldn't have confessed my feelings so early. But is that mistake really worth icing me out and ending everything?"

He stares at me blankly.

"I just can't leave things up in the air like that. I know we started out fake dating, and the plan was always supposed to have a deadline. But," I take a deep breath. "You didn't even come to the gala. That was the plan."

He just continues to stare at me.

"Beau, I really like you. And even if you don't feel the same way, we can still be friends. You don't have to avert your gaze or not show up to things. Don't just ghost me because I told you how I feel," I say with an exhale.

Beau opens his mouth to say something, but nothing comes out. He closes it, and I continue.

"When we hung out, I had so much fun. At the study sessions, the football game, the coffee runs, the skate park, and the drive-in. I felt like we were actually becoming something, so I told you that. And you freaked out."

He finally says something. He looks away and says, "I'm sorry, Marlowe. I just wasn't ready to make that big jump to make things official. And I'm still not."

"But we actually did couple-y things. I mean, at the movie? That wasn't real to you? Because it didn't seem fake at the drive-in," I stammer. "Before my confession."

"I know. And I had a good time hanging out that day. But I just don't see you that way."

If he doesn't see me that way, why did he act the way he did? I've liked him for *years*. But he doesn't even regard me as a friend.

This feeling cuts deep into my chest. My ribs feel like they have popped out of place. My heart is thundering. My ears are ringing. My shoulders are stiff.

Nothing could take away this pain.

He sighs, "I'm sorry I gave you mixed signals. I think I just got swept up in the emotions and the moment. I messed up."

Looking at him with my eyebrows raised, I ask, "Messed up? By kissing me? What about at Maya's party?"

He winces. "I know. I blurred the lines, and I just didn't think things through. I mean, it was clear from the beginning that things were not real between us. I've always just seen you as a friend. And I know that I complicated things when I kissed you. I was just confused."

I don't even know what to say. So he's trying to sweep the past few weeks under the rug?

"You were flirtatious. You leaned in for the kiss. But now you are telling me that you were just confused?" I say, dumbfounded.

He nods. "It's Maya who I really like. It's always been Maya. I just saw you in front of me and our fake relationship, and it messed with how I felt. I was *confused*."

"So you only see me as a friend. And everything before that was confusion?" I ask.

"I know, I know. I shouldn't have done that. I'm really sorry. I shouldn't have even agreed to the whole fake dating plan."

Rubbing my temples, I try to make sense of this. So, he's chalking everything up to the fact that he didn't know what he wanted? Or *who* he wanted?

"But, I mean it would have ended anyway. The gala was the deadline. So even if we went through with it, it would be over by now."

I try to say something, but my tongue feels like sandpaper scraping against the roof of my mouth.

"I'm really sorry. I blurred the lines. That's on me. I realized I messed up when you said you caught actual feelings," he adds. "So I backed off."

"Beau," I say, my eyes welling up. Out of all the ways I pictured the conversation going, this was never an option. "I liked you. I had feelings for you. And you're saying that you were just confused? That doesn't make any sense."

"I know," he chuckles lightly. "Just attribute it to me being a dumb guy."

"No, this isn't funny. You kissed me, Beau. That's a big deal," I say, my voice breaking. *No, no, no. Don't cry. Don't let him see how much he hurt you.*

I don't mention that he was my first kiss *ever*. It just stings too much.

"I'm sorry," he says, scratching the back of his neck. "I know I screwed up at the party. I know that. I just got- I don't know- caught up in the moment."

"I feel so stupid," I mutter.

"No! It's me that should feel bad. This is all on me. Marlowe, you didn't do anything wrong. When you shared your feelings, I realized how much I had messed up. You shouldn't feel bad."

"You don't get to tell me how to feel!" I say, the tears finally breaking past my eyes and falling down my cheeks. "I just-"

"Hey B, I'm out of the shower, and I just changed into your sweats if that's okay."

I look over, and it's like tunnel vision. All I can see is *her*.

Her.

Her wet bleached blonde hair. Her perfect skin. In *his* clothes.

Oh my gosh.

Oh my *gosh*.

Beau's messy appearance. Maya's shower. The clothes thrown in the hallway.

Did they just have sex?

They just had sex.

I feel a catch in my throat. Fidgeting with my fingernail, I can't find the right words to say. Maya's cheeks flush with color as she twirls the ends of her wet hair.

Beau opens his mouth to say something. I can't listen to him right now. I can't listen to that deep voice I almost fell in love with.

Quickly, I say, "Beau, I- I didn't know you had anyone over. You should've told m-me."

Looking at me wide-eyed, Beau says, "I'm sorry. I thought you would be gone by the time she got out."

I grab my purse and start to get up when Maya says, "OMG! Marlowe! No, don't leave just yet."

Maya catches my wrist and pulls me to sit back down on the couch. I'm so out of place that I feel like I could just squirm right out of my skin. I can't stop thinking about the fact that *they had sex*.

"Beau told me about your little fake dating plan," she says, scrunching her nose and smiling at Beau. "Don't worry. Your secret's safe with me!"

Bile rises in the back of my throat. I wouldn't be mad if I threw up on Beau or Maya right now. They deserve it.

I don't think I've ever felt so belittled in my life. I feel like I'm a random zoo animal in a rundown exhibit that Maya visits just to offer me her pity.

I look over at Beau. "You told her?" I say.

He doesn't answer me.

How dare he tell her and then suddenly become mute when I question him?

My stomach coils and twists on itself, as if I had too much greasy food for lunch. My skin is hot to the touch, and sweat pools where the bottom of my scalp meets the base of my neck.

"No, it's fine!" Maya says. "Seriously, I think it is so cute. Like you've always been adorable. But it's just so cute that you would help Beau out like this."

I just look at her. Even though she's made it clear she finds me "cute" and "adorable," I'm not flattered.

To them, I'm an unpaid extra in the background of the Beau and Maya show. I've had this role since I was little. They could never consider me to be a lead character in any way.

But I'm a real person with real feelings. Why don't they understand that?

Maya smiles, "Like, you fake dated to help Beau get with me? That's just so sweet. Seriously."

Nervously, Beau glances at me. Maya continues, "I mean it worked! Kevin and I broke up last week, and Beau and I are dating now."

"Oh," I say with a shaky voice. So Beau's "breather" from me wasn't just a small break. It was a *break-up*. Clearing my throat, I say, "Congratulations."

"Thank you!" Maya squeals. "I really should credit you for the relationship. Ha!"

"I really need to head home."

"Aw no!" Maya says.

"Sorry," I say, standing up.

"I can walk you out," Beau says behind me.

"Bye Marlowe! Seriously, you are the cutest!"

"Bye Maya," I mutter, opening the door. Beau follows behind me and glances back towards the living room.

"I'm sorry about that. I really didn't think you would see her while you were here."

"So, you're dating Maya now? Real or fake?" I huff.

"Marlowe. Don't get mad," he says.

"You made out with me a week and a half ago, and then you went and slept with Maya?! Are you kidding me?"

He doesn't deny that they slept together. *I was right.*

Every time I think of a house party.

A skate park.

A drive-in movie.

My first kiss.

Every time I think of him, I'm going to think of this moment.

Of how he tossed me aside, so he could hold on tighter to Maya.

When he kissed me, was he picturing her lips?

"There wasn't any overlap, I swear. I told you at the drive in I was done," he says softly. "Plus, the only real thing between us was just a kiss."

"It was not just a kiss, Beau. Not to me," I say, with more tears running down my face. I stomp down his front porch steps and call out, "And you knew that."

"Marlowe, I'm really sorry. I didn't mean for all this to blow up."

"Fuck you," I mutter, walking over to my car and driving away.

I don't look back once.

CHAPTER TWENTY

My pillow case is sticky after crying for too long, and I feel a faint headache coming on. Rubbing my temples and sitting up in bed, I look around my room. My purse is slung across my desk chair, and my shoes are on the floor from where I kicked them off yesterday.

When I came home last night, I was so upset that I ran to my room and catapulted myself into bed. Now, I glance at my phone, immediately setting it back down. I have eleven unread text messages and three missed calls.

I feel like I have twenty pound weights sitting on my chest and shoulders. Last night I texted Lenny when I got back to my house.

ME: Beau and I are never getting
back together. It's officially over

Two seconds later, she called me. Right when I picked up the phone she said, "Are you okay? What happened?!"

"He wants to be with Maya," I said in a quiet voice. I was pretty sure Lenny could hear my tears falling through the phone. "He doesn't want to be with me. He wants to be with Maya."

"What?! Do you want me to come over? I can be there in ten minutes,"

Lenny said. I heard some rustling in the background, as if she was putting on a jacket and shoes.

"No, no. I'm sorry I'm just not really fit to see anyone right now," I said and exhaled a breath I didn't even know I was holding.

"Marlowe, I don't care what you look like. If you need me, I'm coming," she said. "*This* is why I'm overprotective. It kills me knowing that you are hurting."

Everything about the situation stung. I was embarrassed that I even liked Beau to begin with. I was embarrassed that I pushed the fake dating idea on him. I was embarrassed that he chose someone else over me.

I was embarrassed about just *how* rejected I felt.

"No. I'll talk to you tomorrow. I just feel really gross," I said on the phone.

"I'm so sorry, Marlowe. I'll give you space tonight. Whenever you are ready to talk, I am here! I love you," Lenny said.

"Thanks, Len. That means a lot. Love you, too," I said and hung up the call.

When my parents came home, I briefly told them through tears what happened. Not about fake dating. I just said that Beau broke up with me because he wanted to date Maya, and they were already a couple. Now looking back, the fake dating plan is even more mortifying. I can't believe I was so head over heels for Beau.

I will take the fake dating secret to the grave.

Talk about a blow to my ego. Every time I think of Beau and Maya together, my skin crawls. I couldn't face Lenny or my parents last night because I knew they wouldn't truly get it. I've had the *ultimate* rejection. I liked Beau. We went on a date- even if he doesn't want to call the bookstore, skate park, and movie hangout a "date."

He touched me.

He kissed me.

I thought he liked me.

After all that, he still abandoned me. It was over in his mind the second I shared how I felt in his car. So, he silently backed off. Beau didn't have the decency to even verbally renounce things with us before he went and slept with Maya.

This is my worst nightmare come to life.

Trying to brush past the memories of last night, I go over to my closet to pick out a giant hoodie and leggings. My feelings are so dim, and all I want to do is be comfortable today. Sliding the hoodie over my head, I am enveloped in the warm and fuzzy fabric.

I check the clock. It's 8:45 AM. I slept in, but luckily I have my first block as a free period. I'll just head into school in time for second period.

I quickly brush my teeth, letting the cool mint swirl around my mouth before I spit it out. I'm slow moving in everything I do, and I feel like I could break down at any second.

Grabbing my keys and bag, I head over to my car. I throw my backpack in the backseat and turn the car on. While I'm waiting for it to heat up, I plug in my phone to play some music.

"Scott Street" by Phoebe Bridgers carries through my car, and her airy vocals are what break the floodgates. While she's singing about being existentially lonely, I can't help but empathize with her.

The guitar strums in rhythm with my heavy feelings. The warmth of my tears run down my cool cheeks. Before I know it, a sob escapes my throat. My brows crinkle together as I try to not completely fall apart.

With a breath catching in my throat, I pull my knees to my chest. I'm still sitting in the driver's seat of my parked car. I haven't even left yet.

"Why?" I cry to myself.

If I wasn't already insecure around guys, this is the nail in the coffin for my low self-esteem. The tears pool under my chin and drop to my shirt. I'm sticky and cold and hot all at the same time.

Turning my car off, I give up driving to school. I grab my phone and call the number that is ingrained in my mind.

"Hello?" Lenny answers.

"Hey," I say, trying to stifle my cries.

"Are you okay?"

"Umm. Not really," I tell her. "I can't drive to school. I didn't know if you could give me a ride. If you can't, it's totally fine. I'll just stay home today."

"No, I can! I'll be there soon," she says.

"Thank you," I say, with tears dropping onto my phone.

I know I probably look like a blubbering mess, but I just can't stop replaying yesterday's events. Beau and Maya getting together is the lowest blow.

"Do you feel ashamed when you hear my name?" Phoebe sings through my car speakers.

Lenny's Honda pulls into my driveway, so I finally climb out of my car. She parks and quickly walks over to me. Before I can even say anything, she swaddles me into a hug. She quietly says, "I'm so sorry, Marlowe."

I tightly hug her back. My shoulders start to shake, and I can't control myself anymore. "I feel so rejected," I sob.

"I know. He's a douchebag," she says into my ear.

"Yeah," I nod. "I just- I don't know. He was my first kiss. My first date. Everything I dreamed of for so long."

"I hate this," she says. I can tell she's hurting with me.

• • •

History was awful. I just sat down in my seat with my arms crossed the entire class period. Beau and Maya came into class after I was already seated. Without even glancing my way, they decided to pick seats together in the back.

LENNY: At least we don't have to sit with them!

ME: Yeah

Each class seems to fly by and drone on at the same time. Walking around school, I feel like a shell of myself. My face feels heavy, and I've got a pretty bad headache from crying so much.

I walk into Leadership with a seemingly dark cloud above my head. Sitting down next to Carter, I don't say anything. He looks over at me, concern crossing his features.

"Are you okay?" Carter asks quietly.

"Yeah, I'm fine," I say. Turning to look at him, I say, "Beau and I are officially over."

"Oh," he breathes. "I'm sorry, Mar."

I shake my head, trying not to let my emotions show.

"I just- Is there anything I can do? For you?"

"No, it's okay. Thank you though," I say.

Carter nods, looking back down at the desk. Mrs. Lin walks in and is about to start class. Quickly, Carter stands up and says, "I have to go to the bathroom."

I nod as he runs out of the room. It takes everything in me not to just run after him and leave school entirely.

Addressing the class, Mrs. Lin says, "I've reviewed your project proposals, and everything looks really good. I'm impressed with how thorough you have been. I've had some questions about if you can make a digital rendering of your project prototype. That's fine, but I would prefer you to make a 3D model. Your prototypes are due in three weeks. Remember, you need to write a five page research essay with the physical or digital prototype."

While I'm writing this down in my notebook, Mrs. Lin adds, "You all can pair up to work on your projects now."

I go ahead and start since Carter isn't back from the bathroom yet. Going to YouTube, I find a few beginner videos from a yoga instructor. I copy and paste the link to Carter and I's shared Google Doc.

The door of the classroom creaks open, and Carter walks in with his hands behind his back. Nodding a hello to Mrs. Lin, he comes over to me and sits down quickly.

"So, Mrs. Lin just wants us to do some more research and-"

Carter moves his hands from around his back and sets an iced coffee on the desk. Sliding it over to me, he grins playfully.

"What?! Is this for me?" I ask him.

"Of course," he shrugs.

"Carter, this is the nicest thing ever. Seriously. And today of all days," I say to him, shaking my head.

"Well, I know you've had a rough day, so I thought you could use a pick me up," he says. "I got your usual: an iced caramel latte."

"Carter," I say, still floored. "I can't believe you got me a coffee."

"It's really no problem. I just snuck down to the cafe," he says. Even though he's trying to brush off his kind gesture, I can see his cheeks redden. He glances over at me with a smile and genuinity behind his eyes.

I sip on the creamy coffee and start to feel significantly better than I did this morning. Carter just has a way to lift my spirits, even when I've hit rock bottom.

CHAPTER TWENTY-ONE

"Ugh, that salad tasted weird today," Lenny says as we head back from the lunchroom. She swats a few pieces of shredded cheese off of her yellow sweatshirt with tiny embroidered bumblebees. "Yeah. Why can't Maya's dads donate money for us to get better food?"

"I don't know," Lenny grimaces and heads up the stairs.

It's the middle of class change, and we've still got a few minutes before I have to head to my next class. Across the hall, I see a group of people lining the lockers, waiting on something.

"What's happening?" I whisper to Lenny. The air conditioning has been abnormally high recently, but I don't think that's the reason I have chills.

"I don't know," she shrugs.

Walking closer to the crowd, I smell cinnamon and leather. I know that smell. Ahem, I *used* to know that smell.

The crowd of students splits ever so slightly, just enough for me to step forward to see what's going on.

He's standing there, with a poster rolled up under his arm. The crowd of students is circled outside of the girls' restroom, as if they are waiting to catch a certain someone leaving the bathroom.

The bathroom door creaks open, and I instantly see a flash of blonde hair. People move back to give her room. She needs space, so she can relish in this moment.

I can't bring myself to move.

Beau unrolls the poster under his arm. On top of the white paper, five words are scrawled with his jagged, boyish handwriting. He hand wrote this. He took the time.

For *her*.

Maya gasps, clasping a hand over her mouth. Her gold bracelets lightly jingle against her slender wrists. With her other hand, she pulls out her phone to video this wholesome moment.

Standing there with his enticing grin is Beau, holding his handmade sign that reads, "WANNA GO TO WINTER FORMAL?"

All eyes turn in my direction, and time has stopped. I feel a catch in my breath, and my palms instantly sweat. This *could have* been me. This *would have* been me.

If only I hadn't messed it all up. If only I kept my mouth shut and didn't say I was falling for him. If only I didn't scare him away.

He would be mine. *He* would be asking *me* to the winter formal.

This can't be happening.

To my right, I see my best friend giving me a look of pity. Behind me is a group of students who have their phones out, videoing every second of my personal hell. Right in front of me stands the most perfect guy in the world expectantly looking for an answer to his question. Beau is so focused on Maya, he isn't even aware that I'm witnessing this proposal. He has no idea that I'm a spectator to this horror show.

I look to my left and see Maya. She looks elated. Overjoyed. Ecstatic.

If only I were in her shoes. If only I could scoot over a mere foot, I would *literally* be in her designer shoes. But instead, I'm the girl who isn't even considered to be asked to winter formal. I've never felt more like the invisible nerdy best friend.

I've thought of this moment a million times. This isn't how it's supposed to go.

"YES, YES, YES!" she gloats.

Maya runs up to him and slings both arms around his neck. Beau drops the poster and grabs her waist, swinging her around in a circle.

I think I'm going to be sick.

Beau sets her down, and Maya thrusts her phone into a random student's hands. "Will you take our picture?" she squeals.

I run behind the amateur photographer and briskly open the door to the girls' bathroom. My chest hurts, and my legs aren't working correctly.

I hear Lenny come into the bathroom behind me. Glancing back at her, my vision is already getting blurry. I'm motion sick. I feel dizzy, and my palms are clammy.

"Marlowe, I'm so sorry," Lenny says.

I shake my head. I wipe my eyes, seeing the black mascara streaks drip off my fingers. I let out a sob.

Girls are coming in and out of the bathroom, but all I can focus on is the pit in my stomach. Lenny steps closer to me.

"I just don't understand," I blubber. "Lenny, I've been passed over my *entire life*. I'm always the second pick. I'm always the afterthought."

"That's not true," Lenny says. "I would never pick you second." She squeezes my arm.

Sniffling, I say, "No, but with guys, that's always what has happened. I don't know what it is about me." I purse my lips.

"You shouldn't let Beau's actions define your self image. You are so much more than that."

I pull my sleeves over my hands and cross my arms. "But how can I define myself, when actions speak louder than words? How can I think that I'm desirable, when I've never been desired in the first place? My entire life is a culmination of rejection."

"What rejection?" Lenny asks gently.

"Every year, I've fallen for a guy. Every single one. And it's never worked out. You've been there to see it! It's never even gotten to the point of an actual date. I've literally been delusional my *entire life*, and I still haven't learned my lesson."

Lenny looks over at me. I can see it in her eyes; she knows it's true.

"Throughout my whole life, I've waited. I've waited on my Prince Charming. I've waited on Mr. Right. And it wasn't working! So, with Beau, I actually made a move. I was actually proactive and put myself out there. And I was *still* rejected."

"But, Marlowe, that isn't true," Lenny says. "You are so much more than the thoughts and opinions of crappy men."

"No, it is true." I shake my head. "Lenny, it's true."

Glancing at the mirror, I see a version of myself that I've tried to ignore. I've tried to forget that this insecure, affirmation-seeking girl is inside of me.

She's the little girl who saw Maya get a bouquet of roses and wished at least one of the guys gave her one. She's the girl who pined over Beau for five summers, waiting for any kind of attention from him. She's the girl who secretly gets envious of her best friend's successful relationship. She's the girl who would be willing to make a fool out of herself to try to get the validation of the male gaze.

She is me. And I'm not proud of it. I need to change, but how do you change something that's been ingrained in your mind for years?

In fairy tales, it's the damsel in distress who needs her Prince Charming to save her. In school, it's the girl who waits for the guy to ask her out, not the other way around. On social media, it's the girl who gets double the amount of likes when she posts with her boyfriend. In girl world, it's *everything* to get the perfect guy.

I've been fed this narrative my entire life.

Ross cheats on Rachel, but she ends up with him in the end. She isn't complete without him.

Even though Ron is super lame, Hermione just *has* to end up with him. We can't have a super smart badass girl who is also single.

Because that's how stories always go.

The guy gets the girl. As if us girls are some kind of object. I've always wanted to be someone a guy would want to *get*.

But I can't keep living like that. I can't keep doing this.

It's ruining my life.

I remember when I was a legitimate *child*, I still wanted a boy's attention. When I was nine at Camp Caelee, I had these rainbow tie dye sunglasses. My mom had taken me thrifting, and I found them while rifling through an accessories bin.

When I saw the glasses, I was instantly in love. They were oversized on my small, little kid face, but that made them more glamorous in my eyes. The lenses were a little scratched, but I didn't care. And because they were rainbow, I was so excited to wear them with every single outfit.

I showed up at camp the next day, sporting my new tie dye sunglasses. While Lenny and I were on the swings, Beau came up to me.

"I really like your glasses," he said with his hands in his pockets.

I remember feeling a catch in my throat, as if his small comment completely took my breath away.

"Really?" I asked. I knew his favorite colors were green, red, and blue, so it shouldn't have been a surprise that he liked my glasses that were full of rainbow swirls. "You can wear them!"

"Oh, cool! Thanks!" he said, holding his hand out. I handed him the glasses, and he ran off to go join the game of kickball.

"Why did you give him those? You just got them," Lenny said.

"Well, he liked them, so I wanted to share," I shrugged.

At the end of the summer day, Beau came back up to me to give the glasses back. "Thanks for letting me wear them," he said.

"Of course!" I said, happy to have another opportunity to talk with him.

The next day, I went up to Beau at the tire swing to give him my rainbow sunglasses. "You can wear them again today if you want," I said.

"Really?" he asked. "Thanks!"

Each day, for the rest of that summer, I let him wear my rainbow tie dye sunglasses. Even though I loved them. Even though I really wish I had them on super sunny days, I still let him wear them.

It made me feel special that he was carrying around something of *mine* everyday. I felt validated that he liked something that I had.

How messed up is that? I gave my favorite sunglasses to a boy every single day in the hopes that that would get him to like me more. As if the rainbow sunglasses contained some type of magic that would make Beau more attracted to me.

Looking into the bathroom mirror now, I see that little nine-year-old who was so obsessed with getting his attention. I was so consumed with the idea of getting any kind of male validation.

And honestly, I'm still that way.

Up until this point, I was waiting to be chosen. I thought I would be the happiest person in the world after I was finally deemed a "relationship girl." But the reality is: who would want to choose me like *this*?

Who would want to choose a girl that has no idea who she really is? Who would want to pick someone that has been hellbent on finding someone to complete them? Because that just shows that I'm incomplete as myself.

Marlowe Ford is incomplete.

Throughout my whole life, I've been searching for Mr. Right. But maybe that was the wrong quest. Maybe this entire time I should've been focusing on growing myself to be *Mrs.* Right. I should've been focusing on bettering myself to the point where I feel like I don't need a man to come and save me. I don't need a Prince Charming.

I pull down a few paper towels from the plastic dispenser and run some cold water on top. I wipe away the watered down makeup that has streaked my cheeks.

"Are you okay?" Lenny asks me softly.

As I wipe off each smear of mascara, I think that being "okay" is a possibility for me. Even if it's in the far future, it's still in the future. It's there.

"I will be," I say.

I'll be okay.

CHAPTER TWENTY-TWO

Bending down to double knot my shoelaces, I take a deep breath. It's the day I've dreaded for weeks. Honestly, it's probably been months at this point. The ACT has been looming over my head, and I just can't wait for it to be over.

It's like this test is the key to a gateway to the rest of my life. And I know I'm not the only one freaking out about this. It's so heavily emphasized by teachers, administrators, universities, and society, but if I complain about it, adults question why I can't handle it. They are the ones putting this pressure on me!

I know my parents aren't worried about my score. But that still doesn't fully take away the nerves. My college career is dependent on this exam. If I don't get a good score, then I may not get into certain colleges. Not to mention, if I actually get into some schools, I may not get a good scholarship without a decent test score.

The ACT is the first step into my college career, but what happens if I trip over that step?

When I woke up, I searched for a ten minute meditation video on YouTube. That helped a little. I don't feel as jittery as I did when I woke up, but I'm still very aware of the exam I am about to complete.

I retie the waist of my sweatpants and straighten the hem of my crewneck sweatshirt. I can't stop fidgeting. I grab my tote bag, and I stuff it full of pencils, gum, and a calculator.

Looking in the mirror, I tuck my hair behind my ears. *I can do this.*

I sling my bag over my shoulder and hop down the stairs. My mom sits at the kitchen table, drawing something on her iPad. Glancing up at me, she says, "How are you feeling?"

With a deep exhale, I tell her, "Honestly I don't know. It's been a whirlwind of the past few weeks."

She nods. "With the Beau situation?"

"Yeah. I'm doing a little better about it. I'm really trying to not let it affect me. I just think that I've been full of stress and worry, so it's hard to try to change that overnight."

"Don't be too hard on yourself. Change takes time. Just know that your dad and I will be proud of you no matter what," she says, getting up to refill her coffee mug.

I grab a banana and a protein bar for breakfast. With another deep breath, I say, "I can do this."

"You can do this!" Mom says, walking over to give me a hug. "I love you."

"I love you too," I say, leaning into her embrace.

"So," she says. "I may have gone a little overboard, but I wanted to make sure you were prepared."

Stepping towards the refrigerator, Mom opens it up and hands me a lunch box. She unzips it and starts pulling out a dozen small reusable containers. Lifting one, she says, "I didn't know if you would want food before or after. So, here are some carrots."

Picking up another, she says, "I also wasn't sure if you would want some fruit, so here are some strawberries and blueberries."

"Aww, that's so sweet. You didn't have to do that," I tell her.

"I'm not done," she says, rifling through the containers. "I didn't know if you would want something sweet. So this one has chocolate chip cookies."

I shake my head at her. "Mom, this is too much," I say.

"No it's not!" she replies. Holding up another container, she says, "I also packed some of your favorite candy in case you weren't in the mood for chocolate. Oh! Here's some cheese and crackers. It can give you a little protein."

"Oh my gosh," I say, baffled.

"Also, here's some trail mix and a bag of potato chips. I just wanted to make sure you had options," she shrugs.

"Thank you," I tell her. "You're the best."

"I know," she winks. My phone buzzes.

LENNY: i'm here!

ME: Sweet!!

"Okay, that's Len. I'll see you tonight!"

"Good luck!" Mom calls out as I head out the door, carrying my giant lunch box she filled to the brim.

Lenny's car is parked in front of my driveway, and I bound down the asphalt to meet her.

"You ready?"

"No, but it's okay. It's just one test," I say to her, but really it's reassurance for myself.

Lenny takes a left out of my neighborhood. "How about we have a movie night tonight? To celebrate the ACT being over?"

"Oh, that would be perfect! It would give me something to look forward to," I lightly laugh. "Should we watch the cinematic masterpiece that is Rebel Wilson as Fat Amy?!"

"Of course!" Lenny exclaims.

This morning I woke up with butterflies in my stomach, but honestly, they feel more like birds flapping around now. It's as if I'm about to give a speech in front of thousands. Or I'm going on a first date with the worst guy I know... *you know who*. Not a good feeling.

After Lenny parks, I grab my bags and coffee, and we walk towards the school. I see some other students walking towards the front doors as well. Some girls have on pajamas, some of the AP kids are carrying three calculators, and the rest of the students look like they could go back to sleep at any minute.

Walking into the school, I see several tables against the walls with students already lining up behind them. We got here ten minutes before the teachers told us to, and I guess everyone did the same. All the students haphazardly lining up does not help my anxiety or claustrophobia.

A teacher I don't recognize stands a few feet away, walkie-talkie in one hand and bedazzled lanyard in the other. Lenny turns to me and says, "I'm going to ask her what we should do. I don't know what these lines are for."

Lenny walks over to the teacher, and I stay where I am. Lenny can still be talkative even if she's nervous. I, however, shut into my shell and just go silent.

"She said we have to sign in and then head into each classroom by last name. So we won't be in the same testing room," Lenny says with a sad face.

I thought I would at least be able to sit next to my best friend during one of the most anticipated moments of my life.

"If you are good over here," Lenny says, "I'll go sign in with the T's."

I nod, and I try to seem normal. "Yeah that's fine."

I should've expected us to be in separate rooms, but since my nerves are already heightened, it really throws me for a loop. With my last name being Ford and her's Taylor, I shouldn't be surprised that we won't be together.

I take a deep breath. *I can do this.*

Standing in line to check in takes forever, and I finish sucking down my coffee while waiting. My chest is heavy, and my breaths feel shaky, as if I could hyperventilate if I inhaled too sharply.

After what seems like ten years, I finally make it through the line. Stepping up to the table, I tell the guy my name. He nods, checks me in, and instructs me to go to room 21A.

"Thanks," I say and glance around to try to find Lenny.

                                                ME: Where did you go??

LENNY: sorry! they told me not to wait around
in the lobby and to go ahead and go to my classroom

ME: Oh okay!

LENNY: sorry! you will do amazing!
i just know it. love you!

ME: Love you too <3

Walking into my testing room, I'm hit with a cold gust of air conditioning. It seems like this school can never get the temperature right. It's freezing in the winter and burning up in the summer.

I take a seat near the front and set my bags under my chair. I can't stop bouncing my foot up and down on the floor. Other students with similar last names start to file in, and it's really hitting me that this is happening.

I am finally about to take the dreaded ACT.

A bald teacher with a bright yellow button down walks into our room. "Hello, everyone. I'm Mr. Thornton. I'll be your proctor today." He sniffles.

Some kids mutter a hello, but for the most part, we just want him to shut up so we can get this over with.

"I'm going to pass out your answer keys for you to fill out your information. Make sure you fill in the correct bubble to the corresponding numbers."

He walks up and down each row, passing out the stark white answer sheets. He sniffles and wipes his nose before handing me a booklet.

Gross.

While I'm filling out my legal name, address, and other random information, I hear the heavy door creak open. Without looking up, I hear Mr. Thornton say, "Can I help you?"

"Sorry. I slept in, so I was running late. I just got here, and the teachers up front just told me to come in here." Oh no, I know that voice.

"What's your last name?"

"Braxton."

The pit in my stomach drops even lower.

"Well, you are in the wrong class, but it's too late to sort that out and try to get you to the B classroom. So you can stay. Here's an answer booklet," Mr. Thornton says. His shoes squeak on the tile as he walks over to give Beau the papers. "You can take a seat."

"Thank you so much," Beau says, and he heads for the only empty seat in the room. Which of course just so happens to be right next to me.

"Oh, hey," he whispers. I look over at him. I'm surprised he even said something to me.

"Okay, so I have to read the instructions before we begin," Mr. Thornton says. *Sniff.*

His nasally voice drones on and on while he covers every single rule and statement from the book. I swear I aged two years by the time he was done talking. I couldn't bring myself to pay attention, so I honestly have no idea what he said.

Sniff. "Okay, I'm going to hand out the test booklets now. We will start with the English portion. You have forty-five minutes to answer seventy-five questions. Capiche?" The overhead lights reflect on his shiny bald head, and I almost go blind.

We nod, and Mr. Thornton tells us we can begin. Forty-five minutes to answer seventy-five questions just seems cruel. He goes up to the whiteboard and writes the start and end time for this portion. The marker he uses loudly squeaks against the board, and it smells terrible.

I carefully open the test booklet, and I take another deep breath. *I can do this.*

The first part I have to answer involves six questions on grammar and a weirdly worded story about contrarian shit, a famous bakery, and chocolate chip pancakes.

I read the first few lines and the first question. I'm supposed to pick the right word choice for the sentence, but all the answers sound fine.

When _____ comes down to it, pancakes are a way to connect people from different backgrounds and all walks of life.

A. its

B. there

C. it

D. they've

I should not be getting this tripped up so early on. I circle the last answer choice and quickly move on to the next question.

Reading the next few lines of the passage, my concentration breaks. *Sniff. Sniff.* I glance up at Mr. Thornton who is reading *Moby Dick* at the front of the classroom. He's sitting at the teacher's desk, and there is literally a tissue box right in front of him.

Sniff. Sniff.

I take another deep breath and slightly shake my head. I can't let this distract me. I try to read the next few sentences.

Banana pancakes, <u>one of the more tastier and more popular flavors</u>, were first introduced to Olivia's Bakery in 1938 in Brooklyn, New York.

A. NO CHANGE

B. one of the more tastiest and most popular flavors

C. one of the most tastier and more popular flavors

D. one of the tastiest and most popular flavors

Literally all the answer choices could work for the sentence. I don't know! And now I'm starting to sweat. I wipe my upper lip and fan my sweatshirt to try to stay cool.

Tap tap tap.

Quickly glancing in the direction of the noise, I see the girl behind me tapping her lime green pencil against the desk. Does she not know proper test etiquette? Who makes this much noise during an exam?!

Tap tap tap.

I'm going to lose it. I set my own pencil down because my hands are starting to get even more shaky. Taking a deep breath, I try to resume my test.

Sniff. Sniff.

Looking up at Mr. Thornton, he's still reading his book and just sniffling away. I stare at him, hoping he'll catch my eye, so I can try to mime the fact that he needs to use a tissue. He doesn't see me.

Tap tap tap.

Sniff. Sniff.

This isn't working. There's just too many distractions. I can't concentrate. My hands are getting really clammy now, and I try to wipe them off on my sweatpants. It does nothing; they just start sweating even more now.

Focusing back on the next question, the words just look like a blur. I'm supposed to decide where the commas go in the sentence. I think?

My skin feels sticky under my sweat set, and I have the urge to just strip down in the middle of the classroom. Tucking my hair behind my ears, I take another deep breath. It doesn't do anything to quiet my pounding heart.

Ba-dum. Ba-dum.

Tap tap tap.

Sniff. Sniff.

My stomach feels like I just went down a drop on a major roller coaster. Now, not only does my skin feel sweaty, it's also starting to tingle. I can't do this right now. I need to get out of here.

Ba-dum. Ba-dum.

Tap tap tap.

Sniff. Sniff.

I try to take another deep breath, but this time, I can't fully inhale. It's like I'm trapped underwater. I give another shaky inhale and close my eyes. My mind is swimming with thoughts, but I can't bring myself to say anything.

I'm paralyzed. Sitting in the cold metal desk, I'm paralyzed. I can't move. I can't say anything. Quick inhale. Long exhale.

Ba-dum. Ba-dum.

Tap tap tap.

Sniff. Sniff.

I look around the room, and I see everyone close to me growing smaller. The walls seem to have doubled in size, slowly inching towards me. I feel like I'm in the scene from *Star Wars* where I'm about to get crushed by the garbage compactor. My vision blurs, and the fluorescent lights make all the colors in the room too bright. The room is definitely getting smaller.

Ba-dum. Ba-dum.

Tap tap tap.

Sniff. Sniff.

I can't do this. I need to get out of here.

What if I fail? What if the next time I take the ACT, I do worse? What if I can't get into college? What will I major in? What college will I go to? What if I disappoint my family?

My breaths are uneven, and my chest aches intensely. I'm not getting enough air. If I keep breathing like this I'm going to pass out. I open my mouth to say something, but no words come out.

I frantically look over at Beau, trying to signal that I need help. My brain won't stop spinning, and I feel detached from my body. I can't do this. I need to get out of here.

Beau looks over at me and gives me a puzzled look. I widen my eyes, trying to telepathically say that I'm dying. That's what this is. I'm dying in the middle of the ACT.

Ba-dum. Ba-dum.

Tap tap tap.

Sniff. Sniff.

Beau furrows his brow and resumes his exam. How can he not see that I'm dying right now? Quick inhale. Long exhale.

Closing my eyes, I try to stop freaking out. Who does this? Who spirals in the middle of a standardized test?

And that's what this is: a spiral. I'm propelling deeper and deeper into panicked thoughts. The spiral just leads me to a dark tunnel with no light at the end. I can't do this. I need to get out of here.

Ba-dum. Ba-dum.

Tap tap tap.

Sniff. Sniff.

Goosebumps line my arms, and I feel a shiver down my spine. I was burning up two seconds ago, and now I'm freezing. This must be what death feels like.

My mind is pinging with thoughts that I can't control. It's like a sink that you didn't turn off all the way so the water just *drop drop drops* into oblivion.

Quick inhale. Long exhale. It's getting worse. I'm sweating again. My eyes are stinging with tears, and the walls seem to just be inching closer to me. Scratching at my throat, I try to get more air.

I can't fully get a breath. I'm suffocating. I'm dying.

Ba-dum. Ba-dum.

Tap tap tap.

Sniff. Sniff.

I can't do this. I need to get out of here.

I swallow, and my throat feels like sandpaper. How can no one notice me? I'm alone. I'm going to die alone in this classroom.

Slowly moving my legs out from under my desk, my shoes feel like they are full of lead. I can barely bring myself to stand up. Tears rolling down my cheeks, I try to stifle my cry. Mr. Thornton doesn't even look up, and he has the audacity to sniffle again.

I turn the handle of the door, and step out into the hallway. My vision is out of focus, and the floor seems uneven. My legs feel heavy, but my head feels light. The hallway lights bounce off the speckled tile like when you see stars after a head rush.

Walking over to the girls' bathroom, I barely make it without toppling over. I'm practically leaning against the wall to support myself. I look in the mirror, and I don't recognize the girl looking back at me.

My forehead is shiny from the hot flash, and my cheeks are flushed. With my eyes bloodshot and my lips a light beige color, I look sickly. This must be what death looks like.

I grab a paper towel and run it under some cool water. I swipe it across my forehead to try to cool me off and calm me down. It doesn't work.

I look at the stalls. I see feet. Other people are in here. Other people can hear me crying. This is so embarrassing.

I can't go back to the classroom. I just left in the middle of the ACT. Is that an automatic fail? Did I just forfeit my chance to take the exam? Should I go back there? No I can't.

I glance at the eggshell white walls, and they are slowly creeping towards me. The room is closing in. Again.

I push through the bathroom doors and head back out into the hallway. I feel dizzy and lightheaded. Quick inhale. Long exhale.

My mouth feels dry. My heart is racing. I'm going to throw up. No, I'm going to faint. No, I'm going to die. That's what this is: death.

I can't seem to anchor myself to reality. I walk the halls, not sure where I'm going. I just walk. Slowly, I put one foot in front of the other. All I know is that I can't go back into that classroom.

Wiping my tears, I keep walking forward. My eyes are like a blurry camera lens- no matter how hard I try, I still can't focus on what's in front of me.

I hear a door close far behind me. Everyone is still taking the exam, and the underclassmen went on a field trip to the history museum. No one is really at school. Everyone is gone or in a classroom. The hallway feels like a ghost town.

I'm still breathing unevenly, and my heart is racing. My sweaty hands tremble as I keep walking forward. I don't even know what I'm walking towards.

"Mar?!" I hear from behind me.

Turning around, I see a flash of red hair. I walk towards him, but my knees start to buckle under my weight. Right before I fall over, Carter catches my arm, steadying me.

"What happened? What's wrong?" he asks me. His wide eyes search my face, trying to decode what's happening to me.

I try to tell him, but I can't get the words out. Quick inhale. Long exhale. Quick inhale. Long exhale.

Carter steps closer to me and wraps his long arms around my shoulders. He rubs my back and mutters in my ear, "You're okay. I'm here. I'm not leaving you. You're okay."

I let out a harrowing sob into his shoulder, not caring if I'm drenching his shirt. His gentle hands rub my back and fall into a soft rhythm with my heartbeat. I'm beginning to step off the ledge.

I pull away from him for a second to look into his jade eyes. I need to tell him why I'm freaking out. I know Carter doesn't care, and he wouldn't judge me. But I still feel the need to explain myself. I'm embarrassed. This isn't normal.

"I was taking the-" I start to say. "I was taking it, and I just can't. I can't do it, Carter. I'm going to fail." My voice automatically goes an octave higher because of the tears. I choke out another sob, letting him see a glimpse of my spiral. Quick inhale. Long exhale.

"It's okay. In my experience, talking about it just makes the panic attack worse," he says.

"No, Carter, I'm dying. I can't get enough air. I'm dying," I say. My body starts to shake as I replay the last hour in my mind.

"It's okay. You're okay, Mar. You're okay," he looks at me intently and grabs my hands. His cool fingers interlace with mine to stop my tremors.

"I'm here. Okay? I'm not going anywhere," he squeezes my hands three times. "I'm not leaving you."

I nod, still breathing quickly. It's like no matter what I do, I can't get rid of the tightness in my throat. Quick inhale. Long exhale.

"Look at me, Mar," Carter says gently. "Breathe. Breathe."

He emphatically breathes at a slow pace so I can try to emulate it. My breath is still faster than his, but I'm trying. I look into his green eyes. They look like a rainforest with sunlight peeking through the canopy. They look like a creamy matcha latte that's been made with love. They look like lily pads scattering across a peaceful pond. They look like *home*.

"Look at me. Breathe."

I focus on his eyes, drowning out the rest of my surroundings. I'm stepping farther away from the ledge. I inhale when he does and follow his exhale.

"You're okay. I'm not leaving you," he says.

I try to wedge a stone into the running gears of my mind. My heartbeat slows to a natural, melodious rhythm. My legs still feel weak, but I'm not at risk of falling over. My hands go from wildly shaking to a small tremble.

"Breathe," he tells me. "I'm here."

Inhale. Exhale. Inhale. Exhale.

I'm off the ledge. If I'm not careful, I could easily regress. But Carter is with me now, leading me down to safety.

I lean into him, wrapping my arms around his torso. He cradles my head in his hands, then folds his arms around my shoulders. Breathing steadily now, I'm enveloped in his scent of fresh laundry, sunny skies, and sweet mint.

"Carter, I-" I start to say.

"It's okay," he whispers.

He's probably four inches taller than me, so that gives him the perfect height to rest his head on top of mine.

I could stand here forever.

He asks, "Do you want to go to the cafe to get an iced water?"

I nod. He grabs my hand and slowly leads us to the coffee shop. Trying to distract me from the spiral I just had, Carter gently asks, "Guess what?"

"What?"

"I think I've convinced my mom to let me adopt Pickles."

"That's awesome," I say quietly, smiling for the first time in what feels like forever. My voice only slightly trembles. "How did you do it?"

"Well, you know my mom. She's a clean freak. But I'll be responsible for him, so she won't even have to worry about cleaning up after him. And if I go away to college, I was planning on working part time. If I worked, I could get an apartment to keep Pickles," he says softly.

"That's so exciting," I tell him, trying not to step back into the whirlpool of my mind.

"She said she would think about it and let me know by Thanksgiving. So fingers crossed."

We round the corner to the coffee shop. Carter steps forward to order an iced water for me. "Do you want anything else? A bagel or something? Caffeine probably isn't a good idea right now."

"Yeah. Just water is fine," I tell him. I can't believe how thoughtful he's being right now. I'll spend forever just trying to pay him back for his kindness towards me.

Carter walks up to the counter to grab my cup of iced water and hands it to me. After leading me over to the overstuffed chairs, we sit down so I can sip on my water. I'm feeling much calmer now, but my eyelids and shoulders feel heavy. That spiral took everything out of me.

I move my hand over to his, webbing his long fingers through mine. I feel pulled towards him after he calmed me down, as if he's my new security blanket or safe space. He rubs his thumb back and forth over the back of my hand.

The iced water does wonders for my sore throat, and after recycling the cup, I say, "I don't know what I should do now. I can't go back there."

"No, don't go back there. Did you drive today?"

I shake my head. "I will probably call my dad to come pick me up."

Carter says, "No, don't worry about it. I can drive you home."

"Wait, were you taking the exam? I don't want you to have to leave just because of me," I say, worry etched across my face. My breath hitches.

"No, no," he assures me. "I didn't have to take it, so we were just working on painting some of the sets for the musical. So I'm totally fine to stay with you. Trust me, I would much rather do that." His upper lip quirks, showing off the small scar from the tire swing fall seven years ago.

I nod and say, "Oh okay. I just didn't want to disrupt your schedule because of my freak out."

"Not at all. I wouldn't lie about that. It's no problem for me to take you home," he says. "I'll just text our stage director. Do you want to head to the front office?"

"Thank you," I breathe. "Yeah, we can head to the front."

"Sweet," Carter says, taking my hand in his without hesitation.

"Thanks, Carter. I really don't deserve you."

Walking up to the front office, Carter holds the door open for me and smiles to himself. He points to the chairs standing off to the side of the office and says, "I'll tell Mrs. Finn what happened. If you want to sit over there, I'll meet you in a second."

I nod and walk over to the blue patterned chairs. Carter knows me so well; I'm sure he decided to fill Mrs. Finn in on what happened, so I didn't have to relive it. Walking back over to me, Carter asks, "You okay?"

"Yeah," I say, really meaning it. I'm physically and mentally drained from my spiral, but at least I'm not on the verge of an anxiety attack anymore.

He nods. "I went ahead and signed both of us out for the day, so we can head to my car." We leave through the front doors of the school, a cool wind rippling through the both of us.

"Do you know what I've been thinking about lately?" he asks, once again trying to distract me from the panic attack I just had.

"What?"

"I want to go back and visit camp. It's been so long, and I've been reminiscing on it more lately. I still talk with Miss Pat because I mow her yard in the summer. So she would totally give me the keys to let us explore."

"Yeah," I say. "That would be so fun. And if you adopt Pickles, we could take him for a walk there."

"Definitely," he smiles.

Climbing into Carter's navy SUV, I scoot into his seats that are worn and soft like a favorite cardigan. Overall, I'm feeling better, but I still feel the bubble at the back of my throat, reminding me of the trapped cries over the ACT. I'm terrified of falling back into the spiral and letting

Carter see me like that again.

Carter gets in and starts the car. He runs a hand through his orange and golden curls. Turning to me, he asks, "Are you ready to go home?"

I nod.

We ride home in a comfortable silence, as I'm starting to feel myself crash from the high of my panic attack. My head feels like it's grown in weight, and my neck needs help keeping it upright.

The sky encloses around us with stripes of gray as Carter pulls into my neighborhood. I catch him glancing over at me to make sure I'm still the same as the last time he looked over at me.

Parking in my driveway, Carter turns off the car and jogs around the front of his car to open my door for me. Smiling to myself, I shake my head. "You didn't have to do that."

He gives me a boyish shrug. Turning to grab my tote and lunch bag, my hand stretches into empty air. My stuff and ten pound lunch box from my mom were sitting under my desk in Mr. Thornton's room. My bags lasted longer with the ACT than I did.

"I left my things at school," I exhale. "I'm sorry. I can ask Lenny to grab it after she finishes the test."

"No, don't worry about it. I can drive back over there later," Carter replies.

"You've done too much already. I can ask one of my parents to run over and grab my things."

Shaking his head, Carter says, "Let's just get you settled inside."

Chewing on my bottom lip, I walk over to punch in the code to the garage. As the door lifts, Carter finds his way over to me, putting a hand on my lower back to guide me into the door of my house.

As I'm coming back down to Earth from my earlier panic, I feel a sickly, twisted feeling in my stomach. Like a snake coiling around its prey, the embarrassment from today makes me want to curl up into a ball under my bed covers.

I glance over at Carter as we walk through the kitchen. He doesn't look mad or anything. I know I *shouldn't* feel guilty for him helping me, but I can't help it.

Stepping up the stairs, I say, "Carter, you can go ahead and go home. Or back to school."

"No, don't worry about it. I'll just stay until one of your parents comes home," he shrugs.

"I don't want you to have to do that. Seriously," I say, heading into my room. "I'm really tired, so I'll just take a nap."

Carter studies me for a second. "Well, let me just go get you another water or something," he says quickly and runs back down the stairs.

Feeling icky with myself, I just can't have him waste more time on me. I dragged him away from his theater prep work. He left school for me. I would be an awful person to make him stay with me until my parents got home.

I throw my shoes on the ground. I flop onto my bed, pulling my weighty quilt up to my chin. All I want right now is a good nap.

Softly knocking on my door, Carter says, "Hey, it's me."

"Come in."

Walking over to me, Carter sets the glass of iced water on my side table and sits perched on the end of my bed. "Mar, I want to stay with you. I don't feel comfortable just leaving you here by yourself. I promise you it's no trouble for me."

I shake my head against my pillow. Looking up at him, I say, "You've done so much for me already. I don't want to inconvenience you more. I'm just going to go to bed now."

Carter lets out a small exhale, running a hand through his hair. When he meets my eyes, there's a wall of sadness behind his expression. "Mar, I told you I wasn't going to leave you. I'm not going to do that now."

"I already feel guilty about everything. Please. I swear I'm fine now. I'm just going to go to bed."

"I don't want to leave you."

I hold his gaze. I feel gross in my own skin. Shuddering at the thought, I try to push back my embarrassed memories from earlier. I can't be more of a burden to Carter.

"It's okay. Seriously. I'm okay. I'm going to take a nap now. Go back to school," I say quietly. "I'm okay."

Carter looks at me for a moment too long. Shaking his head, he asks, "If that's what you want?"

I nod.

"Okay," he whispers. I turn over in my bed with my back facing him. Carter walks over and turns out my bedroom lights. I still feel his presence in my room.

Hearing Carter sigh, it takes him several minutes before he heads downstairs and leaves. I can't fall asleep until I hear his car slowly back out of the driveway.

I know I'm pushing him away, but I can't even think about that right now. I'm just *so* tired. Once he drives away, I finally rest my eyes and fall into a peaceful slumber, trying to forget about the empty ACT test bubbles and answer choices I left at school.

CHAPTER TWENTY-THREE

As we pass by bare tree after bare tree, I yawn and look out the window. Mom is driving me to my first therapy appointment, and my palms haven't stopped sweating since we left the house.

I know something has to change. After my panic attack the other day, I've felt like a shell of myself. I've never surpassed that level of anxiety before. For the past few days, I've just been rotting in bed and watching old episodes of *Hannah Montana*.

Carter and Lenny came over yesterday to check on me since I've missed the past couple of days of school. They were so sweet and caring, bringing me anything that I may need. Lenny brought me a fuzzy blanket from Target, and Carter picked up two pints of Ben & Jerry's ice cream for me.

As I've sat in my room for the past few days, I've heard my parents' hushed conversations from the living room. I know they want what's best for me, and I want that too. It's just that all of this is very unprecedented. Neither of my parents have struggled with this kind of anxiety.

When my mom came home from the studio yesterday, they sat me down to talk. Curled up on the opposite couch from me, Mom said, "So your dad and I have been talking, and we think it would be helpful for you to see a therapist."

I nodded. A part of me didn't want to admit that I needed help, but I couldn't keep doing this alone. I need relief, and I don't want to have another freakout like I did at the ACT.

"Talking with a professional can help you find some coping skills, kid," my dad said.

"Yeah. I mean, I want help. It's just scary."

I am scared of what happened the other day. I'm scared of what it means about me. I'm scared that it's going to happen again. I'm scared that I'm crazy.

Mom pulls into the parking lot of the counseling office. We looked online at the therapists' descriptions to see who would be the best fit. Mom assured me that if I didn't like the lady I met with today, I could easily find someone else.

Unbuckling my seat belt, I head out of the car to the front doors of the building. The weather has turned so cold so fast, and I feel the fall semester slipping away from my fingertips.

My mom and I walk up to the front desk to sign in. The guy working gives us a stack of paperwork, a clipboard, and a pen. We have to fill out all my information before my initial visit.

My mind tells me that I should be nervous about this, but my body feels something different. The lobby smells like lavender fields and chamomile tea. There's a sound machine laying in the corner, filling the room with the relaxing sound of rain on a metal roof. The TV above the sitting area plays a video of an aquarium with multi-colored fish. The ambiance of the office already puts my mind to rest from its earlier apprehension.

Once I'm done with filling every document out, I walk up to the front to turn in my papers. Sitting back down next to my mom, I say, "I'm feeling a little better now. I just don't know what to expect."

"That's completely understandable. It may seem scary, but therapy shouldn't be as intimidating as it may seem. There's nothing wrong with seeing a counselor," Mom says.

"Yeah, I know. It's just that I feel *different*. Like I'm not normal because I need to get someone else's help to figure out all of this."

"That's not true. It's human nature to need help from others. If we don't reach out, life gets very isolating. Look at me Marly- there's nothing wrong with getting help," Mom says intently, waving her hand around.

"Okay," I say.

A few minutes later, a blonde lady with tortoise shell glasses calls out, "Marlowe?"

"That's me," I say quietly. As I stand up, my mom leans over to whisper, "I love you. If you need anything, don't hesitate to come get me."

I nod and follow the blonde woman back to her office. She says, "Hi, I'm Denise. It's nice to meet you."

"It's nice to meet you too," I say, starting to crawl back into my shell.

Denise opens the door for me, and I take a seat on the olive colored couch. She sits down, crossing one leg over the other and says, "Make yourself comfortable."

I look down at the wired basket on the side table and pick up a small green fidget toy. It's a small woven pouch with a marble inside, so I can move the marble back and forth.

"Using a tool like that can help establish a feeling of calm. When you do a repetitive motion, like moving the marble back and forth, your mind slows to a natural rhythm," Denise tells me with a nod.

I nod back to her. Glancing around her beige walls, I adjust in my seat and try to get more comfortable. Tucking my hair behind my ears, I pull both feet into my seat.

"So I understand that you've been dealing with an increase of anxiety lately?" Denise asks me, pushing her glasses up her nose.

"Yes. It's like I've been more on edge this entire semester. I don't know why," I tell her.

Resting her hands in her lap, Denise says, "Junior year of high school can be intimidating for many students. Has there been something in particular that has seemed to be the root of the anxiety?"

"I don't know. I just really started to obsess over the ACT. My school started a study group program, so I have been thinking about it for months now. It has seemed to take up room in my brain for way too long."

Denise nods. Her voice sounds like a running stream of water trickling over a bed of rocks. Her cadence makes me feel more at peace.

She says, "Yes. The ACT can be a big stressor during high school. Other than your study group, have you felt someone or something putting a particular emphasis on the exam?"

"I think just society in general. I want to go to college, and I know that in order to get a good scholarship, I have to do well on the ACT. So, it's kind of the first step in life after high school. My parents haven't really put too much emphasis on it. I know I'm the one putting the pressure on myself," I say.

As I'm saying this out loud, I start to feel parts of my mind click into place. Mom and Dad haven't been the ones stressing about the ACT; it's been me.

"So, what are your parents' attitudes about the ACT?" Denise asks.

"They said they'll be proud of me no matter what," I say.

"How does that make you feel?"

"Good. I mean, knowing that I have their support means a lot. But it wasn't enough to stop me from spiraling," I tell her.

Denise thinks this over and takes a sip of her warm tea, saying, "Reminding yourself of their support can help reassure yourself that nothing is going to take away their love for you. When you were having an anxious response during the exam, what were some of the thoughts going through your mind?"

"I just kept thinking that I couldn't do it. I couldn't take the exam because I would fail."

She nods. "By telling yourself that you couldn't complete the test, you interrupted your positive self-talk."

"My what?" I ask.

"Your positive self-talk. It's when you repeat active, affirming phrases to yourself. It helps establish a better understanding of your sense of self. By repeating these phrases, you can grow your self-image. This would help you stop the self-doubt by naturally gaining more confidence," Denise says.

I nod, still moving the marble back and forth in the fidget toy.

Denise says, "I am capable. I am strong. I can do this. I believe in myself. I trust myself to do this. Repeating these active statements helps your mind focus on the assertion."

"I am capable," I repeat. "I like that one."

"Yes! It can challenge the feeling of self-doubt and anxiety. Using positive self-talk changes your mindset away from the negative thinking pattern," she says.

"I am capable," I repeat again. "So saying these phrases can help stop my anxiety?"

"It won't fully stop the anxiety. But reaffirming yourself with these active statements can help to reroute the anxiety spiral."

I nod, thinking about the other day when I had a bad freakout. Maybe if I had reassured myself, it could have distracted me from the worried thoughts.

Denise asks, "Do you want a note card to write some of these phrases down? So you can practice weaving them into your life?"

"Yes, please," I say. She hands me a note card with succulents around the border and a purple mechanical pencil. Jotting down a few of the active positive self-talk statements, I am already seeing the light at the end of the tunnel. The light is growing bigger, and hope fills my chest.

"So, throughout the next week, you can start putting these coping mechanisms to practice. Repeating those statements can help reassure yourself," Denise tells me. "Does meeting back in two weeks sound good?"

I agree and follow her out to the front, where my mom is sitting. I thank her for meeting with me, and she says, "I'll see you in two weeks!"

Heading out to the car, Mom asks, "So, what did you think? How was she?"

"Really good, honestly. I feel like talking with her validated my feelings, but she also gave me ways to help manage my anxiety," I say. "She's really nice."

"That's so good!" Mom exclaims. "Did she give you things to start working on?"

"Yeah!" I say as she starts the car. "I have some sentences to start practicing each morning. And I think I'm going to start journaling."

"Do you have a journal?" Mom asks.

"I mean, I have some from school."

"Well," my mom starts to say. With a smirk, she asks, "Do you want to go to Target to pick up a journal and do some shopping?"

"Of course," I say. If I'm already missing school today, I better make it worth it. And I'll never turn down the opportunity to go to Target.

Mom drives over to Target a couple streets down. She turns up the volume of the speakers, and "If It Makes You Happy" by Sheryl Crow fills the car. We park and head towards the sliding doors of our happy place.

This trip reminds me of middle school when my mom would pick me up early for an orthodontist appointment. After getting my teeth poked and prodded at, my mom would take us to Target to treat ourselves. I would pick out a book to read, and my mom would grab the random things that we just "had to get."

We round the corner and walk towards the stationary aisle. Multiple notebooks and journals line the shelves, just beckoning me to pick one up. I run my hands over a beige spiral notebook with the outlines of dogs sprinkled along the cover.

I pick up another notebook that is light pink with sage green polka-dots. Flipping it open, I see that the pages are stark white, and I immediately put it back down.

Walking over to the edge of the aisle, I pick up a deep blue journal that's wrapped in a delicate, linen cover. I crack open the spine and feel the buttery soft pages. Not to mention, the pages are a beautiful cream color that's perfect for brain dumping.

"I'm going to go with this one," I say. My mom nods and motions for me to put it in the cart.

We parade through the beauty, home, and food aisles to see if anything is calling our name. Walking back towards the front to check out, we pass a pastel colored aisle.

"Wait!" I tell my mom.

I walk over to the nostalgic shelves and pick up the stuffed animals. Hugging each of them for comfort reminds me of when I was younger where my stuffed animals were my world.

"Oh my gosh," Mom says, picking up a turtle stuffie. "This one is adorable!"

"I think I'm going to get one. I still have some money left over on my Target gift card," I say. I walk down the aisle, holding each animal until I find the perfect one.

The elephant one was too stiff. The dog one was too limp. The tiger one had fur that wasn't soft. The monkey one was too big. The butterfly one was too small.

I almost walked away without any of them, until my eyes landed on a medium-sized, coffee colored bear. It looks like the perfect teddy bear, with floppy arms and legs. I hug the stuffie tightly, and it gives the best hug back. The bear's fur is soft and gentle, and it's the material that gets softer with each cuddle.

I've found it.

"Look at this one! He's perfect!" I say.

My mom smiles, and I'm sure this reminds her of a Target trip we may have taken ten years ago. "Well, let's get it then!"

Walking up to the cashier, I've already decided on a name: Barry the Bear.

Maybe instead of focusing on growing up and the future, I should think back to "simpler times." When I was younger, everything was so easy and pure. I felt like I had my whole life ahead of me.

I know I'm only sixteen, but sometimes I feel like my life is already decided for me. Or that I've lost that light that I had when I was younger. Along with journaling, maybe I need to prioritize connecting back with my younger self. Maybe that can quiet the future "what if" anxieties.

After arriving home, I head up to my room. Getting out my favorite gel pen, I open my new journal and smooth out the first page. Trying to do what Denise suggested, I start writing the active statements she gave me.

I am capable. I am strong. I can do this. I trust myself to do this. I believe in myself. I am capable. I am strong. I can do this. I trust myself to do this. I believe in myself.

It's a start.

CHAPTER TWENTY-FOUR

"Okay, my mom said we can use any of these," I say, opening my tote bag full of craft supplies. I pull out the stack of scrapbook paper, fabric pieces, wooden dowels, and bottle caps. Mom also gave us plenty of glue and tape, so we can craft the perfect prototype for our mindfulness space. Just call it the perks of having an artist as a mother.

Carter and I have to present our proposal and prototype to our class in a month. Our teacher, Mrs. Lin, is having us begin the process early, so if any problems arise we can fix them ahead of time.

We agreed to meet up at Carter's house to begin the crafting process. Jacob and Lenny decided to also come over to volunteer their efforts towards our project. Carter picked up a few pieces of posterboard for us to use as the base of the prototype. We're basically going to try to recreate the room and craft small pieces of furniture, so if our project actually gets approved, we essentially already have a blueprint.

Especially after my panic attack at the ACT, I think a calming space in the school is even more needed. If students have somewhere to wind down, it may be able to decrease their overall stress. I've felt a little better since the ACT, but I would be lying if I said my anxiety fully went away.

I know if I'm feeling this way, there have to be other students who feel the same. We are overwhelmed with schoolwork and the pressure of growing up, and it's just too much. Hopefully, Carter and I's Leadership project can combat some of that student-wide stress.

"Okay, what should we start with?" Jacob asks.

"Maybe you all can start making some of the miniature furniture while Carter and I draw up the room on the poster board," I say.

"Sounds good!" Lenny says, grabbing some of the fabric, stuffing, and thread. "This is my favorite embroidery thread right now. Jacob and I can make some of the little bean bag chairs."

Lenny and Jacob sit over at the kitchen table while Carter and I spread out our supplies on the kitchen counter top. Sheila is out to dinner with Ashley, so we have the whole house to ourselves.

"We should probably sketch it out with pencil first, right?" Carter asks me.

"Definitely. I didn't inherit my mom's artistic genes, so I would mess it up with a Sharpie."

Carter chuckles and hands me a pencil. He leans over the counter to begin sketching, and his auburn hair falls in front of his eyes. His curls remind me of waves in the ocean on a hot July day.

Since the ACT, the memory of Carter calming me down circulates my brain indefinitely. I can't stop replaying how kind he was. How understanding he was. How *Carter* he was.

I lightly drag my pencil over the white paper, attempting to emulate the layout of the room. Trying to steady my hand, I'm very aware of how close Carter is to me. I'm sure I'm still this attentive of him because of what happened at the ACT. This must be my way of thanking him: noticing his every move or how *close* we are.

Not that I'm complaining.

Carter concentrates on making his sketch as accurate as possible, and I see his amber brows furrow together. His long, slender fingers hold the poster board down as he draws the perimeter of the room. Copper freckles line his fingers and the back of his hand. That freckled hand rubbed my back as I was crying. Those fingers interlaced with mine to comfort me.

I need to stop. Carter can not occupy my thoughts this much.

Crafting and sketching like this reminds me of our days at Camp Caelee. Lenny and I loved to make friendship bracelets in the arts and crafts room when it was too hot to play outside.

After a few minutes of sketching with pencils, Carter and I turn to the permanent markers to trace our blueprint. I try to not focus on how close his hand is to mine.

In an attempt to distract my mind from Carter, I push away from the counter and walk over to see what Lenny and Jacob are doing. "Thank you again for helping with this," I tell them.

"Of course! Look how cute these are!" Lenny says. She holds up tiny bean bag chairs and small rolls of foam.

"She may ask your mom to display these in her studio," Jacob jokes.

Just seeing the way they look at each other reminds me that love still exists. They've basically grown up together, and there's something so special about that. Lenny and Jacob are completely comfortable with each other. It's like they skipped the awkward phase and went straight into becoming each other's other half.

I want a love like that.

"Ha! Those are adorable," I tell her. I am really lucky to have friends who would spend their Friday night helping Carter and me with a school project.

Grabbing the remote, I ask, "What do we want to watch?"

"If it were just us, I would say Arrested Development, but I know Len doesn't like that one," Jacob says. "I just got to where Tobias paints himself blue. I almost peed myself laughing."

I giggle and reference, *"I just blue myself."*

"Yes!" Jacob says through fits of laughter.

I end up turning on *The Summer I Turned Pretty*, so we can watch it while we work. Lenny and I have gone back to rewatch the early episodes, and we are *obsessed*. I've always been Team Conrad, and Lenny has been Team Jeremiah. Now, rewatching it, I think I'm actually Team Steven. He reminds me of a certain *someone* related to Lenny, but I can't tell her that.

I *have* to stop thinking of him.

After clicking the *next episode* button several times, the evening slips past us. I can't believe it, but we've been working for three hours.

Sheila, Lenny's mom, comes home, and Jacob leaves to head to his house. After Jacob's car pulls away, Lenny asks me, "Do you want to spend the night? I feel like you haven't slept over in forever."

"Oh my gosh, yes! Let me double check with Mom and Dad, but that should be fine. I don't have anything planned for tomorrow," I say.

After getting the okay from my parents, Lenny and I get ready for our impromptu sleepover.

"Goodnight, Carter," I say.

"Goodnight, Mar," he waves from across the hall.

Lenny and I crawl into her bed, and we burrow underneath her mound of stuffed animals and Disney Princess blankets.

• • •

"I know you cheated," Mr. Thornton yells at me from across the room. He's grown five inches in height, and he stands in front of the class like a tyrant.

"I didn't cheat!" I say. Warm tears stream down my face. I didn't even realize I was crying.

"You cheated! You cheated!" the kids in my class shout.

"No, I didn't! I promise I didn't cheat!"

"We know you did, Marlowe," Beau says, standing up and shaking his head. "And now you are going to fail."

"No! No! That's not true! I didn't cheat. And I can't fail the ACT. I have to pass," I cry even louder. My sobs echo across the white cinder block walls. No one is going to come save me.

I'm utterly alone.

"GET OUT OF MY CLASSROOM!" Mr. Thornton screams and points towards the door. I run out of the room, slinging my backpack over my shoulders. Barging through the front doors, I jog over to my bike that's parked in front of the school.

I climb onto the bike and begin pedaling as fast as I can. I start out riding slowly, but all of the sudden, I'm going 100 miles an hour... on my bike.

"Ahhhh!" I scream. I'm struggling to steer on the road, and cars zip past me. A truck honks, and I get so spooked that I almost fly off my bike.

I keep pedaling and keep pedaling. My heart rate is dangerously high. I have no control over the bike. I'm going to die.

Beads of sweat stream down my face and sting my eyes. I zoom around a bend, and instead of following the curve of the road, I fly off the path. What I thought was a ditch on the side of the road turns out to be a rocky cliff.

Goosebumps spread across my whole body. I'm trying to slow down, but nothing happens. I'm going to die.

I rush off the rocks of the cliff and barrel towards the bottom. Leaves, stones, and branches fly at me as I rush towards the pit. The ground is getting closer. I can't stop the bike. I'm going to die.

The solid dirt floor of the pit comes closer and closer into view. I'm going to die. I'm falling, and I can't stop. I'm going to die.

The front tire of my bike hits the bottom, and I hit-

I jolt awake. I'm panting as if I just ran a marathon. I'm sweating as if I have, too. Looking down at my hands, I see a tremor start to take form. My heart is beating along to the rhythm of a rock concert, and I feel like I'm going to pass out.

I look over at Lenny, and she's sleeping peacefully. She's always been a heavy sleeper, and I hate to wake her now. Reaching over to grab my phone, I see that it's 3:13 in the morning.

Laying back down, I pull her fuzzy blanket around myself, trying to nestle back into a tranquil sleep. My heart is still beating rapidly, and I can feel my pulse in my ears. Balling my hands into fists, I try to stop myself from shaking.

I stare daggers at the wall, unable to calm down enough for sleep. Checking my phone again, I see the time. It's 3:44 AM.

Maybe it's because he calmed me down during my last anxiety episode. Maybe it's because his presence is so serene. Maybe it's because I know he will help comfort me. Maybe it's because I have now begun to think of him as my safe space.

Before I know it, I'm standing in front of Carter's bedroom door.

Tap, tap, tap.

Creaking the door open, I whisper, "Carter?"

"Huh?" he asks, sitting up in bed. I walk over to him and see his rumpled hair and sheets strewn everywhere.

"Hey, it's me."

"Mar? What's wrong?" he asks and rubs his eyes. His gaze travels across my face.

I walk over closer to him. "Um," I start. "I had a nightmare and couldn't go back to sleep."

Immediately, Carter sits up straighter and moves his pillows and blankets over for me.

"Come here," he says.

I climb into his warm bed, and I pull his flannel sheets up towards my shoulders. His hand touches mine lightly, like mist covering the sidewalk in early spring.

"You're shaking," he says. "What happened?"

I scoot closer to him. "I don't know. I've been doing better with my worries. But I just had a really bad dream about failing the ACT and falling off a cliff." My voice breaks.

I know it sounds ridiculous, and I shouldn't be this freaked out over a dream. Deep down, I know that. But even so, he doesn't question it.

Carter takes his arm and wraps it around my body to pull me closer. I take a deep breath. He smells like fresh linen and salt air.

"It was a dream. You're okay. I'm here," Carter reassures me. "You're okay."

I nod and rest my head on his shoulder. "I know. I just got freaked out," I say, my breath hitching. My heart is still beating rapidly.

He strokes my hair and murmurs, "I'm here."

I close my eyes and try to focus on what Denise talked about. I need to distract myself from my near-spiraling thoughts.

I am capable. I am in control. I am okay. I trust in myself. I can do this.

I take another deep breath. It was just a dream. I'm okay. I'm not going to focus on the ACT. It was just a dream. I am okay.

"It was just a dream," I say, reassuring myself. I open my eyes and look up at Carter. He's already looking at me, smiling softly.

"You okay?" he whispers, his hand drawing small circles around my shoulders.

"I feel better," I tell him, nodding into his shoulder.

He brushes away a few strands of hair away from my face, and his fingers graze my jaw. "You are welcome to stay here tonight. I'll take the couch."

"Oh. Um," I stutter. I don't want to be alone tonight. I want *him*.

"Or if you want to go back to Lenny's-"

"Will you stay with me?" I ask. I'm not trying to act like some pathetic codependent teenager, but I need him to stay.

"Of course," he breathes.

I lower further under the covers and nuzzle closer to him. He keeps an arm wrapped around me, and I tuck my hands into his chest.

I'm in a cocoon of his touch, and I never want to leave.

CHAPTER TWENTY-FIVE

Over the past week of school, I've been counting down the days until Thanksgiving break. I've had to break up this semester into chunks in order to digest it. I'm constantly glancing at the clock, and I'm always looking forward to the weekend.

My family and I aren't big on the traditional Thanksgiving. We normally cook a meal full of carbs and then binge watch a show on Netflix. This year we've decided to rewatch *Stranger Things*.

I walk over to the kitchen to pull out my reheated mac and cheese from the microwave. My parents are cuddled together on the couch, with my dad's arm around Mom's shoulder.

Sitting down into the leather recliner, I stir my leftovers from lunch. We just finished the episode where Barb goes missing. RIP!

I pull out my phone and open Instagram. Right at the front of my feed is a picture of a smiling Beau with a laughing Maya. Her rosy cheeks stand out against her pale pink sweater, and Beau's hand is on the small of her back.

Even though it was weeks ago, I think a part of me will always be a little hurt after what happened. I'll mourn what could have been. And I'll always remember Beau as my childhood crush.

I don't want Beau. *At all*. But it still feels like a low blow. He rejected me. He picked her.

I don't miss him. I don't want him back. I'm happy now. But I can't help doing a double take anytime I see a gray Jeep driving on the road. I feel the pit in my stomach when I see Maya post the two of them together. Mom says that should go away with time.

Suddenly, my phone starts ringing, and the picture of Maya and Beau buzzes.

FaceTime Video: Carter Taylor

I answer the call, and I see a familiar looking, scruffy dog staring back at me on my phone. The dog leans towards the camera, licking the screen.

"Pickles!" I squeal. "You adopted him?!"

Carter leans into the frame, and he looks like he's on cloud nine. He says, "Yes! Mom surprised me with him this morning."

"Carter, he's literally the cutest thing I've ever seen," I tell him.

"Thanks." Switching to a baby voice, he coos, "Say, I'm such a good boy. Yes, I am!"

This is actually the cutest thing I've ever seen. Carter gushing over his tiny Chihuahua makes my heart melt.

He asks, "Do you want to come over and see him?"

"Yes!" I say, immediately getting up to grab my things. "Okay, I'll see you soon."

"See you!" Carter says. He picks the dog up and moves him closer to the phone. "Pickles says bye too!"

In the two minute phone call, my cheeks already hurt from grinning too much.

Picking up my jacket, I call out to my parents, "I'm heading to Carter's house! They adopted Pickles!"

"Okay!" my mom says.

It's bizarre to refer to their house as Carter's because normally I just go over there for Lenny. I take my mom's keys and climb into her car to head a few streets over.

While I'm driving, I feel a tickle in my throat as if I'm about to burst into giggles at any moment.

I've sought validation from others for so long, and it feels like a breath of fresh air now that I'm starting to let that go. My search approval isn't fully over, but at least I'm making some steps in the right direction.

Hanging out with people I'm so comfortable with- like my parents, Lenny, or Carter- makes me feel more in tune with who I am. I really don't think twice- or *overthink* twice- when I'm around them.

Pulling into Lenny's driveway, I see Carter standing on the front porch, waving at me. He's holding Pickles, and the pup's tail is wagging back and forth so quickly.

"Carter! Pickles!" I shout, getting out of my car. Carter sets Pickles down, and he comes barreling towards me. Pickles circles my legs, and he licks my ankles. Bending down to pet him, I say, "Pickles! I missed you."

"He missed you too," Carter says, smiling faintly.

I blush. Why does his voice make me feel at peace?

I scratch Pickles' cappuccino colored fur, and he tries to jump up on my legs. Pickles is so short that when he jumps up, he barely hits my calves.

We step into the foyer, and I instantly hear a high pitched squeal. "Marlowe!" Lenny shouts, running down the hallway to meet me.

"Hey!" I say, smelling her signature coconut scent. Her hair is half pulled up into a claw clip, with her strawberry blonde waves flowing past her elbows.

I wave hello to Sheila and Ashley, and we head to the bonus room upstairs. Turning to Lenny, I say, "Ashley came to Thanksgiving? Things must be getting serious."

"Yeah. I like her a lot. She suits Mom really well," she says, nodding.

"Same," Carter pipes up.

"What if you get a new step mom soon?" I ask, wiggling my eyebrows.

"It would be better than the step mom we currently have," Carter mutters. We settle onto the bonus room floor and pull out the new toys Sheila picked up for Pickles. Carter rolls a tennis ball towards his dog, and Pickles sprints to go catch it.

"Carter, don't say that," Lenny chides.

I remember when Sheila found out her husband had an affair when Lenny and Carter were nine and ten. As Lenny's best friend, I tried to comfort her and assure her that everything would be okay. But I had no idea if that was true or not.

Sheila and Paul divorced a few months later, and a full year later he married Evelyn, the mistress. Lenny and Carter were in the wedding, even though neither of them wanted to be involved. Evelyn had Lenny as the flower girl and Carter be the ring bearer, as if they were both toddlers.

"Sorry," Carter mutters. Lenny shoots him a look. "It's just that Dad is pressuring me to go with him next week to a college tour at CalTech, his alma mater."

"I thought you didn't want to go there," I tell him.

Picking at the tassels on the rug, Carter says, "I don't. He planned the tour without telling me, and he doesn't understand why I don't want to go."

"That's awful."

"Yeah," Carter says. "I have to miss a few days of school next week to visit a college I don't even want to go to."

I look at him, but Carter doesn't meet my eyes.

"And Dad is stubborn, so it's his way or the highway," Lenny speaks up. "He wants me to come over during winter break to spend time with him and his new family."

"I'm sorry," I say.

My chest constricts and my ribs ache for them. Seeing them deprived of a decent father figure physically pains me. Everyone says that only-children don't know how to share things, but I would gladly share my parents with Lenny and Carter. They deserve two parents under one roof who love them and love each other.

"It's okay. I'm still trying to get out of it," Carter says with a shrug. "We'll see."

Pickles snorts and then rolls around on the carpet, exposing his pink belly. He looks like a tiny pot belly pig. "Look at him!" Carter says, as his eyes light back up.

Pulling out my phone, I take a 0.5x photo of the four of us. I open up Instagram, and I immediately post the picture to my feed. It feels nice to not have to post a picture with an ulterior motive. To post a picture that's not about a fake relationship, but instead, post it because I'm truly *happy* in the photo.

"Oh wait," Lenny says, jumping up. "We need to listen to the new Wallows album!" She grabs the remote, turns on the TV, and connects her Spotify.

"I waited so I could listen with you all," Carter says.

"Same!" I say.

The drums and rhythmic guitar waft throughout the bonus room, and the three of us slump onto the overstuffed couch. Pickles hops up and immediately burrows into Carter's shirt.

Dylan and Braeden's vocals echo across the cream colored walls. Leaning back into the couch cushions, I close my eyes. Every single Wallows song makes me feel like I'm the main character in an indie romcom. It makes me happy to be alive and glad to be myself.

Even though the past few weeks have been hard, I'm feeling better about myself. I've been thinking back to the past, trying to reconnect with my younger self. I thought back to camp, and it was amazing- aside from my obsessive crush on Beau. And I sleep with my new stuffed animal, Barry the Bear, every night.

My wrist hurts after I journal about my favorite memories growing up. My mirror hears my active, positive statements every morning.

I'm really trying. I'm trying to find myself after a hurdle of anxiety.

By recollecting on the past, I can connect back with who I truly am. It stops me from worrying about the scary future, and it pulls me back into the present.

I'm actually happy.

CHAPTER TWENTY-SIX

finish twisting my hair into a braid, flipping it over my shoulder. Leaning over to wash my face in the sink, I try to wake myself up more. I'm attempting to ignore the fact that it's 3:02 AM.

Paul, Carter's dad, was insistent on Carter flying to visit him. To both of our dismay, Carter wasn't able to get out of it.

He's flying out to Southern California at 7:00 AM, so he needs to get to the airport at 5:00 AM. Carter called me two days ago to see if I wouldn't mind riding with him to the airport, then driving his car back to his house.

I agreed without hesitation.

I swipe on my moisturizer and Aquaphor. I'm not even going to bother putting on makeup today; I don't care if I look rough around Carter. Throwing on my favorite pair of perfectly worn-in sweats, my stomach flips ever so slightly.

My breath caught in my throat when he first asked if I would ride with him. Of course I was honored, but I was surprised that he didn't automatically ask Lenny.

Heading downstairs, I fill up my water bottle with lots of ice and tap water. The airport is almost an hour and a half away, so it's not really long enough to warrant a ton of road trip snacks and drinks.

I grab my bag and water bottle, and I peek into my parents' bedroom. It's the Sunday after Thanksgiving, so my parents are enjoying the ability to sleep in before they have to go back to work tomorrow.

"Psst!" I whisper into the darkness. "I'm about to head on."

"Huh? Oh, okay. Be careful," my mom says groggily within the pitch black void. "Do you want me to pack you some snacks real quick?"

"No, that's okay," I chuckle.

Quietly, I close their door back and do a mental checklist to make sure I have everything. It's so early that my brain feels like it's full of opaque fog. *Buzz. Buzz.*

My phone vibrates, and looking down, I see that Carter is calling me. I move into the living room, and I answer his call.

"Hello?"

"Hey, Mar! I'm like two minutes away," he says. I can practically hear his smile through the phone. Only Carter would be this happy at 3:15 AM.

"Okay, I'll see you soon," I say softly.

Opening the front door, I walk out to our front porch and sit on the wooden swing, waiting for Carter. The chilled wind bristles past me, sending chill bumps throughout my body.

There's something so peaceful about morning darkness. Getting up before the sun sucks sometimes- don't get me wrong- but it's nice to have the freshness of the morning. You can hear the rustles of nature. You beat the sun. You've still got the whole day ahead of you.

It's going to be a good day.

Carter's navy SUV pulls into my driveway, and I caper down the front porch steps. Getting out of the car, he's sporting a vintage Montreal crewneck with navy sweatpants.

"Hey!" I say walking over to him. Carter walks around his car, opening the passenger door for me.

"M'lady."

I snort. "Carter, what are you doing?"

"I'm being a gentleman," he shrugs. Once I get settled, he shuts the door and jogs back over to the driver's side of the car. His car smells like coconut milk and sea salt, fooling me that I'm actually at the beach with him.

"Thank you again for coming with me," he says.

"Of course," I say. I kick off my shoes onto the floorboard, and Carter reaches back to get a bag from the backseat. "I have something for you."

I look at him, surprised. "What?"

"Well, obviously we need some snacks for the road," he says, sounding like my mom. He hands me the plastic bag. Opening it, I see a large bag of Original Chex Mix, a box of Swedish Fish, Reese's Cups, and a pack of spearmint gum. He knows every single one of my gas station snack go-to's.

"Carter, you didn't have to do this."

"I know," he says. "Also, I realized we make the perfect team."

"How so?" I ask.

"Pretzels are my favorite snack, and you hate them. So I'll eat them from your bag of Chex Mix."

It's kind of like the Olive Theory from *How I Met Your Mother*. In the show, Lily and Marshall believe they are the perfect match because she loves olives, and he hates them. They are so compatible because she'll eat all the olives he doesn't want.

"Yeah, I guess that's true! We make a good team," I nod. I didn't even realize that he took notice of me always picking out the pretzels of Chex Mix.

I swear, Carter has the memory of an elephant.

Carter puts his car into reverse, puts a hand behind my headrest, and looks behind us to back out of the driveway.

"So, how's Beauty and the Beast been going?"

"Good," Carter nods. "It's a lot of rehearsing, but it is really coming together. The costume designers finished a mock-up of my costume, and it looks so good."

"Yay! That's awesome. I can't wait to see the finished product," I say. "Can you give me a sneak peek of one of your songs?"

We pull up to the stoplight, and Carter bites his bottom lip, hiding his small white scar. Grabbing his phone, he searches for the soundtrack.

"I'll only do it if you'll be my Belle," he says with a soft smile.

I chuckle and nod, while the stringed instruments from "Something There," play through his car. I can't help but grin when I hear this song; it's just so nostalgic.

Taking my cue from the music, I sing, "*There's something sweet, and almost kind.*" I'm pretty much tone deaf. I'm like those viral failed American Idol auditions from the early 2000's. I'm so off key, but I know Carter doesn't care.

He taps the steering wheel along with the rhythm of the song. When my out of tune part is over, he looks at me sweetly before singing.

"*She glanced this way. I thought I saw,*" he sings. His voice is like a hot honey citrus tea: warm, sweet, and instantly makes you feel better. As he sings each word, I watch his peachy lips move to form every sentence. Every word. Every syllable.

I *need* to stop looking at his lips like that.

The song fades, and turning to him, I say, "Carter, you need to do something professionally with music. Seriously."

"Wait, really?"

"Yes! Do you think you'll do theater in college?" I ask.

"Yeah, I hope so. But I won't have a chance to if I go to CalTech," he mutters, shaking his head.

"What do you mean?" I ask.

He sighs. "I was wondering how long it would take me before I needed to vent about this. It's my dad. It's always my dad."

"Oh," I say. "I'm sorry. You don't have to talk about it if you don't want to."

"No, I want to talk about it. If you're open to letting me rant," he says, glancing sheepishly at me.

"Carter, I'll always be an ear for you. You can share anything with me."

His cheeks crease, his right dimple peeks out. "He just puts so much pressure on me. For no reason. He's been unrelenting about me going to CalTech. I think I want to be a vet, but that doesn't automatically mean I want to go to a STEM school. But he doesn't get that."

"That's ridiculous. Your college decision needs to be that: *your decision.* I forgot your dad became a professor there. Is that why he's so hell-bent on you going?" I ask.

"Yeah, he's worked there for a year and a half now. It's been his most recent personality trait. You know, working at his alma mater is *such* a big deal," he rolls his eyes. "Paul is so focused on me carrying on his legacy or whatever, that he hasn't even bothered to check if I actually want to be a part of that legacy."

"That's messed up."

Carter brings his thumb up to his lips, biting his cuticle. Sheila, his mom, would get so frustrated with him for the habit when we were younger. She said it was unsanitary. I remember her soaking his fingers in lemon juice, keeping his nails short, and painting his nails with a bitter deterrent polish. The habit still sneaks around the corner when he gets nervous. As he bites his cuticle, I can see his fingers tremble ever so slightly.

"Why on earth would I want to go to a school where I would constantly have to see my dad? He's never around now, so I don't understand why he's all the sudden trying to be my best friend and college tour guide."

"Yeah," I say, nodding softly.

"And get this: he wants me to move in with him and Evelyn. He wants me to move into the home of his new family! Is he out of his mind?!"

I shake my head. I can't imagine.

"For one, I've lived in Caelee my whole life. I don't think I want to move thirty-one hours away. I think I want to double major in Biology and Theater. And CalTech isn't known for the humanities. So why would I even go there?"

"Exactly!" I exclaim.

"Lenny is so much better with Evelyn than I am. I just- I don't know. I can't get over how everything went down with them and my mom," Carter says.

"What do you mean?" I ask. I know that the divorce was difficult for Lenny at the beginning, but Carter hasn't opened up to me about his dad like this. When he's mentioned Paul and Evelyn before, it's like he's always biting his tongue, holding back half of what he truly wants to say.

"You know me. I always wanted to be the best role model for all the younger kids at Camp Caelee. I would worry so much about being someone they could look up to. Around the time of my parent's separation, I used to get really anxious about lying. I don't know. It was just a weird spiral I struggled with. Like, I never wanted to be caught lying because I thought it would make me a bad role model or something. I don't know why I obsessed over it so much.

"When Mom and Dad first separated, they didn't tell Lenny and I why. I mean, looking back I'm sure Paul just didn't want to admit to his kids that he had cheated on their mom. So Lenny and I were out of the loop for ten months before Paul told us the truth.

"It's like my brain latched onto that. I couldn't stop replaying the fact that one, my dad had an affair with Evelyn, and two, he had lied about it. I know we were just kids, and they were probably worried that we couldn't handle it, but I felt *so* betrayed. It just made my anxiety about lying so much worse."

"I had no idea. I'm so sorry, Carter," I say. His eyebrows draw closer together, the distress from these memories making an appearance across his face.

"Yeah. And what bothers me is that I still can't be honest with my dad. So that just makes me worry even more. Honesty is so big for me. He's never been honest with us, so even now, I feel my walls go up immediately. I just can't be myself around him," he says. "It's a mind fuck."

I can't imagine feeling that anxiety trap with a family member. With me, my anxiety just surrounds success. Or being good enough. But Carter's is about honesty, and his *dad* is the one who multiplies that anxiety.

"Every time I see him, I think of how he's vanished since I was ten. Every time I see him, I think of that hurt little kid I was after the divorce. I know that's why I can't tell him that I don't want to go to CalTech," he says, taking a deep breath. Carter resumes biting at his cuticles.

I can't help but notice that he feels comfortable enough with *me* to be this honest. Tucking my hair behind my ears, I ask, "And Paul is still pushing for that school even after he's been a terrible father?"

"Yeah," he says, shaking his head. "He thinks I just haven't given it a chance. He thinks he can change my mind."

"I want to punch him in the face."

"Mmm hmm." He smiles gently, with the color rushing back to his cheeks for a moment. "I just- I don't know what I'm going to do. Or even what I'm going to be able to do. Sorry- I know I'm rambling too much."

I look over at him and brush his arm with my hand. There's a heaviness in his eyes that wasn't there at the beginning of our car ride. "Don't apologize. Is there another school you are interested in? Or do you think you'll take a gap year?"

He shifts in his seat and brushes his amber hair away from his eyes. "Yeah, there is another college. They have an amazing theater department *and* animal sciences program. But I don't think I'll be going."

"Why not?!" I ask.

"I don't know. I think my dad just expects me to go to CalTech, so any other option is out of the question."

"What school is it?"

"It's Windermere University, a small liberal arts college. It's about two hours away."

"Whoa, that sounds perfect for you. You need to apply," I tell him.

"I did. But no one really knows. Just Mom and Lenny. And now you," he chuckles lightly. "Paul thinks that I need to just follow in his footsteps. But I don't want to follow him. I don't even want to be on his same path." Carter sighs.

"Yeah! You shouldn't follow down his path. Don't listen to him," I say. Pulling out my phone, I look up Windermere University.

The campus is surrounded by a plethora of dogwood, cypress, and willow trees. On the website, it showcases a stone pathway that descends down to a creek, surrounded by antique metal benches.

I can perfectly picture Carter here.

I swipe through some more photos on the website, and they apparently have an award winning songwriting program, coupled with high level veterinary undergraduate track. This is *so Carter.*

"Carter, this is literally you in university form. Did you see the gorgeous brick buildings? And the stone amphitheater? And apparently they have this huge showcase at the end of each semester for the music students. This is perfect for you!" I say excitedly.

"You really think so?" he smiles.

"Yes! Carter, apparently they have a really aesthetic coffee shop on campus," I say.

"Can't you just imagine me there?!" he says. The light in his eyes has resumed to its normal luminosity.

He's so back.

I scroll through the school's "About" page and point to their mascot. It's a sand colored bobcat with an emerald green shirt. "Look at their mascot! And the university chant is 'Go, cats, go!'"

He chuckles. "I know! I think I would love it. Plus it's not too far from home. I could get an apartment for Pickles and me. I want to get away from home, but I still feel a tether pulling me back to Caelee."

Nodding, I say, "I totally get that. Like, I've lived here my whole life, so this is home. But I feel like I need to experience life outside of our small town."

His fingers tap against the top of the steering wheel, like the swinging rhythm of a pendulum. "I know what to expect. My roots are here. Time moves so damn slow. And I love Caelee because of that. But I also hate it. I need to grow outside of here, so I can really know who I am. It's like my life has just been static. I have had no destination. If I don't leave now, I never will."

I've thought the same thing. There's a certain window in life where it feels like you have to "live it up." I can't waste my youth. If I stay in Caelee my whole life, in twenty years will I be left asking *what if?*

"And California is way too far. I don't want to be that far removed from home. But if I went to school a couple of hours away, I think that would be the perfect happy medium. It's comforting to know that if another town or college doesn't work out, Caelee will still be here waiting for my return," he says.

"I completely understand where you are coming from. Maybe if you mentioned this to your dad, he would get it too."

"I don't know. I don't think so. He picks and chooses when he wants to play the 'dad role' for us. Evelyn and his new kids are the core classes, and Len and I are just the electives. We are an afterthought. So, it's hard for me to trust that he's suddenly coming around to be a good father," he mutters.

"It's completely valid for you to feel that way. He hasn't proven himself to be any different," I say.

"And what's messed up is that deep down, I still want his approval. Even though I hate him at times, I still want him to offer some praise. Some kind of encouragement. Anything," he says, his voice shaking.

"I'm so sorry, Carter," I say quietly.

A beat passes. His lip quivers. His Adam's apple bobs up and down.

"He doesn't even know me, Marlowe. He doesn't even fucking know me," he whispers. A tear falls down his cheek.

His right hand rests on his knee, with his left on the steering wheel. I reach over, lacing our hands together. His long fingers wrap in between mine and onto the back of my hand.

"I see you. I know you. And I like you. Carter, I truly don't know what I would do without you."

He bites bottom lip: his signature move for trying to hide his smile. I squeeze his hand three times.

I can hardly admit it to myself, let alone admitting it to him. Muttering so softly that even I can barely hear it, I whisper, "For the record, I'm not trying to sway you in one direction or the other. If you left, I would miss you *so much*. I can't imagine life without you. But you need to listen to your gut. Whether that's Windermere University or not."

We hit a red light after our exit. Slowing down the car, he swallows and looks at me. Tears pepper his eyelashes like morning dew drops on a spiderweb.

Leaning over, Carter brings his face to the top of my head. His lips brush my chestnut colored hair. Being this close, I can smell his aroma of September air. I look up, giving him a close lipped beam. If I open my mouth, I'll spill about how much he means to me. I can't ruin this moment with my word vomit.

In the last fifteen minutes of our ride, we sit in serene silence. I'm comforted about the words unsaid. The sweet nothings drift in the space between us, wrapping me in a warm blanket.

Nothing needs to be said.

Everything has already been said.

Carter pulls into the parking garage, circling each floor until we find a good parking spot. The muscles in his face have relaxed, seeming much more at ease than earlier.

Opening the car door, I step out and help him with his suitcase. "Thanks," he says quietly, and I have a feeling he is thanking me for a lot more than the luggage.

With my free hand, I walk around to sneak my hand into his. Not in a romantic way per se, but in a *Carter and Marlowe* way. We need each other.

I walk with Carter through the sliding doors of the airport, and he does a mental checklist to make sure he has everything. Sliding his carry-on across the gray terrazzo tile, we head towards TSA.

I wish I could hop on the plane and tell him that everything with his dad is going to be okay. Glancing at my phone, it's 5:03 AM. Time for us to part ways.

We stop, standing a few feet off to the side. Carter puts his bag down and takes a small step towards me. Before I know it, I'm surrounded by his freckled arms.

"Mar, about what I said in the car- I haven't really told anyone all of that before. Other than Lenny," his warm breath tickles across my neck. "Thank you. And for the record, I don't know what my life would be without you either."

My heart gets injected with helium, floating through my chest. I'm so aware of his skin touching mine. I'm sure that when he pulls away, there will be impressions of each of his fingerprints on my shoulders and back.

"Carter," I start to say. He moves his face so he can search my eyes. His jade green irises gleam even under the airport's fluorescent lighting.

"I'll call you. I know I'll definitely need a Marlowe call after this tour with my dad," he purses his lips. "If that's okay."

"Of course," I tell him. Standing on the tips of my toes, I reach back up and wrap my arms tighter around him.

Leaning up to his ear, I whisper the Windermere University chant.

"Go, cats, go."

CHAPTER TWENTY-SEVEN

The metal hangers squeak against the railing as Lenny digs through each dress rack. Jacob officially asked her to winter formal, so we decided to look for a dress at our local boutique. I'm holding seven dresses in my arms that Lenny has yet to try on.

"I just don't know what I'm feeling. What's the vibe?" Lenny asks, holding up a baby blue chiffon dress.

"Wait, that's cute. I don't know. I'm the wrong person to ask," I tell her. I love music and dancing around with my friends, but a formal event has never really been my thing. Maybe it's because I've always been alone or a third wheel for all the school dances.

In eighth grade, everyone was buzzing about who was going with who at the formal. Lenny and Jacob had just started dating, so the upcoming dance was all we could talk about.

I had my eyes on Austin Quinn, and I prayed and begged every day that he would ask me to the dance. We had our Health and Wellness class together, and I caught myself watching his face redden rather than listening to our teacher say that we could get Chlamydia and die.

Every time he walked near me, I felt my heart skip a beat. Turns out, he didn't want to go to the dance with me, but would rather ask out one of the cheerleaders. He asked her with a dozen doughnuts- which was *my* favorite dessert at the time.

At the actual eighth grade formal, I had a fairly good time third wheeling with Lenny and Jacob, but I couldn't stop staring at Austin. He slow danced with his cheerleader girlfriend, and I watched them like a full-on stalker. Not my proudest moment.

Ever since, I've not loved going to school dances, but I'm always down to help Lenny with dress shopping. It reminds me of when we used to play dress up in elementary school.

"Okay, I think this is all we can take into the dressing room for this round," Lenny says, motioning to our rainbow heap of fabric in my arms.

"For this round?"

"Yes. Obviously, I will need to scour the entire store before I say yes to the dress," Lenny chuckles.

Heading towards the back, I see the newly renovated fitting rooms. There's a catwalk-like platform going down the middle, dividing the two rows of fitting rooms. Floor length mirrors line the door to each fitting room. Hollywood light bulbs cast a bright, golden glow down to the fake marble floors.

The people of Caelee County are reluctant to fund the arts (like my mom's studio) but a prom dress store? Forget about it. This is one of the nicest places in town. Again, *a prom dress store.*

Lenny opens the door to a fitting room, and I pile into the small space. Hanging up each dress on the wall, I sort through which dress Lenny wants to try on first.

"Ooh! Let's do the baby blue one first," she says. I grab the gown, unzip it, and help her into the iridescent sky colored fabric. Fixing the clasp, I hear some rustling on the outside of our door.

"Lenny!! You look gorgeous!" I squeal. She does a little spin in the dressing room, knocking over her purse in the process. "Here, let's go outside so you can see it better."

She steps out of the room, and the Hollywood lights immediately cast an ethereal gleam onto Lenny. Doing another princess spin, I take out her phone and catch a video to send to Jacob.

"Walk the runway!" I say, eerily similar to a stage mom.

Looking dead serious, she sets her shoulders back. Lenny emphatically struts along the catwalk and tries to emulate the models on Instagram. We burst into a fit of giggles because it's so unlike Lenny to smolder like that.

The door of the fitting room across from us creaks open and a blur of pink chiffon brushes through the doorway. Simultaneously, Lenny and I look over to see the last person we'd expect.

"Oh. Hey guys," Maya says. She brushes her blonde hair out of her face, and her brown eyes glow under the ceiling lights.

"Hey," Lenny says. Quickly looking over at me, she tries to fill the void of awkwardness. A classic best friend move- coming to my rescue when I don't want to talk to my sworn enemy.

"Are you shopping for formal?" Maya asks, gesturing to Lenny's blue dress.

Lenny nods.

A beat passes.

"Are you going to the dance with Beau?" I ask bitterly. Of course, I know the answer. I saw his romcom worthy proposal in the hallway the other day.

The proposal that *wasn't* for me.

Maya purses her lips together, looking directly at me. Glancing at the mirror beside me, she sighs. Not a frustrated sigh. An I'm-exhausted-of-your-antics kind of sigh. "Yeah," she says.

Lenny looks between us and senses this is a level of discomfort that she can't save with small talk. "Well, I better get to trying on the fifty million dresses I picked out. It was good to see you, Maya!"

"Yeah, good to see you," I mutter and start to follow Lenny into the fitting room. Before I step through the doorway, Maya stops me.

"Marlowe?"

Turning around, she's still on the other side of the runway. She has her hair tucked behind both ears, exposing the pained expression on her face.

"I'm really sorry about everything with Beau. He told me about him basically ghosting you after you shared your feelings. And that you thought you were just on a break, not a break up."

"Um," I start to say. Closing the dressing room door behind me, Lenny locks me out of my best form of escape. I'm stuck on either side of a prom dress store runway with Maya Nguyen.

"I'm really sorry, Marlowe. When I saw you at his house, I thought you knew it was over and that you were done with him. That's why I was so excited to see you. I promise I wouldn't have gotten with him if I had known you thought you all were just taking a breather," she says meekly.

Scoffing, I cross my arms and look at her quizzically. "You wouldn't have?"

"No!" she says, her eyes growing wide.

I don't say anything.

She exhales, "Why do you hate me?"

The question forces me to take a step backward. Maya just pulled away the curtain of what I thought was my perfectly concealed loathing.

"I don't hate you," I say. I can't exactly admit to her face that she's been my nemesis since kindergarten.

"That's not true. You do. You hate me. I see the glances you make at me. The way you actively dismiss me when I talk. And this has been going on way before Beau. What did I do to you?" she says.

I have to remember to close my mouth from shock.

"Well, I didn't mean to do all that directly *at* you. I don't know. I just get annoyed."

Maya asks, "Get annoyed with what?"

"You! I don't know. Your perfection, I guess."

"My perfection? Marlowe, you've known me since I was five. You of all people should know how far from perfect I am."

I gape at her. Does she seriously not realize how loved she is at school? How loved she is by the whole town?

I thought Maya was cool in kindergarten. I wanted to be her friend—just like everyone else. But at some point, I grew tired of constantly being overshadowed by her popularity and limelight. The ripped jeans incident was the final nail in the coffin. By first grade, I officially couldn't stand Maya.

She walks towards me, sitting down on the runway. Motioning for me to do the same, she says, "Here. I want to get to the bottom of this."

I reluctantly walk towards her and follow suit, sitting with my legs crossed on the floor. "Don't you realize that guys think you can do no wrong?"

"What do you mean? Kevin and I fought all the time. So, I obviously did things wrong in his eyes," Maya tells me. "And the same goes for all my other exes."

"No, it's not just been with your boyfriends. It's everyone," I tell her. "Everyone sees you as perfect."

"I still don't understand," she says, shaking her head.

"Maya, I remember thinking this back in elementary school. It was Valentine's Day in fourth grade. I got three roses. You got *sixteen*. You got one from every guy in our class! I was so jealous."

She looks at me puzzled.

I elaborate, "You even got some from previous teachers. Maya, every single guy in the class gave you a rose. You had each of them wrapped around your finger at age nine."

Swallowing, she takes a second before she responds. She looks off at the side wall instead of looking at me. I can't get over how oblivious she's been about all of this.

"I don't even know what to say. I never asked the boys to get me those roses. I was just expecting some from my dads. That was *so* long ago," she says.

"Yeah, but it just shows how much the guys adored you- even when we were younger. They love you," I say.

She huffs. "Okay, let's say they all do love me. Do you know the kind of pressure that puts on *me*? The pressure to stay perfect or else they'll all dismiss me?"

I bite my thumbnail. Honestly, I haven't thought of that. Especially over these past few weeks, I've put an enormous amount of pressure on myself. I can't imagine struggling with that at such an early age.

I say, "But surely the highlight of their attention outweighed the pressure you put on yourself?"

"No. It wasn't like I could just be like, *Oh Kevin likes me. Pressure is gone!* It was always there, haunting me with what-ifs. What if they realize who I really am? What if I lose my novelty?" she says. Maybe it's just from the Hollywood lights around the fitting rooms, but I swear I can see her eyes swell with tears.

"I didn't realize that. I guess I was too busy envying you. I mean, you had what I always wanted," I mutter.

"What- attention from guys? Marlowe, it's really not all it's cracked up to be," she admits.

"You just don't get it," I say.

She shakes her head. "Speaking of elementary school, there were multiple times I remember wishing I was in your shoes."

WHAT?!

"Me? You wish you were in *my* shoes?" I ask incredulously. "Why?"

Maya tucks her hair behind her ears again. "Do you remember the chalk walk we had in fifth grade?"

I nod. Our elementary school started doing "chalk walks" for the students. They lined out spaces on the asphalt for kids to doodle in with chalk. Then, other students would go around and vote on the best ones. The top five kids with the most votes got to pick from a loaded treasure box. Some students won giant bubble kits, Barbie dolls, temporary tattoo mega packs, and a blow-up bouncy ball- aka the lottery for elementary schoolers.

The boys in our fifth grade class thought the chalk walk was "too girly" for them to participate. They all decided to play flag football during the chalk walk recess time. Lenny and I didn't care because that just meant that we had a better shot of winning the big prizes.

"At the time, I was dating Brian, and he was super against the chalk walk. Looking back, it was stupid to oppose it, but I think it was just his way of protecting his fragile masculinity," Maya continues.

I remember. I hated Brian. He was the one who pushed me down the hill at camp. And the one that claimed I cheated when racing on the water slide.

"Well, he insisted on me staying with the guys to be their cheerleader during their game of football. It seems silly, but I wanted to play with the chalk so badly. But every time I walked over to you all, the guys would call me back over to watch the game. I couldn't even do what I wanted to during recess!

"And yeah, I could have said no. But my ten-year-old self didn't want to ruffle any feathers. I just remember wanting to draw more than anything. Plus, I had my eye on the bouncy ball prize. But I didn't even get a chance to win it," Maya says.

Her honest recollection stirs my own memories. Suddenly, I remember that sunny day of the chalk walk. I was so jealous of Maya's attention from the guys. She was their ideal cheerleader. But it turns out that she didn't even *want* that attention.

"I had no idea," I say quietly. When I was younger, I felt the waves of envy overtake my little mind over and over. But I had no grounds to be envious of Maya. She was trapped in a social role that she didn't want to play.

"Yeah. And there were so many other times where I wanted to play on the swing set, talk to you and Lenny, or just get away from the guys," she says.

"You wanted to hangout with us?" I ask. I always assumed that deep down, Maya felt the same dislike for me that I had for her. I thought any kindness she showed me was fake.

I hated feeling left out by the guys in our class. I hated feeling like they never noticed me. And if they did, they didn't see the real me.

And to think that *I* might have made Maya feel the same way?

"Yes! I wanted to have a friendship like you all have. Sure, I have several girl friends. But I've never had the kind of best friendship that you and Lenny had and *still* have. It's almost a sisterly bond," Maya says.

Looking at her, I realize she's just a girl. She's not this ultra queen bee mean girl that I have built up in my head.

Do I even really know Maya?

"I'm sorry. I feel like I never even gave you a chance. No, I *know* I never gave you a chance," I say. "I'm sorry, Maya."

She shrugs. "I mean I think the pressure that comes from guys has always distanced me a little from everyone. Even if that pressure wasn't wanted."

"To be honest, I just always assumed that the male admiration was some kind of orchestration on your part. My jealousy has always put you on a pedestal," I say sheepishly.

Maya pulls her knees up to her chest, the pink fabric billowing over like a waterfall. "I am *not* on a pedestal."

"What do you mean?"

"Marlowe, I'm a Vietnamese American girl living in the south with two dads. I am on anything but a pedestal.

"You haven't gotten the stares that my family has when we go into the small, Boomer-owned stores. You haven't seen how hard my dads had to fight for Caelee to host a Pride festival. Or, you know when I got all those roses from past teachers? In fourth grade?"

"Yeah," I nod.

"My past teachers got those for me because there was a homophobic parent who went off on my dads in a PTA meeting. She was saying how she didn't want her kid around 'my kind of family.' I didn't really understand it at the time. I just remember my dads were upset. My previous teachers sent those roses more to my dads than to me. That was their small act of solidarity," she says.

I gape at her. Thinking back to nine-year-old Maya, I can't imagine dealing with that kind of discrimination. She was dealing with all of that, and my envy completely overlooked it.

"I'm sorry, Maya. I didn't know that. I don't even know what to say," I tell her. Maya has always been herself. I was the one who put the mask of perfection on her.

"I mean, it's fine. I just feel like people don't know the real me," she says, wiping her nose.

Sitting here, I realize *I* don't really know Maya. I don't know her the past superficial things. I've judged a version of her that I created in my head.

Maybe it's because of my new therapist. Maybe it's because I have done a lot of interior reflection lately. Maybe it's because I understand pressure. Maybe it's because I want to be the best version of myself. And that means changing the way I've been towards her.

I don't want to be that girl anymore. I don't want to hate Maya Nguyen.

"I've been so judgmental towards you. Even since kindergarten. I was so insecure and envious, and I didn't even take the time to actually know you. I don't want to be that way now. I want to be better," I say.

Maya nods, and a small smile peeks from her lips.

I breathe. "Maya, can we start over?"

She untucks her hair behind her ears and starts to stand up. Seeing her step towards me, I rise to meet her. She leans in for a hug.

"Of course, Marlowe."

CHAPTER TWENTY-EIGHT

The smell of fresh laundry drifts throughout my closet as I put away my clean clothes. I procrastinated doing laundry for a few days, but I knew it was bad when the last clean pair of jeans I had was two sizes too small.

When Lenny and I got back from dress shopping yesterday, I looked through some of my spring dresses to see if any of them would work for the winter formal. *If* I decide to go.

After about an hour of trying on my old dresses, I concluded that nothing would work. Everything was either too short, too tight around my boobs, or itchy- kind of like every dress Lenny convinced me to try on at the boutique. Nothing worked.

Luckily for Len, she found the perfect dress for her. It's a satiny, floor length, yellow dress that makes her strawberry blonde hair pop. It fit like a glove and was even on clearance! A true romcom moment.

Buzz buzz. Buzz buzz.

Setting down my folded pajamas, I walk over to my desk to answer my ringing phone. I'm not expecting a call from anyone. Although there is a small chance it could be Maya.

We've been texting back and forth, trying to actually get to know each other better. After our heart to heart conversation, I have felt awful about my misjudgment of her. At least we are building a friendship now, even if it's in our second to last year of high school. Better late than never.

Grabbing my phone, it's actually a call from Carter. He's still in California with his dad visiting CalTech. I've gotten a few texts from him, but apparently Paul has planned the itinerary to the second, so Carter hasn't had much time to talk.

Answering the phone, I say, "Hello?"

"Hey, Mar. Do you have a minute to talk?" Carter asks. His voice sounds... *different.*

"Of course. What's up?"

"I just needed to talk. But I don't want to bother you if you are busy," he says.

"Carter, you would never bother me," I tell him.

"It's my dad. I've really been struggling on this trip."

"What happened?" I ask.

"I feel like I'm sightseeing at a zoo or something. I don't know. I'm at the neighborhood park right now, so if you hear cars going by, that's what that is. I just had to get out of that house," he says.

"What do you mean a zoo?" I say, grabbing my phone and sitting down on my bed.

"I don't know, I just feel like there's some kind of glass barrier between us. I'm staying in the guest bedroom, and every time I wake up, I have to walk by the kids' rooms and Paul and Evelyn's room. I feel like I'm doing some type of psych study on a family.

"Do you know that episode in *Parks and Recreation* where Leslie visits Jerry's family? And they are over the top optimistic and fake? That's what it feels like. But I feel like a downer or something if I don't match their energy. It's just that the energy feels fake when it comes to Paul," he says.

"That's totally valid. I mean, Paul has never really been there for you, so I'm sure seeing him super involved with the kids is off-putting," I say.

"Yeah," he sighs. "It just feels so ingenuine. When we were on the tour today, Dad acted like he was The Man or something. He would point stuff out around campus and give facts as if *he* was the tour guide. It was so embarrassing," he says.

I pull the fuzzy blanket on my bed up and around my shoulders. I tell Carter, "Oh my gosh. That's awful."

"And he has all these things planned for me when I supposedly select CalTech as my college. He wants us to go on a road trip over to Malibu with Evelyn and the kids. I mean, they are okay. I just can't look at Evelyn and not think about my dad's affair. It's so screwed up," he says.

"Do you think that planning all this is his way to try to make up for the years of disinterest in you and Lenny?" I ask.

"I don't know. I've tried to understand him so many times, but I just can't. That's why I can't go to school here. Paul decided to leave, and he can't just invite me into his life almost ten years after *he* initially left. That's not how families work," he replies.

"How was he on the tour? Other than acting like he owned the place. Did he sense that you don't want to go there?"

"No," Carter says. I wish I could see his face right now. "It's like he has blinders on and doesn't even care to notice where I actually want to go to school. He introduced me to his old business professor who's still kicking. Like he wanted me to meet the professor because Dad fully expects me to have the same major he had at CalTech. He is confident that I'll go there. There's no getting out of it."

"This is just making me hate Paul more," I say. "And surely he will understand that you don't want to go there. It's *your* college career, not his."

"Yeah, but he's so self-absorbed that all he sees is his own agenda. When we were out today, I felt invisible half the time and under an unwanted spotlight the other half," he says, inhaling a shaky breath. "Mar, why do I have such a shitty father?"

"I don't know. You deserve so much more," I say. I squeeze my fingers around the tufts of my blanket, as if I'm holding his hand.

"I just- I can't do this anymore. Even staying in their house and walking through the hallways makes my stomach drop. It's all pictures of Paul and his new kids. It's not that he has no time to be a dad, he just has no time to be *my* dad," he says barely above a whisper.

My chest aches.

"Carter, I wish I could hug you right now. I am *so* sorry," I tell him.

"And," he pauses, his voice breaking. On the other end of the phone, I hear him breathe in and out.

He takes another breath.

"And he still fucking calls me McCartney."

The words slip into my mind and settle into an old memory that I had almost forgotten. Twenty years ago, when Carter's parents first got together, Paul was a spiky haired stoner whose sole purpose in life was to let loose after constantly studying to get his business degree from prestigious CalTech. To say he had a wild side after his college days is an understatement. Sheila was initially drawn to Paul's free spirit because it seemed like the perfect compliment to her more concrete personality type.

When Sheila found out she was pregnant with Carter, Paul begged and begged if he could name their first kid. He was ecstatic to have a son, and Paul was determined to be the one that would don Carter with his name. Sheila reluctantly agreed.

At the time- and still to this day- Paul claimed that they didn't make music the way they used to. I've never known who "they" is.

Paul's favorite music is not from this century, and it's purely male musicians. So after Sheila labored for nine hours, she birthed her first son, and Paul named him McCartney as a nod to the lead singer of The Beatles and *his* own first name.

Paul and McCartney. Two peas in a pod.

Apparently, Carter hated his name when he was younger. It was long and hard to say, and he was embarrassed by it. It wasn't a "normal" name. So when he started kindergarten, he started going by Carter.

The same goes for Lenny. By the time of her birth, Paul was still dead set on naming the kids, and somehow Sheila let him. Thus, his two children, McCartney and Lennon, were able to carry on the legacy of Paul's favorite band.

Of course, I didn't know Carter when he was in kindergarten. Lenny told me all of this when we met a few years later. Even though Lenny and Carter decided to go by nicknames, Paul has always called them by their original "band" names. Lenny didn't really care, but I remember her saying it always got under Carter's skin.

"He *still* calls you that? Even though he knows you don't like it?" I ask Carter.

His voice shakes, and I hear him sniffle through the phone. "Yeah."

"What is *wrong* with him?" I ask.

"He doesn't even know me, Mar. My own father doesn't even know me," he cries out. The pain seeps through his voice like syrup running over a too-sweet pancake.

"I'm so sorry, Carter," I say. I know I've said it a million times, but it's all I can offer. It's incredibly unfair that Carter is stuck with a dad like Paul. I tell him, "I wish I was there with you."

"I wish you were too," he says. "I haven't felt this bad in a long time."

I shake my head. I cannot imagine what he's dealt with. If I could take it from him, I would.

Carter says, "I don't even know. I just want to leave. Once I graduate and go to Windermere or wherever I end up, I'm intentionally not going to see Paul much. I think being around my dad brings out the worst parts of myself," Carter tells me, his voice quivering.

"What do you mean?" I ask.

"You know how I told you that I got super anxious after my parents' divorce? And I started having my weird anxiety with honesty? It's like even though that was almost ten years ago, that anxiety still creeps in every time I'm around him," he says. "So when I'm around Paul, I *think* I'm the worst version of myself. I can't be honest with him about who I am. I think I'm crazy. I'm anxious. I'm in my head. I'm excluded from his new life. It just becomes one giant spiral."

I want to touch him. I want to hug him. I want to hold him. I want to be with him.

"Everything that has happened between your parents is on Paul. It's *not* on you. And you shouldn't blame yourself for reacting to Paul's behavior. He's proven himself to be dishonest. He's proven himself to be a terrible husband and father. So don't beat yourself up over reacting to this.

"You taught me about my anxiety. About how to cope. About how it doesn't change who I am. Carter, you saw me that day in the hallway. You still cared for me even though I was anxious.

"Right now, I still care for you, even if you are anxious. I still see you. Having anxiety around your dad doesn't mean that you're crazy. It doesn't mean that you aren't still Carter. Your dad doesn't define who you are and aren't," I say. "And I'm here for you. I'm not leaving you."

A beat passes. He lets out an uneven breath. "Marlowe, I-"

Another uneven breath.

"You have no idea what that means to me," Carter whispers.

"I mean it," I say.

"It's just that this whole situation has reminded me of how unprepared

I am for college. I *think* I know what I want to do. But I truly have no idea what will actually happen."

"But is anyone ever ready for college? I think we put so much emphasis on getting our lives together that we forget we don't *have* to have our lives together," I assure him. "I have so much faith in you. Whatever you do- you'll be incredible."

"I don't know," he says. "Earlier today, Evelyn and the kids were watching Alice and Wonderland. I loved that movie when I was younger. But when Alice fell through the rabbit hole, all we could focus on was the magical world that lay before her when she landed."

"Yeah," I say, pulling my blanket tighter across my shoulders.

"It's called Alice and Wonderland. It's not Alice and the Rabbit Hole. But what she didn't tell us- and what we hate to admit- is how terrifying it is to fall," Carter says.

He's right. The entire root of my panic attack during the ACT was fear of failure. I was *literally* terrified of falling behind.

He continues, "It's exactly like Alice and Wonderland. You fall into this dark abyss, and you don't know what lies beyond it. When you think of your future, you look at the end product, not the painstaking process.

"And I kept thinking, when they were watching the movie, that Alice didn't really like Wonderland. She fell. And fell. Yet, she wasn't even fully happy with Wonderland!

"She wanted to go home. So will I? After this process of college decisions. After I go to Windermere. After this season of life. After I reach the other side, will I still be longing for home?" he asks, his voice shattering like a crack in a windshield that fully distorts your vision.

I can hear his spiral. I can hear how much he's struggling.

"Then I ask myself," Carter says. "Will I long for the right now? Will I miss the rabbit hole? Will I miss Wonderland?"

He breathes. "Will I miss it at all?"

His words hit me like a gut punch. I know that kind of worry. I know those frenzied thoughts.

"If I could take *that* anxiety away from you, I would. I wish so badly that I could. All I know is that you are strong, Carter. You are capable. You can do this. I believe in you," I tell him. I hug my knees to my chest, wishing I was hugging him instead.

"I miss you so much," he says softly.

"I miss you, too. I wish I was with you right now," I say.

"You are the source of my homesickness," he says. I feel my breath hitch.

I smile into the phone. "I can't wait to see you tomorrow."

He replies, "Me either."

We sit in a comfortable silence. Carter exhales.

"How are you feeling now? Are you still anxious?"

"Not as much. I'm feeling much better. Thank you, Mar," he says.

"Of course," I say softly.

"I'm so grateful to have someone like you in my life," he tells me. I smile, pinching myself that this is real life.

"I'm not leaving you, Carter."

CHAPTER TWENTY-NINE

"How have you been feeling lately? Do you think seeing Denise is helping?" Mom asks, sprinkling more shredded cheese onto her burrito bowl.

"Yeah, I'm feeling much better than I did a few weeks ago," I tell her. "And I'm trying to journal every night before bed."

My therapist said it would take time to change my thought patterns. The other night, I was working on an essay for English, and I found myself starting to become anxious. Second guessing everything I wrote, I started to feel like I couldn't do anything right. I was teetering on the edge of my spiral, so close to fully diving in.

I stepped away from my computer, trying to remember what Denise taught me to do. When a bike rides on a dirt path over and over again, it starts to pave a new path. That new path makes it much easier to ride along.

But that route may not always be the best way to go. If you're riding on the path, but want to take a detour, it's really difficult to leave the already paved path. When my mind is used to self doubt and anxious thoughts, it's that much harder to switch gears and get out of that mind space.

When I'm feeling anxious, I can follow that path into worry. As I've learned, I have to intentionally make the effort to change my thought patterns in order to cope. I have to form a new path myself.

I am capable. I am strong. I can do this. I trust myself to do this. I believe in myself.

I know I'm not going to change my spirals overnight. But with Denise's help, change doesn't feel impossible.

"We are really proud of you, kid. Seems like things are going pretty well. Do you think so?" Dad asks.

"Thanks," I say, leaning over our kitchen table to grab more salsa. "Yeah, I do. I'm really trying."

"It takes a lot of courage to talk with someone and be vulnerable enough to open up. And it takes even more courage to make the effort to work on yourself," Mom says.

Blushing, I say, "Thank you all. It means a lot."

Mom asks, "What are your plans for tonight? I know you mentioned that Carter was going to pick you up later."

"Yeah, I think he's coming by in half an hour," I say. "And I have no idea what we are doing. He just said he has a surprise for me."

Carter flew in today while Lenny and I were at school, so his mom picked him up at the airport. I haven't seen him since he's been back, but he texted me a couple of hours ago. He said he couldn't wait to see me and asked if I was free tonight.

I wanted to melt right there in the middle of class.

"Okay," my dad says. "Just make sure you are in by 11:00."

"I will!"

"I don't worry as much when you are with Carter," Dad tells me. He has basically watched Carter grow up with me, so Dad has always favored him over the other guys I hung out with.

When I was in elementary school, Carter started to take guitar lessons from my dad. Dad was a guitar fanatic, and Carter's love for music really started to take off at age ten after his parents' divorce. Carter's dad, Paul, knows how to play guitar. But Carter didn't want to learn from him. I think he felt closer to my dad than he did with Paul.

I remember Dad would always shake his head and laugh because Carter could learn a song in record time. In between lessons, Carter would learn an extra song that my dad didn't assign. He said he just wanted to "surprise" my dad with another song.

"Oh! Speaking of working on myself, I talked to Maya the other day."

"You did?" Mom asks.

I nod. "Yeah! Honestly, I have never really taken the time to get to know her. We saw Maya when Lenny and I went dress shopping the other day. I realized I was just really jealous of her. But she's actually cool."

"I'm proud of you for that, kid," my dad tells me.

"That is awesome! Definitely a Barbie movie moment," Mom winks. The *Barbie* movie has become her new personality trait since she's seen it. She can quote the America Ferrera monologue in her sleep.

We need more girls supporting girls. And that can start with me.

I watched a video the other day that said you can't really love someone until you love yourself. I've meditated, I've journaled, and I've moved past grievances with friends. In order for me to find love in the future, I have to get myself in check first.

Finishing up our dinner, I help my Dad with the dishes. Even small moments like this make me so grateful to have the parents that I have. Paul, Carter's dad, is the human equivalent of a pile of dog poop. My heart becomes three times heavier when I think of the dad Carter has versus the dad he deserves.

Wiping my hands on the dish towel, I glance out of our kitchen window. Bright lights shine through the blinds, letting me know that the moment I've looked forward to since this afternoon is finally here.

I run past my dad in the kitchen and past my mom in the living room. Swinging open the front door, I barrel down the stairs as he pulls into my driveway.

"CARTER!"

He puts the car in park, opens his door, and jogs towards me with his arms wide. He didn't even turn his car off.

"Mar!" he yells back. We meet in front of his car's bright headlights, illuminating us like actors on a stage.

He wraps his arms around my waist, and I sling mine around his neck. Picking me up, he swings me around, and I breath in his cool forest aroma. I feel like I haven't seen him in ten years.

His fingertips lightly press into my side as he sets me back down. Biting the inside of his cheek, he tries to hide his smile.

"I missed you," I say, keeping my arms around his neck.

"I missed you, too," he whispers in my ear. My heart does a full somersault.

"You ready?" he asks, smirking slightly.

"I have no idea what to expect," I tell him.

"Guess you'll have to wait and see," he winks.

I giggle and turn around to go close the front door. Before locking it, I call out a goodbye to my parents.

"Bye! Have fun!" Mom yells back, giving me a look as if she's going to start singing the "K-I-S-S-I-N-G in a Tree" song.

I hop down the stairs to meet Carter at his car. He's holding the passenger door open for me, with Pickles in his other hand.

"Part one of the surprise," he says, shrugging his shoulders.

Looking at him, mouth agape, I can't believe I used to put Carter into the box of being my best friend's brother. How could I not notice someone who has been there all along? How could I not notice someone who has grown into my safe space and my home?

I grab Pickles from Carter and settle into the passenger seat. Pickles immediately lays down in my lap, licking my wrist as I pet him. Carter walks around the car and gets in. Eyeing his dog and me, he smiles and exposes his right dimple.

"Okay, so I need to distract you, so you don't notice where we are driving to," Carter says. "On the plane, I kept hearing songs that reminded me of you, so I made a playlist."

"You made a playlist for me?" I ask him, my eyes wide.

"Well, yeah. If that's okay," Carter says.

"If that's okay?! Of course that's okay," I say, turning to him. He looks out of the back window, puts an arm behind my headrest, and backs out of my driveway. "Carter, that's literally the nicest thing anyone has ever done for me."

Chuckling, he hits play on his Spotify playlist, and the gentle strumming of electric guitar spreads throughout his speakers. He knows me so well. "Kilby Girl" by The Backseat Lovers is one of my favorite songs of all time.

"I love this song!" I exclaim. Pickles is completely flopped over in my lap, wanting me to scratch his belly.

I look over at Carter drumming his thumbs on the steering wheel. His golden orange hair is extra floppy today, with one specific curl hanging in front of his forehead.

I've grown up more over the last month than I have throughout the last year. That infamous day of the ACT solidified the connection that Carter and I have. The constant anxiety that I had for approval from guys- mainly Beau- accumulated into an intense need for approval in my school career.

My parents didn't put pressure on me to do well on the ACT. They never said that I had to get a perfect score. I did that.

I was so used to putting that pressure on myself to be perfect socially at school, that it morphed into a need for academic perfection. I can't help but see the correlation between Beau and I's fake relationship and my freak out at the ACT.

With Beau, I was always searching. I was searching for that affirmation and praise that he really *did* like me. I wasn't content enough with who I was to reassure myself. I *needed* Beau's approval.

Fast forward to now, I've put in the work to improve my self image. Seeing Denise and journaling has helped me take the first few steps to distance myself from the girl I was before.

Before I loved myself enough to find the one person who was made for me. Before I really *knew* him.

Before I realized that Carter was the guy I was truly Boysick for.

"Oh, I love this next one," he says, motioning towards his car stereo.

Lucy Dacus's vocals serenade us as Carter drives down the winding roads lined with skeleton trees. The lyrics in "True Blue" by boygenius remind me of a modern, realistic type of love.

"And it feels good to be known so well," Carter sings along with Lucy. *"I can't hide from you the way that I hide from myself."*

I glance over at him, and his peachy lips form a small smile. When I'm with Carter, I get a feeling that resembles when the springtime sun peeks from the clouds after months of gray skies.

"I remember who I am when I'm with you," I sing back to Carter. Taking a hand off the steering wheel, he interlaces his freckled fingers with mine. Pickles snuggles deeper into my lap.

We take a familiar turn to the right as the next song, "Kiss Me" by Sixpence None the Richer, plays in the car.

Carter pulls into the parking lot of Camp Caelee and drives over to the main building. Turning to him shocked, I say, "Campe Caelee?! You're taking me to Camp Caelee?!"

He puts the car in park and grins, "Surprise!"

"I haven't been here in forever," I tell him.

"Well, I still mow Miss Pat's lawn every summer, so I asked if we could have some after-hours access," he says. Carter was always the owner's favorite.

"I can't believe this," I say. My chest swells with excitement. I put Pickles' harness on, and Carter connects his leash. Doing something as simple as dog walking seems like an adventure when I'm with Carter.

Walking across the paved parking lot, we start to head to the backwoods. I'm just following Carter's lead. I walk in line with him, and our arms brush against one another. The feeling of his arm hairs tickling mine sends shock waves through my body, as if I've just hit my funny bone.

"Oh! I had one last song for you," he says, winking.

"What is it?" I ask and try to take a peek at his phone.

He clicks his volume all the way up and the familiar snaps of the song send me back to my childhood days. I'm getting serious deja vu. I'm almost positive I listened to "Cruisin' for a Bruisin'" from *Teen Beach Movie* with Carter at Camp Caelee ten years ago.

He jumps and turns to me, singing. Adding in snaps of his own, Carter croons, *"You better run, run, run, here we come. Revving our engines under the sun!"*

I can't stop giggling. Carter is holding Pickles' leash in one hand, and in the other, he's trying to recreate the dance moves from the movie.

"You're cruisin' for a bruisin'!" he sings, jumping around as Pickles wags his tail.

Even when he's being goofy, Carter can still sing and dance like a professional. He's like my very own redheaded Ross Lynch.

At this point, I'm practically skipping across the gravel path to keep up with Carter's dance-walking. Now, he's miming that he is riding a motorcycle. I don't know if I've ever been more attracted to this man.

"C'mon, Mar! I know you know these lyrics!" he says in between the chorus and the verse.

Trying to emulate Lelah from *Teen Beach,* I sing, *"Bubblegum, cherry pop, go to the hop!"*

I start jumping around like Carter, and Pickles looks between us like we are crazy. Tucking my hair behind my ears, I scream-sing, *"Hanging with my brother cause his friends are so hot!"*

Carter chimes in to sing, *"While they're cruisin' for some bruisin'!"*

His curls bounce around as he does the dance perfectly. Just in time for Ross Lynch's verse, Carter grabs my hands and we jump around in a circle. The setting sun casts an amber glow onto our jam session. I can't help but smile because this feels so nostalgic. I've seen this film before, and I *loved* the ending.

Finishing up the song, Carter's cheeks flush with color, and his grin sends me into an orbit of Boysickness.

As we settle back in line with one another, we keep walking along the rocky path. Looking over at me, Carter smirks and says, "I have one more surprise for you."

"What?!"

"Obviously, I wanted us to take Pickles for a walk across camp. But I wanted us to visit somewhere else while we were here," he says.

Grabbing my hand, he leads Pickles and I over to the wooded area of Camp Caelee. Crunching across the fallen leaves, Carter brings us over to the giant red maple tree in the middle of the woods. I glance up to see that our favorite childhood hangout spot is still there.

They built the caramel colored tree house during my first summer at Camp Caelee. Ten years ago, it was an instant hit among campers. It was the perfect tree house for our imaginative selves. Lenny and I used to pretend it was our life-size fairy house. We would pretend that we were Fawn and Rosette from Pixie Hollow. Carter would climb up occasionally to play with us, and I would imagine he was Terrence bringing us pixie dust.

"It's still here?!" I ask. "I didn't expect it to hold up this long."

"Yeah! Do you want to go up?"

"Of course," I tell him.

"I'll go first in case it falls apart or something when I'm climbing up halfway," Carter chuckles. He picks up the ten pound Chihuahua, and Carter zips Pickles into his sweatshirt as if it's a baby carrier.

"Okay! Be careful," I tell him. He smiles at me as if he's an eight-year-old boy trying to impress his crush. I hope he's trying to impress his crush, and I hope it's me.

Carter climbs up the wooden ladder with ease, and he takes Pickles out of his jacket to set him down on the floor of the tree house. Once they are both up, I start to scale the rickety ladder.

Twelve rungs later, I reach the top. Carter extends a hand to help me up, and my palm fits perfectly into his.

Standing up, I look around my childhood sanctuary. There's still pictures from camp over the years, with several new photos of people I don't know. The smell of cedar reminds me of sweaty summer days filled with popsicles and water guns.

Scanning how much the tree house has aged, I lightly trace my fingers against the wooden walls. Carter watches me revisit the hut that refreshes so many forgotten memories.

Towards the front window lies a bench, just wide enough for Carter and I to sit down. After unhooking his leash, Pickles lies down at Carter's feet. Pickles is such a mood; his favorite things in the world are Carter and sleep.

"He's exhausted," Carter says to his dog, pitching his voice a bit higher.

I scoot closer to him, our hip bones practically conjoined together. I can't stop looking into his jade eyes. They are emerald stones drawing me towards the real treasure.

Picking at the cuticles of his thumbnail, Carter says, "I just wanted to thank you. For being there for me while I was with my dad."

"Carter, that was nothing. You've been there for me so much, and I'm afraid I'll never be able to repay you for what you've done for me," I tell him.

He smiles softly. "I'm so happy to be back home."

"I'm happy you are back too," I say.

"I feel like I'm living in an alternate reality by being here with you right now," he says.

"What do you mean?"

"I mean, when we were younger I was strictly your best friend's brother. I don't want to speak for you or anything, but I feel like now there's something more between us," he says and looks out of the tree house window.

"I think there is something more between us," I agree.

He bites the scar on his bottom lip. "I've wanted there to be something more between us since before I can remember."

"What do you mean?"

"When we were at camp, all those years ago, I knew you liked Beau. I didn't want to ruin that for you or get in the way. You were always so happy when you were around him. But I wanted so badly to just switch places with him," Carter tells me as the sun dips into the horizon. He leans over to switch on the tree house's battery operated lamps.

I gape at him. "When we were kids, you liked me?"

"Yeah," he says, glancing up through his copper eyelashes. "I made Lenny swear that she wouldn't tell you. Because I knew I wasn't Beau Braxton."

"Screw Beau Braxton," I say, shaking my head. "I can't believe you liked me back then. I had no idea."

Pushing his hair back, Carter looks away again. "Well, I didn't just like you then. I like you now, Mar."

The back of my throat tingles, and my eyebrows pinch together. My eyes prick with tears, but I will myself to stop the crying before it happens.

Carter Taylor is *the* standard.

With his face blushing, he tells me, "I like you. I like the way you double knot your shoelaces to make sure that your shoes won't come untied throughout the day. I like how every time I see you, my heart speeds up a little, and it's an instant mood booster. I like the way I can call you at any hour, and I know you are going to pick up.

"I like how you tuck your hair behind your ears and listen to your music at full volume. I like how you pick out the pretzels of every bowl of Chex Mix you eat. I like who I am when I'm with you. I like *you*, Marlowe."

I look at him, shocked. How could such a perfect guy be under my nose this entire time?

"Carter," I start to say. There's no stopping my crying now. My eyes swell, and a tear falls down my cheek like racing raindrops on a car window.

He leans closer to me. He takes his thumb, lightly swiping it below my eye.

"I don't deserve you," I say, my voice shaking. "What about the other girls, like Phoebe from a few months ago? What about all the other girls you've liked before?"

He keeps his hand at my jaw and traces his fingertips across my cheekbones. "Lenny has always given me a hard time about how I could never keep a relationship. I would try to make it work with the other girls, I really did."

"Then what happened?" I ask.

"I wanted you again," he whispers, his green eyes softening.

My lips part to say something, but no words come out.

I bring my hands to his shoulder, and I lightly run my finger across the side of his freckled neck. Electricity runs under my touch.

"I like you too, Carter," I whisper to him. "I like you a lot."

He leans closer to me. I can smell the sweetness of coconut in his shampoo, the salt air aroma in his soap, and the fresh linen scent in his clothes.

The freckles line his nose like stars in the night. In that sky, I see a shooting star. I make a wish.

I move closer to him, our faces inches from each other. Carter brings his other hand to the bottom of my chin. He whispers, and it sounds like the rippling of autumn wind.

"Can I kiss you?" he asks.

Nodding my head ever so slightly, I lean in towards him. Our lips touch softly, and I could melt right here, right now.

The kiss is warm and comforting, like a long welcome after time away.

The kiss is what I've been waiting for my whole life.

The kiss is enchanting.

The kiss feels like home.

I softly run my hand through the back of his hair, his curls wrapping around my fingers. He places a hand on my waist, pulling me closer to him.

His lips flutter against mine like the wings of a monarch butterfly. He kisses the tip of my nose, my cheek, and back to my smiling lips. I kiss the space where the corner of his jaw meets his neck. Goosebumps line my arms, mimicking the freckles that line his.

He pulls back for a second. He lifts his gaze from my lips to look directly into my eyes. He smiles, curling his coral lips upwards and exposing both of his dimples.

"How are you even real?" he says, running a hand through the side of my hair.

I chuckle lightly, taking in the spearmint smell of his lips. "How am I real?! Carter, look at you."

Cupping my jaw, he leans in and presses his lips to mine. With his touch, memories flash before my eyes.

Us playing together at camp. Me at his house watching my favorite romcoms. Us sitting together in Leadership class. Him giving me his car blanket after I fell into Maya's pool. Us taking walks together after school. Him comforting me after my panic attack. Me comforting him after his trip with his dad.

Me.

Him.

Us.

I have not experienced truly knowing someone before us. The us: Carter and Marlowe as a unit. It's as natural as the sound of a songbird or the gentle gust of wind rippling through my hair.

It takes me back in time. It takes me to the future. All that I know is that in every universe, he is mine.

And I am his.

He pulls back, rubbing his thumb across my jaw. Even though it's just the two of us, he whispers, "We should probably head back."

I nod, tucking my hair behind both ears. Carter stands up, waking Pickles from his nap. He picks up the pup and zips Pickles up in his jacket. I follow Carter down the ladder, although it's hard for me to hold on because my hands are shaking so badly. No one tells you the side effects of your dreams coming true.

We walk back to his car in a comfortable silence. Each time I glance over to him, he's got a small smile that mirrors mine. Our new bond surrounds us like a warm cloak.

Heading to his car, Carter opens my passenger door and sits Pickles on the cloth seat. He looks down at his watch and tells me, "It's not as late as I thought it was. Do you want one last surprise?"

"Yeah," I say, biting back an ear to ear grin.

Carter digs around his car and pulls out a BlueTooth speaker. He connects his phone and places the speaker next to Pickles. Leaving the passenger door open, music floats over to us while Pickles just stares at us from the car seat.

"Do you want to dance?" Carter asks. The parking lot street light illuminates Carter's constellation of freckles. He extends his long, slender fingers out to mine.

"Of course," I say, not even bothering to hide my smile.

Hozier's melodic voice fills the space between us as Carter places his hands at the small of my back. His hands nestle into my waist as if we are destined to be together.

I wrap my arms around his neck and shoulders, laying my head against his chest. We sway together slowly under the golden streetlight. I don't even care if the wind has grown chilly; I'm content and warm within his embrace.

Mitski's "My Love Mine All Mine" follows Hozier's verse in exactly the same order as my own "slow dancing in the dark" playlist on Spotify.

I look up into his green eyes, and Carter is already smiling down on me. I ask, "Is this my playlist?"

"I may or may not have stalked your Spotify before tonight," he says.

I reach up and kiss his lips, my smile touching his smile.

We dance under the luminescence of the street light. The golden glow acts as the sun, and we are the orbiting planets.

I want to stay in this universe forever.

Once our waltz ends, Carter walks me over to his car, waking Pickles up. I settle into his seat as if it's my horse drawn carriage taking me home from the ball. On our drive back to my house, he places his hand on my thigh, my skin immediately warming up under his touch.

The car ride ends too abruptly. The night ends too abruptly. He pulls into my driveway, putting his car in park. His eyes stare into mine, as if to say a million thrown out speeches.

He moves towards me, lightly holding my chin. Our lips meet in the middle, greeting each other with one last kiss. I can't get enough of him. I breathe him in, letting his presence engulf me like a cloud of serenity.

"I like you," I whisper to him.

He bites the scar on his lip before his soft smile peeks through. "I like you, too."

Carter walks me over to my front door and squeezes my hand three times before I walk inside. Glancing through the window, I watch him drive away. There's no need for me to say goodbye. We don't need greetings to bookend our meetings; we're timeless.

I quietly walk up the stairs to my bedroom, trying not to wake my parents. Instead of flopping onto my bed like I usually do when I get home, I walk over to my closet. I dig through shoe boxes of knick-knacks and old sweaters that are too small.

My hands trace a plastic, hot pink box from my childhood. Littered with stickers and glitter on the outside, I open it up and find exactly what I'm looking for.

My eyes first catch a small pile of the friendship bracelets heaping in the corner of the box. Pink, green, blue, and purple weave together to recall the years of sitting at the picnic tables to make as many friendship bracelets as humanly possible.

Moving the bracelets out of the way, I see a small French Bulldog figurine that Lenny and I found in the camp's woods one day. Per the "finders keepers" rule, we obviously had to bring it home with us.

At the bottom of the chest is the real treasure. A small stack of photographs beckons me to rifle through each one.

The top photograph is Lenny and I sliding down the giant water slide, with our hair going every which way. The second and third picture is a group of campers and I tie dying some t-shirts under the hot June sun. The fourth picture consists of Lenny and I feeding the ducks at the pond small tears off of a loaf of bread.

The last photograph forces me to set back on my heels. It glows between my fingertips. I walk over to turn on my lamp so I can analyze every detail.

It's a group photo of Lenny, Carter, Beau and I at age ten. We have each of our small arms wrapped around each other, and we still have our multi-colored rock climbing harnesses on.

I'm standing in between Carter and Beau. I'm leaning into Beau, I guess trying to flirt with him. My ponytail almost touches his shoulder. I'm grinning ear to ear at the camera. I remember freaking out that Beau had his arm around me.

But I never noticed the other person who had an arm around me. Carter's sunburnt face isn't looking at the camera like everyone else. His ginger hair is sopping wet from the pool, and I can see his small fingers wrapped around my shoulder.

He's got on a Spiderman t-shirt with his bright red swimming trunks. Leaning towards me, he just looks so adorable. Why didn't I just look over?

In the picture, I'm looking at the camera, wanting to preserve the "moment" between Beau and me. Instead of smiling to the camera, Carter's looking over at me with a wide grin dancing on his lips.

He's looking at me like I'm some kind of jewel. Even in my dorky stage, with my too long arms and buck teeth, he still saw me as if I was this uncovered treasure.

He saw *me*. Marlowe.

I can't go back in time and tell little me to turn and look at him. But I can do it now. I'm choosing to turn to him and truly see Carter for once. Not see him as the guy that lives on the next street over. Not see him as a fellow camper at Camp Caelee. Not see him as my best friend's brother.

I'm seeing him as *Carter*.

I'm Boysick over *Carter*.

CHAPTER THIRTY

With a *slam*, Carter shuts my car door for me, and we walk towards the front of the school. I step beside him and weave my fingers in with his. Looking over at me, his rosy lips form into a small smile.

After our tree house adventure a couple of days ago, I haven't been able to keep Carter out of my head. My stomach flutters and my cheeks pinch into a grin every time I picture his face.

Over the past few days, I have found him every chance I could at school. Seeing him at lunch or in the halls just gives me thrills. After school, we've taken Pickles on walks or gone to dinner. Now that I've admitted to Carter- and to myself- how much I like him, I can't not hangout with him.

I can't even walk beside Carter. I'm so giddy that I'm practically skipping down the school parking lot. The sky is still dark outside, and the handful of cars scattered in front of the school add an eerie feel to the early morning.

Yesterday afternoon, Carter called me to see if I wanted to go for another surprise. He said he had all these ideas he had been saving back in the *chance* that we would get together. Carter even sent me a screenshot of the notes app where he had listed a bunch of date ideas for us. The oldest entry was dated back to three years ago.

Of course, I agreed. I pinch my forearm a dozen times a day, second guessing if this is a dream or not. I'm excited just picturing all of the unspoken conversations that I can have with him.

Today's surprise involves Carter and I waking up super early so we can sneak into the school during the swim team's practice. Administrators open the school up at 6:00 AM a few mornings a week so the swim team can practice before classes start. Carter had the idea to sneak into the school while it's still pretty deserted and try to climb up to the roof.

He said it's on his bucket list for things to do before he graduates. And now it's on my bucket list too because I can do it with him.

Hand in hand, Carter tells me, "Okay, so I'm thinking we can go in through the front door because it should be unlocked for the swimmers. And last year, our stage director told us juniors how to get up on the roof. We just need to get to the elevator, and we'll be good."

"Okay, perfect! And if we run into a teacher or something, what should we say?" I ask.

"I'll tell them that I got to school early to work on sets for theater. And that I asked you to come along," he says. Everyone knows Carter is really involved in the Theater program, so our story should be pretty believable.

Walking up to the two sets of double doors, Carter tries to grab the handle, but the door barely moves. He gives me a puzzled look and tries the other handles. All are locked.

Glancing down at his watch, he says, "It's 6:12. The doors should be open by now."

"Should we check the side doors?" I ask. Carter nods and keeps his hand in mine, pulling me towards the side of the school.

This time, I pull on the handle of the gray metal door. It resists the pull of my arm, leaving us still in square one.

"One of these doors has to be open," Carter says. "Let's check the back."

"No matter what, we *are* breaking into the school," I say.

Carter belly laughs, his voice echoing across the parking lot. I love the way he tilts his chin up when he laughs, and it exposes his wide grin. Or I love the way my stomach flips anytime I see his name pop up on my phone. Yesterday in Leadership, I kept having to physically turn my head away from him, so I didn't just constantly stare at him throughout class.

I pull my dark green cardigan closer to myself and follow the asphalt path to the back doors. When I was at his house yesterday, I felt like we were in some sort of secret club with our stolen glances and stifled laughter.

Carter walks up to the back door, and instead of giving us trouble, the door opens with ease. He looks at me and smiles. "Bingo."

The back door leads us to the cafeteria where we walk past the booths, tables, and chairs. Our steps squeak in unison along the speckled tile.

Carter pushes open the doors that lead out of the lunch room, and he looks around the hallway. I follow his eyeline and see the backside of a janitor, pushing the dust mop across the floors.

Looking at me with big eyes, Carter whispers, "When we shut this door, he's definitely going to turn around. We have to take a run for it."

"Okay," I tell him softly. With the custodian to our right and the corner of the hallway to our left, we have to escape to the cornered hallway.

"1, 2, 3, let's go!" Carter whispers. He pushes the cafeteria door wide open and pulls me to the left of the hallway. We race behind the corner, trying not to make too much noise.

The lunch room door closes loudly, and Carter peeks around the ivory cinder block walls. With a sigh of relief, he says, "He didn't even look back."

"Whew," I tell him. I have to bite the inside of my cheek to keep from beaming ear to ear. Adrenaline races through my veins like the cherry KoolAid we used to chug at Camp Caelee.

His hair is extra fluffy today, and it falls back as we jog down the hallway. Swiveling our heads back and forth, Carter and I make sure no one is following us.

Walking over to the elevator in the center of the school, I push the "up" button. The elevator doors squeak open, and we step inside.

The sliding doors are halfway closed when I hear a nasally voice call out, "Wait!" Sticking his meaty hand through the small space between the doors, Mr. Thornton makes us hold the elevator for him.

Carter and I exchange big eyes as Mr. Thornton stomps into the elevator. "Floor three," he croons. He even has that damn yellow shirt on again.

Giving us a skeptical look, he asks me, "What are you all doing here at school so early?"

Glancing between Mr. Thornton's bushy eyebrows, my mind goes blank. What was Carter and I's story? What was our excuse?

"We are here to work on some sets for the play. You should come see it! It's Beauty and the Beast, and opening night is in March," Carter interjects, lightly touching my arm.

Nodding, Mr. Thornton grunts in response. "I will. You know, back in my day I was in a production of Beauty and the Beast."

Biting his lip to prevent his laughter, Carter says, "Really? Who did you play?"

"I was Gaston," Mr. Thornton says smugly. "So if you need someone to cover that role, you just give me a call."

"Of course," Carter says. He squeezes my hand, trying to suppress his chuckles.

Ding. The elevator stops on the third floor, the doors sliding open. Mr. Thornton turns to us and sniffles. Wiping his nose, he says, "Well, this is my floor. Don't forget about me as an alternate for Gaston."

"Definitely," Carter says, his voice wavering. He purses his lips together, trying not to snort laughter in front of a teacher. Mr. Thornton nods and waddles out of the elevator.

Once the doors creak shut, Carter and I burst into a fit of laughter. Tears fill my eyes, and Carter's face turns a bright red, almost fully concealing his freckles.

"Oh my gosh," I say, trying to catch my breath.

"That man is something else. Can you *imagine* him as Gaston?!" Carter asks me.

"No," I say, shuddering at the thought. The elevator continues to rise until we land on the fifth floor. Walking into the dark corridor, I see piles of party and event supplies. This floor of Caelee High is mainly used for storage for the millions of events we have throughout the school year.

"I've never been up here," I tell him.

"Yeah, it can get kind of creepy. When I was a freshman, one of the football players claimed that he saw a ghost up here once."

Carter flips on the light, and I walk over to a few of the cardboard boxes full of random stuff. Rifling through the banners, unused balloons, and streamers, I pull out a giant plethora of rainbow fabric.

"Is this a rainbow parachute from elementary school?" I say, holding it up for Carter to see.

"I loved those," Carter says and grabs the other end of the fabric. "I bet this is from the Y2k Spring Fling we had last year."

I nod, and push some of the cardboard boxes out of our way. There's about fifteen feet of space around us, which should be enough to stretch out the rainbow tent.

"Do you want to try it?" I ask him.

Smiling, he says, "Of course."

We each take two handles on the edge of the fabric and walk back as far as we can before we hit more boxes.

"I don't know if this is going to work," I say. Normally these rainbow tents are meant for ten people, not two.

Carter counts down. "One, two, three!"

We throw our hands in the air, letting the rainbow tent fill with the air around us. We used to do this so much in elementary school, so the motions come back like second nature.

We pull the fabric down, running towards each other. Plopping down on the ground, I pull the fabric under myself, and Carter does the same.

For three seconds, it works. The giant rainbow fabric forms a tent above us. Since we are right under the fluorescent lights, the colors on the fabric glow like a huge multi-colored lantern. Twinkles of red, blue, green, and yellow shine on Carter's face. I'm transported back to the nostalgic bliss of my childhood.

Suddenly, the tent fails, and the polyester fabric falls on top of us. Carter and I are now swimming in a sea of rainbow. I push the fabric off my shoulder, scooting closer to the middle. Carter does the same until we are a mere foot apart.

"I like you, Mar," he whispers under the canopy.

"I like you, too," I say, and my stomach does Olympic level gymnastics.

We are still sitting on the floor, but Carter inches forward to me. He slides his cool fingers behind my neck and into my hair. Pulling my face towards his, I drown in his emerald eyes.

Carter's lips find mine, kissing me gently. I taste the peppermint of his toothpaste and smell the aroma of morning rain from his soap. Placing my hands on his collarbone, I have to remind myself that this is real life.

Each day it feels like my heart floats through my chest towards the sky. And one day it's going to burst through my chest. I won't be able to contain my admiration for Carter.

He kisses my jaw, whispering in my ear, "You ready to go to the roof?"

I nod, and he plants another quick kiss on my lips. We crawl out from underneath the rainbow parachute and fold the fabric back into the cardboard box.

Carter leads me over to a door at the back of the supply room. He opens it for me, and we walk into a stairwell that looks like it came straight from *Stranger Things*. Some cobwebs line the railing, and there's a layer of dust covering each stair.

"Okay, so Ryan said to just head up these stairs, and then it'll lead us to a smaller storage room," Carter says, coughing from the dust filled air.

We climb up the ancient stairs until we get to the landing with a rustic, dark brown, wooden door. Carter tries the brass handle, but it doesn't budge.

"No," he mutters. "It's locked."

Digging into my jean pockets, I pull out a small bobby pin that I fortunately remembered to bring. "Here! Try this."

"You're amazing," Carter says, with the right side of his mouth turning upward.

After a few moments of jiggling the pin inside of the lock, we hear the faintest *click*. I check behind us one more time to make sure no one is following us, and we are in the clear.

Entering the smaller storage area, the room is automatically ten degrees cooler. Carter turns on his phone flashlight, shining it across the bare walls. This room is just filled with what looks like broken desks and chairs. Rumor has it that the principal, Mr. Brooks, is a hoarder.

I follow Carter and turn on my phone flashlight. "What are we looking for?"

"There should be a smaller door that leads to the crawl space," he tells me.

I point my phone over the back corner and scoot the crumpled wooden desk away. "This?"

"Yes!" Carter says eagerly. He walks over to help me move the other chairs and desks out of our way.

Once the space is clear, I crouch down and pull at the handle. To our amazement, it opens without hesitation. Putting his hand in front of me, Carter says, "Wait, let me go first. In case it's not safe."

I bite back a smile and sit back on my heels. Carter crawls through the tiny doorway, his phone flashlight still in hand.

"Okay, it's all good. Just more dust and spiderwebs," he says.

"Coming," I say, stepping towards Carter. Inside the crawl space is a bunch of insulation and a small wooden walkway. Carter and I are practically folded in half, walking to the other wall.

I balance on the two feet wide wooden plank and try my best not to touch any cobwebs or insulation. Walking a few feet, Carter calls out, "There it is!"

Lifting my head up, I see a latch door on the ceiling in front of Carter. He reaches his hand up, pulling the hatch down. A rickety ladder falls down, and we can see through the opening. The glimpse of a dark blue sky gives us a little light within the crawl space.

Carter straightens out the ladder, placing one foot on it to test its strength. Looking back at me, he says, "Okay, if I fall, just don't laugh."

I chuckle, "I promise." Carter gives me a mischievous grin and starts his ascent.

The ladder holds up well, and Carter hoists himself up through the opening in the ceiling. He makes it look so effortless, I would never have thought there was a chance that he could fall. Looking down at me, he says, "Mar, you have to see this."

I smile, placing my hands on the wooden rungs. Stepping upwards, I move closer and closer to the opened hatch. Carter reaches his arms down. Grabbing his hand, I climb through the opening, and Carter helps pull me the rest of the way up.

Once I'm on the roof, the morning wind ripples through my hair. I scan the horizon, seeing the golden sun peak through the fog. "Oh my gosh," I say breathlessly.

I step away from the latch door and take in the view. The air feels more crisp up here, as if I can breathe ten times easier. As if all my worries and anxieties suddenly melt away.

We got here at the perfect time to watch the sunrise begin. I can hear the sing-song voice of a robin. The sky ranges from a midnight indigo to a lavender purple to an amber yellow. The most talented artist in the world couldn't capture the magic of this moment.

Carter comes over and wraps a long arm around me. I smile at him, leaning my head into the crevice between his neck and shoulder. I have to remember this moment. Pulling out my phone, I snap a picture of the view and take a 0.5x photo of Carter and me.

"This is so beautiful," he whispers.

I like how Carter and I's current relationship is just between us- don't get me wrong. But I also want to shout his name from rooftops and tell everyone about him. Not for my own gain, but I want to show off just how great of a human he is.

I am eternally grateful that Carter and I exist in the same lifetime.

Turning to him, I place my arms around the back of his neck. Leaning forward, I kiss him. I wish I could communicate the depths of my Boysickness in that one touch.

"Every time I go home or we leave for the night, I feel like it's an eternity before I get to see you again," I tell him.

"Me too," he says, his green eyes glowing against the rich daylight.

"Anytime I'm away from you," I say, "I just want you again."

His lips stretch into a smile, moving all of the freckles on his cheek in unison. He moves towards me, kissing me with more passion. Our lips move together like the ebbs and flows of ocean waves.

"I want to be with you," I whisper against his skin.

His eyes move away from my lips as he focuses on my gaze. Running a hand through my hair, he says, "Well, I was going to ask you."

"Ask me what?" I say, trying to conceal how drunk I am off of my emotions.

"I wanted to make things official. I really like you, Mar," he says. I feel my cheeks blush, and my heart jumps to my throat.

"I want to make things official too," I tell him, kissing the tip of his nose.

Now, it's his turn to blush. "You have no idea how happy that makes me."

I grin. I feel like a kid at a birthday party who's on a sugar high after eating too much cake. I feel like I just found a $100 bill outside of my front door, just in time to buy a new book at Barnes & Noble. I feel like I just ran a marathon and came in first place after no training whatsoever.

I may be *more than* Boysick.

"We can tell Lenny first," I say. "I know she'll be supportive."

He nods, "Yeah, I think so too."

Carter looks over the edge of the roof, eyeing the dozen cars that just entered the parking lot. "We should probably head back down before we get caught."

I agree, squeezing his hand three times. Carter kisses the top of my head before climbing back down the wooden ladder into the crawl space. We retrace our steps, trying to put everything back in its place.

Carter and I head down the eerie looking stairwell and into the main storage area. I double check that we put the rainbow tent back up, and Carter turns out the light. He presses the elevator button, waiting for the doors to open back up.

Walking inside, I push the first floor key to take us back down to the main part of the school. I look up at Carter, and he's already smiling down at me.

I want to scold myself for the moments lost before I *saw* him. But now, here I am, wanting to squeal to myself. I want to relish in the millions of moments in the future that are still uncovered by us.

I rest my head and lean into Carter's side as the elevator takes us back down into the real world.

CHAPTER THIRTY-ONE

Stepping up to their front door, I knock a few times, holding Lenny's chai latte in my other hand. I'm a little jittery about telling her. I think it's just that I'm really excited about what is blossoming between Carter and I.

I remember when Lenny started to like Jacob in eighth grade. It was like the perfect little love story. They flirted together and texted a million emoji's back and forth. She told me every little detail of their growing relationship, and I loved living vicariously through her.

Even last year, when Lenny and Jacob had sex for the first time, she told me everything. She told me how nervous and excited she was. And how she kept checking everyone's location to make sure her mom didn't come home early. And how Jacob gently brushed Lenny's hair out of her face when it was all over. She gushed about how tender and wholesome it was.

She was happy. I was happy. Having a best friend you can share every little thing with is so special. And now, I can be on the other side of things. I can gush to Lenny about Carter and I's kisses, and I can tell her how amazing he has been to me.

She'll be able to witness my dreams finally coming true.

Lenny opens the front door. "Marlowe?! Sorry, I didn't realize you were coming over."

"Oh no, you are good! I just wanted to pop by. Surprise!" I say halfheartedly.

"Come in," she says, opening the door wider.

"This is for you," I say and hand her the iced chai. She looks surprised but takes the drink anyway. "Is Carter here?"

"Yeah," Lenny says, right as Carter barrels down the stairs.

"Hey Mar!" he says, coming over to give me a hug. He's wearing a gray sweatshirt, and he just looks so huggable.

His eyes crinkle at the sides, and his cheeks redden ever so slightly. I give him big eyes before burying my face in his shoulder.

"Okay, what's going on?" Lenny asks, looking between us.

"Let's sit down," Carter says, motioning to the living room couches.

"You guys are scaring me," she says.

"No, don't be scared. We just wanted to talk to you," I say, wincing at my words. That makes it sound even scarier. Carter and I take one couch, and Lenny takes the other.

Carter takes a deep breath. "So you know how Mar and I have been spending more time together," he says.

Lenny nods, still looking between the two of us.

"We've been hanging out more, and I've realized how much I like Carter," I say, tucking my hair behind my ears.

"And you know how long I've liked Mar," Carter tells Lenny.

I smile. "After spending so much time together, we've really bonded. And we want to make things official between us."

Lenny looks at us with wide eyes. "Official? As in boyfriend and girlfriend official?"

Carter looks over at me with a small grin and says, "Yeah, boyfriend and girlfriend official." My heart flutters out of my chest.

"Is this a joke?" Lenny asks, her brow creased.

"I wouldn't joke about this," Carter says, confused.

"Yeah, we really like each other," I say. "Lenny, aren't you excited?!"

She still looks at us incredulously. "Excited?! You literally haven't told me anything about this."

"Well, I wanted to figure it out for myself first," I say. "Like, I didn't want to involve you if it somehow didn't work out."

"But, I'm your best friend. Never mind that he's my brother. Why wouldn't you tell me about this?" she asks.

"We just wanted to keep it between us at first," Carter pipes up. "You have to understand that, at least."

"You are two of the closest people in my life. No, I don't have to understand it. Apparently, you don't value your relationship with me enough to fill me in on what's going on in your life," she says. Her face is flushed with color, and her eyes have grown dim.

"Okay, but I'm sure you expected something was up when we were hanging out together," I say. "So this shouldn't be that big of a surprise."

"I definitely thought that was suspicious, but I just assumed you had grown closer after the ACT. But not *romantically* close," she shakes her head.

"We bonded a lot after that and after my college visit," Carter says.

She lets out a groan. "I just can't believe you never told me any of this. I feel so out of the loop."

"I'm sorry I didn't tell you sooner. But aren't you happy for Carter and me?"

She huffs and shakes her head. "I never asked you to get all Boysick over my brother."

Her words force me to sit back. She bit out that comment, and the venom still floats around in the air.

"Lenny," I try to chuckle. I can't seem to lighten the mood. "It's not that big of a deal."

Carter says, "Yeah, we didn't mean anything by it."

She scowls and looks away from me and Carter. Her chai latte sits on the side table, just collecting condensation.

I need to just laugh this situation off. That's what Lenny and I always do. We can always move past things pretty easily.

"Well, I guess while I'm coming clean, I have something to tell both of you," I say, lightly laughing. Lenny's frown doesn't budge.

Carter looks at me confused. "What?"

"Well, you know when I dated Beau? It was all fake," I say.

"Huh?"

"What do you mean?"

"I was too embarrassed to say anything about it at the time. Because it seemed like I was just so desperate that I resorted to a romcom trope. But yeah. Beau and I agreed to fake date until my mom's art show," I tell them.

Carter leans away from me on the couch. "The entire relationship wasn't real?"

"No," I giggle. "He agreed to fake date me because he likes Maya. So we planned for Maya to see us in a relationship, and then she would catch feelings for Beau. And I agreed to it because I wanted Beau and I's fake relationship to turn into something that wasn't fake."

"So everything- the kisses, the Instagram pictures, the dates- it was all fake?" Lenny asks. She genuinely looks shocked.

"Yeah, but then we kind of blurred the lines. I realized he was a douche, and I caught him and Maya together at their house. That was real," I say. "I *was* really hurt because we weren't officially broken up."

Carter just looks at me, stunned.

"But yeah. Not my proudest moment. You all are the first people who know about it. Other than Beau, of course," I add with a shrug.

"I thought I knew you, Marlowe. I knew you were obsessed with Beau, but I didn't know you would go to such lengths to be with him," Lenny says. "It's kind of sad."

"It's not sad!" I say defensively. "It's funny looking back."

Carter is looking down in his lap, not saying anything.

"Guys, I'm trying to lighten the mood. You should be laughing!" I say. Turning to Carter, I tell him, "And don't even worry about Beau. I don't have feelings for him anymore."

"Your whole relationship was fake?" Carter asks.

"Yeah," I nod.

"The whole thing?"

"I mean, yeah. Towards the end I thought things were starting to get real. But all of it was fake," I say.

He looks back down at his hands.

"I'm so disappointed in you, Marlowe. I thought we were so much closer to where you could actually tell me stuff," Lenny sighs.

"We are close! But I was kind of embarrassed about everything. And you would have advised me against it because you weren't crazy about Beau. And I didn't want to hear anything except for the fact that it *was* a good idea," I admit. "If I'm being honest."

"Well, I'm just *so* glad you are being honest now," she deadpans. I've never seen her this way. The tension feels like a humid room that been left without air conditioning for too long. Stale and suffocating.

"Lenny! I don't see why you are so upset about this."

"You were telling me how obsessed you were with Beau Braxton two months ago. And now you like my brother? Marlowe, I can't trust that this isn't just how you are. That you just bounce from guy to guy." She cuts deep and throws salt in the wound.

"No. Everything with Carter is different. And I'm not just bouncing from guy to guy. I genuinely like Carter. It's not just my Boysickness. It's more," I stammer.

"Is it though?" Carter asks, finally looking up at me.

"Is what?"

"Is our relationship more than what it was with Beau?" he says.

I gape at him, tucking my hair behind my ears. "Of course it is. I don't know why you would even think that."

"You just told me about how you fooled everyone into buying into your fake relationship," he says, his voice quivering.

"Yeah, but with you it's different," I reassure him. I want to scoot over, touch him, run my hands through his hair, and take it all back.

"Is everything between us fake too?"

"No!" I say, my heart bucking against my ribs. "The Beau thing was completely different."

A second.

A pause.

An eternity.

"I don't know if I believe you," Carter says, shaking his head.

The lump in my throat falls to the pit of my stomach. I just look at him. I don't even know what to say. My mouth is dry and slimy at the same time.

"Marlowe, I've told you about my anxiety. About how bothered I get about honesty. You kept a huge secret from me. You should see why I'm really hurt by this."

Pressure builds behind my eyes. This isn't how it's supposed to go. Shaking my head, I tell him, "I really wasn't planning on telling anyone about the fake dating thing. I'm sorry."

He inhales, sucking in all the air in the room. Lenny just stares at me.

"It's not that you fake dated Beau. It's really not," he says. "I told you about my dad. I told you about my anxiety. I *trusted* you with that."

I open my mouth to say something, but no words fall out.

"And during that entire conversation, you found no chance to interject? You had no opportunity to be honest about Beau?" he asks.

"I wasn't trying to be dishonest," I say quietly.

"I've wanted this for so long. And now, you're about to tell me that when I finally get it, it isn't even real?!" Carter asks, his voice breaking.

"Just because I fake dated Beau, it doesn't mean that I want to fake date you. I want to *actually* be with you," I say.

"What the hell, Marlowe?!" Lenny says, catching me off guard. Her face is red, and she keeps looking over at Carter worriedly. "My brother isn't some random guy off the street that you can use as your leftovers."

"Lenny, come on," I stammer. "You're my best friend. You know me better than anyone. You should know that I'm serious about Carter."

There's a bitterness behind her eyes that wasn't there before. "Oh, really? Well that's news to me because you've been a terrible best friend lately."

My breath hitches.

She continues, "Marlowe, you've seemed like you are completely uninterested in my life this entire semester. You don't care about my personal life unless it benefits you in some way."

"That's not true."

Lenny nods. "Yes, it is. I've *really* gotten into embroidery lately, and I can't even talk to you about it. When I bring it up, you act so disengaged."

My lips can't form the right words to say.

She gestures to her brown sweatshirt. It has embroidered flowers and vines across the middle, and it mimics Taylor Swift's surprise song piano from the Eras Tour. It's so intricate and colorful- I don't know how I missed it before. Lenny says, "You never notice when I wear something I've made, and the old you would have paid attention."

A speckle of truth tugs at the base of my chest. "Okay, maybe I've been distracted by Beau. It's just that I liked him *so much*. I couldn't think of anyone else. But I'm over him, and I'll be more attentive from now on."

Lenny doesn't look convinced.

Carter takes a deep breath, wiping his hands on his sweatpants. "If you liked Beau for as long as you have, and you got over him this quickly, then what's to say that I won't just be another Beau Braxton to you," he looks at me, eyes glossy.

Oh.

I didn't mean it like that.

I wouldn't move on from Carter like that.

But.

I get how all of this looks.

I can't do that to Carter.

Looking over to him, I try to meet his eyes. I lightly place my fingertips on his forearm. I want him to see it in my face that *I'm sorry*. I want there to be more meaning behind those seven little letters. I want him to see me and know my intentions.

I want him to see me past this.

Noticing his eyes well up nearly sends me over the edge. I messed up. I know I did. This isn't something to laugh about anymore. This isn't a joke. I really messed up.

Almost immediately after I touch him, he pulls his arm back and looks back down at his lap.

Oh.

"I never thought *you* would hurt *me*, Marlowe," he whispers, his voice breaking like sea waves crashing over rocks.

"You need to go home," Lenny says to me, with her eyes still fixed on Carter.

I don't know what to say. My voice is empty, meaningless. All of the words in the world couldn't patch over the gaping hole that exists between the three of us.

"No, I don't want to go just yet. I feel like you all aren't understanding me," I choke out. "I didn't mean any of this to be like that. I was trying to lighten the mood."

Carter gets up and heads up the stairs without saying a word. I frantically look between him and my best friend, trying to figure out how to save this situation.

It's not possible.

"I'm choosing my brother. You need to leave. I need to be with Carter right now," Lenny says forcibly.

"No, I didn't-" I stammer.

"Go home, Marlowe."

"Lenny, you don't understand," I try to tell her.

"Go home."

CHAPTER THIRTY-TWO

I just scheduled my second attempt at the ACT, and I can't even tell the two people I'm closest to about it. I can't even tell the two people who helped calm me down before and after the last one.

The truth is that I don't know where to go from here. This is uncharted territory, and I don't have a compass. I don't even have a map.

I know I screwed up.

When I wake up and when I go to sleep, I think about it. When I'm standing in line for lunch or riding to school with my dad, I'm thinking about it.

The middle of my chest hurts like the stabbing of every small detail that I kept from them. I didn't realize how big of a deal it was. It was just two little secrets.

But honestly, if the roles were reversed I would be pissed.

So I can't fault them for being mad.

I only fault myself. How could I be so stupid? How could I be so wrapped up in Beau Braxton that I treat my friends like discarded trash?

I messed up.

I didn't realize just *how* much I messed up. But I think I do now.

How I kept things from her.

And how I didn't come clean to him.

How I joked about it as if it meant nothing to them.

And how I was so focused on the wrong guy that I destroyed the two people that are most important to me.

This hasn't happened before. My stomach hurts. I can't eat. Every waking thought is about how Lenny and Carter are mad at me.

Or disappointed in me.

Or hurt by me.

I can't live with it.

I've tried to text her a million times. And I rang his phone a million more times. But it's just dead silence on the other end.

Is this how it ends? How I lose my best friend? How I lose the one guy I'm meant to be with?

I'm mourning the relationships that could be over forever. It's been five days since I talked to them. Lenny doesn't sit beside me in our classes together. Carter wasn't even in Leadership.

I know he gets really anxious about honesty. I just didn't put two and two together. I messed up.

I shouldn't have.

I couldn't have.

I wouldn't have done any of this if I knew it would hurt him this badly.

I want to take it all back. Like a vacuum sucking up cracker crumbs in shag carpet. Or how a net catches all the algae and debris in a green-colored pool.

I want to wish it all back and take it all back. But I can't.

I can't talk to them. Is this how it's going to be forever?

I feel stuck in quicksand. I'm thrashing trying to get out. The only way to escape is to grab Lenny and Carter's hands.

That they aren't even extending.

CHAPTER THIRTY-THREE

ME: Lenny please talk to me.

ME: I'm so sorry.

ME: I would be so pissed if I was in your position. I've thought about it so much. If you kept something this big from me, I would be so upset and hurt.

ME: I fully understand where you are coming from.

ME: I won't do this again! Trust me. I've really thought over it, and I know how much I screwed up. Every moment for the past six days, I've beaten myself over and over again. I won't do this to you again.

ME: We've been best friends for over half my life. And over the past few months, I've completely forgotten that. I've acted like we weren't as close as we are. I should've told you about Beau. I should've told you about Carter. I'm sorry.

ME: I know those two words probably don't mean much. Considering how much I messed up. But I really mean them. I'm sorry.

ME: You are literally my other half. I can't lose you. Please don't be mad at me.

ME: Lenny please talk to me.

LENNY: . . .

LENNY:

LENNY: . . .

LENNY:

LENNY: I miss you. But I need more time.

CHAPTER THIRTY-FOUR

"Hope you have a good day, kid," Dad tells me, dropping me off at the front of the school. He gives me a sympathetic smile.

I've told Mom and Dad about everything that has happened with Beau, Carter, and Lenny. When I recount the story, my throat starts to tingle and my head hurts with all of the mistakes I've made. My parents gave me a semi-lecture about what I should've done differently. They didn't fully scold me because I'm sure they could tell I had been scolding myself enough for everyone.

I didn't realize how much I loved Lenny until I didn't have her in my life anymore. It's not even been a week, but I already feel like a shell of myself without her. When I get into the shower, I turn off the lights and let the water fall over myself. Wallowing under the hot water feels like I'm drowning in my own tears.

Today, Carter and I are supposed to do our presentation for Leadership. We have to show our class the research we've done. I called Carter three times yesterday to see if he was okay. I'm assuming we are still doing the presentation together. Even if it is awkward as hell.

"I'll see you later," I tell Dad, closing the car door. Sticking my hands in my pockets, I try to stop my trembling fingers.

Walking into the school's coffee shop, I open up my computer to review Carter and I's slides. I click through each one, rehearsing what I'm supposed to say and leaving pauses for what he is going to present.

I'm in a two person booth at the cafe, but it's just me sitting here. Normally Lenny is filling up the other half of the booth. Now, I'm just left staring at an empty cushioned chair. I check my phone to see if I've missed any texts from her. Still nothing.

While I have my computer out, I pull up my email to see if I have any unread messages. An email with the red exclamation mark is at the top of my inbox.

IMPORTANT: Read Before Class

Marlowe,

Carter has informed me that he is unable to present your project proposal today. He has rescheduled to present to me individually at a later time. For today's class, just plan on presenting your existing slides by yourself.

Thanks,

Mrs. Lin

No. Oh no. No, no, no, no. I'm presenting alone?! So Carter will be there, he just can't present *with me?*

My heart races. My fingers tremble. My brows crease. My stomach falls.

If I think about the depth of his hatred for me, I'm afraid I'll start crying and won't stop. I don't blame him for hating me. But still.

Taking a deep breath, I go back and *re-review* my slides- now with the intention of presenting everything by myself.

I know what this is about. He hasn't spoken to me in a week, so I shouldn't be surprised that he wouldn't want to do a major presentation with me.

I wipe my sweating hands on my jeans and try to rehearse for the one woman show I'm about to perform this afternoon.

Time moves too fast. Before I know it, I've gone through my slides three times, and it's already class change. Grabbing my backpack, I stuff my laptop and notebook inside.

I can do this. I am capable. I trust myself to do this.

I walk down the hall and head to U.S. History. With Lenny and Carter gone, I feel utterly alone. The echoes of what would be Lenny's footsteps beside mine haunt me throughout the hallway. Anytime I see a light purple backpack, I do a double take.

It's never her.

Settling into my U.S. History class, I sit at my normal desk in the rare case that Lenny might sit at her normal one. Over the past several days, she's sat in an empty desk on the opposite side of the room. Maybe today will be different.

Maya walks in, gives me a small wave, and goes to sit next to Beau at the back of class. I'm surrounded by walls of isolation in my fourth period class.

Then, I see the purple backpack and the baby blue sneakers. Looking up to meet Lenny's eyes, I give her a hopeful smile. She returns it with a flat lined expression.

The rest of my history class is filled with mindless doodles and numerous glances at the clock. I can't concentrate. I scheduled my retake of the ACT for tomorrow morning. If I can't even focus right now, how on earth will I be successful with a standardized test? Never mind a standardized test that I've already had a panic attack over?

Once the bell finally rings, I grab my things as fast as possible. If I get to Leadership a little early, I may be able to talk to Carter. If I can talk to him before class, maybe I can convince him to do the presentation with me. Maybe I can convince him how truly sorry I am.

Opening the heavy wooden door to the classroom, I see some familiar faces. But none of them are who I'm looking for. I take a seat and scan the room again.

He's not here. The time limit of class change dwindles down to nothing.

He's not here. Every seat is filled with someone that isn't him.

The door creaks open, and I turn my head. It's not him. Before Mrs. Lin starts class, I call him. The phone rings twice before getting denied.

He's not here. My head aches behind my eyes. I can't do this. All of our work and all of our time is wasted because of me. I was the one who pulled out the trash can and threw it all away.

He's not here. I can't do this by myself.

I halfway pay attention to the other groups' presentations. Each of them has two presenters. One presenter doesn't hate the other. And the other doesn't feel absolutely destroyed with guilt about her actions.

One group finishes up about a fundraising project. They have proposed that the school buy a vintage photo booth, and the school can move the photo booth outside of events. Students can pay for their photo, and the school can pocket the profit from the pictures. It's honestly a really cool and unique idea.

It's just that the two people I would want to take photos with aren't speaking to me at the moment.

With the students walking back to their seats, Mrs. Lin announces the next group that will go.

"Okay, next we'll have Marlowe come up and discuss her project!" my teacher calls out.

I take a deep breath and walk up to the front of the room. I pull up my presentation to project on the board. I wipe my sweating hands on my jeans. Again.

"Um, hi. I'm Marlowe, and I'll be talking about Carter and I's stress mediation initiative," I say, clicking past the title slide. "I don't know about you all, but I've dealt with a lot of school related anxiety this semester. With all the homework, tests, and projects, we students are under a lot of pressure."

I clear my throat, "Yeah, so Carter and I proposed that we transform the old teacher's lounge on the second floor to be a new mindfulness space." I click to the next slide.

"In the mindfulness space, we can have a place for yoga. We'll have a TV to play guided yoga instructions, and we'll set up a place to store all of the extra mats. We also plan to have noise machines, bean bag chairs, and fidget devices so students can unwind," I say, talking too quickly.

I click through photos of our prototype and explain some of the small details we want to add to the actual room. I also show the class some statistics about the average stress of a high school student. My voice keeps wavering.

"Um, yeah. So that's basically it. Carter and I just wanted to create an area where students can relax or help cope with any stress," I conclude. I get a few measly claps while I walk back over to my seat.

This project feels pointless without him. What is the significance of a stress-free space if the co-creators can't even be in the same room?

When school finally lets out, I head over to the front of the school to wait for my dad to pick me up.

I need to talk to Lenny soon. I'm not just sorry because I got caught lying. I'm not just telling her sorry to make myself feel better.

I *actually* feel remorse. When I think about how upset she was, my heart falls to the pit of my stomach. I want to hug my knees to my chest and take away that disappointment and hurt. I want to go back to that bliss and carefree spirit we had as kids.

As I walk to the car rider line, I marinate in my wistful thinking. Putting on my headphones, I play, "If Now Was Then" by Maggie Rogers. The apologetic melody makes me feel less alone. Even though I'm standing by myself outside of the school, thinking about the two people I feel empty without.

CHAPTER THIRTY-FIVE

Mr. Evans' timer goes off, signaling for us students to close our test packets. I take a deep breath. I don't think I aced it or anything, but I finished it.

I just finished the ACT all the way through.

There were *so* many problems that I got tripped up on. And so many times that I wanted to freak out. I wanted to get up and leave so many times.

But I didn't.

I'm really proud of myself. Throughout each section of the exam, I repeated the mantras that Denise has taught me.

I am capable. I am strong. I can do this. I trust myself to do this. I believe in myself.

Mr. Evans walks around, collecting everyone's test booklet and answer key. I'm pretty sure you can see the sweaty fingerprints on every single one of my papers.

Once he gets everything, he goes into the spiel about taking the ACT and the timeline of getting our scores back. With all this talk of numbers, I feel my heart rate quicken and my upper lip sweat.

I'm not going to do this again.

When I feel my mind start to spin and my body grow faint, I rehearse the latest grounding technique Denise taught me.

It helps me get out of my head and focus on what's actually happening around me. As Mr. Evans finishes his conclusion to the exam, I start

Denise's latest exercise.

Five things I can see: I see the white board with the start and end times, I see Mr. Evan's perfectly clean sneakers, I see the bright blue border around the bulletin boards, I see the red exit sign above the door, and I see the green rolling chair behind the teacher's desk.

Four things I can feel: I feel the soft leggings on my legs, I feel my extra hair tie on my left wrist, I feel my necklace against my sternum, and I feel my toes squirm inside of my shoes.

Three things I can hear: I hear the small ticking of the clock, I hear Mr. Evan's deep voice, and I hear someone's chair squeak as they push it away from the desk.

Two things I can smell: I smell the gentle aloe scent of my laundry detergent, and I smell the wooden aroma from the dozen of number two pencils on each desk.

One thing I can taste: I taste the faintest bit of peppermint from my toothpaste this morning.

Slowly, I inhale and exhale. Mr. Evans dismisses us, and I throw my extra pencils and calculator into my tote bag. When I stand up, my legs don't feel like Jello like they did during my first attempt at the ACT.

Walking out to the hallway, I turn my phone on so I can tell my mom I'm done. Once my phone reboots, I see two missed text notifications.

LENNY: hey i know you are taking
the act right now

LENNY: but once you're done,
i'm ready to talk if you are

I close my eyes, and then look at the screen again. Lenny wants to talk to me?! Are we finally going to make the steps towards a resolution?!

I immediately text her with my response.

ME: Hey!! Yes of course!!
I can be there in 15 minutes?

LENNY: that works

Texting my mom an update, I wait outside the front of school and run the possibilities of Lenny and I's conversation in my mind. Does she want me to immediately go into how sorry I am? Does she want me to listen to her first? Will this fix things or make it worse?

Growing up, Lenny and I never really argued. If one of us had a toy the other wanted, we shared it without hesitation. At camp, if someone was rude to me, Lenny would instantly stand up for her best friend. During her parents' divorce, if Lenny needed to rant, I would be an open ear for her.

Would eight-year-old Marlowe and Lenny be disappointed in how I've treated the seventeen-year-old Lenny? People say hindsight is 20-20, but that doesn't fully erase the guilt. Having a better outlook on your actions doesn't diminish the *impact* of those actions.

Saying sorry will only get me so far. If I want Lenny to know that I won't be so selfish in the future, I have to actually show her.

Mom pulls up in front of me with her white Toyota, stopping so I can get in. She looks over at me expectantly.

"Well, how was it?" she asks.

"Not perfect," I say. "But *so* much better than the first time. I did a lot of what Denise has taught me. Like with repeating the positive statements and the grounding exercise. She would be proud."

"Well, *I'm* proud of you!" Mom says. "Your dad and I have noticed that you've been handling things differently."

"Aw, thanks Mom."

"So, you want me to drop you off at Lenny's?" she says.

"Yeah, if that's okay. She said she's ready to talk, and I really need to make things right with her. It's been killing me to not be able to see her," I sigh.

She nods and starts to drive out of the school parking lot. Mom asks me what I'm planning on telling Lenny.

"I honestly don't know. I think I'm going to try to listen to her point of view. Because I messed up by not thinking about her feelings to begin with. So, if I let her rant or share her feelings, I think I can actually understand how to be better," I tell her.

Mom looks over at me with a soft smile. She reaches over and rubs my arm in a very "mom" way. Has therapy helped me that much to where my mom can already tell a difference in how I'm acting?

Pulling into Lenny's driveway, I take a deep breath and grab my bag. Mom wishes me luck, and I walk up to the front porch, ringing the doorbell.

After a few beats, Lenny comes up and opens the front door. "Hey."

"Hey," I say quietly.

Lenny sits on the leather couch, crossing her legs and pulling a blanket over herself. I sit on the opposite couch and pick at my cuticles. The fluttering in my stomach makes me feel like I'm about to fly away.

"So," Lenny begins. "I've thought about everything a lot, and I'm ready to try to talk things out."

I nod. "I want to hear your side and your feelings."

Lenny pauses, biting her lip. "I know I said some hurtful things the other week. It's just that everything was a gut punch.

"I felt like you were so uninterested in me. You didn't care about what I was doing, like with the embroidery thing. When you were going out with Beau, I felt a little left out. You would go on dates and hangout, but I would see more of it from Instagram. I wanted you to tell me all the details like I do with you about Jacob. Marlowe, that's how we've always been. I thought one reason why we were so close is because we can share anything with each other," she says.

She's right. We've always been able to tell each other anything. But I just threw that away. I didn't want to tell her because I knew she would tell me fake dating Beau was a bad idea.

"So I noticed that early on. But I had no idea you were fake dating. And I'm not saying the emotions you felt were fake. I'm really not. It's just that I comforted you during what was basically your first heartbreak, and you *still* didn't tell me the whole story.

"Then, to find out that you were becoming closer with Carter? And *still* didn't tell me? It just makes me feel like this friendship isn't mutual. That I care more about you than you care about me," she says.

I nod. I mean, she's a hundred percent valid. If I were in her shoes, I would feel the same way. Not to mention, it would have bothered me *so* much if she didn't share much with me when she and Jacob got together. I would have felt so left out. But with her, she included me in everything. We would even hangout and *Jacob* was the third wheel.

"And I didn't mean for it to sound like I was calling you a slut or something the other day. It's just that when you've had so many crushes, how do I know you are actually serious about Carter?" she asks.

I clear my throat, stuffing my emotions back into my chest. "Well first off, I completely see where you are coming from. You're right. I was a bad friend and only thought about myself. Lenny, I'm really sorry about leaving you out of the Beau and Carter situation.

"With Beau, I was just really stubborn, and I didn't want anyone to tell me that I was acting stupid. Or that it was all a terrible idea- even if it was. And with Carter, I was so focused on not messing it up, that I completely excluded you. I know it doesn't mean much, but I'm really sorry," I say.

She nods, pulling the blanket tighter over herself.

"I *am* really serious with Carter. You've always said 'when you know, you know' about you and Jacob. And I never really understood that until now. But I *know* with Carter," I tell her. "I don't deserve him- or you for that matter- but I really do like him. I feel complete when I'm with him."

Lenny gives me a small smile. "I believe you. I just don't want to be discarded again."

"You won't. I won't do that again. I'm really sorry, Lenny," I tell her earnestly.

She smiles bigger now.

"Your embroidery is amazing, and I can't believe I acted like it was nothing. So, I have a proposition."

"Okay," she says hesitantly.

I dig into my bag, pull out $150, and lay it on the coffee table. "I worked at my mom's studio last weekend when she was sick. She gave me this, and I want you to use it to buy more embroidery supplies. And

I want it to also be a down payment on a custom sweatshirt."

Lenny thumbs through the cash, shaking her head.

"I promise I'm not trying to bribe your friendship back! I want to support you and show you that I do care about your interests and hobbies. I want to wear a custom Lenny Taylor embroidered sweatshirt," I smile.

"Marlowe, you don't have to do this. This is too much," she says, holding the money towards me.

"No, I want to do it. And if you don't accept it now, I'll just get Sheila to deposit it into your account anyway," I smirk.

"You don't have to do this."

"I feel like a shell of myself without you," I tell her. "I need you in my life. I shouldn't have treated you like that, so this is me trying to turn over a new leaf."

Smiling, she uncrosses her legs. "Thank you for this and for letting me vent. And trying to work on everything. You seem-"

"Less selfish?" I chuckle. "I'm trying."

"I wasn't going to say that," she laughs. "But yeah."

I beam at her. We're slowly ticking towards the clock of normalcy. Lenny and I will be back to normal. We'll be better than normal.

"So, are we good?" she asks.

"Yeah," I say, stepping towards and enveloping us both into a hug. Fifty pounds have just been taken off my shoulders. I can breathe again.

She pulls back, saying, "Also, I was weirded out with the Carter thing at first. But then I remembered back when we went to Camp Caelee. He thought you were so cool. One day, he admitted his crush on you to me.

"I never mentioned anything about it because I knew you liked Beau. But when we were kids, I used to give Carter the hardest time about it. I just didn't realize that the crush followed him into his high school years."

"He told me about how he liked me when we were younger. I just wish I could go back and not even notice Beau. I wish I could've seen Carter so much earlier," I say. "Do you think he'll ever talk to me again?"

She presses her lips together. "I don't know. He's still pretty upset. But over this past week, I was thinking about our camp days. I found something."

"What is it?" I ask.

"Wait here," she says, running towards the stairs.

I wish Carter were here as well, so I could list how wrong I was and try to repair the damage with him. But I don't know if he would even hear me out to begin with.

Lenny bounds down the stairs with something hot pink in her hands. She comes over towards me, and we both sit down on the sofa.

Holding the pink item up, she says, "It's my old iPad! From when we were kids."

"No way! You still have that thing?" I ask.

She nods, clicking the tablet on. Tapping on it for a few seconds, she pulls up a video. "Watch this."

Lenny hands me the iPad, and a grainy video starts to play. There's a younger version of Lenny with a ponytail full of fly aways. It looks like she's in her old teal colored bedroom.

"So, who am I here with?" young Lenny asks. Her voice is so much higher pitched that I do a double take.

The camera points to a young redheaded kid with a red sunburn on his nose. He rolls his eyes. "Carter Taylor."

"And what do you want to tell our viewers?" young Lenny asks. When we were in elementary and middle school, we would film videos as if we were going to post it to a YouTube channel with millions of subscribers. Lenny wanted so badly to be a famous vlogger. But her home videos never traveled from her tablet.

"Nothing," a small Carter grumbles.

"Don't worry. I'm not going to show Marlowe," Lenny says, shoving the camera closer to Carter's face. His cheeks turn so red, they match his sunburn.

"Lenny, not now," Carter says.

Huffing, younger Lenny takes the iPad back from Carter, pointing the camera towards herself. "Carter has a crush on Marlowe! He told me so. Can't you believe it?"

"Lenny, I told you not to tell anyone," young Carter says.

"I'm not telling anyone. Just my subscribers," she says. Looking directly into the camera, she exclaims, "Make sure to comment down below and buy my merch!"

The video stops.

I turn to present-day Lenny, my mouth hanging wide open. Shaking my head, I ask, "Is that video real?"

"Of course it's real," Lenny says. "I found it the other day. I remember filming it at the time. Carter was so mad at me."

"Oh my gosh," I say.

"All that to say, Carter's liked you for forever. I don't think there's ever going to be something that will undo that."

If Carter liked me during my-dorky-and-frizzy-hair-camp days, will he still like me during my-owning-up-to-my-mistakes days?

CHAPTER THIRTY-SIX

Cough cough.

I nearly choke on the cloud of hairspray Lenny just sprayed on her crown braid. I hold up a handheld mirror, so she can see how the back of her hair looks.

Tonight is Caelee High's annual winter formal, even though it looks like it's about to thunderstorm here. Lenny and Jacob are going together, and she's wearing her gorgeous silky yellow dress. She looks exactly like Andie Anderson from *How To Lose a Guy in 10 Days*.

She invited me to tag along with her and Jacob, but I politely declined. I would love to hangout with them, as Lenny and I have resumed our friendship even stronger than it was before. It would all just be too close to home. Seeing everyone have the best time with their lovers would rub it in that one guy I want to slow dance with isn't in my life anymore.

Carter isn't even home while Lenny is getting ready. I think he knew I would be here, so he took Pickles and bolted. I don't blame him.

"Is this too much blush?" she asks, pointing her head towards me so I can see. I shake my head.

"You can never have too much blush," I say.

"That's what I was thinking!" she smiles. "Okay, what do you think?"

She stands up and does a little twirl. With her pastel yellow dress and crown braid, she looks like a perfect cottage core princess.

"Gorgeous!" I exclaim. "Lenny, you are absolutely stunning."

"Thanks," she says, squeezing my arm. She grabs her purse and starts to head downstairs.

As we walk down the steps, I can't help but picture an alternate reality where Lenny and I are getting ready for the dance with our dates: Jacob and Carter.

We meet Jacob in the front foyer. He has a huge multi-colored wildflower bouquet in one hand and a smaller bouquet in the other. His face lights up like a million lightning bugs dancing around a willow tree.

"Oh my God, Len," he says breathlessly. Dropping the flowers, He walks over to wrap her in a tight embrace. "You are so beautiful."

Lenny giggles, her cheeks blushing even more. Seeing them together makes my heart so full. They really are soulmates who met in eighth grade.

Bending over to pick up the flowers, Jacob says, "Sorry. I dropped these."

"That's okay! These are so pretty," Lenny tells him, leaning into his side. Jacob gives her the larger bouquet and turns to me.

"I picked these up for you, too," he says. Looking down at the flowers, I am absolutely stunned.

"Jacob! You didn't have to do that," I tell him.

He shrugs. Lenny pipes up, "I told him to."

"Aw!" I say, giving them each a hug. I want to pinch myself because having them back in my life feels like the opposite of a nightmare.

"Are you sure you don't want to go?" Lenny asks. "You can wear any of my dresses!"

"Really. Thank you, but I'll just sit this one out. You all have the best time," I say. "Hopefully it doesn't rain!"

Lenny thanks me and gives me another hug. We say goodbye, and they head to a nearby park with Lenny's mom and her girlfriend to take some pictures before the storm starts.

I follow them outside and hop into my family's Toyota Camry to head for a drive. I don't want to just wait at Lenny's house for the dance to end and for them to come back home. And staying at my house alone also feels very loser-ish.

Since everything went down with Carter, I've been thinking about visiting our spot. As a last attempt at closure and a way to relish in the good memories before I messed everything up.

I drive to Camp Caelee in silence because I have enough noise from my mind replaying all of Carter and I's memories from the past month and from the past eight years.

Pulling into the parking lot of Camp Caelee, I park away from where Carter and I parked the first time. I'll burst into tears if I'm that close to where we had our first dance.

I grab my phone, keys, and picture from my bag. I brought along the photograph of Carter and I from camp several years ago. It's the one where he's looking at me with the affection of a romcom male lead, even though he was only ten years old.

I can't bring myself to throw it away. But if I keep it in my room any longer, I'm going to spend all of my days just staring at it. I can't keep wasting my time ruminating on how things were.

Locking my car, I start walking the path towards the nostalgic tree house. I decided that I'll just pin Carter and I's photo with the other ones in the tree house. That way, it isn't destroyed in the trash, but I have enough separation from it to where I won't just try to live inside the memories of the photo.

As the gravel crunches underneath my feet, I'm almost to the tree house. The tree house where Carter and I had endless hours of pretend play. The tree house where we made so many memories, stuck together by dried popsicle juice. The tree house where we confessed our feelings. The tree house where we shared our first kiss.

Drop drop drop.

Touching my cheek, I feel a few raindrops fall from the gray sky onto my face. Are you kidding me?! It wasn't supposed to rain for another thirty minutes.

I'm about fifty feet from the tree house. I'm too close to turn around and make a run for my car. I might as well go ahead and pin my photo before heading back.

The rain picks up exponentially, and it's really starting to pour now. Quickening my pace, I start to jog towards the wooden fortress. I read somewhere that running in the rain makes you get even more wet, but at this point, I don't care. I need to take cover.

I slide my phone, keys, and photo inside the back pocket of my jeans and start to climb up the ladder. Feeling my hair grow heavy from the rain,

I brush it out of my face. The wet rungs of the ladder make it difficult to grip on, but I manage.

Ascending to the top step of the ladder, I open up the door to the tree house and hoist myself inside. Toppling over onto the wooden floors, I'm startled by what I see.

By *who* I see.

Carter stands up from the bench in front of the window, his eyes piercing mine. It takes everything in me to stay upright. To not just fall right over and bury myself under the planks of the tree house.

Seeing him knocks the air clean out of my lungs, like when we'd be spinning too fast on the tire swing and get thrown off. As I try to remember how to breathe, Pickles runs up to me.

Inhale. Exhale.

Pushing myself up from my knees, I stutter, "I'm sorry, I didn't know-"

"What are you doing here?"

I fidget with my sleeves. "Lenny and Jacob left for the winter formal. I was just going to take a drive before heading back to my house."

"Oh," he says quietly. A beat passes. The tree house of our childhood is filled with so much awkwardness, I struggle not to suffocate.

"I'll just leave and drive back home," I say, turning to the door, about to lower myself down the ladder.

"Wait," he says barely above a whisper.

I look over at him, an emotion I can't read crossing over his face.

"Can we talk?" he asks.

There it is again. All the air is ripped from my lungs like a baby bird taking a premature flight from its mother's nest.

Inhale. Exhale.

I nod, and he gestures for me to sit on the empty spot beside him on the bench.

"I've been thinking. About everything. And I think I brought some of my own anxiety into the situation. So, I'm sorry," he says quietly.

Shaking my head, I tell him, "No, don't say that. Carter, I really messed up. So don't apologize for feeling the way you did. Your emotions are fully valid."

He nods, still quiet. Pickles curls up at Carter's feet.

"I should be the one apologizing. In fact, I *am* the one that is apologizing," I say, tucking my hair behind my ears. "I'm really sorry. You were there for me in a time where I felt the most anxious I've ever been in my life. And I returned the favor by doing something that would make *you* anxious.

"I don't expect you to forgive me or anything. I really don't. If I could take it all back I would. I wouldn't try to even go out with Beau, for one. And two, I would have told you about it during one of our talks. You shared so much with me, and I did feel comfortable enough to share things with you. I just didn't because I was embarrassed about the thing with Beau," I say.

He nods again. I blink once, twice, three times to fight back tears. I practiced and pictured this conversation an infinite number of times, yet I still feel eternally unprepared.

"I get it if we can't be friends after this. But it just kills me thinking that you hate me," I say, my voice splintering.

He sighs. "I don't hate you, Mar."

My heart flutters. *How can five small words feel like such a lifeline?*

Surprised, I look over at him. "But you have every right to. I didn't think of anyone but myself. And I don't want to do that again."

I'm still holding the weighted shawl of guilt onto my shoulders. Every time hope comes to lift my heart from its cage, shame comes to clamp it back down. I can't shake the guilt of what I put Lenny and Carter through.

"I don't hate you. Yeah, I was really hurt. I wish things played out differently. But-" he pauses, pushing his red curls out of his face.

"Even after it all happened, I kept thinking of all that you've added to my life. I thought about how you were there for me during everything with my dad. I thought about how you didn't even hesitate to support me in trying to go to Windermere University. I thought about how every single time I think of you, I can't help but smile. Even when I'm upset."

"Carter, you don't have to say all of that," I tell him, my heart beating faster. "Really, I get it if you need more time."

"No, I'm being serious," he says, turning more towards me. "Even after everything, I still want you in my life. I still *need* you in my life."

Warmth spreads through me despite my wet clothes. "I messed up though. I don't deserve to be able to just walk back in like nothing happened," I say.

"What I realized is that I *want* to work through anything with you. It's worth it to work things out because it's *you*. Mar, after everything happened, I just kept thinking one thing."

My breath hitches.

"What was that?" I ask tentatively.

"I kept thinking that I wanted you again," he says.

Oh.

Oh my God.

My eyebrows pinch together and my shoulders start to shake like the buzzing of an alarm clock. I can't help the stream of tears from falling. Carter cuts through my emotions, opening me up to how I really feel. Like a key opening a heart shaped lock.

"Carter," I cry, moving towards him. He wraps his arms around my waist, pulling me tighter towards him. I lay my head into his freckled neck and breathe in his comforting aroma.

"I missed you so much," I say into his shoulder.

"I missed you, too," he whispers into my ear.

I pull back, looking into his treasured emerald eyes. Resting my hand on his arm, I say, "Carter, I'm a better person when I'm with you."

He smiles, his cheeks turning rosy. Running a hand through my damp hair, he says, "We'll get through anything, Mar."

I lean towards him, and our lips find each other. We find each other like two halves of a picture finally coming together.

Speaking of pictures, I kiss his cheek and pull out the photograph in my pocket. Unfolding the picture, I show it to him.

"What's this?" Carter asks, studying the photo.

"I found it in my room. It's from one summer when we were younger," I tell him.

He smiles softly, running a finger over the picture. Pickles barks and wags his tail.

"I was going to pin it up here with the other photos," I say, motioning to the pinned pictures on the walls of the tree house.

He smiles even bigger now, his teeth glinting in the moonlight. "Let's do it. It'll be like branding this as *our* tree house. I mean, it is our spot."

I kiss him again. How is this man real?

We stand up, and Carter pulls off a thumbtack from the cork board.

I find an empty spot on the wall, and he nods.

"Perfect," Carter says, pinning the photo into place.

"It is perfect," I agree.

Changing the subject, Carter asks, "Why didn't you go to the winter formal?"

I lightly laugh, telling him, "I wouldn't want to go without you. If I were there right now, I would just be thinking about you the entire time."

"Because I'm just that great?" Carter says sarcastically.

"Uh huh," I say, giving him a small shove. Like Dorothy finding her way back home, I feel so at peace being back with Carter. I run my hand through his curls and trace my fingertips along his auburn eyebrows. "Would you want to go with me?"

"Yeah," he grins. "I want to go with you."

"I don't have a dress or anything."

He shrugs. "Who cares? Besides, Lenny probably has something."

I bite back a smile and kiss the tip of his nose.

I nod, squeezing his hand and taking a mental picture of this place.

Climbing down the tree house ladder with Pickles tucked under his shirt, Carter looks so effortless. I descend- not as gracefully- and he helps me find my footing. Jumping down, we start to jog back to the parking lot to find our cars.

Hand in hand, we race down the gravel walkway, trying not to step in too many puddles. Carter's freckled fingers wrap around mine as we run like little kids around Camp Caelee.

Since we drove separately, we pile into each of our cars and plan to meet back at his house. Right before I start to pull away, Carter runs out of his car. He jogs over to me, motioning for me to roll down the window.

Maybe he's having car trouble? Or he'd rather meet up at my house? Or maybe he's realized it's a bad idea to go to the formal last minute?

When he reaches my car, I roll down the window. Wiping the wet curls away from his face, he pants, "Wait, before you go-"

"What's wrong?" I ask him, concerned.

With a mischievous smirk, he leans into my window, kissing me as I'm in the driver's seat. Thank God I'm still in park because that kiss sent so many butterflies into my stomach, I'm sure the car would've gone flying.

When his warm lips part from mine, he says, "For the road."

Chuckling, I shake my head, "I can't believe you, Carter Taylor."

Shrugging, he starts to run back over to his car. Calling out, he says, "What can I say? I'm pretty amazing!"

I laugh even harder now, my stomach starting to ache from all of the giggling. I really don't deserve him. Smiling to myself, I follow him down the road and mimic the path to his house.

I park in his driveway and head up the stairs of his front porch to meet him. Pickles circles our legs happily. Carter unlocks the door, and before heading inside, he kisses me on the top on my head.

We race up the stairs like little kids dropping their new presents in their room after a birthday party. He goes into his room to pick out something to change into while I walk into Lenny's bathroom to brush out my soaking wet hair.

I'm chilled from the rain, so I open up Lenny's closet to find a dress to wear to formal. Rifling through her hangers, every dress she owns is for a spring occasion. Nothing is heavy weight or suited for winter.

"Hey, Carter," I call out to him.

"Yeah?" he says, walking into Lenny's room. He still has his jeans on, but his shirt is off while he's towel drying his hair. My breath catches as I stare at his smooth chest dotted with copper colored freckles. They look like constellations that I could spend forever finding.

I physically make myself look away and meet his eyes. "I don't think Lenny has anything I could wear," I say.

"Oh," Carter frowns, stepping towards me to look through his sister's clothes.

I rub my arms, trying to erase the chill bumps that are up and down my body. Last time I was this cold and wet was when I was thrown into Maya's pool at her party at the beginning of the semester. At the time, I wanted to put on comfy sweats and bundle up under Carter's blanket.

Wait a minute.

I turn to him, "I have an idea."

"What is it?" he asks, while I walk over to his room.

"Can I wear your sweats?"

"My sweats? To formal?" he asks.

I nod.

Walking to his room, he smiles and pulls out a perfectly folded set of gray sweatpants and sweatshirt. Handing the clothes to me, he turns to pull out another set for himself.

I grab the gray pair and turn around. He does the same thing.

I slip off my wet jeans and soaked sweater. Kicking off my socks, I pull on Carter's well worn pants and top. The fuzzy insides of the sweatshirt surround me in a cloud of warmth.

"Okay, I'm done," I say.

"Can I turn around?" he asks.

"Yeah," I chuckle. Giving him a once over, he looks perfect. His hair is starting to dry now, the ginger curls popping out from behind his ears. His lanky arms fit perfectly into the hoodie which make him look like the love interest in a Netflix romcom movie.

"You are so right. This is the move for formal," he says. "You look really good."

He looks at me as if I've just had the *Princess Diaries* makeover from Paolo. But the truth is that I've got on a half a layer of mascara and comfy clothes.

Pickles curls up in his bed; I'm sure he's exhausted from witnessing the giddiness circulate between Carter and me. I grab a pair of Lenny's socks and shoes as Carter ties up his sneakers. He keeps stealing glances at me with a small smile. I can't stop doing the same thing to him.

Carter grabs my hand as we bolt down the stairs, lock his front door, and pile into his car. His Honda smells like August air, making me feel right at home.

On the way to school, I tease him that I'm going to get the DJ to play "Cruisin' for a Bruisin'" so we can show everyone our dance moves.

He looks over at me and winks. "I'd do it for you."

I have to keep doing a double take to make sure this is actually my life. How did a guy like Carter fall for a girl like me?

We pull into the school parking lot and run out of the car. One, to beat the rain and two, because we can't contain our excitement. It's like we are elementary school kids hopped up on Valentine's Day candy.

Walking inside, I'm hit with the school's intense burst of air conditioning, making me appreciate Carter's sweatshirt even more. He grabs my hand and leads me towards the gymnasium: the iconic place for all school dances.

Before pushing open the double doors, Carter turns to me with a smile creeping along his face.

"What is it?" I ask him

"I like you, Mar," he says.

I giggle. I can't help it. "I like you, too, Carter."

Walking into the gym, I'm surrounded by fairy lights and glowing snowflakes. Orbs of purple, blue, and white lights float around us. It's like Carter and I just walked into a winter wonderland.

"It's so beautiful!" I say, looking around at all the decorations.

"MARLOWE?!?!?!"

Turning my head, I look in the direction of the scream. Lenny barrels towards me with her arms out. "You're here!"

I wrap her in a hug and squeal, "I made it!"

Jacob and Carter do a "bro hug," and Lenny pulls back to look at me and her brother. "Are you-"

"We're back," I say.

"We're so back," Carter tells them.

Lenny squeals even louder, "I'm so happy!"

"Me too," I smile.

Suddenly, the sound of quick guitar strums pours out of the speakers, and the melodic voice of Miss Swift fills the gymnasium.

"You're on the phone with your girlfriend, she's upset," Taylor Swift sings through the speakers.

"I love this song!" I hear Maya scream. Looking over at her baby blue dress, I see her dancing with Beau. She looks really happy, and I'm genuinely glad for it. I call out to her and wave. She smiles and waves back.

Lenny turns to me. "This is our song!"

"It's our favorite!" I squeal, starting to dance around. Carter follows my lead and begins to jump to the beat of "You Belong With Me (Taylor's Version)."

"I may or may not have texted the DJ to play this when she saw us walk in," Carter says to me.

"No way!" I say to him, still jumping and flailing my arms to the song. "You are the best."

He blushes, his cheeks turning crimson. Pushing his hair out of his face, he starts to sing along with Taylor.

He just looks so perfect and so boy next door.

Oh.

Oh. My. Gosh.

He IS the boy next door!

I'm obsessed with the original "You Belong With Me" music video, and I've never realized the parallels to my own life. I have always thought I was Taylor Swift in the scenario- the girl who's ignored by the love of her life.

But I was wrong.

This entire time I have been *Lucas Till* in the "You Belong With Me" music video. I was so concerned with getting with the popular person, Beau- or the brunette and popular cheerleader from the video.

I didn't even notice who was there all along. Carter was Taylor Swift the entire time. Becoming my friend, telling all the jokes, and being there for me when I needed him.

Carter was Taylor Swift. I was Lucas Till.

Now, at the dance together, it sinks in how Carter and I really belong together. It's him and me. It's always supposed to have been that way.

No matter what happens. No matter who or what comes into our lives. I'll know that we can work it out. We belong together.

Because regardless of what life throws our way…

I'll want him again.

EPILOGUE

Sliding down the aisle of auditorium seats, Lenny and I settle in together, with our families on either side of us. This day has been in my calendar for so long, and I can't believe it's actually here.

"I'm so excited to see him," Lenny says.

"Me too," I tell her. "I've helped him rehearse, and he's just amazing. He'll do great."

Sheila, Carter's mom, leans over "Don't forget to turn your phone on silent. Last year, I went to see him in Newsies, and my afternoon nap alarm went off. It was *so* embarrassing."

I chuckle and turn my phone on Do Not Disturb. Sheila's girlfriend, Ashley, just laughs and shakes her head. According to Lenny, Sheila has been asking her and Carter what they would think if she proposed to Ashley. They are over the moon with the idea of Sheila getting engaged.

Looking down, I adjust the collar of my Windermere University shirt. Lenny embroidered little paw prints all over it to match the mascot. She's working with my mom to sell her products in the studio, and I have to restrain myself from buying every new item she makes. I couldn't be more proud of my best friend.

I got the Windermere shirt from Carter and I's college visit a couple of months ago. He officially got accepted a few weeks ago, and I've been so happy seeing him so happy.

We aren't worried about long distance. I'll be finishing up my senior year at Caelee High next year while he's two hours away at Windermere. We've already planned for all the times we can meet up throughout the school year. Carter claims that we need to see each other a few times every month so Pickles doesn't forget about me.

The auditorium lights grow dim, and we all sit quietly in our seats. Mr. Fitz, the Theater teacher, walks out to the front of the stage and introduces the musical, *Beauty and the Beast*.

He discusses how much work the students have put into the play. I've been lucky enough to see all that work firsthand from Carter's dedication. He loves this show, and he wants it to be incredibly successful.

I've even helped him with what I can. On one of our dates, we went to get sushi and then came back to the school, and I helped paint some of the sets. I hope no one in the audience looks at the castle too closely or else they'll see all of my artistic mistakes.

The show begins, and it's just as magical as I always pictured. The lights, the colors, and the costumes come together to transport everyone into Belle's village.

When it's finally time for him to come on stage as the Beast, all of my breath fully leaves my body. He delivers each line with impact, and I truly feel like I'm watching a show at Disney World.

He sings "Something There," and his voice floats through the auditorium like honey. It reminds me of all of our car rides singing along to the soundtrack, even if I'm tone deaf. It reminds me of how there's always been "something there" between Carter and me. And how I'm insanely grateful that we've been able to let that something turn into a blossoming relationship.

He hits the high note with the accuracy and beauty of a Broadway singer. I'm so lucky that I can say that *that's* my boyfriend.

After I give him my bouquet of flowers (because guys deserve flowers too), we take pictures. Ones with just him and me, ones with all of our friends, and ones with his family. I snap a million singles of him because I just am in awe of how amazing he was.

I like him so much that I've realized it may not just be "like" anymore.

His family and my family head to the restaurant for our dinner reservation, while I stay back with Carter as he gets unready from the musical. He wipes off his stage makeup, and his auburn freckles are uncovered again.

Once he's fully turned from the Prince back to Carter, I lead him out to the hallway in front of the auditorium. There are still people around, but most everyone has started to head home after the play.

Grabbing his hand, I pull him to the most recent addition to Caelee High: a couple of vintage photo booths. Our two Leadership classmates were able to get their project started this semester, and it's already been a hit. I'm hoping that the remodeling of Carter and I's mindfulness space will be finished by the end of this semester.

"What's this?" he asks.

"A surprise," I say with a soft smile. Inserting my money, I select the option to get eight photos each.

"Okay, so what faces should we do?" Carter asks me, his green eyes glowing.

"A couple of smiling, then silly faces?" I ask.

He nods, and we get settled into the bench inside of the photo booth. The lights countdown, letting us know that the camera is about to go off.

Carter and I lean into each other, showing off our genuine emotions. We take another one, and instead of smiling into the camera, Carter smiles down at me.

Just like the photo of us from camp.

With six photos left, I turn to Carter. I take a deep breath and say to him, "Carter, I've been meaning to tell you something."

"What is it?" he asks. The flash goes off.

"I like you so much. You are my safe space and my other half. You make me enjoy being who I am, and when I'm with you, I don't try to change into someone else. I'm more Marlowe when I'm with you," I tell him.

His eyes swell with tears. The second flash goes off. Only four photos left.

"I love how my heart pounds out of my chest every time I see your face. I love how when we laugh together, it's like time stops. I love how we can literally just take Pickles for a walk, yet it feels like the most romantic date in the world. I love how I can completely be myself without having to think twice," I say.

He blinks back tears, his smile exposing his dimples. The flash goes off again.

"Carter, I love how when I wake up, you are the first person I think of. I love how we can remember the small details about each other without hesitation." The flash goes off a fourth time.

"It's hit me like a ton of bricks, but what I feel is so much more than just liking you," I tell him, wiping a tear from his bottom lashes. He lets out a breathy laugh.

"I love you, Carter," I say. The flash goes off a fifth time.

He lets out a mix between a laugh and a cry. "I love you, too, Mar."

The flash goes off a final time, as we lean in and press our lips together. Relief, excitement, and now *love* float around in my stomach as we kiss. The best part of all of this is not even knowing that I'm receiving love, but it's being able to love him at my fullest and have it be accepted.

It turns out I'm no longer Boysick.

I'm Lovesick.

ACKNOWLEDGMENTS

First of all, if you're reading this then that means this is no longer a Google Doc but an actual book…. which is insane! If I think about it too much then I'll start crying.

To the people who helped transform this from a file on my computer to an actual book- Vanessa, Tara, and Margaux- you all have been lifesavers in this process. Thank you for your enthusiasm, professionalism, and handling my book with such care. You all are the best.

This book would not be possible without the love I have for Young Adult romcoms. They fill me with so much warmth and nostalgia as reader. To Lynn Painter and Rachel Lynn Solomon: you all are badass women and writing goddesses. You have inspired me more than you know. Your books feel like home!

I am so appreciative of every friend, coworker, and professor who has given me encouragement in this process. And thank you for letting me ask you a million questions about what it feels like to fall in love. You never made me feel silly for chasing my dreams.

To my friends on Bookstagram- you all are the best community in the world. I am forever grateful that we have met- even it's virtually. Thank you for gushing about fictional men and authors with me. I hope you will add Carter to your list of book boyfriends. :)

To Derrick, Hannah, and Shelby- you all have shown me support from the very beginning. You all are such lights in my life, and I wouldn't trade our friendship for the world.

To my STEM girls- where do I even start! You stuck by me when I was more Marlowe than Meredith. I would not have survived high school without you, and I cherish our friendship everyday. YOU are the reason my teenage years were so happy and nostalgic. Thank you for always being there for me and listening to my insane Boysickness. Maryam, Rawan, Camila, Grace, Laura, and Michelle- you've shown me that home is a group of people. I love you forever.

To Belle and Donna- you all are my Lenny. I would not be here today if it wasn't for you. You believed in me before I even came up with the idea for *BOYSICK*. From listening to me rant about terrible guys to lifting my spirits so much to where I'm peeing myself with laughter, you all are my other halves. Your friendship has helped me transform into the young woman I am today. My heart is more full everyday because of you. I love you, and I am so thankful to go through life with you.

To Riya- you're my platonic soulmate. When I met you, it felt like we had grown up together and been friends for years. Not only have you been a huge counsel when it comes to writing, but you've been a sister when it comes to life. You've been the most spirited Carlowe cheerleader, and this book would not be where it is without your feedback and advice. I didn't believe in kindred spirits before I met you. You are the reason the last couple years of my life have been so amazing. To my *Friends* lover and biggest confidant, you are the first person I turn to when anything happens in my life. I love you to the moon and to Saturn.

To my dad- thank you for never doubting me for a second. I would not think it was possible to pursue this dream if it weren't for your support and love. In your mind, I was always going to finish and publish my book. Seeing your support helped me to adopt that same confidence. I am so blessed to have a father like you. I love you, and maybe one day I'll write a Western for you.

To Mary Beth- you are the reason my childhood was so magical. Sometimes I wonder why camp was so wonderful and why I look back at it so fondly, but then I remember it is that way because you were by my side. From us playing the color game in the pool to us building fairy houses in the backwoods, every memory is bright because of you. I wouldn't want to grow up with anyone else. To the Fawn to my Rosetta- I love you.

To Momma- I can't even put it into words. You are my best friend, and I know we have been together in every lifetime. You fostered my love of reading. You make me laugh like no one else. You made countless sacrifices to give me the childhood I had. You're my home base. My lifeline. My role model. My guiding light. You're my human Nankie (no one else will get this but us). You've loved me endlessly through every version of myself. I am who I am because of you. I love you more than you know.

To my dog Henry- you are perfect. You can do no wrong… even when you pee in the house or bark at every motorcycle that drives by. You are my soul dog. I would not have survived my young adult years without you. I love you, your short legs, and your corn chip smell to the moon and back.

Thank you, God. Your Love has been my security and guidance through every high and low. Thank you for bringing these incredible individuals into my life.

Lastly, to my younger self- I want to hug and squeeze you and tell you everything will be okay. I am so proud of you. Keep reading. This is only the beginning.

Stay Boysick,
Meredith

ABOUT THE AUTHOR

MEREDITH MINCEY still lives in her childhood bedroom, nestled in the fields of Corryton, TN. When she's not reading or writing, she's making a dozen playlists that cover her latest music hyper-fixation. Don't mention dachshunds around her or else you'll be stuck for hours listening to her gush about her wiener dog, Henry. Also, she's never been in love. That's right- this romcom author wrote an entire book from her imagination. She's not sure if this is something she should hide from the public or wear like a badge of honor.